# WESTERN

*Rugged men looking for love...*

## Fortune's Holiday Surprise
Jennifer Wilck

## Cowboy Santa
Melinda Curtis

# MILLS & BOON

Jennifer Wilck is acknowledged as the author of this work
FORTUNE'S HOLIDAY SURPRISE
© 2024 by Harlequin Enterprises ULC
Philippine Copyright 2024
Australian Copyright 2024
New Zealand Copyright 2024

First Published 2024
First Australian Paperback Edition 2024
ISBN 978 1 038 93559 5

COWBOY SANTA
© 2024 by Melinda Wooten
Philippine Copyright 2024
Australian Copyright 2024
New Zealand Copyright 2024

First Published 2024
First Australian Paperback Edition 2024
ISBN 978 1 038 93559 5

MIX
Paper | Supporting
responsible forestry
FSC
www.fsc.org
FSC® C001695

Published by
Harlequin Mills & Boon
An imprint of Harlequin Enterprises (Australia) Pty Limited
(ABN 47 001 180 918), a subsidiary of HarperCollins
Publishers Australia Pty Limited
(ABN 36 009 913 517)
Level 19, 201 Elizabeth Street
SYDNEY NSW 2000 AUSTRALIA

Cover art used by arrangement with Harlequin Books S.A.. All rights reserved.

Printed and bound in Australia by McPherson's Printing Group

# Fortune's Holiday Surprise

Jennifer Wilck

## MILLS & BOON

**Jennifer Wilck** is an award-winning contemporary romance author for readers who are passionate about love, laughter and happily-ever-after. Known for writing both Jewish and non-Jewish romances, she features damaged heroes, sassy and independent heroines, witty banter, yummy food and hot chemistry in her books. She believes humor is the only way to get through the day and does not believe in sharing her chocolate. You can find her at jenniferwilck.com.

## Books by Jennifer Wilck

### *The Fortunes of Texas: Fortune's Secret Children*

*Fortune's Holiday Surprise*

### *Holidays, Heart and Chutzpah*

*Home for the Challah Days*
*Matzah Ball Blues*
*Deadlines, Donuts & Dreidels*

Visit the Author Profile page
at millsandboon.com.au for more titles.

Dear Reader,

As a lifelong Jersey girl, the only thing I know about Texas is what I've seen in the movies and hear about in country songs. So when Harlequin asked me to contribute to their Fortunes of Texas series, I was thrilled.

As a writer, I love creating diverse communities where people live, love and laugh together, and where all problems, no matter how big or small, can be overcome. It's essential that my characters find their happily-ever-after and, by doing so, provide hope to my readers.

Hope is especially prevalent during the holidays, and if there were ever two people who needed it more than Arlo Fortune and Carrie Kaplan, well, I haven't met them. Still dealing with the death of his father, Arlo is shocked when his best friend—Carrie's brother-in-law—dies suddenly. Carrie, her newly orphaned niece's guardian, is tasked with teaching her about her Jewish heritage. She's a fish out of water in this tiny Texas town, torn away from the sister she has no idea how to live without.

Welcome back to Chatelaine, where the Fortunes own the biggest ranch in the area. Get ready to celebrate Christmas and Hanukkah as Carrie tries to help Arlo find meaning in the holidays. Stop in at the holiday celebration in the town hall. Admire the decorations and taste the seasonal foods, including the Christmas cookies and Hanukkah bimuelos, the latkes and spiced rum. And if you want to admire the handsome cowboys, well, I'm certainly not going to stop you.

So grab a cup of hot chocolate, turn on the holiday music and dive into this holiday romance. I hope you enjoy Arlo and Carrie's story!

*Jennifer Wilck*

To Debbie & Alyse—thank you for helping this Jersey girl learn about the thriving Jewish communities in Texas. I couldn't have written this book without you.

## *PROLOGUE*

ARLO FORTUNE STARED at his best friend's front door and blinked hard. Only a week and a half ago, Isaac Abelman and his wife had died in a freak gas explosion while on a business trip overseas. Arlo had endured a funeral worse than any other he'd attended, including his own father's. And now, seven days later, he'd come to pay a condolence call to Isaac's grieving sister-in-law, someone he barely knew. He pulled at the clasp of his bolero tie and wondered if he should knock on the blue oak door or ring the black iron doorbell.

Once upon a time, he'd opened the door without a care, yelling hello to Isaac, kissing Isaac's wife, Randi, on the cheek and tickling the chin of their toddler daughter, Aviva. Hell, going back even further, to his and Isaac's childhood, he couldn't remember the last time he'd knocked or rung before entering.

But now?

He grimaced and didn't realize anyone was walking behind him until a throat cleared, and a man and a woman said, "Excuse me," before moving past him, walking up the steps to the front porch and opening the door.

Despite the grief that slowed his thoughts and body, Arlo quickened his pace and followed the couple into the house.

He expected Randi to greet him, Aviva on one hip, a grin

on her face. Instead, one of his neighbors nodded to him. From the front hall, Arlo glanced into the full living room on the right, filled with murmuring voices and subdued laughter. On his left was the dining room where he and his friend had shared many a meal. Today, the maple table was covered with a white cloth and loaded with platters of food and trays of dessert. More people gathered around it, helping themselves and huddling in groups.

He'd fiddled with his tie so much it probably needed fixing, but the mirror in the front hall was covered, probably a Jewish mourning custom he didn't know, so he smoothed his hand down his front and wandered into the fray.

Snatches of conversation drifted toward him.

"...so sad about the baby."

"...such a freak accident."

"...going to stay here..."

Arlo scanned the room, trying to find someone he knew. He'd never paid a shiva call before, and he didn't know what was expected.

Spotting one of his friends across the room, he started to make his way in his direction when a voice interrupted him.

"Ladies and gentlemen, if everyone could come into the living room for the minyan, please."

*Minyan? What was that?*

Someone handed him a book, open to the beginning. There was English and Hebrew writing on it, but the book was backward. He frowned. The rabbi he'd seen at the funeral walked to the front of the room and began to read.

The English was meaningful, the Hebrew chanting beautiful, and it brought into focus the importance of being together in this time of grief. As he listened to the prayers murmured around him, he looked at the people in the room.

Many of them were neighbors and townspeople he recognized. Some were people he'd grown up with. Others were strangers to him.

His gaze stopped when it landed on Randi's sister. Arlo remembered her name was Carrie. Isaac had mentioned her occasionally, and he'd seen her at their wedding five years ago, but this was the first time he'd really had time to notice her.

She was pretty, with long dark hair she had twisted up in some kind of knot, big brown eyes filled with sadness and pale skin.

She looked...alone. Despite everyone joining her in mourning, there was a wall around her. He didn't know if it was of her own making or maybe his imagination. But sympathy tugged at him.

In the middle of the service, Aviva began fussing. Carrie reached for her, and he thought he saw fear in her eyes, but he blinked and it was gone.

What must it be like to have parenthood thrust upon you like that? Aviva was adorable. He'd always had a bond with her, but even still, taking care of a two-year-old out of the blue? What kind of life change must that be?

He wanted to go up and reintroduce himself to her, see how she was doing and check on Aviva. But when the service ended, a swarm of people crowded around her, and he was forced to wait. He wandered through the living room into the kitchen, stopping to greet people he knew.

"Terrible tragedy," his friend Jim said. "I talked to him the night before he left. Never thought it would be the last time, though."

Arlo's throat thickened. "Yeah." His voice croaked, and he made a fist with his hand at his side. He hadn't spoken to Isaac since a month before he died, and when he had, they'd argued. He'd had many arguments with his friend, but they'd always made up afterward. This time, they never would. He wanted to scream and shout at the unfairness of it all.

The rabbi walked past him, nodding to those he knew, and approached the table full of food. All of the guests treated him with respect, appropriate for a man of God. Arlo shook his head. How could he believe in a God who left a two-year-old parentless? What possible reason could He have for taking away his best friend and that man's wife? He huffed out a frustrated breath. For that matter, what kind of God took *his* father and left him with more questions than ever before and no way of getting answers?

Nope, he didn't want to interact with the rabbi, no matter how nice of a service he'd led. He turned away from the dining room and ran smack into Carrie.

Reflexively, he reached out to keep from knocking her over.

"Sorry about that." He removed his hat and held out his hand. "Arlo Fortune. Isaac was my best friend. I'm sorry for your loss."

The sorrow he'd seen in her eyes deepened, the dark brown reminding him of his polished leather saddle.

"Thank you." Her voice was soft. "I'm sorry for yours as well."

Something about her expression made him want to continue the conversation, to ask how she was holding up, what she was doing about Aviva, and to offer his assistance, if necessary. But before he put those thoughts into words, another mourner approached. With a tip of his hat, he retreated a step and soon the crowd swallowed her, and he turned and left.

# CHAPTER ONE

*One month later...*

EVERY TIME CARRIE KAPLAN walked into her sister's cheery kitchen, her stomach hurt. She'd avoid the room if she could—as a nutritionist and health/wellness writer with syndicated columns across multiple online sites, she was an expert on how to take care of yourself and do what's best for yourself—but this was no longer her sister's kitchen.

The yellow kitchen with white curtains was now hers.

Only a month ago, this had been her sister's house, the place where she lived with her husband and adorable daughter, Aviva. Carrie had packed a weeks' worth of clothes and arrived excited to babysit her niece while they left on a business trip.

Killed tragically in their hotel, they never came home.

Now, as Aviva's guardian and new owner of her sister's house, she faced a life completely different from the one she imagined.

And walking into this kitchen several times a day gave her a stomachache.

"Me hungwy," Aviva said, tapping Carrie's leg.

Despite her sadness, she smiled down at her niece before lifting her to her hip and nuzzling her cheek.

"Well, then, we should feed you," she murmured.

"Yes, pwese."

As she'd done a thousand times since moving in here, Carrie wanted to tell her sister how adorable Aviva was, especially when she used her manners. She blinked back tears as she placed the little girl in her high chair next to the big bay window overlooking the grasslands of the nearby ranches.

Between the cold December weather and the early morning, no one was on the road, other than trucks delivering supplies. If her brother-in-law were still alive, though, he'd be pulling into the driveway with treats from the nearby bakery before heading upstairs to work in his home office. With a sigh, she opened the fridge and pulled out some fruit. In the freezer, she grabbed a frozen waffle and stuck it in the toaster.

"What color plate would you like today?" she asked Aviva. "Pink or orange?"

"Owage."

Carrie cut up the fruit into toddler-sized bites and placed it on the plastic dish. When the waffle popped, she added that to the plate, making sure to cut it up as well. Then she put the breakfast on Aviva's high chair tray, added her sippy cup of milk and sat down next to her.

"Auntie Cawwy eat, too?"

Crap. She wasn't hungry, but she needed to be a good role model.

She smacked her forehead. "Oh, my goodness, I forgot!" She widened her eyes and dropped her jaw, making Aviva giggle.

She grabbed herself a yogurt and spoon and joined her niece at the table.

"What shall we do today, kiddo?"

"Swings!" Aviva gave a wide, toothy grin as she answered with her favorite activity.

"You always say swings."

*"Swings!"*

Carrie cleaned Aviva's mouth, hands and high chair tray

before unstrapping her and placing her on the ground. "First, let's get dressed." She looked down at her own pajama-clad self. She needed to get changed, too.

It had taken her a little while to learn to balance caring for a toddler and herself, but the two of them had developed a routine.

Carrie appreciated routine. It gave her a sense of control and prevented her from curling up in a ball with her grief. And now that she'd sent for her clothes and most of her things back in Albuquerque—even if it was only for the time being—she was starting to feel a little more like herself.

She followed Aviva upstairs to her bedroom. The little girl ran over to her dresser, opened drawers and pulled clothing onto the floor. Carrie stood in the doorway, watching the flurry of activity. After a couple of minutes of marching and bending and tossing, Aviva stood up, triumphant.

"I want to wear this," she said.

Carrie nodded, impressed. Although the items didn't come close to matching, they were weather appropriate. The child had picked a pair of bright orange leggings with a pink and blue tunic top. Once again, she silently thanked her sister for only keeping seasonal clothes within reach.

"You will be one colorful kid," she said, folding up the discarded items and replacing them in the drawers, before helping Aviva to put on her clothes.

When she was dressed, with an orange bow in her hair—Carrie needed *something* to match—she brought her into the guest room, sat Aviva on the bed with the TV turned on to the latest kiddie show and got herself ready for the day.

A commercial for a store with Christmas sales came on, and with a jolt, Carrie realized Hanukkah was coming, too.

In addition to naming Carrie as Aviva's guardian when she was born, Randi had requested that Carrie help impart Jewish customs and traditions on her niece. At the time, Carrie had been thrilled with the task. She remembered her grandmother lighting the Shabbat candles and reciting the blessings on Friday nights, going to synagogue in their best clothes, and cooking delicious food. She and Randi had grown up with her grandparents, now long dead, and they had shown both Carrie and Randi the importance of Judaism. Carrie had looked forward to celebrating the holidays with her niece.

She'd never planned on being the only one to carry on the tradition, though.

With Hanukkah approximately a month away, Carrie had a lot to prepare for.

Her sister and brother-in-law's bedroom door was shut. No matter how much time Carrie had spent here, and how many of Randi's things she'd gone through, she couldn't make herself tackle their bedroom.

"Mommy Daddy room," Aviva said, rushing over and reaching for the handle. Her little body stretched, but it was just out of her reach.

"That's right, Vivie. Let's go downstairs, though, okay?" Her throat was thick, but she pushed the words through anyway. With Aviva so young, Carrie couldn't explain too much about her parents' deaths, but had relied on some simple storybooks and lots and lots of love to do her best to cushion the impact of their sudden disappearance from her life.

"Otay."

Thank goodness Aviva was so easy.

"Come on, kiddo, let's go outside." The thought of spending all day inside the house, going through her brother-in-law's things, oppressed her. She'd wait until Aviva went down for a nap. In the meantime, it would do them both good to get some fresh air.

After bundling her niece into her jacket and strapping her into her stroller, Carrie walked into downtown Chatelaine.

She laughed to herself. "Downtown Chatelaine" was really just one road with a one-pump gas station at the town line proclaiming "Welcome to Chatelaine. The town that never changes. Harv's New BBQ straight ahead."

Her phone rang, and Carrie answered with a smile. "Hey, Kelsey." Her best friend from Albuquerque called her almost every day to check on her. Actually, several of her friends did, stepping in to be her family when her grandparents who raised her had died. She didn't know what she'd do without them, especially now that Randi was gone, too.

"Whatcha up to?" Kelsey asked.

"We're taking a walk through the one-horse town," she answered with a laugh.

"Air is good," Kelsey said. "What about people?"

Carrie shrugged. "Haven't seen a lot of them, but then again, I haven't really gone searching for them, either."

Her friend's tone turned serious. "Don't cut yourself off from everyone, Car. You need people."

"Which is why I've got you, and Emma and Olivia." The four of them had been a group all throughout school. Even now, they remained close.

"Yes, you'll always have us," Kelsey said. "But you're not in Albuquerque any longer. You need to make friends in Texas, too."

She sighed. "I don't know, Kels. I'm probably not staying here much longer. Only as long as it takes to get Randi and Isaac's estate settled and Aviva's adoption finalized."

"You never know," Kelsey said. "Just promise me you'll try."

"Okay, I will."

Carrie hung up the phone and thought about this town Randi and Isaac had lived in. Growing up outside Albuquerque, Carrie had thought her hometown was small, but it was a thriving metropolis compared to Chatelaine. It also had a thriving Jewish community of which she'd been a part. Still, this place had charm. As much as thoughts of the funeral pained her, Carrie had been touched by the presence of what seemed like the entire town at the service and shiva afterward. Although her brother-in-law wasn't observant and the funeral itself had been nondenominational, his parents had thought having mourners gather after the service was a lovely idea, and the shiva had enabled Carrie to grieve with her Jewish faith in mind. And the townsfolk had agreed.

As she walked down the street, she chatted to Aviva, pointing out the dogs on leashes, the birds in the sky and the different cowboy hats they saw.

They paused outside the local bookstore. A weathered sign with Remi's Reads in robin's-egg blue lettering welcomed them. A woman with long sleek brown hair who appeared close to Carrie's age looked up from where she was fluffing pillows on the benches outside. She stood by the doorway, her porcelain skin flushed, and she waved them inside.

"Hey, y'all, come on in." The woman bent down and smiled at Aviva. "Aren't you just the cutest little thing." Rising, she held out her hand to Carrie, sorrow darkening her long-lashed deep brown eyes almost to black. "I'm Remi. I'm so sorry for your loss. Your sister used to come in and browse all the time. She loved mysteries and playing with Aviva in our children's section." Remi blinked before continuing. "She was a doll. Such a tragedy."

"Thank you. She talked about how much she loved your bookstore." Carrie's eyes filled, and she forced her tears away. Although everyone seemed to know everyone else in this town, she didn't, and she felt weird sharing her sorrow with strangers, no matter how kindhearted they might be.

"How are you adjusting to living here and taking care of your sweet niece?"

Carrie shrugged. Ideally, she wanted to return to Albuquerque in the near future, but she wasn't going to confess that here. "She's wonderful, and I love her to pieces. I haven't figured out what I'm going to do yet, or how, though."

Remi nodded. "You've got time. Don't rush anything."

Her neck tightened. *Time.* Her sister and brother-in-law were supposed to have time, too. She shook her head, trying not to let the grief overwhelm her.

"If you'd like to browse, we've got lots of new releases over here," she said, pointing to a tall, labeled bookcase. "Unless you're going somewhere special?"

Carrie didn't know if Remi knew she needed to change the subject or was just naturally curious. Part of her was grateful for the segue, another part of her was hesitant to answer in the face of such blatant curiosity. She tried to squelch that part.

"We're just getting some fresh air."

"It's a shame you weren't here a half hour ago. Arlo Fortune was in. Poor man looked so sad. It must be terrible for him to lose his father and best friend, one right after the other. I feel so bad for him." She brightened when Aviva started bouncing in her stroller. "I'll bet he'd have loved to see Aviva."

Everyone in Chatelaine and the surrounding area knew the Fortune name. Even Carrie, who only came by to visit her sister, recognized it. She knew from chatting with Randi that Arlo had been a good friend of her brother-in-law's. She vaguely remembered him from the crush of people at the funeral. Tall, longish sandy hair, sorrowful green eyes.

"Another time," she said.

Remi nodded. "Don't hesitate to stop by if you need anything or just want some company."

Carrie thanked her before waving goodbye and exiting the store. There were so many things she needed; it was overwhelming. And as nice as it was to have people offer to help her, the one person she relied on for help—her sister—was gone. Without her, Carrie didn't know what to do.

ARLO FORTUNE LEANED back in his brown calf-leather desk chair and rubbed his eyes. He'd stared at the computer screen, going over the Fortune Family Ranch's expenses for what seemed like hours. His eyes were gritty, and his head ached.

The good news was that Dahlia's plans for the new sheep

were on track. With the first shearing of the herd taking place in the spring, she'd be able to sell the wool in bulk as well as spin it into yarn to sell. Arlo was comfortable telling Nash, his brother and ranch foreman, to expect a profit in the next two to three months. His brother would be happy.

Arlo should be as well, but his heart wasn't invested in the ranch at the moment. Even though it should be. When he'd first found out his mom had bought the ranch from an older couple who'd retired to Arizona, he'd been thrilled to put his skills to work in building the spread into a successful venture. The fact that it would have ticked off his dad, who expected his kids to go into business like him, was an added bonus. But his heart was aching—in anger at his late father and in sorrow for his best friend. The anger was nothing new. He'd been pissed at his dad for what seemed his entire life. Casper Windham was a ruthless bastard who put business before his family. His mom might have accepted it, but he never would. To think his father might have betrayed his family, though? And to be unable to confront him about it? He fumed.

Usually, he'd talk to his best friend, Isaac. But the last time they'd talked, they'd argued over his father's potential betrayal. And then Isaac had died. He closed his eyes. Even after a month, it still hurt. Seemed like all his relationships were up in the air, unable to be resolved. If only he could let them go.

Shoot, it had been a month, and he hadn't checked on Aviva, his best friend's daughter, or Carrie, the sister-in-law who was now her guardian. The last time he'd seen either of them had been at the shiva. He'd been filled with sorrow and good intentions, but while the grief lasted, the good intentions had disappeared into thin air.

With a sigh, he pushed away from the desk and walked outside. Taking a walk into town earlier and stopping at Remi's Reads hadn't helped him. Maybe talking to the animals might.

Midday, the sun was high overhead, and although it was only in the midfifties, he was comfortable in his shirtsleeves.

He left the main building where his office was and walked along the dirt path from the cream-stucco office building to one of the red barns. On a sunny day like this, he'd usually spend time admiring the beauty of the ranch, but today, he just didn't care. With the doors wide open on either end, a refreshing breeze aired it out. The weak sunlight highlighted dust motes and pieces of hay floating in the air. The cattle in their stalls huffed and stomped, knocking their feed trays.

He paused in the doorway and inhaled the scent of hay and sawdust, wood and manure. Although he never imagined himself as a rancher, there was something about being in the barn that centered him.

If his father could see him now.

The mood that was lifting now soured. Casper had hated everything about ranching. It was "beneath him," and he'd thought Arlo was wasting his time. He never would have understood this feeling. Shaking his shoulders as if by doing so he could rid himself of the uncomfortable memories, he strode the length of the barn, checking in on the cattle inside, stopping to pet a nose or to exchange a word or two with one of the ranch hands.

"Hey, Arlo," Heath Blackwood, his soon to be brother-in-law, called out. His sister Jade was head over heels in love with him, and Arlo couldn't be happier for the newly engaged couple. Her happiness was the one thing capable of piercing his overwhelming sadness. The tall man stepped into the main corridor of the barn, the sun glinting off his sandy hair. "How's your drone analysis going? Did you get a chance to look into the supporting documents I gave you?"

Arlo nodded. "I'm really impressed with how AI technology can help kill weeds without pesticides."

The other man's blue eyes gleamed. "Yeah, me, too. I think it might give the industry a profitable way to go green."

Arlo leaned against one of the stall doors, absently petting the nose of one of the many horses they kept. "I've started to read up on it, and I love the idea of getting rid of pesticides," he said. "I'm just not sure how it helps ranchers like us. If we were farming crops, I'd be fully on board. Any chance you can get me more information on how it applies to us?"

Heath nodded. "I get it. I was skeptical, too, at first. I'll send what I have over to you today. I want to make sure we have this handled before Christmas. I don't want to mess up your holiday plans."

Arlo scoffed. "No worries. I'm not doing anything for Christmas this year, so nothing you do will mess me up."

"Not celebrating Christmas?" Heath's eyes widened. "Why not?"

Why the heck did he open his mouth? He could have just volunteered to get the work done in plenty of time and not brought up the holiday. Now, not only did he have to answer the man, but the entire family would probably hear about it and make his next month a living hell.

"Don't mind me, Heath. I'm just grumpy today."

His sister's fiancé stared at him long and hard. "You sure that's all it is?" he asked.

Arlo nodded. "Trust me. And don't worry, we'll get everything finished before Christmas."

He wasn't fooled into thinking the matter was settled, but Heath let him off with a nod, and Arlo exited the barn before the man had second thoughts. He walked along the drive, trying to air out his melancholy. In the distance, Christmas lights decorated the barbed wire fencing. Up against one side of the barn, an old tractor tire was painted green, and someone had tied a huge bright red bow on it. And out by the petting zoo on the other side of the barns, bales of hay were painted white, piled on top of each other, and decorated to look like snow men.

His family thought the decorations made the ranch look festive.

As for him? Well, he thought it looked like a mischievous elf had thrown up Christmas dust everywhere.

With a growl, he stalked back to his office, shut his blinds and stared defiantly at his computer. He was aware of his mood but didn't care. Isaac used to be able to tease him out of it, but his best friend wasn't here anymore. He didn't care who disagreed with him. He wasn't celebrating the holiday this year.

WITH AVIVA FINALLY down for her nap, Carrie stood outside Isaac's home office, staring at the closed door. It was time to tackle the beast, but she'd been putting it off for way too long. Even going through her sister's closet had been preferable to entering Isaac's office. She'd sorted Randi's clothing, given most of it away, but kept a few pieces that held memories of the time she'd spent with her sister. She'd also kept a few maternity pieces to show Aviva when she was older, in case she wanted them as mementos of her mom, in addition to a few random scarves and shoes for the little girl to play dress-up. Although the items were personal, somehow she was able to convince herself she was doing a mitzvah by donating the clothes her sister would no longer wear, and therefore, even though she'd cried, she'd also laughed, remembering the good times they'd had together.

But Isaac's office? Ugh.

The only reason she had to go in there was his death. She'd yet to decide whether to sell the house or make it her own, but she couldn't do either if she didn't clean it out. Time was passing, though, and Aviva would be waking from her nap soon, so no matter how much she wanted to avoid the chore, she had to do it. Better to tackle the job on her terms.

Taking a deep breath, she opened the door to his home office. The drapes were closed, leaving the room in darkness, and a month of being shut up tight left it with a stuffy, musty smell. She opened the navy drapes, letting the winter light into the room. She wanted to open a window, but the chill outside made her pause. Dust motes floated in the light. A hint of Isaac's aftershave permeated the room.

She surveyed the space, deciding to tackle first what she dreaded most—his desk. The large oak piece of furniture took up a good chunk of one wall. A brown leather chair still held the imprint of his body. It didn't feel right to sit in it, but then again, it felt wrong to be in here in the first place. With a sigh, she sat on the edge of the chair, whispered an "I'm sorry" to Isaac's spirit and examined the surface of the desk.

A leather inbox sat in the upper right corner, filled with mail. She took the papers and sorted through them, making notes to check bank accounts and forward necessary pieces to his business partners.

She took the photo of Aviva—a smiling close-up showing two teeth and a little drool—and put it in the keeper pile. She pictured it in her bedroom on her dresser. The other photos, a framed copy of their wedding photo and a candid of Randi at a barbecue, made her tear up. She'd display them somewhere so Aviva could see them. She didn't want the child to forget her parents.

Finally, it was time to look inside the drawers. Invading Isaac's privacy still bothered her. She'd never been involved in his business, didn't know what he did other than financial consulting. But what if she discovered something she shouldn't?

She loved her brother-in-law, but everyone had bits of themselves they kept hidden from the rest of the world. What if he had a secret that changed how she thought about him? She'd never be able to ask him to explain what she found and would have to live with her interpretation of the news. Carrie bit her lip. The idea of asking someone else to go through his things flitted through her brain, but she tossed it aside. His colleagues had gone through his office at work already. It was her job to go through his private desk, no matter how distasteful the idea might be.

She took a deep breath before she opened the front drawer of his desk. On the left was his tablet. She smiled. Isaac had never been without it for long, constantly using it to jot down ideas for whatever project he was currently working on. It had been a bone of contention between Randi and him, although she'd always complained in a loving way about how he could never escape from his job. When Aviva was born, he'd used it as a camera as well. After trying a few password ideas, Aviva's birthday finally unlocked the tablet. She nodded as she scrolled through the apps and photos. Placing it on the desk in her keeper pile, she continued to sort through the drawer, digging through office supplies until she came to a yellow legal pad. Even a techie like Isaac had to go old-school once in a while.

The first page was a handwritten letter to Arlo.

*Dear Arlo,*

The first few lines were crossed out, and she couldn't make out the words, but then,

*I want to set things right between us. Our friendship means more to me than any argument. I never should have given—*

The letter stopped there.
Frowning, Carrie turned the page.

*Dear Arlo,*

*We never should have fought over*—the lines were crossed out.

The name, Arlo, was uncommon enough. Did he mean Arlo Fortune? She'd learned that Fortune was a big name in Chatelaine, and Arlo had paid a shiva call. She vaguely recalled him at the funeral, too, although that day had been a blur.

Her throat thickened. Had Isaac died with Arlo angry at him? She leaned back in her brother-in-law's desk chair. Isaac had always grabbed hold of what he wanted. He was loyal and defended those he loved. She couldn't imagine his letting an argument go without resolving it, especially with a friend. Carrie shook her head, saddened at the unfinished business, then moved the pad to the side and found a white envelope peeking out from the bottom of the drawer. The envelope was addressed to Arlo Fortune. There was no address given, but she recognized Isaac's handwriting. How many times had she seen it on notes written to her sister or birthday cards he'd sent to her? She traced the writing with her finger, missing the kind man who'd never failed to make her laugh. She flipped the envelope over, but it was sealed.

Her eyes welled with tears. Was this the letter he'd been writing but never sent? Was he waiting for the right time or having second thoughts? He'd died before he could send it. Her shoulders shook with silent grief as she cried about all the opportunities Isaac and Randi missed.

Holding the letter in her hand, she wondered what argument could separate good friends. Randi hadn't mentioned anything to her, even though they had spoken daily. Her sister was her best friend, and it killed her they could no longer talk to each other. Her sympathy for Arlo swelled.

She had no idea what they'd argued about, but she had to deliver the letter to him. Clearly, Isaac had been trying to patch things up between them. Maybe he'd tried unsuccessfully in person, and this letter was his last resort. Or perhaps he was trying to start the conversation with him by writing him a letter, intending to talk face-to-face later. He'd died before any of those events could happen.

She owed it to Arlo to give him the letter in person. Right away.

Still uncomfortable using Isaac's computer, she punched in Aviva's birthday again, and when it succeeded, she shook her head at his poor computer security and opened her laptop to search for Arlo's address. Randi had told her the Fortunes bought a huge ranch on the far side of Lake Chatelaine last summer. It had been the talk of the town, and she remembered her sister's conversations about it.

*"Carrie, you wouldn't believe the opulence," Randi had said one afternoon while they were chatting. "All the Fortunes live right on the lake in these big fancy cabins. Ha, not that they're the kind of cabins you or I would think of, though."*

*Carrie had pulled away from an article she was writing about energy drinks and rubbed her eyes. Staring at a laptop all day killed her eyes, and she'd been thrilled to take a break and chat with her sister.*

*"Really? Do you ever see them in town? What's the family like?"*

*"I only know one of them, Arlo Fortune. He's Isaac's best friend and is a really nice guy. Smart, too. They call him the 'ranch whisperer.'"*

*"Why? Does he whisper to cows or something? That seems kind of strange."*

*Randi had laughed. "No, but he takes failing ranches and turns them around. Even the most hopeless ones. And Aviva loves him."*

What would Randi think of her bringing the letter to Arlo? Carrie smiled through her tears. She'd probably insist on going just so she could take a look at the wealthy area.

Carrie paused. Showing up unannounced was odd. Maybe she should check to see if she could find a phone number for him, to let him know what she found and to find out if he wanted her to give him the letter. He hardly knew her, even if she was Aviva's aunt. Some people didn't like surprises.

Just then, the monitor squawked to life with Aviva's voice.

She walked into the toddler's yellow and white nursery. Ducks painted on the border of the walls right below the ceiling had always made her smile. Aviva sat up in her white toddler bed with the guard rails and gave her aunt a toothy grin.

Her blond curls were mussed from sleeping and tumbled all over her head.

"Hello, muffin," Carrie said, joy shooting through her body. Somehow, the little girl always made her smile.

"Wo. Up. Up now."

Carrie chuckled. "Yes, you want to get up now. I see that."

She lowered the guardrail and let Aviva climb out of her bed. Knowing the routine, the toddler wobbled to the changing table and grabbed a diaper, the tush of her pants sagging.

"Change now, pwese."

Some toddlers' favorite word was *no*. Aviva's was *now*. At least she said please.

"Yes, ma'am."

Aviva giggled her way through the change and then brought her stuffed elephant with her downstairs with Carrie.

Carrie fixed her a snack of bananas and cheese cubes and sat her in her booster seat at the kitchen table. She brought her milk in her blue sippy cup and, once the child was settled, opened her laptop in the seat next to her.

She entered Arlo Fortune's name in the search bar, hoping to find a phone number, but nothing came up other than his address. Frowning, she tried again, without any luck.

With one eye on Aviva, she scanned the room. Where would Randi and Isaac keep Arlo's phone number? She didn't doubt they'd had it, but they'd probably kept it in their phones, and unfortunately, those had been destroyed in the accident.

She sighed.

Aviva leaned over and patted Carrie's shoulder.

"Iss okay," she said in her little voice. "Iss okay."

Carrie kissed Aviva's head. "I should be saying that to you, little one."

Aviva scrunched her face. "I big girl."

Laughing, Carrie responded, "Yes, you are." She pretended to try to lift Aviva up and groaned. "Oh, my goodness, you *are* big!"

Peals of laughter echoed in the kitchen, filling Carrie's heart with joy. Cleaned off and out of her booster seat, Aviva raised her arms over her head.

"Big, big, big," she chanted as she marched around the room.

"Well, then, it's time to take this big girl on a ride."

"Wide?" Aviva asked.

Carrie nodded. "Ride." If she couldn't call Arlo, then she was going to have to hand deliver the letter. She just hoped he wouldn't mind a surprise visitor.

## CHAPTER TWO

ARLO WAS SITTING at his desk, buried in strategic plans for the ranch, when Maria, the part-time receptionist, knocked on his office door.

"Yeah," he said, his eyes glued to his computer. He had one more piece of information to work out before he could sign off on the plans, and he hated to break his concentration.

"Arlo, you have a visitor," Maria said.

He looked up, and his eyes widened at the sight of Carrie. He rose when he saw Aviva in her arms.

"Thanks, Maria. Carrie, Aviva, this is a nice surprise." He ushered them into his small office and looked for a place for them to sit. The ranch offices were located in a 1950s ranch-style home, where the original owners had lived before they'd expanded. When the Fortunes had taken over the property, they'd renovated the house into workspaces, and Arlo's office was in the former utility room. Usually, it suited his needs fine. He preferred working in his house on the lake, but when he needed to interact with his sisters and brothers, he worked here.

But his office wasn't set up for visitors. The room was small, with a simple metal desk and ergonomic chair. The two chairs on the other side of his desk were filled with paperwork that he hadn't yet gotten around to filing. That was to be his project during the holidays, when the rest of his family were off celebrating.

He swept one chair clean, piling the papers and folders on the floor in the corner.

"Here, sit down," he said.

Carrie looked amused. "I didn't think you'd recognize me," she said.

"I remember you from the funeral and shiva."

A frown flashed across her face, disappearing as quickly as it appeared. She looked around the office.

"You have an interesting filing method," she murmured.

He huffed. "It's not my strong suit."

He stared at the pretty woman seated across from him. The last time he'd seen her she was deep in mourning, with sadness etched into her face, her eyes deep with misery.

Now, well, he suspected she was still in mourning, but she hid it better. Carrie's dark brown hair was pulled back into a ponytail, with a few strands escaping around her oval face. Her hands were graceful, her nails polished pale pink, and she held Aviva's chubby hands in hers.

*Aviva.*

He smiled at the rosy-cheeked toddler, seeing his best friend in the shape of her mouth and the dimple in her chin.

"What can I do for you?"

Discomfort crossed Carrie's face. She began to unzip Aviva's jacket, and Arlo wasn't sure if the task was for the child's benefit or to give her something to do.

"I was going through Isaac's desk and came across these items. I thought you'd want them."

She handed him a yellow legal pad and a sealed envelope. He'd recognize that handwriting anywhere.

His chest tightened.

Grief and regret mingled and caused him to lash out. "What are you doing with this? Did you read it?"

Aviva hid her head in Carrie's shoulder. Guilt flooded through him.

"I read the legal pad because it was out in the open, and I was trying to figure out what it was," she said matter-of-factly. "And like I said, I was going through his desk at home."

He and Isaac had been best friends as children. He should have figured there might be things for him in Isaac's possessions. But the thought of this woman going through them felt like a violation of privacy.

He didn't want things. He wanted his friend.

"What gave you the right to read any of it?" He knew he shouldn't lash out at her, but he couldn't help it.

Carrie's eyes widened. She straightened, tightening her hold on Aviva. "He was my family."

Arlo paused to gather his thoughts and his breath. He looked at the envelope. Still sealed. Rationality returned. She wasn't prying; she was going through the horrible chore of sifting through her sister and brother-in-law's things.

The rest of his anger fizzled, like a soda pop going flat.

"I'm sorry," he said. "I shouldn't have jumped on you like that. I was wrong."

"You're in mourning, too," Carrie replied, her voice low. She rubbed Aviva's back, the repetitive motion soothing.

For a moment, the thought of her soothing *him* flashed through his mind, gone as quickly as it came.

"Isaac was my friend, but he was your family. I appreciate your generosity."

She nodded as he swirled his hand over the handwriting on the legal pad.

*Dear Arlo,*

*I want to set things right between us. Our friendship means more to me than any argument. I never should have given—*

He stared at the words as they blurred before his eyes. Isaac had wanted to apologize. Waves of grief overcame him. What a waste. Instead of spending weeks angry at each other, they could have worked out their differences and had extra time. He'd give anything for even an hour or two at this point, and to think he could have had an entire month.

A tap on his knee brought him back to the present. Aviva was touching his leg and holding out her arms to him. He forced a smile, leaning down to pick her up. As he gave her a hug, her sweet toddler smell washed away some of his sadness.

"Hello, pretty girl. I haven't seen you in a while. I'm sorry."

"Sowwy."

"That's right, I'm sorry."

He glanced at Carrie. Her wariness unsettled him, but then, with how angry he was, he shouldn't be surprised about her nerves around him.

Aviva lifted her arms up, and he laughed. Rising out of his chair, he lifted her up over his head and placed her on his shoulders. She squealed.

Carrie rose, looking like she wanted to pull Aviva off him, but he adjusted the child and held on to her feet.

His smooth, confident movements must have put her at ease because she sat down again.

"What animal should I be today?" he asked Aviva. It was their favorite game to play together, and even though it had been a while since he'd last seen her, and longer still since they'd played this game, she remembered.

"Chicken!" she yelled. "Cwuck, cwuck!"

His office was small, and with Carrie sitting across from his desk it felt even smaller. But he squatted and shuffled around in a circle, yelling, "Cluck, cluck." The child's peals of laughter soothed his soul, and even made Carrie smile.

Or maybe she was smiling at his ridiculous actions.

He certainly didn't look like a chicken, although he did feel like one. His mood darkened, but he tried to hide it from

Aviva. He hadn't liked what her father had said, and instead of listening to him or considering his suggestion, he'd gotten angry and walked away. And then, instead of being a mature adult and apologizing, he'd done nothing.

It was his fault they hadn't made peace with each other before Isaac died, and all because he was a coward. Suddenly, the game wasn't fun anymore.

CARRIE WATCHED IN equal parts fascination, discomfort and humor as this man she barely knew clucked like a chicken, waddling around in circles in this small, barely-big-enough-for-an-office space. His tall, muscular frame made his ridiculous movements look easy. His green eyes crinkled when he smiled, and his cheeks had sexy dimples. *Sexy?* She shook her head in equal parts confusion and denial.

Nothing had gone the way she'd expected today. The lack of control made her antsy.

Arlo knew who she was even before she introduced herself, which was odd since they barely knew each other. Back home in Albuquerque, that didn't happen, but she was quickly learning Chatelaine, Texas, was a far cry from New Mexico.

Even so, who would have thought a Fortune would know her? Yet he had and didn't think it was strange she was stopping by unannounced.

What kind of a wealthy investor had a tiny office barely big enough for antics he apparently was used to performing? Wouldn't you think he'd have kept that in mind when he'd set up his office in the first place? Or hadn't he planned to cluck like a chicken at work? Maybe he saved that behavior for his off hours. It was a good thing Aviva hadn't asked for a giraffe.

Her niece was so at ease with him, a small sliver of jealousy sliced through her. And then she took herself to task. She wasn't about to be jealous of Aviva's love of this man. There were few enough of those in the two-year-old's life, and she wasn't about to take this away from her. Her heart seized.

What would happen if she moved back to Albuquerque with Aviva? One of the best reasons to do so was to give her sister's child a bigger Jewish community. But would Aviva form such a connection with other men she met there, ones who were complete strangers?

With a mental shake, she looked on in amusement as Arlo continued to cluck and waddle in circles. She wasn't sure what to do. Aviva's laughter was contagious, and a part of her wanted to participate, to do something to cause the tyke to laugh with her, too. But she'd never been one to let down her guard enough in front of strangers, and he *was* kind of a stranger to her.

As she stood there watching the two of them play together, a shadow crossed Arlo's face. His step hitched, but he recovered before she had a chance to say anything, or even wonder if she should say something to him. A couple minutes of play later, he swung Aviva off his shoulders.

"Whew, this chicken is tired!"

Setting Aviva on the floor gently, he made sure the toddler had her balance before he looked over at Carrie.

"You must think I'm crazy," he said.

"You mean like a chicken without his head?"

He laughed, and Carrie admired this handsome man who wasn't too full of himself to play with a child and act the fool.

"No," she added. "I don't think you're crazy. I'm glad Aviva has someone in her life like you." She rummaged in her bag for a container of Goldfish, opened the top and handed it to the little girl.

"Here you go, sweetie."

"Tank you," she said.

"You're welcome." She didn't know a lot about raising a toddler, but she'd figured out that if she encouraged and modeled manners, they'd continue.

"You're very good with her," Arlo said as he watched the child munch the cheesy crackers.

"You are, too."

His green eyes pierced hers, filled with sorrow. "I'm very sorry for your loss," he said, his deep voice scratchy. He cleared it, an endearing action that filled her with sympathy. She'd received a lot of consolations during this past month, but Arlo's felt different. Like he was almost as affected as she was.

Like he understood.

Squatting next to her niece to make sure she didn't make a mess of the small office, she looked up at him.

"Thank you. I'm sorry for your loss, too. It's hard to lose a friend."

He nodded. "Especially when we—"

At her quizzical look, he swallowed before continuing. "We fought before his death and never made peace. He'll never know how sorry I am, or how much his friendship meant to me."

Carrie's heart melted, even as her throat thickened with tears she couldn't allow herself to shed. Not here, and not in front of Aviva. The girl had been around way too much sadness in her short life.

She cleared her throat and tipped her chin at the letter in Arlo's hand. The one she hadn't opened.

Neither had he.

"Maybe reading the letter will help."

He stared at it, moving it from hand to hand, turning it over and over, like Torah students searching for hidden meanings.

Without overthinking, she reached for his hand and squeezed it. Not for any other reason but to share some sympathy. She didn't expect to notice how strong his hand was, how large, how warm the skin.

She didn't expect him to squeeze back.

ARLO STILL HELD the letter in his hand after Carrie and Aviva left his office. He'd walked them to the door and watched them leave, the attractive woman and the tiny child. With their departure, his office felt small and airless. All the joy disappeared with them. He sighed, the letter weighing on him more than its actual few ounces.

He stared at it. What if reading it made him feel worse?

Shaking himself off, he silently rebuked the thoughts crowding his mind, almost hearing his father's voice scoffing in the background.

*You'll never know if you don't open it. And maybe it will actually make you feel better.*

Closing his door for privacy, he sat behind his desk, grabbed a gold letter opener with an engraved *W* on the handle—one of the things he'd taken from his father's personal belongings—and slit open the seal.

He clenched his teeth and began to read:

*Dear Arlo,*

*Your friendship means a lot to me. I had no right to try to make you look at the situation with your dad and the misdelivered toys differently. Yeah, you're right, I wanted that to be about something else. But you know I had issues with my own father, and making peace with him before he passed changed me for the good to the point that I soon met the woman I would marry. I'm a husband and father because I let my own past go. I just want the same for you. But I'm sorry for trying to bulldoze you about it. Let's put it aside.*

*—Isaac*

He dropped his head onto his desk. His breath whooshed out of him like a deflating balloon. Isaac had apologized to him. Although he'd never be able to tell his best friend he forgave him, just knowing Isaac's thoughts prior to his death was a huge relief. Memories of the day of their fight swirled in his brain, but this time, others drove them away. Their first day of rodeo camp, when Arlo had reassured Isaac that the horses were friendly; s'mores-eating contests…and getting sick afterward; the cowboy song they'd created and sung together. There were also more adult memories—visiting each other over college breaks; conversations about investing strategies; Isaac's excitement at finding "the perfect place to live near camp," and then his surprise and pleasure when Arlo and his family moved here.

So many wonderful times together. He wished there could be more.

He remembered his friend's nuptials. It had been the first time he'd attended a Jewish wedding, and he'd been fascinated by the customs—stepping on a glass, the bride circling the groom, the wedding canopy. Isaac and Randi had looked joyous. He remembered being pleased for them, but there were also shards of jealousy, wondering if he'd ever find someone who made him as happy as they made each other feel.

He still wondered that sometimes.

Sighing, he raised his head and flattened the letter on the desk. Thanks to his friend's words, he could look back at their relationship with less pain than he'd felt in more than a month.

If he couldn't have settled things between Isaac and himself before the accident, at least he knew his friend had forgiven him. It wasn't perfect, but it was much better than before.

When Isaac and Randi had moved to Chatelaine, they'd raved about small-town life. When Randi had gotten pregnant, Isaac had talked to Arlo about the prospect of teaching his child how to ride a horse.

Well, Isaac was gone now, but *he* was here. Maybe he could talk to Carrie about getting Aviva horseback riding lessons someday. Heck, he had an entire ranch filled with his siblings who worked on it. His sister Dahlia was a sheep farmer. Jade led children's workshops and ran a petting zoo. Even his brother Ridge was a cowboy. One of them could come up with something. Plus, he needed to thank Carrie for giving him the letter.

## CHAPTER THREE

ARLO DROVE INTO TOWN, past GreatStore, Remi's Reads and the Cowgirl Café. They were decorated for Christmas, with lights strung around their windows. A sign in the window of GreatStore advertised the yearly Christmas cookie contest to be held at the local church. Everywhere he looked, there were signs of the holiday. He turned off the main road onto Carrie's street. As it happened every time he pulled into the driveway, his mind couldn't grasp that Isaac and Randi were gone. He expected them to open the door and give him a hug and a clap on the back as they always had. But when he exited his truck, loped up the front steps and rang the doorbell, they didn't answer.

Carrie did.

"Arlo," she said, surprise showing on her face. "Come in." She opened the door wide, and he stepped into the familiar-but-not front hallway, removing his cowboy hat and placing it on the hall coat rack, as usual. Carrie had left the rack but changed the hallway, adding photos of her sister and brother-in-law on the entryway table. The sight of them gave him both pleasure and pain. He hadn't fully thought this through.

To his right, in the living room, Aviva sat on the floor playing with toys.

"I hope I'm not disturbing you," he said, rocking back and forth in his boots.

Carrie had her dark hair tied back in a loose ponytail. Wisps on either side of her face had escaped. She wore tight-fitting jeans that showed off her long legs, and a soft-looking pink sweater that made her cheeks glow.

"Not at all." She turned to her niece. "We love company, right?"

Aviva put her hands on the floor and stood up, then ran over to Arlo and grabbed his leg.

Grinning, he swung her up in the air. "Hello, munchkin!"

She squeezed his neck, and he inhaled her little-girl smell. The more he saw her, the greater the pull he felt for her. She was the living, breathing embodiment of her parents.

"Would you like to come in?" Carrie asked. Her voice brought him back into the moment.

He looked at her, and he thought he saw understanding flash across her face, but it was gone before he could be sure.

Nodding, he followed her into the living room. She motioned to the deep gray suede couch, and he sat. Aviva wiggled out of his grasp and returned to her toys on the gray-and-green-striped rug. He scanned the room. Once again, there were photos of Isaac, Randi and Aviva everywhere.

"I don't want Aviva to forget them," Carrie said.

"So, you're going to stay?"

"For now."

The answer pleased him. "I'm happy to hear that. It gives me more time to spend with Aviva." Being separated from the child had been especially hard during his estrangement from Isaac, and he was looking forward to making up for lost time.

Turning his thoughts from Aviva to her aunt, he glanced at Carrie sitting on the corner of the couch. She was quieter than most women he knew. On the ranch, his sisters were constantly in motion, Dahlia working with her sheep and expanding the dairy farm, Sabrina crunching the numbers and Jade leading children's workshops. But Carrie was still. At least, her *body* was. He'd bet there was a lot going on in her brain. There was something about the way she observed everything that spoke to him.

"I wanted to thank you for bringing me the letter and the legal pad," he said, when the silence had stretched a moment too long. "They were really helpful."

Her expression softened. "I'm so glad. I don't know what the letter said, but based on what I saw written on the legal pad, well, I hope you were able to get some closure."

He ran a hand over the top of his head. "Closure. That's a tough word. I don't know if that's possible, but after reading the letter, I feel better knowing Isaac forgives me."

His stomach clenched. He hadn't meant to blurt that out.

"How are you doing?" he asked. It was a long overdue question.

She redirected her gaze to Aviva, who continued to play with her toys. "I don't know," she admitted. "I love Aviva more than anything in the world. I thought I was coming here to babysit for a week. Next thing I know, I've lost my sister and brother-in-law, I'm living in a small ranching town, and I'm responsible for raising her and for teaching her all about her religion. It's such a huge change. I haven't had a moment to breathe, let alone think about how I'm doing."

Gosh, he should have checked in on her sooner. Of course, she was overwhelmed. Meanwhile, he'd been sitting with his head up his butt like a rodeo clown.

"I remember Randi being so excited you were coming. And Isaac, who had been nervous about leaving Aviva for a week, relaxed as soon as Randi told him you'd be babysitting." He turned to look at Carrie. "They had a lot of faith in you."

Her dark eyes welled with tears. "Thank you. That's nice to know."

"Tell me about Randi," he said quietly. "What was she like as a big sister?"

"Bossy," Carrie answered with a laugh. "No, I guess that's not true. She always looked out for me when we were growing up. It used to annoy me at times, but then when she had Aviva, I realized she was just a mothering type. It wasn't in her nature to let those she cared about suffer, so she was always trying to help me."

Arlo nodded. "Yeah, I understand that. I have five other siblings, and one of them was always trying to boss someone around. Usually me, since everyone but Ridge is older than I am."

"How did you and Isaac meet?" she asked. "I remember he was so excited to be moving here near where he went to camp."

"We met at a rodeo camp when we were seven." He chuckled. "We were the unlikeliest rodeo cowboys you'd ever met, at least that first year. We were both small and skinny and hadn't been around horses before."

Carrie laughed, and Arlo warmed to the topic. "Isaac grew up in Dallas and was a total city kid, and I grew up in a small town outside Dallas without any knowledge of horses, either. So, I guess we decided teaming up together was our best course of action."

Nodding, Carrie said, "I'll bet."

"By the end of the summer, we were horse crazy. We kept in touch all during the year, even though my dad thought rodeo horses were beneath me." He swallowed. "As we got older and returned to camp yearly, we started to be known for our skills not just with horses, but activities involved with running the camp. As adults, we turned that knowledge into our businesses."

"Wow, you got all of that experience at a rodeo camp?"

He nodded. "You'd be surprised how well horse skills can translate into other ones."

"How so?" Carrie asked curiously.

Arlo adjusted his body and got comfortable. "Well, I can look at a horse—his movements, his eyes, his breathing—and know how reliable that horse is. That skill translates to people. I can get a good sense how trustworthy a person is based on their body language. And when I'm taking a look at the books on the business side, I use my knowledge of the people—as well as the animals they use—to determine how successful that ranch is going to be."

"That's incredible."

"Not really. You just have to understand a ranch is more than just numbers." He rolled a ball to Aviva, who rolled it back to him. "What about you? What do you do?"

"I'm a writer. I write health and wellness articles for a variety of online sites."

"Really? That's cool. What kinds of articles?"

"A lot of food and nutrition, with some mental health thrown in as well." She looked around before continuing. "I'm actually considering pitching a grief journey series to my editors. Unfortunately, I've learned a lot about that in the past month, and I think my experiences could help others."

"I think that's a great idea," Arlo said thickly. "Maybe it will give you an outlet, help you process everything. I know that's been my struggle."

He paused. Had he really just confessed that to her, almost a complete stranger? He studied her. She wasn't *really* a complete stranger. In some ways, he'd been more open with her than he had been with his siblings. And nothing about her hinted that she'd use anything he said to her advantage. She oozed kindness and compassion.

"It's something that's been tough for me, too. Which is why I want to write about it, even if no one publishes it." She focused on Aviva for a few moments. "Now I just have to find the time to do it, right, cutie?"

"Pay wif bocks?" Aviva asked, holding one up.

As Carrie took it and started to build a tower, Arlo marveled at her strength. She'd lost her sister and brother-in-law, had taken over the care of her niece and had to learn to juggle single-parenthood and a job, as well as her own grief. Yet she wanted to help others, too.

He shook his head as the differences between the two of them stared him in the face. While he'd turned inward, she'd turned outward.

Regret nudged him once again. He really should have offered to help her long before now.

Carrie rose. "I'm getting her a snack. Can I offer you anything to eat or drink?"

"I'll take a Coke if you have it."

She nodded, and he played with Aviva, rebuilding the tower she'd knocked down while Carrie left the room. A few minutes later she returned with a sippy cup and a container of Cheerios for Aviva and two Cokes.

They both drank and watched Aviva for a few moments.

"Are you entering the Christmas cookie contest?" he asked to break the silence. At her quizzical look, he continued. "The town council sponsors it every year. People bake their favorite holiday treats, and the mayor and other town leaders judge. The entry fees go to help the poor. Winners receive a monogrammed apron and a certificate." He grinned. The prize was a little ridiculous, but the cause was good.

Carrie looked thoughtful. "I didn't know about it. I could make *bimuelos*. They're a Hanukkah treat. Do you think that would be okay?"

Arlo nodded. "I'm sure they would. What are they?"

"They're puffed fritters with an orange glaze. It's a Sephardic Jewish tradition for Hanukkah."

"Sephardic?"

Carrie nodded. "Jews who come from Eastern Europe are Ashkenazi, and they have their own foods and traditions that they brought over from Europe. Jews from the Middle East and Spain are Sephardi, and although we have the same religious traditions, our culture reflects where we're from geographically."

"That's fascinating," Arlo said. "I guess now that I think

of it, different countries celebrate Christmas differently, too, whether it's food or when we open presents. But I never spent a lot of time considering the differences."

Carrie smiled. "It's so interesting to learn about other cultures and traditions. And sometimes, we even find similarities that we didn't know about."

"Tell me more about Hanukkah," he said. "Those *bimuelos* sound delicious."

"They are," Carrie said. "The holiday, although relatively minor on our calendar, celebrates the miracle of the oil and a military victory from back in ancient times. A small tribe of Jews, the Maccabees, beat a huge army who destroyed their temple. After the battle, the menorah only had enough oil to last one day, but it lasted eight, enough time for the oil to be found and replaced. Since then, we light a special candelabra, called a menorah, one candle each night for eight nights."

"I learned some of that," Arlo said. "I joined Isaac's family once or twice, and they gave me a brief overview. I remember thinking lighting the candles were cool, and you know, eight days of presents had its appeal." He laughed. "Maybe you can teach me more about it."

"Of course." Carrie's face lit up. "There are so many fascinating traditions to being Jewish, and a lot of them involve food."

Arlo rubbed his stomach, making Carrie laugh. "We eat jelly donuts during the holiday because they are fried in oil. When we light the candles, we recite a psalm in honor of the rededication of the Temple. And, since we are Sephardic, coming from the Mediterranean countries rather than the Eastern European ones, we have a big celebration—a *merenda*—on the last night of Hanukkah."

"Looks like Randi chose the perfect person to teach Aviva about her religious culture," he said.

"Thank you," she said. "That's such a nice thing to say. I really want to make sure Aviva doesn't feel alone in her heritage." She released a breath. "And maybe you could share some of your Christmas traditions with me." She gave him a smile that blew him away.

He was so speechless, in fact, that all he could do was nod. When she smiled, it was as if a magnetic field formed around her, drawing him in and making him never want to see that smile dim. Without thinking, he blurted, "My father sent a box of toys to someone right before he died."

"Who'd he send it to?"

"That's just it, I don't know," he muttered. "It was addressed to someone named Stevie Fields, but the address he wrote down doesn't exist. The postman brought it back to the ranch, saying the address was wrong and the mail forwarding listed Windham, our old name, in the system. He was trying to do the right thing and bring it back to us to figure out."

"And did you?"

Arlo shook his head. "Nope." He stared off into the distance. His dad was a mystery, and the box didn't clear anything up. He sighed, focusing on Carrie once again. "I couldn't exactly tell the postman that we'd all moved to Chatelaine to start over, changing our name from Windham to Fortune when my mom found out she was related to that family. Heck, I'm not even sure why I'm telling you, except…" He hesitated. "You're easy to talk to. But the box reminded me of everything I'm trying to forget, and everything I can't fix."

Carrie reached for his hand. "For the past few years, I've been so focused on my writing career, I neglected my family. There were so many times Randi invited me here to spend a weekend to catch up, and I never took her up on it. I always said I was too busy, even though my career was the kind I could do anywhere. It's only now that she's gone that I realize what I missed." She leaned forward. "Have you looked inside the box?"

He nodded, exhaling a deep breath. "It's a box of toys, with a note that said, Dear Stevie, Enjoy these! Casper Windham.

My dad was sending toys to some little kid, so that has to mean he had an affair with a woman in Chatelaine and this kid is his second family." He scoffed. "It's just like him to add another mysterious layer when I can't confront him."

"Oh, wow, that must be heartbreaking for you," she said softly. "What do your siblings say? Did they know anything about this?"

He shook his head. "I didn't tell them. They all have their own issues with my dad." He rose and paced the room, hands in his pockets. Confusion swirled through him. "I did tell Isaac, though. That's what we fought about. He was trying to convince me the box of toys could be something completely harmless, but *come on*! This isn't my first rodeo. He was trying to get me to look into it before I jumped to the wrong conclusion, but he didn't know what he was talking about. My dad was a cold, ruthless businessman who always put his company before anyone in his family."

Footsteps behind him warned him Carrie approached a second before she put a comforting hand on his shoulder.

"My dad cheated on my mom when we were young, so I understand the betrayal you're feeling," she confided. "It was the worst time of my life." Her voice grew thoughtful. "We lived outside Albuquerque at the time, and it seemed like everyone knew what happened. They either gave me and my sister pitying looks or whispered behind my mom's back. I was so glad when we moved to Albuquerque proper so I could start over."

Arlo's chest tightened at the image of the childhood Carrie painted. He'd had his family to rely on when his world fell apart, even if he hadn't been the most gracious about accepting their help. In the back of his mind, though, he knew with bone-deep certainty that his siblings and his mom would do anything for him, just as he would for them. Looking back at his upbringing, he realized his mom had always shielded him and his siblings from his dad's life choices. Wendy had supported him and kept him from knowing what other people said, if they'd said anything at all. He still didn't know.

His heart ached knowing Carrie hadn't had that same protection as a young child.

He didn't understand why fathers would put their children through this. Weren't they supposed to love and nurture them? What was wrong with some men? He looked at Aviva. If he were a dad, he'd do everything possible not to hurt his children.

"I just don't get it," he gritted out.

Carrie turned, and he realized he'd spoken out loud. "What don't you get?" she asked.

Once again, whether it was her sympathetic expression or her similar experience, he felt the need to bare his soul.

"I don't get why some men are such jerks when it comes to their families." His fisted his hands at his sides. "And I'll never know why my dad did what he did. Isaac was right, the *not knowing* is killing me. He kept pushing me to look into it, as if finding out whether my dad had an affair or an illegitimate child is going to make a difference."

He heaved himself off the sofa and paced the room. "Isaac just wouldn't let it go. He kept insisting I look up Stevie Fields and that his own good life was testament to the idea that the truth sets you free." He scoffed. "I stalked off and now he's dead." He whispered the last part, his throat aching.

Sniffling made him look back at Carrie. Her eyes were filled with tears, and guilt pierced him. *Great, she's in mourning, and I'm making her cry.*

He'd leave, but it would be even worse to abandon her while she was upset.

"I don't want to butt in, or make you feel worse, but maybe Isaac was right," she said, wiping her eyes. "At least if you know the truth, you'll be able to feel the proper emotions. Look at Isaac. He was adopted, but his adoptive parents kept that a secret from him until he was much older. Not knowing his true past made it hard for him to trust anyone. He was angry at his parents, especially his dad, who had insisted on the secrecy, but they finally talked it all out." She paused for a beat before continuing. "Knowing his background didn't make up for everything, but it helped him realize there wasn't anything wrong with him, and once he learned that information, he and Randi were able to make a wonderful life together."

She turned toward him again when he sat on the sofa. There was something about her voice that calmed him. "If nothing else, it will help you know what to do with those toys," she said.

He groaned. "You're right. And so was Isaac." He ground out those last words, his throat feeling like sandpaper over the admission.

He needed a break. Looking around the room, he noticed things he hadn't before. Like nail pops in the walls near the doorway into the kitchen and scuffed paint on the baseboards. The bookshelf next to the fireplace looked crooked, and he rose to check it out.

"Careful," Carrie warned. "It's getting a little wobbly. I need to get that fixed before Aviva pulls a book off the shelf and the entire thing topples."

"This is dangerous," he stated, looking around to see if there was something to secure the bookcase. "Don't leave her alone in this room."

Carrie's eyes flashed. "I know how to take care of my niece."

He realized how his comment had come across at about the same time Carrie blushed.

"I'm sorry," he said, softening his tone.

"I am, too," she added. "I didn't mean to jump on you. You're right about the bookcase. In fact, I've got a list of the repairs I need to make around here. I'm still getting used to being in a small town where everyone is in everyone else's business."

She held up her hands in apology. "Not that I object to your help in keeping her safe. Do you know any reputable repairmen?"

He nodded. "I get it. At the risk of making you even more uncomfortable, would you let me help out with that list of repairs? Isaac tried to help me, and I brushed him off. I can't apologize to him, but it would make me feel better if I could work on his list. It's a way for me to make amends, I guess?"

"Of course," Carrie said, a look of relief on her face. "That would really help me out. And how about, as a thank-you, I make you some of my famous Hanukkah *bimuelos*?"

He grinned, patting his stomach. "I wouldn't refuse."

CARRIE LOOKED AROUND the living room, trying to see it through Arlo's eyes. He was right; there were a lot of things that needed minor repairs. Randi had decorated it with an eye toward hominess and comfort—light gray walls, green and blue pillows on the sofa, colorful family photos on the white fireplace mantle and wood furniture stained a dark gray. It was calming and definitely family friendly, but, as Arlo pointed out, things needed repairing. Even Isaac had kept a list in his desk of repairs that needed to be made. She was happy to accept Arlo's help, especially if it meant he'd be around more often.

Just watching him with her niece gave her a sense of joy she'd missed these last few weeks. Aviva clearly loved him, and he seemed to return the feelings. Right now, he'd moved onto the floor with the toddler, handing her blocks for her to build a tower. She'd build it, knock it down and chortle with glee.

Carrie settled back onto the sofa, content to watch the two of them together while she got some of her own work done. The more often he was here to fix things, the more he and Aviva could continue to strengthen their bond. Without a father, it was more important than ever for her niece to have a strong male figure in her life.

And Arlo was definitely strong. He might be involved with the business side of the ranch, but his forearms were muscular, his shoulders wide, and he appeared to handle any physical tasks she gave him with ease. But as much as she admired his outward strength, there was more to him than met the eye. He was confident and clearly willing to put his own work and troubles aside to help others. Those were traits she admired, but she didn't want whatever was bothering him to fester. Maybe if she spent more time with him, she'd be able to convince him to investigate the relationship between his father and Stevie Fields. Because as she'd written time and again in her articles, true peace didn't happen until a person had worked through an issue. And the only way that would happen for Arlo was if he stopped running from what "might be."

Not to mention, focusing on helping Arlo helped her gain control of her own grief.

Aviva started rubbing her eyes, and with a start, Carrie realized it was nap time.

"Hey, baby girl, it's time to go *durme*."

Arlo frowned in confusion.

"It's Ladino for sleep," Carrie said. "Ladino is a combination of Hebrew and Spanish."

He shook his head. "That's so interesting."

Aviva held out her arms to him. "Arwo."

Carrie wasn't sure who melted more, her or Arlo. All she knew was her own heart turned to mush as the muscular man lifted the sweet child into his arms, cradling her against his broad chest as she rested her head on his shoulder and stuck her thumb in her mouth.

She must have sighed out loud, because Arlo glanced her way. Her pulse raced at the look he gave her, like they were part of something. Together. Blinking, suddenly thrown into something she didn't quite recognize, she blurted, "I'll show you the way."

As soon as the words escaped her lips, she flushed. He'd been here before, so surely, he knew which way was Aviva's bedroom.

His eyes glowed, like he smiled from within, but instead of

correcting her, he simply whispered to Aviva, "Which animal should I be today?"

Her niece answered in a sleepy voice. "A sheep."

As Arlo bahhed his way out of the living room and upstairs to Aviva's bedroom, Carrie struggled to collect herself. This man who was so aloof was perfectly fine turning himself into an animal to please a two-year-old? And somehow, in the process, he made her feel she was part of their special group.

Because the two of them—this man who seemed to appear right when she needed him, and this little girl who brightened up even Carrie's darkest day—had a bond.

While Carrie pulled down the blackout shades in Aviva's duck-themed room and made sure her toddler bed with the white eyelet cover was ready for the nap, Arlo deposited the child on the floor before getting down on all fours and continuing to play the sheep. He nudged her with his face, making her giggle. Once she climbed into bed, Arlo suggested he read her a story.

Carrie sat in the maple rocker—the same one their mom had used when she and her sister were babies—and listened while he told Aviva a story about a lamb who was looking for just the right spot of grass to snack. Every place she nosed, she didn't like. One area was too minty, another too mossy, until finally she found the perfect blades of grass, under a tree where after she ate, she could nap.

By the time he finished reading, Aviva lay curled in her bed, eyes drooping, thumb in her mouth. Carrie didn't know whether to laugh at his antics or ask him to teach her how he did it. Her niece never went down as easily for her.

They left the room together, and, in the hallway, she spoke to him. "You are the toddler whisperer," she said.

He shrugged. "Toddler whisperer, ranch whisperer, I'll take whatever you'd like to call me."

"You're clearly multi-talented."

He followed her into the kitchen and waited while she put a kettle on to boil.

"Isaac used to call me ranch whisperer because I have a knack for turning struggling ranches around."

"Randi told me. I heard you and your family recently bought a ranch on the other side of town."

He nodded. "We did. And I'm doing my thing and making sure it's as successful as possible for our family."

She handed him a mug. "Isaac used to talk about you, you know. Said you were the only finance guy he'd trust, other than himself."

"That was mighty nice of him." He paused for a moment, before walking around Carrie and opening the cabinet above her.

The position of his body hemmed her in and made her aware of him as a man. He smelled like pine and soap, reminding her of her grandmother's kitchen during Passover cleaning. She would have taken a deep breath, but her lungs were constricted by his large presence. Hyperaware of him, the hairs on the back of her arm rose as his biceps came within an inch of her. He never touched her, but his proximity did things to her. Things she shouldn't think about, not when she was alone in the house with a toddler to take care of.

His breathing echoed in her head, making strands of her hair billow. It would be easy to lean back, just a fraction, to feel his body against hers—hard muscle, soft fabric, prickly whiskers. She'd been strong and on her own for so long. All she wanted was to give in for one minute.

What would he do if she leaned back? Or better yet, turned around and let their bodies touch?

Then his stomach rumbled, and the spell was broken. She closed her eyes, grateful she hadn't given in to her weakness... or her desire. This was Arlo, her brother-in-law's best friend. He was here because of Aviva. Just like him, her focus needed to be on her niece.

"I thought we might need plates," he said, his voice gravelly. "In case you wanted a snack to go along with your tea."

Did all men think only about food or was it just Arlo? "I guess you're hungry," she murmured.

Turning, she met his green-eyed gaze. Once again, the color seared itself into her brain, reminding her of Lake Chatelaine on a stormy day, when the wind whipped up and the sky turned that greenish-yellow gray right before a tornado.

What kinds of thoughts were racing through his brain to turn his eyes that color? They couldn't be just for food, could they?

He remained silent long enough for her to realize she was right, he wasn't thinking only about food. Carrie replayed her comment in her head, and her body heated. She suspected her face was turning red.

*Lovely.*

He stepped away and finally responded, "I could eat."

*Thank goodness.*

The situation was slipping away from her, something she couldn't afford to let happen. She poured tea into the two mugs and slid them toward Arlo while she searched the fridge for snacks. The refrigerated air cooled her cheeks, and by the time she'd pulled out hummus, cheese and cut-up vegetables, she felt more in control. Grabbing pita crackers from the pantry, she arranged everything onto a tray and brought it back into the living room.

His eyes widened. "I didn't mean for you to go to such trouble."

"No trouble. Besides, this is what happens when you tell a Jewish woman you're hungry." *Or when she needs a minute to collect herself.*

"Noted," he said. He dipped a raw carrot into the hummus and stuck it in his mouth. Her throat dried as she watched his strong jaw and throat move as he chewed and swallowed.

So much for cooling off and collecting herself.

"Have you put up your Christmas tree yet?" she asked, searching for a topic of conversation to distract herself.

He sipped his tea before shaking his head. "I'm skipping the tree this year."

Carrie was taken aback. "Why?"

"I'm not in a festive mood, no matter how many ads I see, or how many stores try to convince me to get into the Christmas spirit. I don't think half of them would recognize the meaning of the holiday if they fell over it."

He couldn't really mean to skip Christmas, could he?

"I've noticed Chatelaine is really getting into the holiday spirit," she said. "All the restaurants and stores are decorated and—"

"Don't forget the sales," he said, his voice bitter. "It's not Christmas if you can't spend money on things no one needs. I swear," he said, "people become like my dad at this time of year, so caught up in the materialistic side..."

His hands were fisted on the table, and he wasn't looking at her, but off into the distance. His body was taut with tension.

She wanted to reach across and cover his hand with hers, to ease whatever was troubling him. But she didn't know him well enough, and besides, he might not want that. Just because his attitude about Christmas made her feel bad didn't mean she could assume she knew what was best. She gripped her mug of tea tighter.

He shook his head. "Sorry about that. You didn't deserve that outburst."

She blew on the tea before answering. "You don't have to apologize to me," she said. "It is easy to get caught up in shopping during the holidays and forget about the meaning behind it. I get it. I'm responsible for Aviva's Hanukkah celebrations this year—both the religious rituals and the fun, present-y ones, and there's a huge side of me that wants to buy her everything I see." Part of that desire was to make up for what she'd lost, as if somehow a toy could make losing her parents less awful.

"What stops you?" His gaze bore into her.

"You mean besides the fear of bankruptcy?" she deadpanned.

He huffed in response, his gaze brightening.

She smiled and continued. "I keep thinking about the meaning of the holiday and how Randi asked me to help teach Aviva about her heritage. Hanukkah's a pretty minor holiday, but it has lots of traditions. So, although I will buy her presents, there are so many other activities that we'll be doing, and I'm trying to focus on all of them."

He nodded. "As I mentioned before, I know a little about Hanukkah," he said. "Mostly that potato pancakes are delicious. Although," he paused. "Isaac and Randi always invited me to dinner the last night of Hanukkah."

She laughed. "Clearly the way to your heart is through your stomach. That dinner is called a *merenda*." His gaze intensified, and she looked away before continuing. "Although I already told you the story of Hanukkah, I'm happy to teach you, along with Aviva, more about the holiday, especially since you'll probably be here during a lot of our activities. Your first lesson," she said with a smile, "is that it is about way more than potato pancakes. I'll have to make you some *cassola* and *keftes de espinaca*. They are delicious!"

He pushed his plate away and leaned back on the sofa. "I think I've had those, but I'd love to learn. And clearly, I'm going to have to drag out the repairs needed around here, since I need to try all the food, even though I don't understand half of what you're saying."

Carrie laughed, glad to see Arlo's mood changing. She hadn't been sure she'd be able to dredge up enough holiday spirit to teach her niece, but maybe she could help the two of them and herself at the same time.

"*Cassola* is a sweet cheese pancake and *keftes de espinaca* are spinach patties. Sephardic Jews make them at Hanukkah because they're deep-fried in oil."

Arlo patted his stomach. "Sounds good to me. I'll take as many as you want to make me."

She took a sip of tea and replaced the mug on the table again. "On second thought, maybe I'll teach you to make them." There was nothing sexier than a man cooking. Her cheeks heated, and she brushed the thought away. "In fact, why don't you come for dinner one night this week? We can have a mini-Hanukkah food-making lesson, and then you can try all the delicacies. And maybe tell me a little about your Christmas celebrations."

*Oh, gosh, had she gone too far?* Her only intent had been to make him feel better and to get him to want to participate in the holidays.

But the smile that lit him from within eased her fears. "I'd like that."

Her stomach fluttered with excitement at the thought of dinner with Arlo. "Great," she said. "And thank you."

He frowned. "For what?"

"You're helping me get into my own holiday spirit."

Rising from the sofa, he brought the tray of snacks into the kitchen. She followed him, and almost bumped into him when he turned. He held on to her arms to keep her from falling over. His scent, his proximity, his touch, sent shivers down her spine. Time stopped as he looked at her, his thumbs making circles on her skin. The silence lengthened. She licked her suddenly dry lips, and like the crack of a starter pistol, he pulled back.

"Anything I can do to help." One corner of his mouth turned up before he grabbed his hat and left her house.

THE SHORT DRIVE to his brother Ridge's house was not nearly enough time for Arlo's thoughts to settle. Indeed, his heart still pounded, and his palms were slick on the steering wheel as he thought about how close he'd come to kissing Carrie.

*Kissing Carrie.*

It had been the only thought potent enough to cut through his bitterness. As far as he was concerned, the holidays should be canceled this year. He was in no mood to celebrate them or humor the commercialization gods.

He'd even let some of his feelings bleed into his conversation with Carrie. But somehow she'd managed to wiggle past his defenses, show her compassion and entice him all at once. From the moment he'd entered her kitchen, all he'd wanted to do was take her in his arms and kiss her.

Was that even allowed? She was still in mourning for her sister. Yet he'd swear she'd looked at him like she wanted to kiss him, too. She smelled like flowers, and being near her had made all his rational thoughts evaporate.

He shook his head as he turned off the ignition. He was supposed to be helping Carrie, not jumping her bones, no matter how enticing she might be. This wasn't the time to start something with her.

He stayed inside his truck for another a minute, thinking about her. The woman amazed him. In the face of all her hardship, she was still able to look forward and find joy. And despite his initial protests about the holiday, she'd even made him eager to celebrate pieces of it with her. How did she do it? Maybe it was the responsibility of taking care of a child. Because she took that responsibility seriously. It would have been easy for her to do what was best for herself, regardless of her sister's wishes. But she was intent on carrying out her promise to Randi and Isaac and celebrate the holiday, no matter how sad she was.

He shook his head. Responsibility might explain Carrie's eagerness for Hanukkah, but he had responsibilities, too, and they were doing nothing to get him in the holiday mood. Helping ensure his family's ranch success was hard work. When his mother had bought the ranch, he'd been all for working here, as had his siblings. But instead of giving him joy, all the ranch did was remind him of his father and his best friend. Every success he had on the Fortune Family Ranch made him want to say, *"See, Dad?"* It also made him want to go out and celebrate with Isaac or ask his financial advice. He had to find a way forward, but he didn't know how. That's why he'd driven to his brother's house.

He looked through the windshield toward Ridge's cabin. Two stone square pillars with a plain bronze-looking gate sat at the entrance to his gravel driveway. The gate and pillars were similar to his own in simplicity, although Arlo's stone pillars were lower and wider, and his gate was wood. Since the family owned the entire thirty-five-hundred-acre ranch, they rarely kept the gates closed, and Arlo drove right through.

He pulled his pickup truck up to his brother Ridge's cabin. Similar to his own, the center part of the structure was a wooden A-frame, with wings on either side and a large front porch that faced the ranch. But he knew from experience that the back of the house was the impressive part, with almost an entire wall of windows overlooking Lake Chatelaine.

He climbed out of his truck and grabbed his hat. Maybe Ridge could help. As kids, they'd stuck together. As teenagers, they'd gotten into trouble together. And as adults, they'd looked to each other for advice. When Arlo had a problem, he'd always talked to his younger brother. But still, he didn't move. Somehow, when faced with the need to do something to solve his problems, paralysis struck.

He scoffed. Sitting in his truck wasn't helping matters. With a sigh, he climbed out, grabbed his Stetson and made his way up to the front door.

Like everyone else, his brother's cabin was decorated for Christmas, with a big wreath on the front door. He knocked on Ridge's door, all the while wondering what outdoor decorations, if any, Carrie planned for her house for Hanukkah. He hadn't asked her about decorating. He'd have to remember to do that tomorrow.

A female voice to his left startled him.

"Hi," Hope, the woman who was staying with Ridge while she recovered from losing her memory, greeted him. She held her seven-month-old daughter, Evie, in her arms.

"Hi, Hope," Arlo said. "How are you?"

She gave a shy smile. "Okay, thanks. You?"

"Pretty good," he answered.

The front door swung wide, and Ridge answered the door.

"Arlo." The two men slapped each other's backs. "Come on in," Ridge said. He looked at his auburn-haired houseguest and an expression passed across his face. "Hope, did you need anything?"

"No, I was just going to go to the grocery store. I'm out of milk."

"I've got plenty inside. Come on in." He made room for Hope and the baby to pass by him, before addressing Arlo. "You just caught me. I was about to go back out and talk to Bender about sheepherding. Can I get you anything?"

Arlo shrugged. "I just wanted to say hello." He watched Hope head into the kitchen, noticing how similar she looked from the back to Carrie when she held Aviva. They both turned their faces into the baby, they both arched their backs the same way. Maybe it was a mom thing, even if Carrie wasn't quite a mom.

"What's up, Arlo?" Ridge's expression changed from fondness as he looked at Hope to concern as he focused on him.

His brother cared for that woman.

Arlo shook his head and paced around the room. He'd loved being with Carrie, but now he was antsy and didn't know why.

"My head's just in a weird place, you know?"

Ridge nodded. "It's only been a month since Isaac died, and less than a year since Dad did. Your head is going to be messed up for a while."

"I shoulda made peace with Dad before he died. And now…" He shrugged.

"Why didn't you?"

This was a mistake coming here. He couldn't tell Ridge, or any of his siblings, what he'd found in that box. It would mess up those who'd made amends with the man, and not help those who hadn't. He had to shoulder this burden alone.

"Stubborn, I guess." He needed to change the subject. His gaze bounced off the Christmas tree in the other room.

"What are you getting Hope and Evie for Christmas?"

Ridge held his finger to his lips before pulling out his phone and showing Arlo a picture of a diamond key pendant.

Arlo grinned. "That's beautiful, but a little fancy for a seven-month-old."

His grin faded as Ridge nudged him with his shoulder. "Jerk."

Rubbing it, he nodded. "Nice. And how about the baby?"

"That's more Hope's department."

"What's Hope's department?" Hope asked as she returned to the great room. She handed Evie to Arlo while she poured the milk into a bottle.

Arlo shook his head when she reached for Evie again. "That's okay, I like holding her. Right, Evie?"

Evie gurgled and gave him a big smile.

His chest warmed. Something about babies always made him feel good. It was weird. He'd never have thought of himself as a baby lover, but between Evie and Aviva…

"I was asking what you're getting Evie for Christmas."

Hope's face brightened. "It's her first one, so I want it to be special. But she's so young, it's not going to mean much to her. Probably a couple of cute outfits and a toy or two."

Ridge turned to her. "Maybe more than a toy or two, but we'll see."

Hope looked up at him and smiled.

An idea crossed his mind. "I don't suppose you'd know what to get a two-year-old for Hanukkah?" He wasn't sure where that question came from, but suddenly, he wanted to add Aviva, and maybe even Carrie, to his holiday list.

Hope's eyes brightened. "Two-year-olds are fun, and with eight days of gifts, you could buy all sorts of things," she said. "You could get developmental toys, like puzzles, or stacking toys. Books are always good, too, like *The Very Hungry Caterpillar* or *Goodnight Moon*. Or even a stuffed animal—"

She froze, and, confused, Arlo glanced at Ridge in alarm, while squeezing Evie against his chest.

"Hope, what's wrong?" Ridge asked.

Her eyes were wide, but she remained silent, as if she was somewhere else. Seconds ticked by, with Arlo watching Ridge as his face crinkled in concern.

Finally, she blinked, before reaching for Ridge and burying her face in his shoulder. Her shoulders rose and fell while they waited for her to speak. Finally, she turned, tears in her eyes.

"I remembered being in a man's embrace," she whispered. "I was loved, cherished." She touched the ring finger on her left hand. "I was wearing a wedding ring."

Arlo glanced at his brother. Ridge's face was white, his throat working convulsively. Sympathy washed over Arlo. His brother cared for Hope, but if she was married… Where was her husband? Would she remember who he was and leave?

Arlo looked at her bare ring finger. How come there wasn't a ring? Did she take it off? Why?

That question hung in the air, suspended in the kind of fragile shield no one dared break. But from the glances between Ridge and Hope, he knew that question was top of mind.

Arlo shouldn't be here. He should leave them to deal with this together, without any interference. Except he was holding Evie, and handing her back to them might draw more attention to his presence. The baby was drinking her bottle in peace, and it was one less thing they had to deal with right now.

So, he sat at the table in silence, wondering how Ridge could handle not knowing Hope's background. Knowing at any moment this life he was considering with her could come crashing down around him. How did he wrap his head around the magnitude of unfinished business? As usual, it was another lesson for him, if only he could learn from it. But he couldn't ask his brother for advice. Not now, while he was in the thick of it. That wouldn't be fair.

Ridge and Hope stood together for a few moments more, before separating and looking at Arlo apologetically.

"I'm sorry," she said. "These memories come back at the most unexpected, and inconvenient, times. What were we discussing? Oh, right, gifts." She gave him a weak smile, and his heart broke for her.

"No, no, it's fine," he said.

She reached for Evie, and he handed the baby back to her, taking care not to dislodge the bottle.

"I should leave you two alone," he said, rising.

His brother gave him a grateful look and led him to the front door.

"Thanks, man. I'm sorry about that," Ridge said.

Arlo took him by the shoulders. "You have nothing to apologize for. Neither does she. You're both in an impossible situation. Go be with her. I'm okay."

"You sure?"

Of course not. But he couldn't tell his brother that. A vise tightened around his chest. His brother and Hope, Carrie and Aviva. They were all grieving, trying to find their way. He was, too. How was he supposed to help any of them if he couldn't even help himself?

## CHAPTER FOUR

THE REST OF Carrie's day passed in a fog, as thoughts of Arlo consumed her. *Anything* he could do to help? *Help?* What exactly did he mean? She threw laundry into the washer, wondering if he was volunteering to clean her clothes. She blushed as she hung her lingerie to air dry. *No thank you, sir. Or maybe yes, please.* Jeez, how desperate was she to jump into a full-on flirtation with the first guy who caught her eye. She was here for a reason, not a vacation.

Sitting at her computer and working on an article on vitamins for her health and wellness sites, her mind lingered on Arlo. Or rather, his stomach. He loved to eat. What vitamins did he take? Did he work out? He was trim, and she'd admired his muscles at various times. She'd assumed he got them from ranch work, yet he claimed to mostly be involved in the behind-the-scenes office work. Like Isaac. Did he go to a gym? Or work out at home? A vision of him with sweat trickling, muscles defined, skin flushed, came to mind, and she fanned herself. This was ridiculous.

When Aviva woke from her nap, Carrie read her a story about a dreidel. But instead of seeing the brightly colored pictures on each page, she visualized scenes from their time together this morning—every look Arlo had given her, every clearing of the throat, every brush of his body against hers.

She shook her head to clear it.

"No, no, no," Aviva said, shaking her head also.

Carrie laughed, and the little imp repeated the action.

She swung her up in the air and blew on her belly. They descended into silliness, and slowly, Carrie's tension faded away.

Deciding to take advantage of the good weather, she brought Aviva outside to play. Isaac and Randi had put up a play set in the backyard, one of those timber ones with two swings, a slide and a little playhouse at the top. She pushed her niece in the baby swing, watching her cackle with glee and yell "higher" with each push.

Once again, her thoughts turned to Arlo, but this time, she was more rational. Maybe she was reading too much into it. Sure, he was good-looking, and yes, there might have been some chemistry between them, but probably not as much as she imagined. The man was in mourning, just like she was. Who was it who said, "Don't make any decisions within the first six months of someone close to you dying"? Well, he'd lost his father and his best friend. If he was interested in her at all, it was probably for a quick fling, and while she was flattered, it wasn't what she needed right now. She needed to focus on Aviva and on getting all of the legal paperwork completed for adopting her niece. She also had to figure out how to make a stable home for the child and somehow learn to live without her sister. Arlo was a great friend, and she was happy to try to help him deal with his grief. But anything more than that just wasn't in the cards.

Her phone rang, and she put in her earpods.

"Hey, Emma, how did your show go?" Emma was an artist, and she'd had her first gallery showing in Albuquerque last week. Carrie had wanted to be there, but it hadn't worked out.

"It went great! People actually showed up, other than just my family."

"Woo-hoo, that's terrific!" Carrie said.

"Woo-hoo," Aviva cried.

"Did you hear that?" Carrie laughed. "My niece agrees with me. And I don't know why you're surprised. Your art is amazing."

"Thanks. A couple people bought some of my prints, and the gallery agreed to display the rest for another month."

"Oh, I'm so happy for you, Em. I wish I could have seen it. Maybe when I come home..." She pushed Aviva on the swing.

"Are you still planning to come home in the New Year?"

Carrie paused before answering. "As soon as I get everything settled here."

"Oh, I sense a hesitation in your voice," Emma said. "What's going on?"

"Nothing, why?"

"Because any other time we've talked, you've been whole-heartedly set on coming home ASAP. But you hesitated just now. Why?"

*Had she?* "Aviva's life is here..."

Emma's voice gentled. "She's two, Carrie. She'll be okay wherever you are. Have you met people? Kelsey said she keeps pushing you to make friends."

"Just a guy—"

"Aha! That's why you hesitated," Emma crowed. "Okay, tell me about him."

"It's not like that, Em. Arlo was good friends with Isaac and is great with Aviva."

At the mention of her name, the child turned her head and looked at Carrie.

Carrie smiled at her, phone balanced on her shoulder.

"And?" Emma stopped talking, forcing Carrie to fill in the silence.

She hated when that happened.

"And I feel bad for him because he's going through loss, too."

"What else?"

"What do you mean?" she asked.

"I mean what's he look like, do you like him, all the juicy details. Come on, I'm an artist. I'm a visual person."

Carrie laughed despite her annoyance. "He's good-looking. Tall, muscular, sandy blond hair. Green eyes." She disappeared into images her mind created until Emma brought her back to the present.

"So, he's a gorgeous cowboy and you're falling for him."

"What? No, I'm not! I don't have time to fall for him, Em. I have too many changes in my life going on right now. The last thing I need is a gorgeous cowboy."

"Says you," Emma said. "I think a gorgeous cowboy is exactly what you need."

THE NEXT DAY, Arlo woke up early, after not getting much sleep the night before. His mind had been racing with what ifs. What if he'd made peace with his dad? What if he found out the truth about the box of toys?

What if he'd kissed Carrie?

After being woken from a dream in which a rodeo's worth of bucking broncos jumped out of the box of toys and trampled Arlo's siblings to death, he sat up drenched in sweat and decided to get out of bed. He dressed in jeans and a work shirt and trod barefoot into his home office. Sitting behind his desk, eyes gritty, he texted Ridge to check in. After yesterday, he wanted to be sure his brother was okay. Then he followed up with Nash about bringing Ridge in to help him learn more about ranch management, especially on the horse side of the ranch. They also discussed Nash's strategic three-year plan for the ranch.

By ten in the morning, he'd finished his immediate work and was ready to head over to Carrie's house to start on her repairs. While he was there, he'd see if he could tell if any of Hope's gift suggestions might work. Yawning, he added stopping for coffee to his list and drove over to the Daily Grind, across the two-lane highway from the Longhorn Feed & Seed.

Inside, he waved hello to Miss Callie, the owner, who was serving one of her famous apple pies, and glanced across the dining room to the back corner. Sure enough, Beau Weatherly sat at his usual table with a sign, Free Life Advice. He scoffed. The man was great and all, but this is how he chose to spend his retirement? At age thirty, retirement was rarely on his mind, but Arlo knew that when he eventually stopped working, he wasn't going to spend his free time sitting in a coffee shop spouting life's wisdom to others.

He stood at the front counter and pointed to his coffee cup, waiting until Sylvie, the waitress, filled it. Then again, Beau was smart and friendly. And he'd been a successful investor. Maybe he'd have a suggestion for him.

Silently calling himself every ridiculous name he could think of, he headed over to Beau's table.

"Mind if I join you?" Arlo asked.

The old man's face creased in a smile. "Not at all." He swept his arm across the gingham tablecloth toward the empty seat, and Arlo sat. They drank their coffee in silence for a little while as he gathered the nerve to talk to a stranger about his problems.

But talking to those he knew didn't seem to help. Isaac's letter, the box of toys he intercepted, his dad, Carrie. Everything weighed him down, and he didn't know where to start.

He sighed. "Beau, what would you say if I told you I was right about something—"

Beau laughed. "You sure you want my advice, or should we just jump to the end where we shake hands?"

Arlo laughed. "Really?" He raised an eyebrow.

"Hey, my advice may be free, but that doesn't mean it doesn't come without commentary."

"Maybe I should rephrase," Arlo said.

"Go ahead, I'm listening."

"I have a problem, but I'm afraid if I pursue it, I'll open a can of worms and make things worse. If I'm right, nothing is going to come out of stirring things up unnecessarily. But if I'm wrong, which I don't think I am, I might find peace. But I don't know if it's worth potentially hurting others."

Beau grunted before taking another drink of his coffee. He flagged down the waitress, who topped both mugs off before leaving them alone again.

"Well, son, I'm a big believer in leaving well enough alone."

Arlo's chest lightened.

"However, this doesn't sound like one of those times."

Shoulders slumping, Arlo waited.

"The truth is everything. You sound completely torn up. And I don't think you're going to get closure, or find peace, or get that horse back into the barn, until you pursue whatever it is that's troubling you."

*Goddammit.*

He was afraid, and he hated being afraid. But he hated being stubborn more. He sipped his coffee, thinking if his family could read his thoughts...

That would be awful. He *was* headstrong, but that trait had made him a successful investor. He knew which things and ideas to stick with, even when others would have abandoned them long ago. But when stubbornness prevented him from moving forward?

His brothers and sisters had often accused him of that, and maybe they were right.

Beau chuckled softly behind his mug of coffee. "Hurts when you have to admit you're wrong, doesn't it?"

What, the man was a mind reader, too?

"It's not that I don't want to admit I'm wrong," Arlo said. "It's just I'm not used to it. I know that sounds terrible, and I don't mean to be all holier-than-thou. But usually, I'm a good judge of character, of what ideas have potential and what ones don't. So, it's hard for me to take a step back."

Isaac used to help him with this. He'd been his sounding board, keeping him in line when he'd been inclined to chase his idea a little too far. His bullheadedness had cost him the last month of his best friend's life. If ever there was a time to make an adjustment, this was it.

Beau nodded. "It's always harder to change yourself than it is to change others."

Arlo put his coffee cup down on the table, reached into his pocket for his wallet and put a twenty down.

"You're right. I have to find out the truth, no matter how painful it might be. Coffee's on me today, Beau. Thank you."

Beau nodded again and smiled at Arlo as he left the coffee shop.

Arlo couldn't ask his dad about Stevie. The only way to find out the truth and get closure was to go hunt the little boy down.

Outside, he was about to climb back in his truck when the bright-colored display window of the GreatStore caught his eye. The store carried everything. Surely it would have something he could get Aviva. Thinking about Hope's suggestions for Hanukkah gifts, he entered.

The store was festooned with Christmas decorations. Above the door was a huge wreath with red and white bells. Silver garlands outlined the doorway, and white lights surrounded each of the huge picture windows. The checkout lanes had red garlands wrapped around the number poles. Christmas tunes played over the loudspeaker. There was a giant sled filled with wrapped gifts in green, red and gold, with a sign that said This Way to Santa. A huge section of the store had been organized with everything you could possibly need for the holiday, including an entire aisle of trees and ornaments. Even the employees were dressed up like Santa's elves. For the first time, Arlo paused. What must it be like being Jewish, or any other religion for that matter, when everyone around you celebrated Christmas in such an in-your-face way? Isaac had never complained about it, at least not to him. Randi hadn't mentioned anything to him, either, but he was starting to understand why Randi had made a point of making Carrie in charge of teaching Aviva about her religion. As he walked through the store toward the toy aisle, he realized how hard it must be for her.

He wandered the aisles, paying special attention to the toys. There were several toddler toys that looked age appropriate, but he couldn't remember if Aviva had them or not. He'd have to investigate while he was at their house today. The store had an aisle dedicated to books of all kinds, with mostly bestselling books for adults, but there were also a few rows of children's volumes. Again, there were a few board books, including titles Hope had mentioned, and Arlo made a mental note to check what Aviva already had. Maybe Remi's Reads had more. Just as he was about to leave, he noticed a small display of bright-colored dreidels. He stopped, pleased.

One of the elf salespeople must have noticed his shock, because she pointed to them with a smile. "The colorful tops are so pretty, aren't they?"

He didn't bother to correct the young worker but nodded and walked forward to take a closer look. There were all different kinds and sizes and styles of dreidels. Some of them, on their own, were beautiful pieces of artwork—ceramic with painted flowers, or wooden with carvings. Before meeting Carrie, he probably never would have stopped to take more than a cursory glance, but now, they piqued his interest.

"Do you think any of these would be good for a two-year-old?" he asked the elf.

"What about this one," she said, holding up a colorful wooden one.

"Perfect." Arlo paid for the dreidel and returned to his truck.

When he arrived at Carrie's house, he took his toolbox and the bagged dreidel from the cab and rang the doorbell.

"Hey," Carrie said, answering after a few moments. "Come on in."

He removed his hat upon entering and hung it from the

hook before handing the bag to her. "I saw this in a store and thought of Aviva," he murmured. "Is it okay if I give it to her before I get started working?"

Carrie's face lit up, and Arlo was struck with not only how pretty she was in her simple jeans and light blue top, but also how easy it was to make her happy. The dreidel wasn't an expensive gift. It wasn't even for her. But the expression on her face made it seem like he'd dedicated a brand-new, prize-winning heifer in her honor.

"This is wonderful!" she exclaimed. "Where did you find it?"

Arlo stuffed his hands in his pockets. "The GreatStore in town."

"I had no idea they carried Hanukkah merchandise." She gave him a hug. "It's so nice of you to pick it out for her. Of course, you can give it to her."

Arlo remained standing in place, still wrapped up in her floral scent and the feel of her arms around him. Her hug was spontaneous and...intoxicating. He would have liked it to last longer, to see what holding her felt like. But she'd released him and backed up, only making him realize it had happened after the fact. So, if it was so quick, why did he miss her? At her curious stare, he mentally gave himself a shake. He was making more of it than was meant. Clearing his throat, he took the dreidel back from her and followed her into the living room.

Once again, Aviva sat on the floor in orange leggings and an orange and purple top, playing with her toys.

"Vivie, look what Uncle Arlo has for you," Carrie said.

"Arwo," the toddler cried, standing up and running over to him.

"What's cookin', good lookin'?" he asked, swinging her up over his head and making her giggle.

"Not cookin', pwayin'," Aviva said.

"What are you playing?"

"Wif my toys."

"Your toys? Show me."

He knelt on the floor as Aviva toddled around, picking up different toys and showing them to him. After a couple of minutes, he said, "I have something for you."

She tipped her head to the side, her blond curls tangling across her forehead. With one hand, he brushed her hair out of her eyes. With the other, he held out the bright red wooden dreidel.

"Wed!" she cried. "I wike wed."

"You do?" he asked, pretending to be shocked. "I didn't know that."

"Aviva, do you know what that is?" Carrie asked.

He'd almost forgotten she was there. Craning his neck, he watched her kneel down next to him, take the dreidel and spin it like a top. Aviva's eyes widened, and she lay down on the floor, watching it spin.

"Do it again, pwese," she said.

Carrie repeated the spin. Each time the dreidel landed, she pointed to the Hebrew letter on the side and told Aviva what it was. Arlo paid attention, too. He'd have to ask her about the letters later. For now, he let Carrie lead.

"Arwo spin," Aviva implored.

He and Carrie's gazes met over the toddler's head, and she seemed to ask him if he wanted to without saying a word. Nodding, he took the dreidel in hand and spun it. It didn't spin as well as Carrie's had, but he didn't embarrass himself. When it stopped, Aviva pointed to the letter and said, "Gimel."

"That's right," Carrie said. "Good job! Now you spin."

Aviva took the dreidel, but it skidded across the floor. Frowning, she tried again. After three times, she shook her head and gave it back to Carrie.

Arlo's chest tightened. He hadn't meant to frustrate the child.

But she seemed satisfied having Carrie and him spin, with

her calling out the letters. She was smart. Isaac and Randi would be proud.

He looked over at Carrie. She seemed to feel the same if her expression was any clue. She looked at him and nodded. Warmth flooded through him. He'd never had any wordless communication with a woman before, and certainly not twice.

"You want to see something cool?" she asked Aviva.

The toddler nodded.

This time, when Carrie spun the dreidel, she spun it upside down, on its stem, rather than on its bottom. Arlo wasn't sure who was more amazed, Aviva or himself.

"Whoa," he said, as it bounced in the air before spinning and eventually falling to its side.

"Whoa," Aviva mimicked. She clapped her hands, handed the dreidel back to Carrie and said, "Do it again, pwese."

Carrie repeated the trick a few more times before saying, "Okay, no more for now."

Aviva took the dreidel and turned it over in her hands, laying it on its side and yelling out the letter.

"Vivie, are you going to thank Arlo for your gift?"

She raced over to him and squeezed his neck in a hug so hard he couldn't breathe for a second. "Tank you."

"You're welcome."

He'd dallied with them long enough. It was time to get moving on the repairs, but he didn't want to break up the cozy scene they'd created. He sighed to himself as he rose. Didn't matter what he wanted, he'd made a promise, and he was going to keep it.

"Where would you like me to start?" he asked Carrie.

She rose as well. "Actually, could you start in her room? The ceiling fan makes noise when it runs, and I'd like the outlet covers switched to child-safe ones. Plus her closet door is off the track and I can't seem to get it back in line. She loves picking out her own clothes, and I'm afraid she might get her fingers caught."

"No problem."

She led the way upstairs into Aviva's bedroom. He remembered when Isaac was painting it. A pale yellow with ducks along the ceiling, and cows along the bottom.

*Arlo walked into the room to see Isaac on the ladder and Randi, one hand on her belly, giving instructions. He laughed.*

*"I didn't know you were an artist," he said, turning around in a circle.*

*Isaac shook his head. "Randi's the artistic one. She painted the animals. I'm just the roller dude."*

*"Roller dude," Arlo said with a chuckle. "You've completely changed him, Randi."*

*She nodded, a satisfied smile on her face. "One day, Arlo, someone's going to change you, too."*

Now, as he followed Aviva, he wondered if he'd ever be as lucky as the two of them were.

"Hewwo, duckies. Hewwo, cows," Aviva said as she walked into the room. "This is my woom," she announced to Arlo.

"I know that, silly. Quack, quack."

Her eyes brightened. "Quack, quack," she replied. "Moooooo!"

He looked around the room and had an idea. "Would you like to be my helper?" he asked Aviva.

She nodded.

After looking over at Carrie for permission—he probably should have asked her first—he set up the step stool that Carrie had provided underneath the fan.

"Can you make sure the step stool doesn't wobble," he asked the toddler. The step stool was secure. There was no way it was going to wobble, not with his weight on it. But Aviva didn't know that.

She nodded again and held on to one side of the stool, her pudgy hands pressed down on it as he got down to business.

Pulling tools from his pocket, he tightened the fan blades, which had come loose and were causing the noise. Careful not to step on Aviva's fingers, he warned her. "Okay, I'm coming down now."

The child pressed against the stool, her face reddening in her efforts. When his feet hit the floor, he knelt down in front of her. "You did great," he praised. "You're a terrific helper."

Aviva jumped up and down, before running over to Carrie and hugging her leg. "I'm helping."

Carrie looked down at Aviva and tousled her curls. "Yes, you are," she said. "You're doing a wonderful job."

Watching Arlo and Aviva together melted her heart, and although she had her own work to do, she didn't want to move from this spot. No matter how Arlo acted when the holidays were mentioned, he clearly had spirit. His purchase of the dreidel proved it. All they had to do was help him get past his concerns about his father's second family, and Carrie knew he'd enjoy the season.

He turned to her, wiping his hands on his thighs. "What's next?" he asked.

She pulled her gaze away from his thighs. "Let me get my computer," she said. "I made a list."

Before she embarrassed herself further by being caught staring, she walked quickly into the bedroom and grabbed her laptop off the nightstand. Returning to Aviva's room, where Arlo and her niece were once again playing their animal game, she opened up the laptop and pulled up the repair list. She scanned it.

"We should probably move on to the bookcase downstairs that you noticed. Just in case this one gets too close," she said with a smile.

"Right," Arlo said. He looked at Aviva. "Ready to be my helper again?"

Aviva nodded.

"I don't want her getting in your way," Carrie murmured.

"She's not," he answered. "Besides, this way you can also get work done."

This man was so thoughtful. For the first time since her sister died, she didn't feel quite so alone. And letting him help her didn't scare her. In fact, she wanted to help him, too.

They all went back downstairs, and while Arlo set up his tools around the bookcase, Carrie logged onto the health and wellness site. She kept an eye on Aviva, but Arlo had things under control. He and her niece were taking the books off the shelves, and Aviva was helping him make piles. As Carrie worked on her grief article, she was cognizant of the two of them and couldn't help smiling at their bond.

"I spoke to Beau Weatherly this morning," Arlo said, pulling her attention away from her article.

"Who is he again?" she asked.

"He's kind of a town fixture. A kind, older man who sits at his table at the Daily Grind every morning from seven to eight thirty, offering 'free life advice.'" He put finger quotes around the words. "I've never been sure if he was wise or lonely, but after today, I'd have to say wise."

"What advice did you ask him for?"

Arlo paused while he nailed a brace into the bookcase. "There, that should keep it steady," he said. "Just a general question about closure." He gave her a sheepish look. "He also said I needed it."

Carrie paused. She was glad he'd talked to someone about his dilemma. Just as she was learning about herself, sometimes it helped to have an outsider's perspective. Arlo, who was used to taking care of everything and everyone around him, needed time to sort things out.

"You know, you could just google Stevie Fields on Buckers Road and see what comes up," she said. "Or I can—"

"No! I'll do it."

Aviva jumped at Arlo's raised voice.

"Sorry, I didn't mean to shout," he said to both of them. He gave a quick, reassuring smile to Aviva before turning again to Carrie and expelling a deep breath. "I know you're just trying to help. I appreciate it."

Carrie swallowed. She shouldn't have pushed him. Just because she needed control in order to deal with things in her life didn't mean he did. The decision to find out about Stevie Fields should be his alone. "I didn't mean to push you," she began. "I just thought—"

He came over to her. "You didn't do anything wrong." Letting out a sigh, he pulled his phone from his back pocket and sat next to her on the sofa. "It's just that if anyone is going to google the name, it should be me."

Relief filled her. "Of course."

She returned to her article, once again keeping an eye on Aviva and Arlo at the same time, and basically getting nothing done.

He frowned after a couple of seconds.

"The only Fields on Buckers Road I can find is a Lynne Fields. She's probably Stevie's mom and the former mistress of Casper Windham," he ground out. "This is stupid."

"No, it's not," Carrie said. "You don't know who Lynne Fields is. Maybe you're right, but maybe not. And you're never going to know unless you do something about it. Why don't we take the box over to her place right now, tell her it was sent to the wrong address, and see what she says?"

"Okay, okay," he mumbled. "You're probably right."

"What's that?" Carrie asked. "I didn't hear you."

Arlo laughed.

"That's better," Carrie said.

"Alright, I'm out of my funk. And yes, we can go, but not today."

She smiled.

"Or tomorrow," he added.

Instead of feeling frustrated with him, her insides warmed. He was getting there, on his own timetable. Hopefully soon, he'd go through with investigating Stevie Fields and maybe even feel better. In the meantime, this good-looking, kind-hearted man was in her home making the repairs she had yet to get to. She had an adult to talk to, and she was going to make the most of it.

She looked over at Aviva and was delighted when she saw that the child was playing with the dreidel.

"Tell me about your Christmas traditions as a kid," she said, putting aside her laptop.

Arlo stepped back a few feet and examined the bookcase before answering. A faraway look crept onto his face, softening his features and removing all trace of the grumpiness she saw before.

"My mom loves Christmas," he confided. "She was poor and raised by a single mother. They never could do much for Christmas, so when my mom married my dad, she made a huge deal of the holiday, especially as we all came along. My dad, of course, wanted to put on a big show to impress everyone with how rich and successful he was, but my mom kept it personal with little touches she knew we all loved." A brief scowl crossed his face before smoothing out.

"The main Christmas tree, the one my dad insisted on, was professionally decorated. I hated it. But my mom made sure there was another one, a smaller one that we picked out and cut down every year and strung with popcorn and handmade ornaments. Same with our stockings. We each got a stocking that represented our current obsessions or favorite colors. Mine was always blue, even though my dad thought they all should be red and green and matching."

"That sounds lovely," Carrie said. "Were you Christmas Eve opening presents people or Christmas Day?"

His smile stretched wider. "Both."

She laughed. "Really?"

"None of us had any willpower or patience, so we had a kind of white elephant, but with books, on Christmas Eve, and then the rest we opened on Christmas Day."

"Fun! What was your favorite holiday fare?" she asked.

"Anything sweet," he said. "I was never picky, but I guess I favored... Christmas cookies. Honestly, I don't know if it was the taste or what they looked like or just that they meant Santa was coming soon." He patted his totally flat stomach.

Carrie swallowed. She'd never cared much about men's bodies, only their personalities. But looking at Arlo these past few days, and now noticing how his work shirt emphasized his broad shoulders and taut abs, made her wonder what he'd look like shirtless.

And what he'd *feel* like.

"I've always had a weakness for cookies," he confided.

*"Cookies?"* Aviva looked up eagerly, making them both laugh.

Saved by the toddler.

Carrie wasn't sure if she was relieved or not.

Aviva stood up, tush first, and ran over to Carrie. She placed her hands on Carrie's knees, gave her a big grin and asked, "I have cookies? Pwese?"

"Yes." As she walked with her niece into the kitchen, she said over her shoulder, "See what you did?"

Arlo laughed. "I have no regrets."

He followed them, swinging Aviva into her booster seat and buckling the straps as Carrie pulled out animal crackers from the pantry. She gave her niece apple juice in her yellow sippy cup before leaning over the counter.

"How about a mini latke-making lesson? We can have them for lunch if you'd like to stay."

Carrie's tummy flipped. It wasn't that she didn't want him to stay for lunch, she just hadn't expected to blurt out the invitation like that. Usually, she thought out exactly what she was going to do and say beforehand. But somehow, Arlo made her do things without thinking. And so far, nothing bad had happened with a little spontaneity.

His face split into a wide grin, making his green eyes sparkle.

"I'd love to."

She nodded, not only pleased with his response, but with how easy it happened. Why, she'd think about later.

"Great. First thing is to peel the potatoes. That's your job."

She pulled out several large potatoes from the vegetable bin and handed them to Arlo with a peeler. Folding her arms across her chest, she leaned against the counter, one eye on him, the other on Aviva.

"Wait, you're not going to help me?"

She shook her head. "Don't forget to wash them. And no, that's what you get for creating a cookie monster out of her."

"I didn't realize you were so mean," he said, pretending to pout. He turned on the water and scrubbed the potatoes.

"I'm not mean," she corrected. "Mean would be making you peel the potatoes and not allowing you to eat them."

With a bark that passed for a laugh, he dried the potatoes and began peeling. "Yes, ma'am."

While he peeled, she watched his hands. They were strong, his movements sparse and sure. Before long, he finished. She filled a bowl with cold water and placed the potatoes in it.

"What's that for?" he asked.

"So they don't turn brown."

She plugged in the food processor and then grabbed a large onion from the fridge.

Arlo held up his hands. "Oh, no, don't make me peel those."

Laughing, she took care of it and sliced it into quarters. "No worries, you've redeemed yourself. The first thing we do, after all the peeling, of course, is to alternately shred the potatoes with the onions."

The whirring motor made Aviva cover her ears. To entertain her, Carrie and Arlo did the same thing.

Once they shredded all the potatoes and onions, Carrie added flour, salt, pepper and egg, and mixed the concoction together. Then she placed a large frying pan on the stove, filled it with oil and heated it.

"That's a lot of oil," Arlo remarked.

"I know," she answered, opening the kitchen windows. "If we don't open the windows, the whole house will smell of oil for days."

"Let me help," he said. He finished opening them, before telling her their locks needed repairing as well. While he went to get his toolbox, she waited for the oil to heat.

"Now we drop small amounts into the oil and let them brown."

Carrie made the first batch. When the latkes were just about ready, she lined a tray with tin foil and then paper towels, before placing the first batch on them to drain and cool.

Arlo reached over to grab one, burning his fingers in the process. It didn't deter him, and he popped a hot one in his mouth.

His eyes widened as he chewed.

"You're going to hurt yourself," she cried, handing him a glass of water.

He gulped it before speaking. "It was worth it," he said. "They're delicious!"

He reached for another, but she shooed his hands away. "Go get applesauce, sour cream, avocados and lox out of the fridge."

That man couldn't be trusted around food, clearly. Someone needed to protect him from himself.

She pointed to the table, and he put out everything he'd gotten from the fridge, along with plates, cups, napkins and silverware.

When he finished, she expected him to try to take another latke. Instead, he stood across the kitchen island, watching her. While his attention was diverted with setting the table, she'd had a nice rhythm going—a forkful of potato mixture, drop into the pan, move the cooking latkes around the pan, flip and remove. But now that he stared at her, her face heated, and she was so distracted that her hands didn't grip the oily spatula as firmly as before, and she dropped a latke on the floor.

He grabbed it. "Five second rule," he said as he popped it into his mouth.

He chewed, emphasizing the cut of his jaw as the muscles worked. He licked his fingers, and her stomach clenched.

She looked away, but not before she caught the twinkle in his eye. *Great, just great.*

"You don't mind that I ate that, do you?" His voice drawled, emphasizing the Texas accent. All he needed to do was add "ma'am" at the end and tip his hat, which was hanging in the hall by the door.

She cleared her throat. "No, I suppose I don't."

Aviva leaned over in her booster seat. "Me want!" she cried, opening and closing her hand as she reached for the latkes.

"Just a minute, sweetheart," Carrie said, arranging the potato pancakes on a serving plate. "They're just about done." She handed the platter to Arlo before rummaging in the fridge for drinks.

Returning with two bottles of water and a sippy cup, she looked around at the table and the two people already sitting at it, waiting expectantly. "Alright, let's eat," she said.

As the three ate latkes, and compared which way they preferred to eat them, Carrie struggled to drag her focus away from his hands, from thoughts about those hands on her... She blinked, and turned toward Aviva, whose face was covered in applesauce, potatoes and grease.

Arlo leaned back in his chair and sighed contentedly. "Mmm, mmm. That was delicious."

Aviva leaned back in her booster seat and imitated his action. "Mmm, mmm."

Carrie and Arlo laughed. They continued to chat as he helped himself to seconds. When he finished, Arlo pushed away from the table and grabbed all three plates. "I'll clean up," he said.

Carrie shook her head. "It's not necessary. You're already fixing things around my house. You don't need to do dishes, too."

He placed his hand over hers. The warmth spread up her arm, and for the first time since her sister died, she felt something other than grief. Hope mingled with red-hot desire.

Glancing into his eyes, she thought she saw a glimmer of the same thing before he blinked.

"You cooked, I do dishes," he said, clearing his throat. "That's the rule."

She frowned. "Whose?"

"Mine."

"But…but what if you don't do it right?" she asked. She gripped the counter and tried to tame her racing heart, suddenly panicking at the loss of control.

He looked at her askance. "Let me get this straight. You trust me to fix things around your house that are falling apart and could hurt you if I do it wrong, but washing dishes and possibly missing a speck or two of grease throws you off?"

He moved closer to her, his large body making her feel tiny. His green eyes pinned her in place, as if convincing her to answer him.

She took a deep breath. When presented his way, it sounded ridiculous. Still, she hated to give up control. It was the one thing that had kept her sane since her sister died. But it was only *dishes*. There was keeping her walls up out of self-preservation and then there was falling down the rabbit hole and never letting anyone do anything for her again. Ever. Plus, it was Arlo, the man who made her insides squishy.

She looked into his endless green eyes and blinked. "I guess when you put it that way…"

While Carrie let Aviva out of her booster seat, Arlo began to wash. "Would you like to inspect?" he asked after washing the frying pan.

Him? Oh, yes.

But he was holding out the pan, and ignoring it would make this already awkward situation even worse.

She took it from him, rubbing her fingers along the surface. No grease. She smiled. "Thank you."

"I'll try not to let my fragile male ego, or my dislike of gender stereotypes, get in the way," he said as he continued washing.

His smirk gave his humor away. It also showed a side of him to Carrie she hadn't expected.

"How about I make it up to you?" she murmured.

He arched an eyebrow. "How?"

*"Bimuelos?"*

His eyes widened, and he grinned. "You're on."

# CHAPTER FIVE

As THE SUN dipped through the trees, Arlo finished fixing the pipe under the master bathroom sink, his mind on Carrie as it had been the entire day. The more time he spent with her, the more he liked her. Aside from being a terrific cook, she was funny and smart. Emotionally strong, too. As he put his tools away, a citrusy sweet smell wafted from the kitchen below, making his stomach growl. He closed his toolbox, peeked into Aviva's room to see if she was there and jogged down the stairs.

He paused in the doorway of the kitchen. Carrie stood at the counter with Aviva sitting next to her. The two of them were patting dough and forming it into balls. He admired the graceful movements of Carrie's arms as she worked the dough. The kitchen light shone onto her dark hair, giving it reddish highlights. And the smile she gave Aviva as the two chatted melted his heart.

He stepped into the kitchen. "I smell something yummy," he said, striding over to Aviva and tickling her tummy.

She giggled and held up her sticky hands. "Bimwos!"

He snagged one, popping it into his mouth and rolling his eyes in delight. "What are you doing this evening?" he asked.

She gave a rueful smile. "Same thing I do every evening.

Putting Aviva to bed and either going through Randi's and Isaac's things or curling up with a book."

Arlo shook his head. "Not tonight you aren't. Tonight, you're going out with me."

She looked at him askance. "Oh, really?"

"Yes, ma'am. Have you seen the lake yet?"

"I've driven by."

He scoffed. "That's a no, then. We're going to the lake."

She pointed out the window. "You do know it's winter, right?"

"Yep."

"And what about Aviva?"

"Bring her."

"But…"

Arlo gripped Carrie's upper arms. They were soft, yet he knew they were strong. Her brown eyes gave away her worry and also, for a split second, desire. Did she want him as much as he was coming to want her? The look was gone before he knew it, but the worry was still there.

"You both deserve a break. And a change of scenery. Please? I promise we'll be back in time for Vivie's bedtime."

He waited, sure she was going to refuse. Just as he was about to let her bow out gracefully, she relented.

"Okay."

Joy surged through him. "I'll pick you up at five."

Pushing away from the counter, he packed up his tools, grabbed a last *bimuelos*—gosh, they were good—and returned to the ranch. He checked in at the office at the main house to make sure there wasn't anything he needed to do right away. And then he got ready for the evening.

At four fifty-eight, he pulled his pickup truck into her driveway. The asphalt needed patching, and he mentally added it to his to-do list. He laughed to himself. If his father could see him now. The man had thought manual labor was beneath him, and here Arlo was, leaning into it. He shook his head to clear it. He didn't want to think about Casper tonight. Glancing into the back seat, he triple-checked there was enough room for Aviva's car seat before getting out of the cab and loping up to Carrie's front door. His hand hovered over the bell, but before he could press it, the door opened.

His heart stuttered. Something about this woman took his breath away. Her shiny brown hair was cascading around her shoulders. She wore jeans that hugged her hips and a V-neck sweater in a light blue color that emphasized her eyes. Her necklace, a gold Jewish star, drew his attention to her chest, but he wasn't about to ogle her. Not when she held Aviva on her hip.

"Arwo!" the toddler cried, holding out her pudgy arms to him.

He took her from Carrie's arms.

"Hello, little one. Hi," he said to Carrie, wondering why he was tongue-tied.

She smiled softly. "Hi."

She reached for a bag with what he presumed was for Aviva, and he took it from her. Their fingers touched, and once again, heat shot up his arm. Their gazes met, and this time he was sure she felt it, too.

"You've got your hands full with her," Carrie said. "I can carry the bag."

"Go open the back seat of the truck," he insisted. "I'll take care of this."

Nodding, she grabbed a jacket from the hook next to the door, locked the door behind her and rushed over to the truck.

"Pway game?" Aviva asked.

"Hmm," he said as he sat her in her car seat. "We're owls," he said. "Hoot, hoot. They're night animals." He widened his eyes.

"Hoot, hoot," Aviva replied, bugging her eyes out, too.

Arlo opened the door for Carrie, who laughed as she climbed into the truck.

"Okay, owls, it's time to go," she said.

He glanced at the sky through the windshield as he backed out of her driveway. They'd just make it.

"You said the lake," Carrie said. "Where exactly are we going?"

"My cabin."

Out of the corner of his eye, he saw Carrie stiffen.

"Don't worry, we're headed to the dock behind my cabin," he clarified, hoping to put her at ease. The last thing he wanted was for her to think he had anything untoward in mind.

A short time later they arrived at his place and he parked in the driveway. When she unlocked her seat belt, he smiled over at her. "Follow me," he said.

Arlo had chosen his cabin—one of six that he and his five siblings moved into, because of its view of the lake. Entering from the front, he led Carrie through the flagstone foyer into a huge great room, with the kitchen on the right, a huge sitting area in the center and his office and guest rooms on the left. But it was the back of the house that caused Carrie to gasp.

The back wall was all windows. The views of the lake were spectacular. While she and Aviva stood at one of the windows, he grabbed two blankets and exited the back of his house. Making sure they were still with him, he brought them down to the dock, where two large chairs, made from logs just like his home, sat facing the water. He sat and motioned to Carrie to do the same. When she was settled, he handed her a blanket before pointing to the sky.

"Now watch," he said.

The air was cool, the lake smooth as glass. As the sun began to set, the sky turned shades of pink, red and blue. The colors reflected off the water, turning the world a rainbow hue and making it seem as if the sunset was endless.

"This is...beautiful," Carrie whispered.

The awe in her voice made Arlo smile.

"It is." It's why he'd insisted on a wall of windows at the

back. He looked over at her, though, instead of the sunset and thought to himself, *So are you.* He didn't dare say the words out loud. After her stiffening in the car at the idea of going to his house, he didn't want to push his luck and scare her off. He watched her snuggle under the blanket with Aviva.

Was it his imagination, or was she sneaking glances over at him, too? In profile in the waning light, it was hard to tell. But a few times, when he thought their gazes may have met, her mouth quirked in a smile. Then again, it could have just been the presence of Aviva. He wasn't sure.

When the sun had set and the colors had muted to black, she turned to him.

"That was one of the most gorgeous sunsets I've ever seen. Thank you." She glanced around the lake for a few more seconds. "You and your neighbors must love living here."

He nodded. "We do."

At her quizzical look, he continued, "The ranch is owned by my family, and my siblings all live on the property, along the lake."

He'd already pointed out Jade's and Nash's houses as they entered the property. "You can't see them from here, but Ridge, Sabrina and Dahlia live farther down. We have golf carts to travel from one cabin to the other."

A wistful expression crossed her face. "It must be nice to live so close to each other."

His heart squeezed with sympathy. What would he do if he lost one of his siblings? He'd thought burying his best friend was awful. He couldn't imagine losing one of his brothers or sisters as well.

"I'm sorry," he said thickly. "I didn't mean to make you sad."

She shook her head, wiping a tear from her cheek.

He made his hand into a fist so as not to catch the tear on his fingertip. He could only imagine how soft her skin would feel.

"It's okay," she said. "I'm glad you brought me here."

He reached across the space between their chairs and squeezed her hand. To his delight, she squeezed back.

"It's getting chilly," he told her. "Would you like to come inside for dinner?" He'd been so sure of himself this afternoon, almost cocky. But now, although still confident, he was aware how skittish she was, and he didn't want to do anything to push her away. So even though she'd agreed to come out with him this afternoon, he checked in with her now, to make sure she was still on board.

He'd bring her home if she wanted…but he hoped she didn't want to leave.

"That would be nice," she replied, her voice shy. She cleared her throat. "I think Aviva is getting cold."

Arlo stood and reached for Aviva, keeping her wrapped in the blanket. With his other hand, he helped Carrie up, and the three of them walked toward his house. He would have liked to hold Carrie's hand longer, but she let go of his, and he didn't try to take it again.

Inside, he lit the fireplace for warmth and then went into the kitchen to check on the beef ribs he'd put in the slow cooker earlier in the day.

Although he wasn't a gourmet chef, he'd wanted a kitchen that was spacious and functional. With red cedar cabinets, copper pendulum light fixtures, black marble countertops and a slate tile backsplash, the room was cozy yet modern. Even Arlo, who didn't like to cook, enjoyed being here. And when he had guests over—usually his family—the open, adjoining dining area and open living area made him feel part of the get-together, even when he had to prepare a meal.

Speaking of which, the barbecue smell wafted up, and he inhaled.

"That smells delicious," Carrie said next to him. "What can I do to help?"

"How about a salad?" He looked across the open kitchen to the living room, making sure Aviva wasn't near the fire. She was sitting on the couch, reading one of the books Arlo kept around for the little ones in his family.

Something about the way her little legs stuck straight forward on his brown leather couch, with the oversize cushions practically swallowing her whole, stirred something in him and made him yearn for a family.

"—you want?"

Carrie's voice startled him, and he turned toward her.

She held two heads of lettuce in her hands.

He blinked.

"Which do you want?" Her lips twitched. "In your salad."

"Sorry, wasn't paying attention."

"Clearly."

"Romaine. I think there's Caesar dressing in the cabinet." He walked into the kitchen and reached around her to the pantry. Her hair brushed his nose, and he inhaled the floral scent of her shampoo.

He cleared his throat. "Here you go."

As he handed her the bottle, their hands touched, and this time, he searched her face for a response.

*Success!* His chest swelled as he watched her bite her lip, her gaze alternating between their fingers and his face in rapid succession.

Despite his desire to continue the contact—keep savoring the warmth of her fingers against his—he let her go, a small smile his only sign that she'd felt the spark, too.

"Thank you," she whispered.

Flashing lights drew Arlo's attention away from Carrie to the slow cooker on the counter.

"Perfect timing," he said, with only a little sarcasm.

He lifted the lid, releasing steam and the aroma of barbecue ribs into the kitchen. Pulling out corn bread warming in the oven, he brought everything to the oak table in the dining room and began setting the table while Carrie finished dressing the salad.

She called Aviva over, got her settled in before taking a look at the food. She closed her eyes and inhaled, then glanced at Arlo, a gleam in her eye.

"Wait a minute. Can you even call yourself a Texan if you make ribs in a slow cooker? I thought you all were big barbecue people."

He chuckled. "That would be y'all, not you all."

She shrugged. "My question still stands."

Arlo let the silence stretch while he served Carrie so she could cut up the rib meat into bite-size pieces for Aviva. Then he took a bite of his corn bread while formulating his answer.

"Well, you see, yes, Texans love their barbecue, and I'm no different. But we also appreciate reality. And if I'm working all day, I can't devote the proper amount of time to my barbecue, so then I use the slow cooker."

Leaning on her hand, Carrie's eyes widened. "Does that mean you're just like the rest of us mere mortals?"

"Oh, honey, don't you know everything is bigger in Texas?"

Her shoulders shook before she dropped her head and laughed. When she looked at him, tears streamed down her face.

"You cwying?" Aviva asked. Her lip quivered.

"Oh, no, sweetie," Carrie said, quickly wiping her face. "I'm laughing. Arlo made a joke."

The little girl frowned, looking between the two. And then, as if she didn't want to be left out, she laughed, too.

Her forced laughter made Arlo laugh, and Carrie joined in as well.

"All this laughter reminds me so much of the big dinner my family had every Hanukkah," she said, a wistful look on her face. "We'd have my grandparents, aunts, uncles and cousins, and the house was always filled with laughter."

"I've heard of Christmas dinners, but never Hanukkah dinners," Arlo admitted. "What are they like?"

"As I'm sure you've figured out, lots of Jewish holidays

revolve around food," she said with a smile. "We have a big celebration the last night of Hanukkah, called a *merenda*, to mark the end of the holiday," she said. "Probably similar, but on a much larger scale, to the dinner you were invited to. All our relatives came, like I said, as well as our friends. The dinner was potluck, but my grandma always made the *bimuelos*. Everyone would bring their favorites, and somehow, although no one sat and organized anything, we always ended up with the right number of dishes."

"So, no three pots of brisket and zero vegetables?"

Carrie laughed. "Nope. The celebration was always noisy, especially because we made sure to invite people we'd fought with during the year so we could make amends."

Arlo sat back. Would Isaac have invited him to a *merenda*? Would he have attended? Gosh, he hoped so.

"Wow."

Nodding, Carrie continued, "As the sun set, my grandpa would light our family menorah, everyone would eat dinner, and it was just a wonderful time."

"That's a great tradition. You should do that here," he said.

"How exactly?"

"I don't know," Arlo confessed. "But I'd certainly come."

"Anything for *bimuelos*," she teased. "By the way, this is delicious."

"And you made fun of me for not barbecuing."

"Okay, maybe I was wrong." She looked around the room. "Your home is beautiful, by the way. I didn't know people lived along the lake on this side."

"Thank you. My mom really lucked out when she purchased this spread. The former owners built the houses my sisters and brothers and I live in, and when we saw the views of the lake, we were hooked." He laughed. "Funny thing, we were told they were log cabins." He turned in a circle. "I don't know about you, but when I picture a log cabin, this is not what comes to mind."

All of the "log cabins" were huge A-frames with decks and huge windows overlooking the lake. The only thing "log" about them was the wood they were made of.

Carrie nodded. "No, me neither. But if the rest of them are anything like yours, they're stunning."

"Thanks. The lines are similar, but there are differences in style and decorating, especially as we've made ourselves at home."

"What about your mom?" Carrie asked. "You said she lives on the ranch, too?"

"Yes, that's right. Plus, she owns the Fortune Castle, which she's renovating and turning into a hotel and spa."

Carrie's eyes widened. "Wow."

Arlo nodded. "It's a crazy story," he said. "Maybe Randi mentioned it to you?"

Carrie nodded. "Yeah, she said something about your family inheriting the castle."

He toyed with his napkin. "My mom discovered she was the secret illegitimate granddaughter of Wendell Fortune. Apparently, the woman who raised her, the one I've always thought was my grandmother, was actually a babysitter hired to take care of my mom for a brief time while her real mother and father went off to elope." He took a long swallow of his beer before continuing. "But her parents died in the Chatelaine mine disaster in 1965, and the babysitter—Gertie Wilson—thought she'd been abandoned and raised her as her own. My grandmother left the truth in a letter that my mom opened after Gertie passed away, and she ended up meeting Wendell right before he died. He left the entire ranch and castle to my mom and now she's fixing it up."

"Oh, my, that *is* quite a story." She met his eyes. "And turning the castle into a hotel sounds like quite an endeavor."

"It is, but she is doing an amazing job with it," he told her proudly. "She goes back and forth between the two places a lot while overseeing the renovations but is currently residing in the main house on the other side of the ranch property. Actually, we all live here, which makes our jobs much easier."

"I'll bet it does," she said. "I envy you living so close to your family."

Sympathy filled Arlo. Carrie and Aviva were all alone here. He wanted to cheer her up. Actually, he wanted to take her in his arms and reassure her that she wasn't alone, but he suspected she'd pull away. He needed a distraction.

"Would you like a tour?"

Carrie looked around the kitchen, which was separated from the adjoining dining area by a huge marble island. "If the rest of your home is as impressive as this, yes please!"

"Yes pwese, yes pwese!" Aviva clapped her hands, making Arlo laugh.

"I'm glad you like it. Come with me." He led the two of them from the kitchen to his sunken living room. The huge fireplace, which he'd lit earlier, was framed by the same slate as the backsplash, stretched almost to the ceiling, with a black marble hearth and mantle.

Carrie paused in the middle of the room and sighed.

To their right, facing the lake at the back of the house, were floor-to-ceiling windows, which followed the peak roofline. Although long past sunset now, his backyard was illuminated by lanterns, as was the dock on which they'd stood earlier. With the full moon reflecting off the water, it was brighter than normal. As usual, Arlo was stunned by the view as well.

He glanced at Carrie.

She was even more stunning. Her hair was pulled off her face with a clip, her sweater hugged her curves, and her jeans... well, they hugged her, too. The look of wonder softened her facial features.

"I don't think I'd ever get tired of this view," she whispered.

"Me, neither."

He responded without thinking, but when she glanced at him, a puzzled look on her face, he swallowed. "I mean, I don't."

"Do your siblings have a lake view, too?"

"They do, although we're all spread out with about thirty acres each. Still, if you look over there—" he stood behind her, one hand on her shoulder, the other pointing in the distance "—or there, you might be able to see their lights."

While she searched the shoreline, he enjoyed being close to her. Since he was tall, the top of her head reached his chin. Holding her like this was almost an embrace.

"Oh, yeah," she said. "I can see them over there." And then she shifted her posture, enough to add space between them, and the moment was lost.

"You'll have to come back in the daytime so I can show you the outside and the ranch itself. Plus, that way, Aviva can see the animals at the petting zoo. We have ducks and pigs and some baby chicks. My sister Jade runs it. She used to have a lamb in the zoo, but he got stressed, so she moved him into the barn with a goat for company."

Aviva's face brightened, and he held up his hand for a high five.

"We'd love to," Carrie said.

"Then it's a date." As soon as the words left his mouth, he froze. His blood rushed in his ears. He hadn't meant it the way it sounded…but at the same time, a date with Carrie, well, he wanted nothing more.

And yet the look on her face told him she wasn't ready.

Shoot, had he messed everything up?

"We'll have to put it on the calendar, so we don't get distracted by everything else we have to do," he said, the words sounding odd to his own ears.

But her relief was palpable.

"That would be fun," she agreed, giving Aviva a squeeze. "We'd like that, wouldn't we, Vivie?"

"I wike amals," she said. "Baa, baa, baa."

He tousled her hair, glad of the distraction, as Carrie laughed.

"So do I." He winked, looking at the toddler. Carrie hadn't refused the idea. It would take some time, but maybe she'd give him a chance.

THE NEXT DAY, while Aviva played with her toys and Arlo caulked some of the upstairs windows that were letting in drafts, Carrie worked at her computer. Her editors had loved the idea of a grief journey series and wanted to include such topics as the stages of grief, how to help someone going through the process and where to find help. Carrie put together a portfolio of articles and advice for distribution.

But all the while, thoughts of Arlo distracted her.

He'd been so kind last night, seeming to understand her discomfort and respond to it in exactly the right way.

And then he'd suggested the "date." She'd been taken aback at first, so he'd brushed it away as a time on the calendar, and now she didn't know what to do.

Her friend Emma was right. Carrie was attracted to him, there was no doubt, but the thought of focusing on a man when she was still grieving seemed wrong.

However, she couldn't deny the sparks of attraction that zinged between the two of them. From the tone of his raspy voice to the warmth of his flushed skin, she suspected—*no, knew*—he felt the same. And ordinarily, she'd act on it. In fact, a part of her wished he'd given her a little longer to come to terms with the idea before backpedaling.

But she also had Aviva to consider. The two-year-old was enamored with him, which should have lessened her concerns, but with so many changes going on in her young life, Carrie was hesitant to add anything else to the mix.

But oh, mama, he was hot. And the way he interacted with Aviva? Her ovaries convulsed every time. She wished Randi was here to talk to, but if she was, Carrie would be back in

Albuquerque and most likely wouldn't be fighting this wild attraction for her brother-in-law's best friend.

Although she missed "home," Chatelaine was growing more appealing by the minute.

She sighed and opened her email. Her lawyer needed information for the adoption papers, and Carrie tried to focus on the task at hand.

"Earth to Carrie."

She jumped.

Arlo leaned forward. "I'm sorry," he said. "I didn't mean to scare you."

Swallowing, she tried to even out her breathing. "No, that's okay. I don't know why I'm so jittery."

Well, other than having a sexy man in her new home.

"Did you need something?" she asked.

"I'm running out to pick up a few things for your window. Need anything while I'm gone?"

*You.*

"Um, no, thanks, I'm good."

She breathed a sigh of relief, if only because she didn't have to worry about embarrassing herself in front of him.

Finishing her email in response to her lawyer's questions, she put away her laptop and made Aviva lunch.

"Okay, sweetie, nap time."

Aviva shook her head. "No nap."

"Okay, how about we read a story?"

"Yes!"

She followed Aviva over to the newly repaired bookcase in the living room and watched while her niece looked at all the books, finally pulling one out and handing it over to Carrie.

"Come, we'll read upstairs."

Slowly, they climbed the stairs together. Once in Aviva's room, Carrie sat in the maple rocker, removed Aviva's shoes and socks, and cuddled with her as they read the book she'd chosen. It was a story about a little girl and her *abuela* who hid her Jewish identity but incorporated it into her own customs at Christmastime. The subject was way above her niece's understanding, but Aviva loved the colorful pictures, and Carrie adapted the story to fit a two-year-old's mind. She kept her voice low and soothing, and thanks to the steady rocking of the chair, Aviva fell asleep before Carrie finished the book.

"That's an interesting story," Arlo whispered as he stood in the doorway.

This time, he hadn't scared her. He entered and helped her lift Aviva into her toddler bed, tucking her in, a tender expression on his face.

They stood over Aviva for a few minutes in silence before tiptoeing out of the room and shutting her door.

"Some of our ancestors came from Spain and had to hide who they were," Carrie said as they talked in the hallway. "They settled in this area, and most of the Jewish traditions were lost, but some still remained. The book is a little advanced for her, but I guess Randi wanted her to know about that part of our history."

"That's fascinating."

"Yes, they're called 'crypto-Jews' or 'Marrano Jews,'" Carrie explained. "Some are eager to embrace their Jewish heritage today, and others still don't."

"Wow, I never knew that."

Carrie smiled. "Did you get what you needed?"

He held up his paper bag. "Yup. But I'll have to finish tomorrow. I've got to get back to the ranch to talk to Nash about implementing some of his plans for the ranch, as well as Heath's new technology. I need an update about our bottom line, and well, other stuff." He looked sheepish. "I don't mean to bore you."

Carrie tried to hide the pit of disappointment in her stomach. Her sister's house—*her* house—wasn't big, but she'd grown accustomed to having Arlo around.

*Liar,* her conscience said. *You like having him around because you think he's sexy.*

"No problem," she said. "I really appreciate your time here. I'm sure you have a ton of your own work to do."

He shook his head, following her downstairs and grabbing his cowboy hat off the hook in the hallway.

"I enjoy doing this." He looked down at her, sincerity shining in his green eyes. "Like I said, it makes me feel good to help you out."

"Thank you." She watched him jog down her porch steps, shutting the door before he drove off in his car.

The next day, Arlo returned early in the morning. So early, Carrie was still in her T-shirt and pajama shorts, cooking pancakes.

"Knock, knock," he called, before letting himself inside. "Oh, man, I smell something good."

Carrie sucked in her stomach, hoping, somehow, he wouldn't notice her lack of bra. "Blueberry pancakes. Want some?"

"Does a bear—"

He paused, his face reddening, just as Aviva said, "Roar!"

Carrie burst into laughter, as did Arlo.

"Saved by the toddler," she said to him as he sat at the table next to Aviva. "Again."

"Sorry about that. Must have been overcome with hunger."

When he turned away, she reached for a sweater, before she served him three large pancakes and nodded toward the maple syrup. "Wouldn't want you to starve, then, would we?"

As the three of them ate breakfast, Carrie wondered what it would be like having breakfast with this man all the time. He easily joined in conversation with her and Aviva and helped the toddler with her food and drink.

Since Aviva had made the bear noises, he peppered their meal with various animal sounds, adapting their game since they were sitting down to a meal.

"I swear, I'm going to gain a thousand pounds if you keep cooking for me," Arlo said as he finished.

"Well, then, you should probably avoid my house until Hanukkah is over. I'm planning to make lots of special foods."

His eyes lit up.

Was he always this appreciative of food, or was it her cooking? And did he just think she was a good cook, or was a budding attraction to her coloring his opinions?

*And why do I care?*

She wanted to shout at herself, to tell herself she was being a fool. But a small part of her liked the attention.

As Arlo went off to continue his work on her window, Carrie decided to cut herself a little slack. Yes, she was lonely. She grieved for her sister. But she also missed her life back in Albuquerque and her friends. Talking to them on the phone was harder to do the busier she became, and she missed them. And she definitely missed the Jewish community. Being with Arlo, however, softened those feelings, and being with someone who understood her grief was soothing. He was a wonderful man in so many ways, especially in his willingness to learn about her traditions.

It was time to stop analyzing every moment and just breathe.

Aviva ran over. "Cawwy, dwadel." She held out the red dreidel Arlo had given her.

Smiling, Carrie bent down. "You want to play dreidel, lovey?"

Aviva nodded.

"Okay, let's go find our pennies."

Taking her niece's hand, they walked into Isaac's office. Carrie swallowed in the doorway but pushed her way into the room. By now, she'd removed her brother-in-law's personal things, and while it still looked like an office, it could be anyone's. She was even considering transforming it into her own, but she wasn't sure.

Since Aviva liked playing the dreidel game so much, Carrie had begun collecting pennies and tossing them into a jar, which she kept on the desk. She pulled it closer.

"Here you go. How many do you think we need?"

Aviva reached her hand into the jar and pulled out a fistful. Some of them dropped on the floor. Carrie picked them up, took the remainder from Aviva's hand and nodded for her to take another handful.

"That's perfect," she said.

As they exited the room, Aviva cried, "Bye, Daddy."

Carrie's breath hitched. A lump formed in her throat. Tears pricked, but she didn't want to shed them. She didn't want Aviva to associate sadness whenever she mentioned Isaac or Randi. So, she swallowed and whispered, "Bye."

Back in the living room, she cleared her throat. "Are you ready?"

Aviva nodded.

Carrie spun the dreidel. It landed on *shin*.

"Shin, shin, put one in," Aviva cried, clapping.

"Good job!" Carrie said as she put another penny in the middle.

The next spin showed a *hay*. "Hay, take half," Carrie said and split the pile of pennies in half.

She spun again and landed on *nun*. "Nun means none." She frowned.

"None, none, none," Aviva cried.

"That's right."

One more spin, and this time, the dreidel landed on *gimel*. "Gimel is gimme all of them!" Carrie took the whole pile and laughed when Aviva clapped her hands.

Aviva's joy was infectious, especially when she grabbed all the pennies and slid them toward her. The child took to the game immediately.

She continued giggling as Carrie made a game of pretending to take Aviva's pennies, and Aviva tried to take Carrie's. She was having so much fun with the little girl, she didn't notice Arlo return until suddenly he was right next to them, smiling.

"What, no pennies for me?" he asked.

Aviva pushed herself up and gave Arlo all her pennies.

"Hey," Carrie cried. "What about me?"

Aviva shook her head no before hiding behind Arlo's leg. Carrie pretended to pout, but then the little girl peeked her head around and shouted, "Boo!"

Somehow, the game morphed into hide-and-seek, with Carrie and Arlo playing along.

Carrie wasn't sure what she enjoyed more—Aviva's contagious joy or Arlo joining in. Her senses spiked into high alert. Every time her arm brushed against Arlo's, or she exchanged a glance with him, time slowed, her skin prickled, her insides clenched.

*Every. Time.*

She didn't remember Hanukkah games being this interesting when she was a kid. Clearly, things were different in Texas.

ARLO HAD RUSHED through his paperwork in an effort to get back to Carrie and Aviva sooner. Maria, the ranch office assistant, had left him a pile of papers to sign. He'd had emails to read and return. And Ridge and Nash wanted to meet with him. But his attention wasn't on the ranch, it was on the two females playing Hanukkah games, and his attempts to clear off his desk failed.

While he'd signed all the documents, he'd read only half his emails and responded to none. He'd pushed Ridge and Nash off another day or two and flown out of the office and back to Carrie's house before anyone could argue with him. He expected at least one or two annoyed texts or phone calls, but he didn't care.

What he did care about was spending as much time as possible with Carrie and Aviva. Only with them did the all-consuming grief and guilt not press down upon him. Only with them did he smile and find himself forgetting his concerns. Only with them did he enjoy holiday preparation.

So yesterday, when he knocked on Carrie's door and no one answered, and when he opened the door to sounds of laughter, he couldn't help himself. He joined in.

And today?

Today he was sitting at her kitchen table watching her and Aviva make Hanukkah candles. Never mind that he should be outside fixing the mailbox that listed to the side. Never mind that the only candles he'd ever heard of being made from scratch were last made in colonial times. He sat at the table and stared at Aviva's chubby hands rolling beeswax into lumpy, misshapen, beautiful candles.

As one, he and Carrie praised the little girl's efforts and laughed at her rainbow-colored hands.

When they finished making the candles, Arlo helped clean up while Carrie left the room. He heard her steps retreat upstairs, but the running water while they washed their hands drowned out any other sound.

"All clean," he declared after inspecting each of Aviva's ten fingers.

"Aww cwean," she echoed, turning his hands over and scrunching up her face.

Carrie entered the kitchen, a pained look on her face.

"I found Randi's Hanukkah box," she said.

Arlo's chest ached. "You okay?"

She nodded, although her eyes looked misty.

"I was looking for their menorah."

She placed the box on the table and opened it. Arlo lifted Aviva into his arms so she could see—but not touch—the items.

Inside the box was a velvet case. Carrie opened it and ahhed.

"Look at this, Vivie." Her voice cracked, but she kept going. "This was Mommy and Daddy's menorah."

The nine-branched candelabra—one for each of the eight

nights, and the helper candle—was a wave of rainbow-colored glass. Even with Aviva's misshapen candles, it would look beautiful when lit.

"Pwetty," she said, her mouth open. She reached her hand out to touch it, and Arlo guided it so she wouldn't break it.

"Let's see what else is in the box," Carrie suggested.

She pulled out several glass and ceramic dreidels. "Oh, these are beautiful," she said. "But they're just to look at, not to play with, okay? If we play with them, they'll break."

"I hold?" Aviva asked.

Arlo's pulse raced. This was asking for trouble. But Carrie was patient.

"Yes, but you need two hands."

Arlo put the toddler down, and Carrie cupped her hands to show Aviva what to do. Aviva copied her. Then Carrie placed one of the dreidels in her hands.

Arlo smiled, but Aviva sat almost frozen, staring at the dreidel with a big smile.

"No more," Aviva said, after a few seconds.

Not knowing if the child was going to drop the dreidel or what, Arlo took it out of her hands and gave it to Carrie.

The smile she gave him warmed him. "Thanks."

"What else in there?" Aviva asked, pulling at the box flap and trying to stand on tiptoe.

"How about I lift you up?" Arlo asked, lifting her before she could answer him. Somehow, he suspected it was safer for her in his arms than near the box of fragile things.

"There are tablecloths and tea towels and some china trays with gelt on them." Carrie pulled them out and showed them to everyone. Nothing held Aviva's interest for long.

"Down pwese."

Arlo put Aviva down once again, and she ran to get her red dreidel. As Carrie placed the items around the house, Aviva added her toy dreidel from Arlo to the shelf where Carrie displayed the other dreidels.

"What a great idea, Vivie," Carrie said.

Aviva clapped her hands.

Arlo's chest swelled thinking how much the little girl liked the gift he'd given her.

"Just remember, we can't play with the other ones, only your red one."

"Onwy wed."

Carrie nodded. "That's right."

"Want help with the tablecloth?" Arlo asked.

He didn't know why that question popped out of his mouth. Really, out of everything he could have asked, that was probably the most ridiculous. But here he was, having already spoken the words and now waiting for an answer.

"I'm going to wash them first."

And now he felt even more stupid, although he couldn't explain why. He stuffed his hands in his pockets. She didn't need him for this stuff. She *did* need him for repairs, and if he was smart, he'd get going on those things.

He pointed to the door. "Yeah, so I'm just going to get to work—"

Before Carrie had a chance to answer, he left the house, grabbing his tools and getting to work on the listing mailbox. Aviva's laughter echoed in his mind. *Gosh, that kid is smart.* He didn't know a lot about children, but he didn't think there were too many two-year-olds who understood so many things and spoke so well, even if she had a hard time pronouncing her *r*'s.

His chest tightened, thinking of all Isaac was missing. He remembered talking to him about his hopes and dreams for his baby when Randi was pregnant.

That man deserved to be a father. He would have loved every second of their Hanukkah celebrations.

He shook his head. Life wasn't fair. Then again, it wasn't fair his own father had possibly ruined two families—his own and Stevie's. Because now that Casper was dead, there was another child without a dad...

He pounded the nail into the wood so hard it cracked the rotting shelf. He swore under his breath, and turned to go find another piece to replace what he'd ruined. Inside the house, the smell of fried onions made his stomach rumble, and he followed his nose into the kitchen.

"What are you making?" he asked, hoping the awkwardness from before had disappeared.

"I'm making *keftes de prasa* and freezing them ahead of time for Hanukkah." Her cheeks reddened. "I should have asked you first if you'd like to try some. They're fried leek patties."

She looked at the pan sizzling on the stove. "I'll have another batch ready in a minute, if you want to wait."

She was always cooking, this one. "They smell delicious, but if I don't get work done, this house will fall down around your ears." And he'd never get over the guilt of failing his friend.

She nodded. "Well, they're here if you're hungry."

He was always hungry, but hunger didn't fix listing mailboxes. After he found another piece of wood, he returned outside and finished the repairs, determined not so shirk his responsibilities like his father had done. He straightened, looking between his truck and Carrie's house. Swallowing, he realized that's how he thought of this place now. If only he could be sure she'd stay.

He was about to go inside to say goodbye when she and Aviva appeared on the porch. Carrie put a tray with two mugs of hot chocolate and a sippy cup down on the table.

She nodded to the mailbox. "That looks so much better. Thank you. You know," she said, patting the rocker next to her, "Randi mentioned a mine to me. Do you know anything about it?"

It was like she'd read his mind—if she were interested in the town, maybe she wanted to remain here.

"Back in 1965, my great-uncles Elias and Edgar Fortune owned a secret gold mine, ignored warnings that it might be unstable and, as a result, caused a mine collapse that killed fifty-one people."

Carrie gasped. "Oh, my goodness. That's terrible."

Arlo nodded. "Yeah, the two brothers were pretty awful. They slunk out of town without taking any responsibility for the accident and supposedly died in a boating accident in Mexico. My great-grandfather, Wendell, was their older brother. And my grandmother was the fifty-first person killed in the mine."

"Oh, now I get it," Carrie said.

"Anyway, the mine didn't actually have any gold, only silver, but it's the source of our family wealth. Or it was. Now it's just a historical and tourist site."

"So that's why the town was originally founded?" Carrie asked.

"Yep. The castle belonged to my great-grandfather, who, as I'd mentioned, left it to my mom. Chatelaine Hills is where my family and some of the wealthier people settled as they arrived. You've probably seen the country club, right?"

She nodded.

"The townspeople are friendly and hardworking. Luckily, they don't seem to have a problem with my family and I, since they've been pretty welcoming to us since we arrived."

He wasn't big on gossip and hated to connect himself to the horrible relatives who had caused so much grief to so many people. Growing up with his father, he'd hated the idea of people talking about his family, and once he found out about his actual family history, he was even more careful. But he must have done something right because by the end of his conversation, Carrie was nodding.

"I can't wait to get to know these people now that you've painted such a vivid picture."

He tipped his head in acknowledgment, and inside he gave a mental cheer. If she wanted to meet people in town, she definitely wasn't planning on leaving anytime soon.

"You'll meet a lot of them if you join us for the holiday party," he said.

"Oh?"

"It's in ten days and held at the town hall. Practically everyone in town goes. There's music and holiday festivities. It's fun." He paused a moment. "You should come. With me."

There, he'd said it. He swallowed, wondering if she'd say no.

"I'd love to," she replied with a smile. "It sounds fun."

He took a drink of the warm liquid to compose himself. She wanted to go to the party. With him. Excitement made his body warm, his disappointment in his dad from earlier disappearing. If Carrie stayed, if he took her and Aviva to the festival, he'd have more opportunities to be involved in both of their lives. He could help Aviva get to know her father. His heart turned over.

She turned to him. "You've got something on your chin," she said.

He touched his face, but she shook her head. "No, here."

She dragged her finger across his jawline to his chin, and swiped a dollop of whipped cream. The contact sizzled. Before she pulled away, he reached for her hand and held on to her wrist. She froze, as did he. Around him, the silence thickened, except for the sound of his pulse pounding in his ears. Her lips parted and her chest rose and fell as her breathing increased. Her skin was soft beneath his. His fingertips pressed against her skittering pulse point.

He wanted to pull her close and feel her body against his. To nudge her hair away from her neck with his nose and press a kiss at her nape. To take the finger against his chin and bring it to his mouth and lick it.

But Aviva was nearby. They were seated on the front porch, where anyone could walk by and see them. And Carrie was still grieving.

Instead, he squeezed her wrist, a wordless promise of sorts. *More later if you're willing.* And he released her.

Her finger remained suspended near his chin for a few seconds, as if she didn't know what to do with it.

Or as if she wanted to stay close to him.

But then she lowered it to her side and turned away from him.

He waited for her to speak, watching her for any sign that she wanted him as much as he wanted her. His reward was the sight of her sides expanding and contracting, thanks to the snug fit of her shirt. He smiled to himself.

When she finally did speak, all traces of her desire were gone.

"Would you mind getting me several sheets of paper towels, please?"

He swallowed before doing what she said.

She took the towels from him and continued with what she was doing. And he made a decision.

"How about a break from it all?"

She looked at him, askance. "From what 'all'?"

"All the work you've been doing. Let's take tomorrow off, with Aviva, and go for a drive?"

"A drive where?"

"San Antonio."

Her eyes widened. "That's two hours away!"

"It'll be worth it, I promise."

She finished the last of the leek patties in silence, and he waited for her to say no thanks to his offer.

The idea, still formulating in his mind, had popped out of his mouth. But the more he thought about it, the more he wanted to get her away from here, with all the memories of her sister and brother-in-law, with all the pressures to pass down holiday traditions to her niece, and to just have a day of fun. With him.

"Okay," she said.

He was so caught up in his own thoughts, he almost missed her answer. But then he replayed the last few seconds and smiled. He'd have a whole day with her, away from the responsibilities and memories of this place.

And maybe a chance to make new ones.

Together.

# CHAPTER SIX

THE FOLLOWING DAY, Carrie was up with the sun. She'd flown in and out of San Antonio before but hadn't explored it. She knew nothing about the city, nor did she know Arlo's plans. Without anything to go on, she dressed in jeans and a long-sleeved light blue top and tied a heavier sweater around her waist. She left her hair down and slipped on a pair of sneakers. Not leaving anything to chance, she'd packed a bag for Aviva with some toys and books and a variety of jackets and sweatshirts, pull ups and an extra pair of leggings.

"I wish he'd told me where we were going," she muttered to herself as she got breakfast ready. "Or that I'd thought to ask."

But at the time, she was reeling from being so close to him, from controlling her longing for him. All she'd wanted to do yesterday was pull his head forward and kiss him. Or wrap her arms around him and hold on tight. He'd grabbed her wrist, and they'd locked eyes, and she'd fallen deep into a well of desire. And then when he'd suggested spending the day together? Well, her brain and her heart and her body had thrown a party, and all she could do was nod and say yes. Luckily, she'd thought enough to make sure Aviva was included. But anything else useful would have to wait.

Ages had passed since she'd done something fun, something

that wasn't a required task for either her sake or Aviva's. She didn't really care what they did today. She just hoped she was sufficiently prepared.

When Arlo showed up at ten, he came to her door, knocked and let himself inside. She'd grown to like that habit of his. It was starting to feel like he belonged here, which was weird, because it was she who was the outsider.

But with Arlo, she didn't *feel* like the outsider. She felt like she belonged.

"Are you ready?" he asked, entering the kitchen.

"Arwo!" Aviva cried. She ran over and hugged his leg, making Carrie smile. She was getting used to having him around, too.

"I'd be more ready if I knew what we were doing," she said. "But yes."

She pointed to the bags by the front door.

"I know it looks like we're moving, but toddlers need a lot of stuff."

Arlo laughed, swinging Aviva up into his arms and kissing her cheek before planting her on the ground again. "No worries, I have a big truck. Come on, kiddo, we're going for a ride."

"A wide? Yay!" Aviva jumped up and down.

They filled the two-hour trip to San Antonio with singing, pointing out the sights and laughter. Before long, they reached their destination.

"First stop, the San Antonio Zoo," Arlo said. "Who wants to see the animals?"

*"Me!"* Aviva yelled at the top of her lungs and bounced in her car seat.

Carrie smiled. "You sure know how to make her happy."

He flashed her a smile and squeezed her thigh, before getting out of the truck and going around to Carrie's side to open the door. He was still smiling, and Carrie could have spent all day looking at him, his green eyes lit up, his dimples flashing. But Aviva was about to burst with excitement, so Carrie got the stroller while Arlo got her.

Once they had the child strapped in they entered the zoo.

"Which animal should we visit first?" Arlo asked.

"The zebwas!"

"Zebras coming up," Carrie said while Arlo pretended to be a zebra and galloped in front of Aviva.

When they reached the designated area, Arlo bent down to take Aviva out of the stroller and swung her up on his shoulders. His muscles bunched beneath his blue plaid shirt, and for a moment, Carrie wished she was in his arms. But the giggles and squeals from Aviva brought her back to reality. The little girl tapped Arlo's head with excitement, and Carrie exchanged a rueful glance with him.

"My niece is going to give you a headache," she said.

He shrugged, and they spent the next few minutes watching the black-and-white-striped creatures. Then it was on to the camels, the giraffes and the rhinos.

By now, Carrie was starving, and they stopped into Longnecks Bar & Grill, where they had a quick bite before resuming their walk.

"Okay," Arlo said, "we have time for two more animals. What should they be?"

"The wions," Aviva declared.

"The lions? And what about you, Aunt Carrie? What do you want to see?"

"She wants to see the monkeys," Aviva said.

"She does?" Arlo asked.

"I do?" Carrie echoed.

Aviva nodded.

Laughing, they walked to the lions, with Arlo roaring in Aviva's ear.

The toddler loved when the lions yawned, and she jumped when one roared a little too close to her. Carrie comforted her and they moved on to the monkeys, who were swung from the trees.

"I wike them," Aviva said, watching them in their enclosure.

"I like them, too," Carrie said. "Look how long their arms are."

Aviva tried to stretch her arms, and Carrie laughed. "I don't think that's going to work, Vivie."

"Alright, ready for our next adventure?" Arlo asked.

Carrie and Aviva nodded.

"Where are we going?" Carrie asked.

"Well, you can't visit San Antonio without visiting the Alamo," he announced. "Have you been?"

Carrie shook her head. "Nope."

"Excellent."

They drove to the tourist destination and visited the living history encampment. Although Aviva was young for the demonstrations, she watched, wide-eyed, as people walked around in costumes. She covered her ears at the musket demonstrations, and by the time they were halfway through, she'd fallen asleep in her stroller.

Carrie loved learning about the history of the site, and about the early years in Texas.

"I would not have wanted to get sick back then," she said, after listening to a demonstration about early medicine.

Arlo nodded in agreement. "Me, neither. Do you mind if we go into the church? I reserved free tickets, but we don't have to use them."

"Of course not," Carrie said.

Arlo gave a sheepish smile. "Good. I wasn't sure if you'd want to…"

She paused, touched that he cared, but wanting to set the record straight. "Just because I don't worship in a church, doesn't mean I don't find them interesting," she said. "And this one has so much history attached to it. I wouldn't want to miss it." She pulled at his elbow. "But I do appreciate your checking with me."

They entered the hushed building. He was so considerate, Carrie thought as they wandered around inside. When he pushed the stroller and ushered Carrie around, she felt taken care of, for the first time in a long time. Maybe as part of her guide to healing-after-grief series, she should suggest finding a cute guy.

Scratch that—handsome, sexy rancher.

Who would have thought this nice Jewish girl from Albuquerque would fall for a cowboy?

She took a deep breath, for the first time in a while feeling relaxed and hopeful.

When they'd seen everything there was to see at the Alamo, Arlo led her outside. By now, Aviva was awake.

"Ready for our last stop?" he asked.

Carrie looked at Aviva, and they both said, "Yes."

This time, Arlo pointed them away from the car. "We'll walk this time."

Aviva swung her legs in the stroller while Carrie kept pace next to him. She looked at everything on their short walk, trying to take in as much of the trip as she could.

Arlo had been right. She'd needed to get away.

"Here we are," he said, pointing to the entrance. "The River Walk."

By now, the sun was beginning to set, and colorful lights filled the trees along both sides of the river. Holiday displays were everywhere, reflecting off the water and casting rainbow hues along the sidewalks and building facades.

"Wook, wook!" Aviva cried, pointing to the shimmering lights. "Pwetty!"

Aviva was right, Carrie thought. They *were* beautiful, actually. It was like walking through a multicolored fairyland.

Aromas of Texas barbecue, spices and sweets mingled, making her mouth water. Restaurants had installed space heaters for guests to sit outdoors. Colorful umbrellas covered tables, and small tour boats cruised the river, enabling tourists to float as well as walk. Strains of Christmas music projected from speakers and added to the festivities.

"This place is magical," Carrie murmured, turning to Arlo.

"I thought you'd like it," he said. "Although I'm sorry there aren't any Hanukkah decorations."

"I don't mind," she said. "I like experiencing your holiday like this."

Somehow, without her noticing at first, Arlo had taken her hand, and as they walked along the river, exploring shops, examining menus and admiring the holiday decorations, Carrie kept her hand in his, enjoying for the moment their time together. She didn't know what he intended by taking her hand. Was it an unconscious action, the first step of a plan, or merely the result of the festive mood on the River Walk?

She sneaked a glance at his profile. The lines and planes of his face emphasized his confidence. At this moment, the signs of grief and guilt were gone. They were two people, spending the day together.

Carrie wanted more. The realization shocked her, but it was true. She wanted more than a day. When her sister had been killed, she'd dreaded a future without her. She still did. But in addition to that deep sadness, she finally wanted to see what her future held. And being with Arlo had helped her to see that her life hadn't ended when her sister died.

"Thank you," she whispered.

Arlo turned to her. "For what?"

Hope filled her chest, almost making her blurt out her feelings. But they were new, and she wanted to savor them herself for a little while longer.

"For today. For everything you're doing to help me. For your kindness to Aviva..." Her voice trailed off.

He squeezed her hand. "Thank you for letting me."

Now that she knew he was holding her hand on purpose,

her joy increased. They continued along the river, showing Aviva the sights.

When the food aromas got to be too much, she pointed to a Mexican restaurant. "Want to stop?"

He nodded, and they settled at a table on the riverfront.

"Is it wrong of me to feel guilty for enjoying myself as much as I have today?" she asked him after the waitress took their order.

"I was actually thinking the same thing. I have so much on my mind, so much that's unsettled, but today? Today was just about perfect."

Carrie smiled. "Just about?"

He lifted one side of his mouth in a small grin.

The waitress arrived with drinks, interrupting the flow of conversation.

"I know Randi wouldn't want me to spend my days crying," Carrie said after the waitress left. "And everything has felt so overwhelming. But today, with you, was the first time I've felt myself in what feels like forever."

"I'm glad I could help," Arlo said. He reached for her hand across the table. "You've helped me, too. Somehow, being with you lightens the weight of my father's death, wondering about his other family, everything. I feel better equipped to confront things, and to learn to live without my best friend."

This time, she looked him straight on when their fingers touched. There was no mistake. His gaze was intense. Her desire was reflected in his eyes. A delicious thrill stole up the back of her spine at the realization he liked her as much as she liked him.

"I enjoy spending time with you," Arlo said. His smooth voice reminded her of the melodious sound of the cantor singing during Friday night Shabbat services—deep, rich and smooth. "I'd like to spend more time with you—free time—going forward."

"I'd like that, too."

He scooted his chair around, so they were on the same side of the table. Not releasing her hand, he cradled her face with his other hand, drew her close and kissed her.

His hand was warm, his lips firm, his kiss glorious. She closed her eyes, leaning into him, her skin flushing. His thumb made lazy circles against her cheek and sent shivers down her spine.

"Me, too, me, too," Aviva cried, puckering her lips.

With a laugh, they each kissed one of her cheeks. She gave them a huge smile.

"Well, this is going to be interesting," Arlo said, his eyes dancing.

"I can't wait," Carrie said with a wink.

ARLO LEFT HIS office a few days later after another meeting with Heath to discuss his technology improvements. Numbers and technical terms jumbled in his head as he thought about Ridge's latest idea and how it would help the ranch succeed.

Running feet behind him made him pause, just as he was about to leave the building.

"Arlo, wait," Heath said. "Can I talk to you a minute? In private?"

Nodding, Arlo looked around before turning back to his office and shutting the door. He pointed to the chair across from his desk, and Heath sat, folding one leg over his knee and resting his ankle on it.

He steepled his fingers and focused on his sister's future husband. "What can I do for you?" The man was intelligent with a kind heart, perfect for Jade, and Arlo was willing to do whatever he needed.

"It's more of what I can do for you," Heath said.

"What do you mean?"

Heath expelled a breath. "We've been so focused on business, we haven't had a chance to talk much. And..." He rubbed the back of his neck, an awkward expression on his face.

"You've been through a lot these past few months, especially after your friend died. I just wanted to check in with you. Jade and I are both worried about you."

Arlo's heart pounded and his face warmed. He didn't know what to say. He opened and closed his mouth a couple of times, and then froze when Heath smiled.

"Yeah," Heath admitted, "it's a little weird coming at you out of the blue when we don't know each other well." His gaze sharpened. "But I know what it's like to lose people you love and to have the foundation shift beneath you. I know you've got lots of people to talk to, but I guess I just wanted to offer myself as one of those people if you need it."

Silence built in the room, until Arlo finally found his voice. "You've no idea how much your concern means to me," he said. "Not that I was ever concerned, but I couldn't have picked a better guy for Jade if I went looking for her match myself."

Heath's posture softened. "Thank you."

"No, thank you. You're right, it's been tough these past few months, and I've had a lot on my mind. It's nice to know you're here for me."

"Anything you want to get off your chest?"

He studied the man across his desk. If anyone would listen without judgment, it was him.

"I don't know, to be honest. I've found out something about our dad, and the secret is killing me. I don't want to make the rest of family feel even worse than they do, but I'm not sure how to handle it." He huffed. "I'm sorry for being so vague, but since you're with my sister, I don't want to put you in an awkward position, either."

Heath pinned him with a sharp gaze. "I appreciate that. You've all had complicated relationships with Casper, I get it. But there's no reason for you to suffer in silence, either. The thing I admire most about you Fortunes is you stick together. It's up to you whether or not you tell them what you've found out, but don't for a minute think they can't handle it or that you have to shoulder the burden yourself. You Fortunes are strong, a lot stronger than you think."

Heath was right. They were strong. Some of the burden that weighed him down, lifted.

He rose, as did Heath, and the two men hugged quickly, slapping each other on the back.

"Thanks, I appreciate it," Arlo said. "Really."

With a tip of his hat, Heath left.

Arlo was still ruminating on Heath's advice when his phone rang. He smiled when he saw the screen.

"Hey, Carrie."

"Hey, any chance you were planning to come over today?"

They'd been talking on the phone nightly before they went to sleep, and of course, during the day when he was working on her house, but he hadn't been there for a day or so.

"Why, do you need me?" Oh, the loaded words. He missed her, and honestly, *he* needed *her*, but he also had a job on the ranch he couldn't ignore.

"It's fine. I can do it myself."

"Wait, what's going on?"

He was on his way back to his house, and he sat in his golf cart, ready to drive it the short distance to his home.

"It's not a big deal. I didn't mean to bother you. I have to go to the lawyer's office regarding the adoption papers—"

"Whoa, that's a huge deal!"

Carrie huffed. "Well, yes, it is. I just meant I can bring Aviva with me. I don't want to take you away from working."

"What time is your appointment?"

"One o'clock. But, Arlo, if you have work on the ranch…"

He quickly figured out his day in his head. "Let me clear up some things now, and I'll come to you by twelve thirty. Okay?"

"Are you sure?"

"Carrie, there's no one I'd rather spend time with than you or Aviva." He meant it.

"Thank you."

His pulse raced with the anticipation of seeing Carrie later, and an idea formed. Driving into town, he stopped at Great-Store, compiling a list in his head of the items he needed. On his way out, he bumped into his sister, Dahlia.

"Hey, there," he said, giving her a hug. "What are you doing in town?"

"I needed a few groceries. Feel like stopping for a quick cup of coffee?"

He looked at his watch. He had a little time before Carrie needed him.

"Sure."

They walked into the diner and grabbed a seat at the back. After fixing their coffees, Dahlia took a sip, while Arlo contemplated the advice Heath had given him. Should he talk over his dilemma with his sister? She'd been close to their dad. Maybe she'd have some insight.

"So how are you and Carrie getting along?" she asked.

He smiled. "I'm seeing her later. And Aviva." He filled her in on the adoption status.

Dahlia's face softened. "You're really attached to that little girl."

*And her mother.*

"Yeah. I am. She makes me feel closer to Isaac."

Dahlia reached into her bag and pulled out a sheaf of paper. "Do you think Carrie would mind if I made Aviva a blanket to celebrate Aviva's adoption?"

"I think she'd love it."

Dahlia smiled. "Good. I saw this pattern and thought it would be adorable."

He nodded. "Hey, how are you doing with Dad's death? I haven't checked in with you in a while, and I should have."

She stiffened before taking a deep breath. "I miss him. I know I'm probably the only one—"

"No, no matter our feelings for the man, we're all grieving. We just do it differently."

Heath might have been right about not shouldering all the responsibility, but Arlo wasn't sure Dahlia was the best person to tell his suspicions about their dad's second family.

That being said, as he said, everyone dealt with grief in their own way—his siblings, himself, Carrie. He'd do well to remember that, and maybe give everyone, including himself, some slack.

A FEW HOURS LATER, he knocked on her door, shopping bag in hand.

"Hi," Carrie said as she opened the door. "What's in the bag?"

He walked with her into the kitchen.

"I had an idea."

"Uh-oh."

He nudged her. "Go sign your papers."

"I have a couple minutes. Tell me about your idea."

For some reason, he was self-conscious. Part of him wished she hadn't noticed the bag, and that he could surprise her with his efforts when she returned.

With a sigh, he pulled out candy molds and handed them to Carrie. Her features softened as she looked at them. "Dreidels and menorahs and coins. You're going to make gelt?"

He nodded. "I thought Aviva would have fun. We'll melt chocolate in the microwave and pour it into the molds. They'll refrigerate, and then she can have them for Hanukkah."

Carrie dropped the mold on the counter and hugged him tight. Then, she kissed him.

Man, if she was going to kiss him every time he had an idea, he'd ensure he turned into Albert Freakin' Einstein.

Her kisses were sweet and tender, but with a promise of more. His senses exploded as he tasted her sweetness, tangled his tongue with hers, and let the softness of her lips carry him away. She massaged his shoulders as she deepened the kiss, and his thoughts floated away. He grasped her waist, wanting more. He groaned as she stepped back.

"That's such a nice idea!" Sighing softly, she gazed up at him. "I have to go. I should be back in an hour or two. Thank you for all of this." She said goodbye to Aviva and left.

"Okay, kiddo, let's make chocolate!"

For the next hour, he helped Aviva make gelt. Or rather, he helped her make a mess. The gelt was a byproduct. But boy did he have fun. The two of them laughed and poured and melted and laughed some more. They were just cleaning up— seriously, two-year-olds could get chocolate in the weirdest places—when Carrie returned from town.

"Oh, my," she said as she walked into the kitchen.

Discarding her bag and her coat, she stood in the doorway and shook her head. "Any chance any chocolate ended up in the molds?"

Arlo walked to the refrigerator and pulled out a tray. "Ta-da!"

"Ta-da!" Aviva repeated.

He cracked the molds and turned the candies onto a dish.

"Wow," Carrie said. "I see dreidels, and a menorah or two, and some coins." She smiled. "Nice job, guys."

Aviva frowned. "I not a guy. I a girl!"

Arlo burst out laughing. "Yes, you are, sweets."

He turned to Carrie. "How'd your meeting go?"

"Really well. We have to go back in a few days—both of us—and appear before the judge, and then we're set."

"Congratulations. That's wonderful." Arlo's chest filled with happiness for them, but Carrie had a pensive look on her face. "Is there a problem?"

She shook her head. "No, it's just the final adoption makes it all real. I mean, I know it is, but it really hits home that there's no chance that my fantasy of Randi and Isaac showing up and saying, 'Surprise,' will happen. It's more final, even, than their funeral."

He put an arm around her, pulling her against him. She buried her face in his shoulder, and he held her while she breathed. Running a hand up and down her back, he warmed at her coming to him for comfort. She fit perfectly against him, and he was prepared to spend the rest of the day holding her if that's what she needed. But after a few moments, she pulled away. He brushed her hair away from her face and cupped her cheek.

"Do you want me to go with you? It's a big deal, and I could give you moral support."

She shook her head, her eyes bright. "No, I think it's something I have to do alone." She expelled a large breath. "But thanks for today."

"Don't thank me until you're satisfied with the cleanliness of your kitchen. I had no idea chocolate could get in so many places."

"Oy." She laughed. "I appreciate the attempt, though. You should probably get back to work?"

He didn't want to. He wanted to remain here, with this beautiful woman and this amazing child. They filled him with hope and light, something he'd lacked recently. But he had work to do for Ridge, and he couldn't postpone it any longer.

"Call me later?" he asked as he put his Stetson on his head and his hand on the front door.

"Of course."

CARRIE STOOD AT the top of the town hall stairs a few days later. The building was a one-story adobe brick building with a weathered red roof. The cool wind made her shiver in her dress and heels. Aviva's nose was red from the cold.

*Aviva. Her daughter.*

She longed to have someone to share this momentous occasion with…like Arlo. But she'd been right when she refused his company. No matter how alone she felt, she had to do this by herself. Eventually she would be leaving Chatelaine and returning to Albuquerque. She couldn't always rely on Arlo.

She tipped her head back and closed her eyes, letting the wind ruffle her hair. The adoption was final, and Aviva was hers.

She knelt before the stroller. Aviva clutched the bear the judge had given her. "I promise to do the best I can," she said to the little girl. She looked up at the sky and mouthed *I promise* as well.

"My beaw," Aviva cried.

"What are you going to name it?"

"Beawy."

Carrie laughed. "That's a wonderful name. Welcome to the family, Beary."

Despite the chill in the air, Carrie was in no hurry to go home. The town hall was across the street from the GreatStore and Harv's New BBQ. She hadn't checked out their Texas barbecue yet, although everyone raved about it. Still, she wasn't hungry right now. Maybe she'd take Aviva to Remi's Reads, the local bookstore. As she stood on the stairs, trying to figure out which of her errands she should do, a woman walked up the stairs holding a stack of papers in her hand. She stopped in front of Carrie.

"Hi, do you know about the Chatelaine Holiday Celebration?" She handed Carrie a flyer.

Carrie skimmed it. "This sounds like fun. We'll be sure to come." She sighed.

The woman, even though she'd never met Carrie before, looked concerned. "Is there anything I can help you with?"

She was a little taken aback. This woman didn't know her. "It's nothing. I'm just being dramatic."

Leaning in, the woman whispered, "That's okay, sometimes it's necessary. Happens to me all the time."

Looking at the woman, approximately the same age as herself, with her hair in a ponytail, her face devoid of makeup, and wearing practical jeans, a gray turtleneck and a puffy vest, along with the requisite cowboy boots, somehow, Carrie doubted her statement. Still, it was nice of her to try to make her feel better.

"Are you sure I can't do anything for you?" she asked again. "By the way, I'm Rita. I'm on the committee."

"Hi, I'm Carrie Kaplan, and this is Aviva, my daughter." Carrie swallowed. It was the first time she'd said those words. It felt weird, but right, yet somehow still filled her with more emotions than she could process. Certainly nothing she would express here.

Recognition followed by sorrow crossed Rita face. "Oh, you're Isaac Abelman's sister-in-law. I was a good friend of Randi's. I'm so sorry for your loss."

Swallowing, Carrie nodded. "Thank you."

"She was such a sweetheart. Are you sure I can't help you with anything?"

"It's not a big deal. I was just hoping there might be something having to do with Hanukkah at the holiday celebration. I'm trying to teach my ni—I mean my daughter—about her heritage." *And feeling very alone.*

Rita's eyes widened. "Oh, my word, that's right, you're Jewish. We're having a bake sale to raise money for the poor in our community. We'd love it if you brought some Hanukkah baked goods. And I'm sure we can find some Hanukkah music to add to our playlist. In fact, I'll put that on my to-do list right now."

Carrie smiled, touched by the automatic inclusion. "I'd love to bake some treats. Thank you!"

"You're welcome." Rita looked her up and down. "You know, if you ever want to grab a quick bite, give me a call." Before Carrie could say anything, Rita wrote her number on one of the fliers and handed it to her, before waving and heading up the stairs into the town hall.

Carrie folded the paper and put it in her diaper bag. Not yet wanting to return home, she wandered to the GreatStore, where she browsed among the aisles.

An elderly woman sat at the entrance of the store, greeting customers like old friends as they entered.

"Welcome to GreatStore," she said. "My name is Doris. Hello, little one, I love your bear!"

Aviva hugged the bear to her chest and smiled as Carrie greeted the friendly woman and continued walking. A manager, whose name tag read Paul Scott, nodded to her as she passed, and suggested she and Aviva check out the store's new photo studio. That sounded like a fun activity, and Carrie headed toward it.

"Hi, I'm Alana. Are you interested in getting your photos taken?"

Carrie looked at the woman who appeared to be close to her age. "I'd love to. The adoption just came through for us, and I'd like something special to commemorate it."

Alana's eyes brightened. "Oh, my goodness, congratulations! Come on over and we can pick a background for the two of you."

Carrie pushed the stroller over and looked at the options for a photo shoot. There were lots of Christmas decorations and plenty of options to turn the photos into a Christmas card.

"I don't suppose you have anything with a blue background?"

Alana nodded and showed her a dark blue drape with silver snowflakes. Since Carrie and Aviva were both wearing shades of pink, it was perfect.

In no time at all, Alana had taken several shots of Carrie and Aviva together, as well as several with the toddler holding her bear.

"These look great," Alana said. She handed Carrie a ticket. "Come back next week to pick them up. And congratulations, again!"

Ready to go home, Carrie headed back toward the entrance of the store. A middle-aged woman waved to Aviva and told her how much she liked her bear. And multiple salespeople said hello, offered her assistance and talked about the weather with her. She kind of liked the familiarity. Some of her earlier loneliness lessened. And aware that Aviva was always listening, Carrie made sure to carry on friendly conversations and be extra polite.

There were a lot of things to be aware of when you were a mother.

*A mother. She was a mother.*

Waves of joy and guilt crashed against each other, taking Carrie's breath away. Spots floated before her eyes. Her knees shook, and she leaned against a shelf. Eyes closed, she tried to get ahold of herself.

"Cawwy? Cawwy?"

Aviva's voice called through the fog.

"It's okay, Vivie. I just need a minute."

She needed more than a minute. She needed her old life back, her sister and brother-in-law…and Arlo.

Her breath hitched at the thought of him. Why hadn't she let him join her today? She wished with everything she had that he was here now.

"Ma'am, are you alright?" A young salesman looked at her, worry crossing his face.

"I… I'm fine." Her face heated. She hated making a scene. "I just need to catch my breath."

He spoke into his radio, but she didn't pay attention to what he said. Instead, she focused on calming herself down. But tears had started to fall. She tipped her head, hoping no one would see them. She was falling apart in the middle of the GreatStore in a small town where everyone would see and hear.

"Oh, honey, come with me." A woman's twang sounded close to her ear. "Let's get you out of here, okay? Winston, go open the office door. This woman needs to sit a spell."

"Thank you," Carrie whispered.

The woman patted her back as she led her into the back.

"You just sit right here and take as long as you need to get ahold of yourself. I'll be right back."

"Cawwy, why you cwy?"

She tried to wipe her face, but the tears wouldn't stop falling. Sobs built up in her chest, and she was afraid to speak for fear of scaring Aviva. So she took her hand and squeezed.

"Here you go," the woman said. She'd returned with a glass of water. "And I think the little one needs a c-o-o-k-i-e?"

Overcome by the kindness, all Carrie could do was nod.

"Sometimes the world gets to us and we just have to let it all go. Especially we women, who have to manage everything."

The older woman's wise words penetrated Carrie's grief. She needed to get ahold of herself. Just a few more moments and then she'd take Aviva and somehow get themselves out of the store with the minimum of embarrassment and go home, where she could cry in solitude.

They sat in silence, punctuated by Carrie's sniffles with her eyes closed and her head in her hands, until heavy footsteps sounded in the background and there was a knock on the door.

The chair legs scraped against the linoleum floor as the woman rose from her seat next to Carrie. Muffled voices sounded, and then, the voice she'd longed for.

"Carrie?" Arlo's low voice made her open her eyes. "I hear you're having a rough time."

Before she could react to his sudden appearance or to ask how he knew, he took her in his arms. His warmth and strength surrounded her, held her together as she fell apart.

He pressed his lips to the top of her head and rubbed her back as he comforted her. His presence loosened the tight hold she'd kept on her emotions and sobs wracked her body. She gripped his shirt, and he tucked her against him, letting her burrow and soak his shirt without complaint.

After an endless amount of time, the tears stopped. Her breaths stuttered as she tried to calm herself, embarrassment returning. But still he held her, like it was the most natural thing in the world. Like needing him was okay.

When she finally pulled away, he looked into her eyes and brushed the hair out of her face.

"Hey," he whispered.

"Hey."

She looked around, fear knotting her chest. "Where's Aviva?"

"Myra took her to get a drink."

"Oh, no."

"It's okay. She's grandma to about sixteen kids at this point. I'll get Aviva when we leave. It's perfectly safe, I promise."

"Thank you." She crumpled again. "Look at me. I can't be a m-m-mother."

He gripped her hands. "Why not?"

"I'm not supposed to…be one now. I'm supposed to be an…aunt. Randi is her mother." Her breath chopped. "I can't replace her."

He drew her to him once again. She shuddered in his arms. "I can't do this. I don't want to do this." She hit his shoulder with her fist, and he hugged her tighter. "I love her…more than anything. But it's not supposed to be…me."

"But how lucky is she that you're there to step in?" Arlo's voice whispered across the back of her neck.

She shook her head. "I'm going to…mess this up."

He took her by her upper arms and held her out in front of him. Staring into her eyes, he waited until she met his gaze. "You're an amazing woman. Of course, you're going to mess it up, lots of times probably, but you're not alone. There are so many of us who are here to help. Including me."

"I feel so alone." *And I shouldn't need so much help.*

He shook his head. "I know. But you're not. I promise. Look how everybody helped when they saw you having a tough time."

The band around Carrie's chest loosened. "I made a great impression as the crazy lady in the GreatStore."

Arlo smiled. "Nah, there've been others way worse than you." His expression grew serious. "I know it's overwhelming, but you're *not* alone. And I'd be honored if you'd allow me to help you."

She took a shaky breath and nodded.

"Think you're ready to go home?"

The thought of walking back through the store to her car filled her with embarrassment. It was one thing to cry in front of Arlo, which for some reason didn't bother her at all. It was something else to have to face the entire town of strangers. She closed her eyes.

"How crowded is it?" she asked.

"Doesn't matter. My truck is parked back here, and I have a car seat for Aviva." He pointed to the door next to them. "No one will see a thing."

Relief flooded through her.

He handed her a couple of tissues, and she blew her nose. When she nodded, he helped her up and walked her to his truck. "Wait here," he said, before disappearing back into the store.

She leaned her head against the headrest, shutting her eyes. She hadn't expected to fall apart. Today was supposed to be a good day. But somehow, as excited as she was to have the adoption finalized, the reality had hit her, and she hadn't been able to stop it. Even thinking about it now made her wobbly.

Arlo returned to the truck with Aviva.

"Wook what I got," she said, holding out a rainbow sprinkle cookie the size of her head.

"Oh, my goodness, that's huge."

Aviva nodded and gave a crumbly grin.

"Someone also got a lollipop and a toy horse," Arlo said.

Carrie's eyes widened. She'd have to thank the woman...

What was her name? Myra. She'd have to thank Myra later. Never mind the incredible sugar high.

"You're one lucky girl."

"You feel better?" Aviva asked.

Carrie's heart beat hard in her chest. "Yes, sweetie." Guilt burned through her. While she understood the child hadn't known what was happening, she did know Carrie was sad.

Back at her house, Arlo got Aviva settled while Carrie went to her room to sort out her face. She was a red mess. Her mascara was almost completely gone.

*Great, just great.*

That meant it was probably all over Arlo's shirt. That would teach her to move back to waterproof mascara permanently. She'd thought a month after Randi died was safe.

Nothing was going to be safe again.

She cleaned herself up as best she could and then sat on the edge of her bed, shoulders slumped. This was supposed to be a joyous occasion. How was she supposed to celebrate when the entire reason she'd gotten to this point was the death of her sister?

A soft rap on the door made her look up. Arlo stood in the doorway of her bedroom. His blond hair was finger combed. And his shirt, as she suspected, had tear stains and mascara smears. He held a glass of water.

"May I come in?"

She nodded. "I'm sorry about your shirt." Her voice was hoarse from crying.

He entered and handed her the water. Then he looked down at his chest and shrugged. "No biggie. Kind of adds character." The cold water soothed her parched throat. She placed the glass on the nightstand before looking at Arlo once again.

"You're very kind," she said.

He joined her on the bed.

"Maybe."

Turning toward her, he ran a hand through her hair and down the side of her neck.

This time, his touch wasn't as comforting as before. Not that it was bad. Oh, no. It was good. Her head and neck tingled at the contact, and she arched toward him. His eyes were green, like emeralds. How had she never noticed their shade before?

"I like your lashes natural," he said, a glimmer of a smile on his lips.

"So does your shirt." Carrie touched the marks on the fabric, lingering as she felt the hard muscles of his chest. She started to move her hand away, but he clasped it against him.

They sat together for a few moments, the only sound their breathing. Then, very slowly, he leaned forward to kiss her. His lips met hers. Their gentle exploring made her yearn for more. He tasted like mint. He kept his hand on top of hers, but with his other hand, he cupped the back of her neck and brought her forward, so there was hardly any space between them and nowhere for her to go.

Which was a good thing because she didn't want to move. She wanted to know more about him—the texture of his skin, the slope of his shoulders. She ran her free hand through his short hair, the waves curling around her fingers, and then over his sculpted shoulders to his back.

He never stopped kissing her, and when she sighed against his mouth, he continued exploring with his tongue.

Carrie moaned, before pulling away. "Aviva," she said.

"Is napping," he answered.

With a smile, she pressed her lips against his. This time, with both hands free, she wrapped her arms around his waist.

He placed his hands on her hips, giving her freedom to move, but making sure she knew he wanted her to stay right here. And she had no desire to leave.

His shirt was soft from wear and untucked. She played with the hem of the cloth, and before she had time to think about her actions, she'd slipped her fingers beneath the shirt and against his warm skin.

He deepened his kiss, as if telling her he liked what she was doing.

Good.

Kissing sideways was giving her a crick in her neck and preventing her from savoring him as much as she wanted. She climbed onto his lap, and he smiled against her, a deep-throated growl expressing his pleasure.

All of her sorrow and embarrassment and bewilderment coalesced into desire. She wanted him, and she wanted to forget just for one minute how her life had changed.

Gripping her tighter, he fell back against the mattress, bringing her with him. Sprawled on top of him, their bodies pressed against each other, Carrie let all her cares drift away. Surrounded by his strong arms, possessed by his mouth, she wanted nothing else but to disappear. As he hardened beneath her, demonstrating his need for her, desire coiled.

"I want you," he whispered.

His eyes darkened with desire.

"I want you, too," she answered, barely willing to pull away long enough to speak.

He smiled, before rolling her to the side and lifting her shirt over her head. Exposed to the cool air in the room, her skin developed goose bumps, and he drew her to him once again, rubbing his palms over her back and arm.

"I want to see you undressed," she said as she lay on his chest, listening to his heart beat beneath her ear. The request increased his heartbeat, and he fumbled with the buttons on his shirt until he ripped the clothing off and flung it across the room.

His chest was muscular and tan, and she trailed her finger over it until he shuddered. She gave him a wicked grin before planting kisses all along his bare skin.

"Enough," he ground out, taking her by the upper arms and flipping her onto her back. "My turn."

He did to her what she'd done to him, and she marveled at how he'd remained on the bed. Beneath his touch, she arched and moaned, and that was just when he stroked her with his fingers. When he repeated the process with his mouth, she gasped. His kisses were hot and wet, and her body trembled with need. When she couldn't take his torture any longer, she pushed against him, once again, taking the upper hand.

As he lay back on the bed, a grin on his face, she pulled at the snap of his jeans and unzipped his fly before he had a chance to stop her. His grin turned to shock as she took him in her hands, running along the length of him. His skin was smooth and warm to the touch, yet beneath he was hard.

He stared at her, eyes glittering, until she leaned forward and kissed him.

"I want to see you naked," he rasped.

While she kept her hands on him, he sat up and removed her clothes. Finally, they were both naked. They paused, each drinking in the sight of the other.

"You're beautiful," he whispered.

They came together. His skin was rougher than hers, his muscles more defined. But they fit perfectly, and they quickly learned each other's rhythm. Before they got too carried away, Arlo paused and grabbed a condom from his jeans that were still partially on the bed.

Carrie took the foil packet from him and slid the condom on, enjoying how her touch unraveled him.

Finally, they were both ready. Carrie stared into his eyes, drowning in their green depths. He discovered all her sensitive places with his hands and his breath—beneath her chin, under her left rib, above her right knee. Heady with sensation, she mapped his body with kisses, lingering at the notch in his collar bone and the indent of his right pelvic bone. Her skin was on fire, her nerves sending jolts of electricity throughout her limbs, until she didn't think she could take it anymore.

When she was just about to scream in a combination of frustration and need, he flipped her beneath him, supported himself on his straightened arms on either side of her and, with a nod from her, eased his way into her. Her body welcomed him, expanding around him but never completely losing the tension. He gritted his teeth as he pushed farther and farther, until finally they were as close as two people could be. Once again, Arlo asked her with only his eyes if she was ready, and when she nodded, he began to move. She followed him, adapting to his rhythm as if this wasn't their first time together, as if this wasn't a momentous, extraordinary event.

Carrie could barely hold on to a thought, but the "rightness" of this moment and this person with her enveloped her. He was her safe harbor, her "yes, you can" when she was sure she couldn't. He was sexy and smart and fun. And he was hers, for the moment. As their bodies performed an age-old dance, she let herself go, matching his movements and straining as she got closer to her peak of desire. She grabbed hold of him and arched her back. As he drove into her one more time, she crested the wave, sparks dancing before her eyes, and she shouted her release. He thrust a couple more times before joining her as they both spiraled out of control. Minutes later, as their breathing eased and their sweat dried, he turned to her.

"You're amazing," he said.

She gave him a serene smile. "It was wonderful. Thank you."

He cradled her in his arms, and they lay peacefully, drifting in the hazy afterglow.

"Thank you for being there for me when I fell apart earlier," Carrie whispered.

He turned and caressed her cheek. "Always. You never have to thank me. And thank you for tearing me apart just now." He winked at her, and she elbowed him in the ribs.

"Oof," he said.

She laughed, turning on her side and draping a leg over him.

"Are you feeling better?" he asked.

"Now that I've elbowed you? Much."

Chuckling, he added, "You know what I mean."

"I do," she said. "And I am."

"Feel like celebrating Aviva's adoption later?"

Joy, the piece that had been missing from earlier in the day, filled her. "Yes, I'd like that."

"Great," he said, sitting up and swinging his legs over the bed. He began to dress.

Carrie eyed him, wondering why he was in such a hurry. "What are you doing?"

"I have things to get."

"Like what?" she asked.

He shook his head. "Things."

She rose and started to get out of bed. "Well, I have cooking to do if we're celebrating," she said, reaching for her shirt.

At that moment, Aviva cried out, and Carrie hurried up.

Arlo held out his hand. "No, you stay and relax. Aviva and I will take care of everything."

"Even the cooking?"

"*Especially* the cooking," he said. "Seriously, relax and take it easy."

He strode to her side of the bed, leaned down and kissed her. "We'll be back."

He turned to the door. "Coming, Aviva!"

## CHAPTER SEVEN

ARLO SWUNG THE stroller around as he walked around the lake by his house. After a tumultuous day, Carrie needed rest more than ever. And he loved spending extra time with Aviva. They'd made shapes of the clouds, admired the different trees and wildflowers on the water's edge, and even collected a few rocks to bring back to Carrie.

"Hey, Arlo!"

Dahlia's voice pulled him up short, and he waved to his sister sitting on the back deck of her house. He turned the stroller her way and met her at the edge of her property.

"Morning," he said, bussing her cheek.

"Hey, cutie," Dahlia said, kneeling down next to the stroller.

Aviva was shy, but Dahlia soon got her to open up, and pretty soon his sister and Aviva were jabbering and laughing together.

Rising, Dahlia turned to him. "The blanket is almost done," she said. She nodded with her chin. "Just needs a red border, since clearly, that's a favorite."

Arlo laughed. "It is."

"I wove wed," Aviva said.

"I can see that," Dahlia said, pointing to the toddler's red shirt and red bow in her hair.

"She picked her outfit today," Arlo said.

Dahlia's eyebrows shot to the middle of her forehead. "Oh, really?"

Arlo's face heated. He'd just given away that he spent more time at Carrie's.

"I'm glad to see the two…three of you getting on so well."

He nodded. "I'm happy." His chest expanded. For the first time in a long time, he meant it.

Reaching toward him, Dahlia pulled him into a hug. "I'm so glad, little brother" she whispered in his ear. "So glad."

He pulled back, looking into her eyes, and hoped he wouldn't disappoint her when he found out the truth about their father. But for now, he'd take it.

Giving her a last squeeze, he said goodbye and continued on his way. They had a busy day, and it was time to get moving.

Back at Carrie's house later that afternoon. Turning off his truck, he released Aviva from her booster seat and gave her a small bag to carry to the door. Then he grabbed the rest of the bags and made his way to Carrie's front porch, where he somehow managed to get the front door open without dropping anything.

"Whoa, you guys have a ton of stuff," Carrie said, peeking among the bags in Arlo's arms. "I almost didn't recognize you. You're like bags with legs."

Aviva giggled her way toward the kitchen and put the bag on the floor. Arlo followed her, putting his bags, and then Aviva's, on the counter.

"We have a lot to celebrate, so we needed a lot of stuff. Plus," he said, kissing Carrie, "two-year-olds don't exactly understand the term 'moderation.'"

"Neither do you, it appears," she said, nodding toward everything. "What in the world did you buy?"

"Wainbows!" Aviva cried.

"Rainbows?" Carrie swung Aviva up in her arms. "I love rainbows."

"Me, too," she said.

"That's a *lot* of rainbows," Carrie mused.

Arlo propped his hands on his hips. "Go sit in the living room, or go to work, or whatever. I've got this."

"I already worked while you were gone. I don't want to sit. There's nothing wrong with me. Let me help."

"Alright," Arlo relented. "How about you and Aviva put up decorations in the dining room?"

"That sounds fun." She smiled at the child, who was jumping up and down. "Wait, though. What are you going to be doing?"

"Something else. Now shoo."

Rolling her eyes, she took the bags he pointed out and left the room with Aviva. Their voices carried throughout the house as they decided what to decorate where. Now was his chance. Excitement raced through him. He opened his laptop, pulled up the website for the Chatelaine Bar & Grill and placed an order for home delivery with his cousin Damon. Adoption day was a big deal. His heart expanded as he thought about how much he'd grown to care about Carrie, and how special Aviva was. His pulse raced with the chance to share in the celebration. He wanted Carrie and Aviva to feel special. As great a cook as she was, he didn't want her having to do any food prep tonight. He looked at the time, figuring out when the delivery would arrive. Then he walked into the dining room.

"Looks great," he said.

Carrie was standing on a step stool, hanging red streamers—Aviva's choice—and signs saying Happy Day and Welcome. Aviva was holding the decorations out to her and wrapping herself up in them at the same time. All the little girl needed was some glitter, and she could be the centerpiece.

Which, when you thought about it, was true. Maybe if Carrie looked upon it as a way to celebrate Aviva, rather than emphasizing the awful thing that happened, she'd feel better. He'd have to find the right time to suggest it to her.

He paused. Was there a way for him to change his perspective when it came to his father and Stevie? He'd have to mull it over later. They were celebrating now.

"Thank you," Carrie said as she climbed down off the step stool. "Okay, Vivie, what's next?"

"This one," she said, holding out another sign.

"May I?" Arlo asked.

When Carrie nodded, he took some tape and attached the sign to the window. He turned and saw Carrie shaking out a rainbow tablecloth. Grabbing the other end, he helped her spread it on the table, while Aviva smoothed out the wrinkles—or made more, depending on your perspective. Finally, all that was left were the red balloons. He grabbed one from the bag and began to blow it up. Carrie joined in. The first balloon was Aviva's, and she chased after it, letting the adults finish their job alone.

Carrie looked around. "This is—"

"—very red?"

She laughed. "I was going to say festive, but you're not wrong."

He winked. "I suppose it could be worse."

"Yes, she could have chosen a glitter theme. I might have had to murder you."

"No glitter, gotcha." He pretended to take notes, and she laughed, which filled him with warmth. He was happy he'd been able to cheer her up.

"What do you think?" she asked. "Are we good with balloons?"

"That's up to you," he replied. "I think we are, but you're the boss."

"Actually, I think Aviva's the boss. Hey, Vivie, do we have enough balloons?"

The toddler scrambled over, still playing with the one they'd first given her. "Yes!" she cried. "I wike bawoons."

"I know you do, sweetie," Carrie said, scooping her up

in her arms. "And this party is for you, so all these balloons are yours."

Aviva's eyes got big. "Yay!"

The doorbell rang, and Carrie turned to Arlo, a frown marring her smooth features. "Are we expecting someone?"

He kissed her cheek—Aviva was right there—and headed toward the door. "Don't worry. It's part of the surprise."

"Arlo, I'm not dressed for guests," Carrie protested, following him into the foyer.

He looked her up and down, his pulse quickening at the sight of her. She was wearing leggings and a sweatshirt with the neck enlarged so it hung off one shoulder. He wanted to lick it.

"You're dressed perfectly," he said. He opened the door and took the food bag from the delivery person, handing him a tip and shutting the door. "Besides, it's just dinner."

"You ordered food?"

His mouth dropped open. "You can't have a party without food! Do you want us to starve?"

Shaking her head, she followed him back to the kitchen. "God forbid."

"Good thing I'm in charge of food," he said.

"You seem to be in charge of everything."

Turning to her, he pulled her into his arms. "Anything you'd like me to change?"

She shook her head. "No, it's perfect."

"*I'm* perfect, you mean." He winked at her, and she kissed him.

It was a brief kiss, but it filled him up inside.

"At the risk of stoking your ego, yes," she said.

He whooped, making Aviva laugh. Carrie rolled her eyes, but he wasn't fooled. She liked the mischievous side of him. She was more relaxed than he'd ever seen her.

"Go sit down, and I'll bring out the food in a minute."

"That's silly," she said. "I can help."

"Nope, this party is for you as well. You and Aviva go sit down."

They disappeared through the doorway into the dining room, and he quickly got to work putting all the food on the serving trays he'd bought. He didn't want her to have to do any dishes afterward, and he wanted everything to look festive. One by one he brought everything to the table with a flourish—roasted root vegetables, boneless BBQ ribs, chili, fried potatoes and a salad. The Chatelaine Bar & Grill was one of the nicer restaurants in town, known for its delicious food, and he hoped Carrie would like the traditional Texas meal.

When everything was presented to his liking, he sat across from Carrie and Aviva. He poured red wine into his and Carrie's glasses and made sure Aviva had juice in her sippy cup before raising his tumbler in a toast.

"To the two of you. One, a strong and compassionate woman. The other, a smart and vibrant girl. Together, the two of you will make a formidable team and a wonderful family. Aviva is a very lucky little girl, and you are right where you belong."

Carrie's eyes welled, but she clinked her glass against his and Aviva's sippy cup and took a drink. Gosh, she was beautiful. He shouldn't be thinking that during such an emotionally charged moment, but sitting across from her, he couldn't help himself. And he was privileged to be here with the two of them on adoption day. She could have thanked him for his help and told him she wanted to be alone. But she'd let him stay.

How did he ever manage his days without her? The thought of filling them with work, as much as he enjoyed what he did, felt unimaginable, if Carrie and Aviva weren't there, too. He wanted to say something, to tell her how he was feeling, but he hesitated. She was overwhelmed. This day was about her and Aviva. No matter how badly he wanted to say something, he had to wait.

They ate their meal in a companionable silence, breaking it now and then to entertain or tease Aviva.

When they finished, he looked at the little girl's face and laughed. "I think she has more barbecue sauce on her face than was on the ribs," he said, chuckling.

Carrie looked at Aviva and joined in. "Oh, my, I'm not even sure a bath can get you clean. Is that sauce in your hair?"

The child took her sticky, saucy hands and reached for her head. Realizing her mistake just a moment too soon, Carrie jumped. Arlo started to say something, but it was too late. The once blond curls were red and matted to her scalp.

"It is now," he said dryly.

"I don't suppose I could hose her down?"

He shook his head. "I wouldn't advise it. We need a photo of this."

Carrie's eyes lit up. "Oh, we do! And I'll have to show it to whomever she chooses to marry someday, too."

"Okay, but only after the vows. You don't want to scare anyone away."

"Aww, even with this face, no one will run away," Carrie said, reaching over and getting mere inches away from the messy toddler.

"How about we save dessert for after the bath?" Arlo suggested.

"There's dessert, too?"

"Of course. You can't have a celebration without dessert. It's against the rules."

Carrie shook her head. "You're like a child sometimes, you know that?"

He grinned. "That's why Aviva loves me, right?"

"I wuv you, Arwo. I wuv you, Cawwy."

"Aww, I love you, too, sweetheart," Carrie said. "Now, let's figure out how to get you into the tub without getting me saucy."

Arlo slipped around to the other side of the table to help and whispered in Carrie's ear, "But I like you saucy."

She swatted him away, laughing. Arlo removed Aviva's tray and strap, while Carrie carried her with arms outstretched into the bathroom. As he got the bath ready, she stripped the child of her clothes and deposited her gently into the warm water. Together, he and Carrie washed her until all traces of the barbecue sauce were gone. While Carrie dried her and got her into pajamas, he returned to the kitchen to clean up and prep dessert.

He and Aviva had stopped at the GreatStore's bakery while they were out and picked out a cake. Somehow, Aviva had kept its presence a secret, and now, he thrilled at the thought of the surprise.

He brought the cake out to the dining room just as Carrie and Aviva were sitting down.

"Cake!" Aviva cried, clapping her hands.

"Oh, that's so nice," Carrie said, reading the inscription on the top of the chocolate cake. "Happy Adoption Day!" She looked at Arlo. "Thank you."

"I hope it's appropriate," he said, suddenly nervous. What if she didn't like it? Or what if it was wrong in some way?

"It's perfect," she assured him. "And I know a prayer that I'm going to say. It's called the *Shehecheyanu*, and we say it on the first day of something new." She looked at Aviva and then back at him. "I don't know if it's the 'rule,' but I think it's appropriate."

Arlo listened as she recited the blessing to Aviva. The Hebrew words were foreign to him but had a musical quality coming from Carrie. Even Aviva was enthralled...for a second. And then she wanted cake.

Carrie sliced pieces for everyone. "Oh, no, I'm going to have to bathe you again, aren't I?" she asked as she gave Aviva a piece.

"How about I feed her?" Arlo offered.

When she nodded, he scooted around to the toddler's side

of the table and alternated between feeding himself and feeding Aviva, while Carrie ate her piece.

When they finished, Carrie cheered. "Yay, no mess. By the way, that cake was delicious. Where did you get it?"

"From the GreatStore. When in doubt, go there."

"Good to know."

They finished cleaning up after dinner and put Aviva to bed. Arlo didn't want to leave, but he didn't want to force Carrie to be with him if she wanted time alone.

"You've had an overwhelming day," he said when they left Aviva's room.

"It's been a lot," she agreed and turned to him. "But thanks to you, I got through it." She rose on tiptoe and kissed him.

Relief and desire flooded through him, and he pulled her close as he kissed her back. Pulling away, he searched her expression. "I don't want to overstay my welcome," he said. "So, if you want me to go, tell me."

She leaned against him, the top of her head against her chest. "I don't want you to go, but I think I need you to."

Now he was confused. "Why?"

"Because I need to know I can handle all this alone. You saved me today, but I have to save myself, too. So as much as I'd love you to stay here, I haven't really been by myself lately, and I think I need to be. In the silence, where all there is to do is think. Do you understand?"

He did, as much as he didn't want to. If he were honest with himself, he'd avoided spending time by himself so as not to think about his own issues. He respected her for her independence, as well as her acknowledgment of what she had to do. "I do. I don't like it, but for selfish reasons."

He kissed her again before grabbing his Stetson off the hook, followed by his jacket. "Call me if you need anything. Anything at all."

He left her, looking over his shoulder as he made his way back to his truck and over to his home. The large house was empty. *Too* empty. As he grabbed a beer from the fridge, he thought about how happy he'd been in Carrie's small home, with laughter and messy sauce and a happy occasion. Even with glitter and tears, he would have been happy.

He sighed. He'd done the right thing, not telling her how he felt. He still had his father and Stevie's past to figure out before he focused on his future. But he was going to have to do it soon.

As CARRIE AND Aviva pulled up to the town hall in Arlo's truck three days later, she gasped. Someone had decorated the town hall with rainbow-colored lights along the roofline. White lights wrapped around every fence post and tree in the vicinity. And two tractors on either side of the building sported *Happy Holidays* wreaths, and lights decorating them.

"Wow, this town goes all out for the Chatelaine holiday party," Carrie said, climbing out of the truck and unbuckling Aviva from her car seat. She stood next to the cab holding her daughter, transfixed by the sight. There was something about holiday lights that brought her joy, even if they weren't celebrating her holiday. It was the season.

Arlo came around to her side and put an arm around her. "Not bad."

She poked him in the ribs. "Don't tell me Mr. Grinch likes it," she teased.

His mood had lightened recently, and she was pretty sure he'd take her words for the joke she meant them.

"We'll see," he said. The corners of his mouth twitched, though, and a glimmer of joy shone in his eyes.

She'd take it.

They carried the platters of food she'd made for the party— sweet cheese pancakes, *bimuelos* with orange glaze, spinach patties, leek patties, fried pastry frills and chocolate gelt.

"I can't believe they asked you to make all of this," Arlo

grumbled as he balanced the trays and navigated the door at the same time.

"They didn't," she said. "I couldn't sleep last night, so I cooked more than what I promised."

He eyed her over the pile of food but remained silent.

Inside the town hall, the holiday decorations continued. Lights outlined doorways, wreaths hung on doors, there were multiple decorated Christmas trees in the foyer, and the display case that usually highlighted Texas artifacts displayed a Hanukkah menorah, a Kwanzaa kinara and a snowman. Music piped in over speakers, and paper snowflakes hung from the ceiling.

To their right, tables covered in silver clothes displayed holiday foods, so Arlo and Carrie headed that way.

Carrie spotted the woman she'd seen on the steps a few days ago. "Hi, I don't know if you remember me, but I'm Carrie, and I offered to bring Hanukkah food."

Rita's eyes widened. "Of course, I remember you! Holy cow, you brought a lot!"

"I hope it's okay. There are so many tasty treats that I couldn't decide which to make."

"We will never turn down food," another woman said as she started moving other platters around to make more space. "By the way, I'm Shirley. It's nice to meet you."

Once the food was set, Carrie and Arlo and Aviva explored. The library sponsored a holiday story time in one of the meeting rooms. In another one, people could make and display holiday crafts. And in a third, there was a gingerbread house contest. Tables lined the walls of the room, and each table held a trio of different and elaborate gingerbread houses. Some were traditional and others were out-of-this-world creative. The three of them oohed and aahed at the gingerbread spaceship someone had created. Aviva clapped her hands at a gingerbread zoo, complete with candy animals. And the gingerbread ranch in the center of the room, with moving parts including a

Santa popping out of a barn door, wowed them all. They spent some time at the story time, and Aviva listened to a story about Kwanzaa. In the craft room, they chose to make a menorah out of empty toilet paper rolls and colored tissue paper.

"See, there's the glitter," Arlo quipped.

"Thank goodness it's here and not at home," Carrie added as Aviva dumped a ton on her menorah. While the menorah dried, they wandered over to the gingerbread houses.

"These are so pretty," Carrie said.

"Look at this one." Arlo pointed. "It's like a mini ranch. I wonder who made it?"

Carrie searched for a name, but there was only a number. "I guess they want to maintain anonymity for voting," she mused.

After studying the rest of the houses, they returned to the foyer to taste some of the food. The sweet and savory scents combined to make Carrie's stomach growl. Grabbing plates, they filled them with a variety of foods, including some of what she had made.

Arlo's face showed pure bliss. "Oh my gosh," he said with his mouth full. "This is so good."

"Is my math whiz brother eating again?" A deep male voice sounded from behind Carrie's shoulder.

A smiling man—tall, lanky with dark brown eyes—and a woman with a baby stroller approached.

"Hi, I'm Ridge, Arlo's brother." He held out his hand and Carrie shook it.

The woman beside him had long, dark auburn hair, and her baby looked to be about seven months old.

"If Carrie cooked for you, you'd know to grab these while you can," Arlo said, punching his brother in the arm.

Carrie's face heated at the compliment.

"From the look on Hope's face, obviously, I have to try them," Ridge said. He reached over and took a bite of a leek patty from Hope's plate.

His eyes widened. "I see what you mean, bro. Carrie, these are wonderful."

Hope pulled her plate out of Ridge's reach. "These are mine," she said with a laugh. "Get your own. Hi, Carrie. I don't think we've met before, but Arlo has spoken about you and your beautiful daughter."

Carrie smiled at her. "So nice to meet you. And your baby is just precious."

"Thank you. You're going to have to share the recipe with me," Hope said. "I've had some of these before, I think, but yours are way better."

Warmth spread through Carrie. When Arlo put his arm around her shoulders, joy coursed through her. "Thank you. I'm happy to share my recipe with you, for these and everything else I brought."

Ridge jerked to attention, and Hope's eyes widened. "Wait, you brought *more*?" she asked. "Show me."

Carrie brought her closer to the table, trying not to cut in front of anyone who was getting food. She pointed at her platters and explained what each thing was.

"Ridge!" Hope called.

He rushed over.

"We need all of those," she said. "If these leek patties were this good, can you imagine what everything else will taste like?"

"On it," he said.

Tipping his hat to several of the neighbors in line, he rushed to do Hope's bidding. Arlo joined him.

"He really cares about you," Carrie said, nodding toward Ridge.

Hope smiled. "He's wonderful, although I'm sure he's just being polite." Her expression turned pensive. "And so understanding."

Carrie wanted to ask what Hope meant, but she didn't know the woman well enough.

"Arlo is clearly into you, too," Hope added, brightening.

The old Carrie would have been uncomfortable discussing with a stranger whether or not a guy was into her. But Hope wasn't pushy, and Carrie had started the conversation.

"Do you think so?" It couldn't hurt to get an outside perspective. Carrie didn't know much about his past, and she missed the sisterly connection forged by being able to discuss things with Randi.

Hope nodded. "Absolutely. His expression when he looks at you, the way he just casually put his arm around you. And he's lost a lot of the sadness that's been dogging him recently.

"Speaking of which…" Hope put her arm on Carrie's shoulder. "I'm so sorry about Randi and Isaac."

The condolences still stung, but she was starting to get used to them. "Thank you. I'm glad I've been able to help Arlo get through this. He's certainly helped me."

Hope's eyes grew misty, her smile soft. "You two make a wonderful couple."

The men returned, and Hope looked at Ridge appreciatively. "Thank you."

"Anything for you. Can I have some, too, though?"

The four of them laughed.

"Yes, if you insist."

Arlo held out his plate to Carrie. "Take whatever you'd like."

She drew back. "And prevent you from eating? No way."

Ridge chuckled. "She's got your number."

Hope took a bite of the fried pastry frills and closed her eyes. "Oh, my, this is—"

She gasped, dropping her frill and staring straight ahead.

"Hope," Ridge cried. He pulled her against him to shield her. Around them, there were murmurs. Someone found a chair and placed it behind her so Ridge could lower her into it. Someone else moved people out of the way so the four of them could have some space. A third rocked the baby's stroller to keep Evie calm.

Carrie looked on helplessly, gripping Arlo's hand. After what felt like forever, Hope blinked and burst into tears. She buried her head in Ridge's shoulder, and he held her. The rest of the people in the foyer of the town hall moved away to give her privacy.

Carrie was touched. Seeing how they cared for one of their own, how they made themselves helpful without interfering, impressed her.

When Hope calmed down, Ridge spoke. "Do you want to go home?"

"No. I, uh…remembered things. I was in a house and there were lots of people around." She squinted. "I think it was my house. There were photos of me with the man who'd kissed me, although I still couldn't see his face." She reddened and squeezed Ridge's hand.

"Go on," he said gruffly.

"His face was blurry, but he was familiar. There was a ton of food…" She looked at Carrie, mouth agape. "Your frills were there! I mean, not *yours*, but I think that's what made me remember."

Carrie nodded. "Is that a good thing?" she whispered to Arlo.

"Yes," he said. "She needs to remember. It's the only way she and Ridge can be happy."

"What else did you remember, Hope?" Ridge prompted in a gentle voice.

"Someone came up to me and apologized." She looked at him. "She said my husband was so young."

Hope gasped, and her eyes welled. She blinked her tears away and touched her belly. "I was pregnant."

Carrie, Arlo and Ridge looked at Evie before returning their focus to Hope.

"Did my baby's father die?" Hope sniffled. "I recall that middle-aged couple coming over to me. They were crying, and they hugged me."

She looked at Ridge, confusion etching her features. "They seemed so nice. But then why am I so afraid of them? Why were they ominous in other memories that I have? Who *are* they?"

"I don't know, but you did great, Hope," Ridge said, rubbing her back.

"When am I going to remember everything?" she moaned.

Someone brought them all water. "Don't rush it, Hope," the person said. "You'll figure it out eventually."

She rested her forehead against Ridge's shoulder. "I hate this," she said.

"I know." His deep voice was soothing.

"Can we go home?"

He stood up and helped Hope to her feet. Arlo and Carrie followed, pushing Evie's stroller as well as Aviva's. Ridge ushered Hope outside and into his truck. When she was settled into the cab of the truck, he shut the door and turned to Arlo.

"Thanks." He looked at his brother, his eyes speaking volumes. Carrie's heart broke for him.

She stood with Arlo as the two pulled away. The luster had been rubbed off the holiday celebration, and Arlo's look of grief was back. But this time, she knew it was for his brother. She wrapped her arm around his waist.

"What can I do for you?" she asked quietly.

He shook his head, stiffening. "I need to be with my brother. Do you mind if I take you home?"

Carrie swallowed. He was doing the right thing by going after his brother, but it hurt that he wouldn't let her comfort him. Her arms almost physically ached to pull him close to her and soothe him. She broke eye contact and nodded, her chest tight.

"Of course."

In silence, they climbed into his truck after getting Aviva settled and drove back to Carrie's house. Arlo said a quick goodbye before backing out of the driveway in a rush, heading toward his brother's house.

"Come on, Vivie, let's go inside."

The rest of the day took forever to pass. Aviva was cranky, Carrie was out of sorts, and her mind kept straying to Arlo and Ridge and Hope.

How awful must it be to lose your memory? Her heart squeezed at the thought of not remembering her sister. She recalled their childhood arguments, playing dress-up together, stealing her clothes when she wasn't looking, and late-night phone calls asking advice about everything. It was bad enough she had started to forget what her voice sounded like. But to completely forget her existence?

And how did Ridge deal with wanting someone who might not be free?

Then there was Arlo. She cared for him. Maybe too much. Her foot bounced. She had a sneaking suspicion she was falling in love with him. Seeing Ridge and Hope together and comparing how Arlo and she were had shown her the similarities between all of four of them, and how she'd grown to depend on him. Was she losing her own independence? Her stomach fluttered. Listening to Hope confirm that Arlo's attention was real and meant something helped to solidify her feelings for him in her mind. But watching him leave without her, not to even consider asking her to join him, hurt. It shouldn't. She was an adult, and if he wanted alone time with his brother, she should understand. And she did. Sort of. But she wished he'd asked her how she felt about it.

She sighed, frustrated with herself. The man had spent almost all his free time with her. He was entitled to as much time with other people as he wanted.

Maybe she was relying on him too much. She'd come to Chatelaine determined to settle her sister and brother-in-law's affairs and take Aviva back to Albuquerque. She'd never intended on forming a relationship with anyone here.

By the time she put Aviva to bed, Arlo still hadn't called. She missed him. Another sign she needed him too much? She sank down in front of the TV, searching for something to watch. Her attention wasn't on anything. She found a Christmas movie on TV and put it on for background noise if nothing else. The movie took place in a small town, making her laugh at the coincidence.

She'd never wanted to live in a small town. Albuquerque had always been her home. She had friends, a thriving Jewish community and amazing restaurants, among other things. Not to mention the anonymity. She missed it.

But, after seeing how everyone behaved today, there was something nice about a town where everyone knew you and looked out for you. That would never have happened in Albuquerque. The people at the celebration today hadn't butted in but had been helpful and respectful of Hope's privacy. Kind of like Myra at the GreatStore the other day with her. They'd even added Hanukkah touches for her. Carrie remembered her conversation with Rita beforehand and made a mental note to thank her if she saw her again.

The truth was, the more she thought about going home to Albuquerque, the less appealing it was. Despite how much she missed her friends. She'd started to like this town, and after meeting Hope today, she thought they might develop a friendship. Other people at the fair had been friendly, too. Her mind raced. Positives and negatives danced in her brain and overwhelmed her.

There was no Jewish community, but Randi and Isaac had been okay. Maybe she could be, too. Did she want to be? And maybe she could find a Jewish community to join, whether virtually or not too far away. She'd have to look into that soon. *If* she stayed.

Finally giving up on the movie, turned off her phone and went to bed. She'd stop by Hope's in the morning to make sure she was okay. That's what friends did, right? If she wanted her to be her friend, now was the time to act on it.

ARLO SAT IN Ridge's home, nursing a beer while he waited for his brother to come back. Ridge had gone with Hope to get her settled. The woman was exhausted.

His brother returned and the lines on his face showed his stress. He made a beeline for the fridge, grabbed another beer and plunked down on the overstuffed leather chair across from Arlo. He didn't speak but drank from the bottle in silence.

Arlo let him, knowing full well his younger sibling had a lot to process.

Other than some creaking of floorboards and the faint hum of appliances, the house was silent.

"Let's get some air," Ridge said, rising and striding out of the room.

Arlo followed him onto the porch.

Ridge leaned his forearms on the railing and stared out over the ranch.

"I wish all the memories would just flood back at once," he said.

Arlo paused. With every memory Hope recalled, there was a chance she'd find out her history and have to return to her family. His brother was falling for her. Arlo could see it every time he looked at Hope.

"Why?" he asked carefully. "Aren't you afraid of what you'll find out?"

Ridge took a slug of beer and nodded his head. "Yeah. Terrified. But this not knowing is killing me. Killing *her*. If we knew her story, we could take action one way or another. It's the uncertainty that's leaving us in limbo."

Arlo's heart ached for the two of them.

"I want to be able to help her, regardless of what it means for me, personally." Ridge looked at Arlo, his gaze haunted.

"But I can't protect her if I don't know what I'm protecting her from."

"I wish there was something I could do for the two of you."

Ridge took another gulp of beer. "Just be glad you're not in this position. And if you ever are, remember what I said about knowing what you're facing."

They looked out at the property, the millions of stars showing in the clear night. The monochromatic beauty of the place struck Arlo.

"You ever think about Dad?" he asked Ridge.

"All the time. What brought this on?"

"I don't know. The beauty of this place. Dad's dislike of anything having to do with ranch life. How he missed out on all this..." He used his beer bottle to point to the sky.

Ridge nodded. "He missed out on a lot. So did we."

The familiar anger churned in Arlo's belly, and he forced his grip to loosen around the glass bottle.

His brother turned to him. "You know, one of the best things I ever did was make peace with Dad before he died."

Arlo froze.

"Not for any other reason than it freed my mind and brought me some sort of closure."

"So, you just forgave him?" Arlo asked.

"Not exactly. I talked to him and told him why he'd hurt me. I still don't agree with how he treated all of us, but I made my point. It took away a lot of the hurt and put an end to things. I guess you could say it gave me closure."

"And you're okay with him now?"

Ridge leaned his back against the porch railing. "Do I agree with what he did or understand it? No. But talking to him took away the power it held over me."

Thinking over his brother's words, Arlo pressed his hands into the porch railing before looking up at the sky. Sometimes, all he wanted to do was run screaming into the night—his feet pounding the earth, his voice echoing through the open expanse, the wind flying in his face and making his eyes water.

But he kept it all inside, hoping his anger and loss would somehow disappear.

It hadn't happened, yet.

Looking at his brother, he saw the worry lines around his eyes. The man's shoulders were tense with stress. Yet, he looked peaceful. Certainly, more content than Arlo felt. If Ridge could attain that peace despite what was going on with Hope, maybe all wasn't lost for Arlo.

"You know you can talk to me about anything, right?" Ridge asked.

Except he didn't know what Arlo knew. Ridge wasn't aware that their father probably had a second family. He hadn't seen the box of toys with the address written on it.

Arlo didn't want to tell his family what he'd found, not until he knew what it meant. Right now, the knowledge would just shatter their peace of mind. And those of them who'd found it didn't need to lose it so quickly.

"I know," he said. "And I appreciate it. The same goes for you. You and Hope need anything, you let me know."

He finished his beer and hugged his brother. Nothing else needed to be said.

At home, he reached for his phone to call Carrie, but his battery was dead. Swearing under his breath, he plugged it in, then looked at the time. She'd probably be sleeping, and he didn't want to risk waking Aviva. He left it charging on the counter and went to bed.

The next morning, he made coffee and checked his phone.

He frowned. He hadn't spoken to Carrie, and she hadn't contacted him, either. His missed her. Longing to hear her voice, he called her.

"Hey, pretty lady. How are you?" he asked.

There was a small pause before she answered. "How are Ridge and Hope?"

"They're okay," he said, "but you didn't answer my question."

She was quiet.

"Is something wrong, Carrie?"

She sighed. "Yes. Well, no. I'm not sure. I... I think I need some time to myself."

Arlo's stomach rolled. "What's wrong?"

"I'll talk to you later, okay?"

Before he had a chance to respond or even say goodbye, she hung up.

His body tightened, and he jumped up, ready to race over to her house. But she'd said she needed time alone.

It was the last thing he wanted to give her, but echoes of Heath's and Ridge's offers to talk if he wanted, and his own unwillingness to do so, played in his head. As much as it pained him, he had to respect her request.

At least for a little while.

A LITTLE WHILE? Arlo scoffed as he looked at his watch for what had to be the fortieth time in three days. He knew it was three days, because he'd picked up his phone at least one hundred times, checking to see if he'd somehow missed a text or call from Carrie. He hadn't.

And the radio-silence was killing him.

Ridge must have gotten all the Fortune patience, because Arlo's ran out. Day three of giving Carrie space was three days too many. And if that made him less understanding, or more reckless, well, he'd work on himself later.

Work. Ha! He'd gotten nothing done.

His eyes stung from sleepless nights, worrying about Carrie, thinking about his father, missing Isaac and wondering if by giving Carrie space he was hurting Aviva.

Oh God, Aviva. Her parents left her. Would her toddler brain think he left her, too?

This was ridiculous. He grabbed his hat, stuffed it on his head and strode out the door. Something was wrong with Carrie, the woman he cared for, and he wasn't waiting any longer. He broke every speed limit in Chatelaine as he rode to Carrie's house, slammed the door and raced onto her porch.

Gripping his hat in his hand so tight he'd probably dent the brim, he rang her doorbell.

Her look of surprise when she answered almost hid the desolation in her gaze. She straightened her shoulders.

"Arlo?"

He'd missed that voice. He'd missed everything about her.

"I know you said you wanted space, but it's been three days. Please don't shut me out any longer."

Her eyes filled, and his heartbeat battered his ribs. He was making her cry.

She blinked before backing up and letting him inside.

He exhaled in relief, and followed her into the kitchen.

He sat down at the island in his kitchen. "Please, Carrie, you can talk to me."

Groaning, her words came out so fast he had to concentrate to understand everything. "I wanted to go with you to Ridge's the other day, but you clearly didn't want me to, which was fine, but I still felt bad. And then I started thinking that maybe I've grown too dependent on you. That led to me reevaluating every part of my personality and all the decisions I've made since Randi died, and I don't know. Everything has changed so fast and I don't want to lose myself as I become a mother, and you've got things to settle in your life, and..."

She paused for breath.

"You asked," she said. She fingered the hem of her shirt, not looking at him. "You probably regret that now."

"Regret you? Never." Sorrow pressed down on him. "I'm sorry. I never meant to hurt you. I should have included you, and I'm not even sure why I didn't."

She still wouldn't look at him. His heart cracked open.

"I'm used to being alone, I guess," he said. "I don't know why I didn't include you, but I swear there was no intent behind it. And I never, ever meant to make you doubt your ability to take care of yourself. If my trying to help you is doing that…"

Finally, she met his gaze and shook her head.

"It's not. I'm so grateful for your help. I just need to make sure I can stand on my own. I don't mean to be needy. It's so not a good look. And it's a bad lesson for Aviva."

He reached for her hands. "You're the least needy person I know," he said. "It's okay. And if you still want time to yourself, I'll go."

"I think I've had enough," she said, a small smile breaking through. "I've had a lot of time these past three days to let everything settle. I'm less panicky and hopefully more confident."

He reached for her and held her. They stayed that way in silence for several moments. Arlo's stress lessened, his heart beat normally once again, and the dread of being without Carrie lessened.

Finally, he pulled away. "Speaking of needy, though." His voice turned serious. "You've helped me realize something. I think it's time I figured out what's in that box and why my dad was sending it. I don't want to go alone, but I can't ask anyone in my family to come with me. Would you go with me?"

"Of course, I'll go with you." She paused. "You're doing the right thing, you know."

He expelled his breath in a whoosh and rubbed the back of his head. "I hope so. What if I make things worse?"

"How exactly?" she asked.

"Right now, nobody in my family except me knows about the box of toys. It's an easy secret to keep. But if I find proof he had another family, or something equally horrible, I'll have to tell them. I can't keep something like that to myself. And then I'm destroying them."

"You're not responsible for your father, Arlo. And if for some reason, what you find out is truly as bad as you think it might be, we'll figure it out together."

He didn't know if it was the relief of letting out his fears or her response and her use of "we." Maybe it was his conversation with Ridge last night and the fact that he'd slept better after that conversation than he had in months. Whatever the reason, his confidence soared. He could do this.

And knowing Carrie would be with him made it even better.

"When do you want to go?" she asked.

"As soon as possible. Are you free today?"

"I am, but what about Aviva? Are you okay with her coming with us?"

He loved Aviva and spending time with her was never a hardship. But the last thing he wanted to do was introduce her to his father's second family.

"I have an idea, if you're up for it," he said. "Would you be okay if my mom watches her? She loves kids. Heck, she raised all of us."

The silence stretched between them. "Would she even want to? I mean, she doesn't know me or Aviva…"

"We'll leave that up to her. Give me a few minutes to call her and ask, and I'll let you know. Okay?"

When Carrie agreed, Arlo dialed his mom.

"Oh, Arlo, honey, bring her right over. We'll have a grand time while you and your girlfriend spend some time together."

"She's not my girlfriend, Mom." *She wasn't, was she?*

They hadn't discussed their relationship, even though they'd had sex. He frowned. Meaningless sex with a woman like Carrie didn't sit well with him. He wanted something more, and she deserved more. With Aviva gone today, it would be the perfect chance to discuss their relationship. Provided, of course, whatever they discovered wasn't a complete disaster. He groaned silently.

When his mom laughed, he groaned aloud.

"May we drop her off in about an hour?"

"Absolutely. I can't wait to meet her. Aviva, too."

Arlo hung up the phone to the sound of his mother's laughter.

Just great.

"All set with my mom. She'll be ready for us in forty-five minutes."

Now that he was actually planning to solve the mystery, his nerves were on high alert. Multiple times, he wanted to cancel. Or at least put it off until later. But before he knew it, it was time to leave.

"Arwo, I pwetty!" She was dressed as a princess, and he picked her up and tossed her in the air.

"You are the most beautiful princess in all the land," he exclaimed as he put her down.

He looked at Carrie. She looked almost as nervous as he felt, and he grasped her hand. "I promise it's going to be fine."

"I know. I just haven't left her before."

They drove to his mother's home at the main ranch house, which was constructed of weathered light-colored stone with wood finishes and a metal sloped roof. A covered porch extending on either side of the front door had a white railing and six posts.

"I've never seen anything other than the barns and office at the front of the ranch," Carrie said. She craned her neck to see through the front windshield. "I never even knew this was here."

"It's a good thing it is, since my mom can't live in the castle—as I mentioned before, she's renovating it to host guests with a spa and all kinds of amenities. Luckily, this house was also on the property, so she has somewhere to live. Wait until you see inside, and of course, the view from the back," Arlo said. He held open Carrie's door and waited while she took Aviva out of the truck. He followed behind them, watching Carrie grip the toddler's hand.

His mother met them at the door. She was tall and willowy, with blond hair and a quiet, confident air about her. He could tell Carrie immediately felt at ease.

Wendy's face lit up. "Did an actual princess come to visit

me today?" She curtsied to Aviva before kneeling down to her level. "I can't wait to spend time with you."

Aviva got shy and hid behind Carrie's leg. Rising, his mom turned to Carrie. "Hi, I'm Wendy. It's so nice to meet you. I was sorry to hear about your sister and brother-in-law."

Carrie shook her hand. "Thank you. And I really appreciate you watching Aviva today. Everything she needs is in her bag. I hope you're not too inconvenienced."

Wendy took the bag from Arlo and gave him a hug. "Are you kidding? I love playing with little girls, especially one dressed like a princess."

Aviva peeked her head out from behind Carrie's leg.

"Tell me," Wendy said, leading them inside her home. "Does Aviva like cookies?"

Carrie's eyes sparkled. "I don't know." Arlo studied Carrie as she glanced around the front foyer, which led straight into a huge great room, with a stone fireplace and an open stairway leading upstairs.

Aviva nodded, her fingers in her mouth.

"Hmm, I wonder if she'd like to bake some Christmas cookies with me," Wendy said, addressing Carrie.

"Maybe," Carrie said. Arlo noticed Carrie's shoulders relax as she took in the furniture in the room—sturdy wood and leather. It would probably survive her toddler's antics for the day.

Once again, Aviva nodded, and she took a step out from behind Carrie's legs.

Arlo was enjoying watching his mom convince the two-year-old to trust her. She'd always been great with kids, and he loved seeing the joy on her face.

"I was also thinking we could decorate them with frosting and sprinkles. Does she like sprinkles?"

Before Carrie could answer, Aviva said, "Yes."

"You do?" Wendy asked.

Aviva nodded again.

"Then would you like to come with me to make the cookies and decorate them? And I think I have some books that we can read."

Aviva stepped forward and took Wendy's hand. She looked over her shoulder at Carrie.

"Bye, Vivie," Carrie said. "Have fun!"

"Bye, Aviva," Arlo added. "Thanks, Mom!"

He ushered Carrie out the door before the little girl had a chance to get upset or change her mind. Having Carrie to himself made his heart beat a little faster. He always loved spending time with Aviva, but there was something special about having Carrie all to himself.

"I hope you don't mind her decorating Christmas cookies," Arlo said. He placed a hand on the small of her back. It felt right.

"Not at all," Carrie said. She looked behind her before climbing into the truck. "But I hope your mom knows what she's getting into."

Arlo laughed as he started the truck. "Are you kidding? She is so excited to play with Aviva today. She probably should have asked you first, though, about the Christmas thing."

Carrie laid a hand on Arlo's forearm. The heat of her hand permeated his flannel shirt. "I don't mind her learning about other holidays, especially when she's going to be around so many people who celebrate Christmas. I want her to appreciate all of the winter holidays while being proud of celebrating her own."

"Does this mean you're thinking about staying here?" His heartbeat quickened. Spending so much time with Carrie and Aviva brightened his days. His mood was lighter when they were around. He hadn't meant to ask Carrie this question yet, though. He didn't want to push her, but it had just slipped out.

She took her hand away, and his heart dropped. He tried to cover his disappointment by starting the truck and backing out of the driveway. Of course, she wasn't going to stay. She had a life and friends back in Albuquerque.

"Yes," she said. "I'm thinking about it."

His foot pushed harder on the gas pedal at her quiet comment, and he slowed down to normal speed. He couldn't stop the grin from spreading across his face. "I'm glad." He wanted to show her how thrilled he was, but before he had a chance to pull over, she changed the subject.

"How far away do the Fieldses live?" Carrie asked.

Her question doused some of his excitement. "Not far," he said. Which would make it awkward and uncomfortable if they turned out to be his dad's second family.

He scowled.

"You know, this might turn out better than you think," she said, her voice soft.

"Hmm," he grunted. He hated to be so pessimistic, but he didn't see how there could possibly be something good to come out of this. Other than getting rid of a box he was continuously tripping over.

She squeezed his arm once again, and they drove the rest of the way in silence.

Arlo looked one last time at the map on his dashboard, then out the side window at the house he approached. He slowed the truck, his stomach in knots.

"I think that's it," he said, pointing to the modest house set back from the road. It was two stories, with yellow aluminum shingles and a roof that looked like it could use a repair. A tree next to it sported a tire swing, and an old car sat in the driveway.

Arlo shook his head. This was how his dad took care of his second family? He had a hard time believing the man he knew who had been so concerned with appearances could leave people he cared about in a house that clearly needed work.

"You ready?" Carrie asked.

*No.* "Let's get this over with," he said.

He grabbed the box of toys, waited for Carrie to catch up with him then walked with her to the front door. The cement walkway seemed endless, but too soon, they reached the front door.

Taking a deep breath, he rang the doorbell.

A few moments later, an older woman with gray hair wearing a house dress answered the door. Her face was lined but kind, her eyes inquisitive.

"May I help you?" she asked, peering through the screen door.

"Ma'am, my name is Arlo Fortune. This box was addressed to the wrong house and was returned to my house. I looked up Stevie Fields and came up with this address. I was wondering if maybe it belongs to you or your son?"

The woman's face creased in a wide smile. "That wonderful Casper Windham. Such a generous man. Please, come inside, won't you? I'm Helen, Stevie's grandmother."

Arlo's chest tightened. *Wonderful? Generous?* Was this woman actually talking about his dad? Carrie's hand on his back helped propel him forward, and he entered the dark foyer.

"I just need you to keep your voices down if you don't mind. Little Stevie is upstairs napping. You can leave the box of toys there," she said, pointing to the spot next to the front door. "I'm sure he'll be thrilled with them when he wakes."

She led them into the kitchen, a cheerful room with a big window and peach-colored walls.

"Can I get you something to drink? Coffee, tea, water?"

Arlo was about to refuse. All he wanted was to get out of here now that he'd delivered the box to his father's other family, but Carrie piped up.

"That would be great. Two coffees, if you have it."

He tensed, ready to refuse, but she caught his gaze and nodded toward a chair at the table. He sat, wondering why he was bothering and what she thought could be gained by remaining here when he had his answer.

Helen knew his father. What else was left to discover?

She brought their coffees, and hers, to the table on a tray, along with sugar, cream and spoons. Then she joined them.

"Casper was your father?" she asked Arlo.

He ground his teeth. He didn't want to tell this woman anything about himself or his family, but the manners that had been drilled into him since he was a child overruled him.

"Yes, ma'am."

She shook her head. "That wonderful man saved my daughter Lynne's life, you know. She's at the hospital getting her chemo treatment. Treatment she couldn't afford until that man came along."

Leaning forward, her eyes glistening with tears, she continued. "While he was a patient at the cancer center, he paid for every patient's care, and arranged for toys to be sent to every patient's kids. Did you know that?"

Arlo shook his head, stunned.

"No, of course not. He swore the hospital to secrecy, of course, but my daughter found out when she went to pay her bill, which is how I know. Stevie and Lynne will have a lovely Christmas now, thanks to your father."

"I… I don't understand." He forced the words from his suddenly parched throat. "My father did this?"

Helen nodded. "He did. He saw how easy it was for him to get treatment, but how hard it was for others, and knowing how little time he had, he decided to use his money to help others."

"How do you know?" Arlo asked. "Did you know him?"

"I didn't have the pleasure. But my Lynne did, and she told me how kind and thoughtful he was. You're a lucky man to have had such a father."

Arlo's throat clogged.

The woman's phone rang, and she patted his hand before rising to answer it.

"Are you okay?" Carrie asked, her voice low.

*Was he?* He had no idea. "How do we get out of here?"

"I'm sorry about that," the woman said. "I'll call them back."

"No, it's really fine," Carrie said. "We've taken up enough of your time."

"Are you sure?"

"Yes. We're so glad to have been able to deliver the toys to Stevie. And thank you for telling us about Mr. Windham."

The older woman bustled about as they headed for the front door. "No problem at all. My condolences to you and your family," she said to Arlo as they exited the house.

Arlo remained silent until they reached the truck.

"Would you rather I drive?" Carrie asked gently.

"No, thanks." He opened her door and then climbed into the driver's seat. Once out of sight of the Fieldses' house, he pulled to the side of the road and bowed his head over the steering wheel. He remained like that, taking deep breaths and sorting his thoughts. Carrie stayed next to him, silent but supportive. Finally, he raised his head.

"Thank you," he rasped. "Thank you for making me do this and for coming with me and for getting us out of there. I could never have done this on my own."

"You're welcome. How do you feel?"

He mentally probed himself, trying to digest everything the woman had told him, and finally smiled. "Actually, I feel good. Really good. A huge weight has lifted off me. My father wasn't a great dad, but he tried to change and become a better person. And the things he did for the people at the hospital? How amazing was that?"

Cassie's smile brightened her face. "I'm so glad."

He banged the back of his head against the headrest. "I can't believe I'm going to have to tell my brother he was right."

"And me. Don't forget me." Cassie winked.

Arlo's blood heated. "Oh, I couldn't forget you. Ever." He leaned over, slid his hand behind her neck and pulled her toward him. Their mouths met. All of his emotions coalesced into hunger and need and joy, and he put everything into their kiss. Tongues and lips and teeth and the very air they breathed together. She wrapped her arms around him and pressed against him. Their bodies were as close as they could get with the truck console in between them. Their noses bumped as their kiss deepened, until finally, he pulled away.

"I love you, Cassie."

She stared at him, as if memorizing is features.

"You don't have to say it back," he said, his words tumbling out of him. "But I wanted you to know."

Putting a finger over his lips, she hushed him. "I love you, too. I think I have for a while now."

"Even though I messed up the other day?"

She kissed him. "Even though."

She suddenly drew back, concern etched on her face.

"What?" he asked. She'd helped him so much; he wanted to help her, too.

She bit her lip before speaking. "I want to make sure you're not speaking out of some adrenaline rush. You've gone through an emotional rollercoaster, and it's perfectly natural to feel all kinds of things, but when things settle..."

He pulled her closer to him. He liked it better when she was near. "I've loved you for a while. Finding out about my dad maybe hastened my telling you my feelings, but it didn't *create* the feelings."

He caressed her cheek, waiting for her response. After a few moments, she nodded, and he kissed her again.

"We should probably get back," he murmured. "I don't exactly want to have to explain to the cops why I'm pulled over and making out with my girlfriend."

Her cheeks reddened, and she laughed. "Not to mention, you have no idea what I'd say."

Raising an eyebrow, he pulled out onto the road. "Hmm, I may have to rethink this."

She elbowed him. "I dare you."

Their ability to joke in such a carefree manner as he drove

them back home filled him with happiness and relief. For the first time since his dad died, he felt as if he was truly free to move on with his life. He pulled his truck into his mom's driveway and parked by the front door.

Carrie was out of the truck before he had a chance to come around and open her door.

"Mom, we're back!" he yelled as they entered her home. He inhaled, the smell of baked cookies permeating the house. "And something smells delicious!"

"Cawwy, Arwo, wook!" The toddler's feet pounded on the tile floor, and she plowed into their legs a moment later.

Carrie lifted her in her arms. "Hello," she said.

"Wook at my cookie." She held out the cookie, and Carrie opened her mouth wide.

"Oh, my goodness, it's beautiful!"

"Twy it?"

She stuck the cookie in Carrie's mouth before she had a chance to answer. Arlo laughed as Carrie took a quick bite and chewed.

"It's delicious. You did such a good job."

Aviva leaned toward Arlo, and he took a bite as well.

"Yummy," he said.

He walked with Carrie and Aviva to the kitchen. It was situated in a nook on one end of the great room, with an island counter in the center, a brick backsplash over the stove, white marble counters and stainless-steel appliances. Wendy had set up an area at the island for Aviva to sit and decorate.

"There's my best helper," Wendy said. She walked over and kissed Arlo on the cheek and smiled at Carrie. "She was such a great girl, and we had so much fun, didn't we?"

Aviva bobbed her head, making her blond curls bob.

Wendy did a double take. "Arlo, you look happy." Her voice was filled with shock.

Pain over the worry he'd caused his mother stabbed him.

"I am, and I'd like to tell the family why." He looked around at the lack of Christmas decorations.

"How about we have the family over tomorrow to decorate, and I'll tell everyone what I learned today?"

She frowned. "You mean I have to wait?"

He nodded.

She looked between him and Carrie and then back again. "Okay." She smiled. "I'm so glad to see you happy, I'd probably agree to anything."

Arlo texted his siblings in their group chat, before rubbing his hands together in mock glee. "Good to know."

## CHAPTER EIGHT

THE NEXT DAY, Arlo's siblings poured into Wendy's house, astonishing Carrie with their boisterous behavior.

The brothers—Nash and Ridge—and the sisters—Dahlia, Sabrina and Jade—clapped Arlo's back, hugged and kissed him, and exclaimed over his complete change in attitude. Even the siblings' significant others noticed.

Carrie appreciated it as well. The cloud hanging over his head had disappeared, lightening his voice, straightening his shoulders and bringing into sharp focus all the traits she'd come to love about him—his eagerness, devotion and compassion for others.

And the Christmas decorations? Wow.

The Fortune family took decorating seriously. Even Arlo, who'd expressed no interest prior to this, was eager to trim his mother's tree.

Carrie was a little overwhelmed. She and Aviva sat on one of the chairs in Wendy's living room and watched the bustle of people. The room was at the back of the house—and as Arlo had warned, the back of the house was the most impressive, with huge windows overlooking the lake and a multilevel deck and patio. The living room had another fireplace—there were several in Wendy's home—with a brandy-colored mantle and turquoise marble. The floors were made of gray stone, and the walls were painted a similar shade of turquoise as the fireplace marble. White trim outlined the windows and molding. The effect was dramatic but warm. Their Christmas tree filled a back corner of the room. As each of Wendy's kids and their loved ones had arrived, they'd helped to carry a box or two of decorations into the living room. Or they'd brought their own. By the time everyone was present, Carrie was pretty sure bringing a lively two-year-old with her had been a mistake. There was no way she wasn't going to get into everything and probably break something.

"Okay, Arlo, we've been patient long enough," Wendy said once everyone had settled into the oversize golden velvet sofas. "What did you want to tell us?"

Carrie squeezed his hand, and he rose, walking over to the fireplace and looking around the room.

"Almost two months ago, the mail carrier brought a box that had been misaddressed back to the ranch. It was from Dad, addressed to Stevie Fields. Inside the box were toys."

Confusion marred everyone's faces.

"Who is Stevie Fields?" Dahlia asked.

"And why was Dad sending toys to someone?" her twin, Sabrina, added.

"I had the same questions," Arlo said. "I was convinced Dad had a second family somewhere, and I didn't want to tell any of you because I didn't want to upset you."

Wendy gasped. "Arlo!"

He held up his hand. "I was wrong," he acknowledged. "About many things. First, I should never have kept the news from all of you. It was too much to bear alone. I talked to Isaac about it, and he tried to convince me I was wrong and should find out more information. We argued, I refused and then he died."

"Oh, gosh," Jade said. "I wish you'd told us."

He nodded. "Again, I was wrong. Heath suggested I tell you

all—not that he knew anything, just the general idea of a secret I was keeping—and I wanted to, but I didn't know how. Thanks to Carrie and Ridge and a few other things that unfolded, I decided to find out once and for all what was going on."

He took a deep breath. "Dad did *not* have a second family. He was paying for patients' chemo at the hospital who were going through treatment at the same time he was, and he was delivering toys to their children so they could have a festive holiday."

The room went silent. Through the reflection in the windows, Carrie saw everyone digesting the information. And she stared at them in astonishment. Not that they shouldn't be shocked, but the noise level prior to this had been so loud, their ability to quiet down surprised her. But it didn't last. Chaos erupted. She watched as everyone spoke at once, disbelief and confusion covering their faces like masks during Purim celebrations. Arlo answered the questions flying at him in quick succession. And finally, their faces brightened.

"Dad had a change of heart," Nash said. "I'll be darned."

Ridge's face shone. "I knew it." His voice wasn't loud, but still, the room heard him.

As one, they turned to Wendy. She had remained silent, and it was to her that everyone seemed to look to for the official conclusion.

She held the room with her silence, until finally, she spoke. "Your father was far from a perfect man. But I'm glad that, in the end, he returned to the person I first fell in love with. I hope all of you are able to make peace with him now, in time for the holidays."

They all murmured their agreement.

She turned to Arlo. "Thank you for trying to spare us more pain," she said. "I know it wasn't easy. The toll it took on you." She walked over to him and took his face between her hands. "Do not ever feel you have to do that again."

Everyone rose, hugged Arlo, and continued to decorate their mother's home for Christmas. Dahlia festooned the fireplace with fir boughs and tiny bells. Sabrina began decorating the tree. Jade, Hope and Nash's fiancée, Imani, hung wreaths and mistletoe on all the windows. Nash and Ridge, as well as the other men, went outside to begin stringing the lights on the house and the deck.

Wendy came over to Carrie and took her hands. "You have brought me the best Christmas gift of all. My son's happiness."

Her hands in the older woman's, Carrie felt tears come to her eyes. "The feeling is mutual."

"I hope you'll join us on Christmas Eve for our book exchange," Wendy said. "We'd love to have you share in our tradition."

Carrie inhaled, surprised but also delighted by the invitation. "I'd love to, thank you."

"Wonderful. Arlo will have to give you all the details."

After they hugged again, Wendy's face brightened. Putting her arm around Carrie's shoulders, she turned to the group. "Sleigh ride, anyone?"

Carrie frowned. "Sleigh ride?" She looked toward the bank of windows. It was a clear night, with the moon shining off the lake. "I never knew it snowed out here."

Arlo's mom squeezed her shoulders. "No, honey, this is Texas. We don't get snow down here. We do, however, love Christmas, and I thought it would be fun to offer our guests a Texas-style sleigh ride."

With the rest of the family clamoring to go, Carrie nodded. She made eye contact with Arlo. Striding over to her, he pulled her away from Wendy, and the two of them followed the rest of the family outside.

"Need a rescue?" he whispered in her ear.

Just being in his arms was enough for her. "No, but I'm curious about what your mom has planned."

Outside were two hay wagons, dressed in fir boughs, red

ribbons and bells. Four horses, two per wagon, were harnessed, and two ranch hands sat in the driver's seat, wearing Stetsons with holly and bows.

Carrie smiled. "Now I get it."

The family divided themselves between the two wagons, pulling red and green plaid blankets over their laps, sitting on bales of hay and drinking thermoses of hot cocoa the ranch hands had offered.

Carrie snuggled against Arlo as she kept a protective arm around Aviva. "Where are we riding to?"

The ranchers clicked their tongues, and the horses began to trot, the bells on their harnesses jingling.

"Around the ranch, along the lake and back. Are you ready for some good, old-fashioned Christmas-y fun?"

"More than ready!" Carrie murmured. "And the more time I get to spend with you, the better."

He bent his head to kiss her, their mouths coming together and sending shards of warmth through Carrie.

"I could get used to this," he whispered.

"Me, too."

THE NEXT EVENING, after spending the day tackling all the ranch business he'd ignored, Arlo returned to his house, alone. Carrie was with Dahlia and Sabrina at Jade's house for the sisters' annual Christmas cookie baking extravaganza in preparation for the annual cookie contest. She was showing them how to make *bimuelos* and fried pastry frills. He was thrilled she'd been accepted into the family so easily. Tomorrow, he'd take her over to Remi's Reads to purchase books for his family's Christmas Eve exchange. He sat on his back deck, staring up at the stars. Perseus twinkled in the northern sky. For the first time in months, he was at peace. He didn't mind being alone because he wasn't uncomfortable with where his thoughts would take him.

And those thoughts were filled with Carrie and Aviva. Carrie had given him his soul back. She'd shown him that it was okay to have faith in the goodness of people. That not everyone was going to disappoint you. And thanks to her, he'd come to terms with his relationship with his father. He'd learned that although the man might not have been the best father, he wasn't a horrible person. He'd finally been able to forgive the man. And he'd been able to appreciate the joy in the world around him again.

Carrie was smart and sexy. He admired her ability to persevere despite horrible tragedies. And she let him help her, despite her independence. He knew how hard that was. God knew, he had trouble leaning on people, too. But she'd let him in, confided in him and showed him how to be a better person in the process.

And Aviva? She was a joy. He'd play animals with her every day for the rest of his life if she'd let him.

*The rest of his life?*

Yes.

He walked down toward the lake, thinking about the adorable toddler. He couldn't wait to share Hanukkah and Christmas with her. Since Hanukkah started on Christmas day this year, she was going to be totally overwhelmed with presents and sugar and fun, and he looked forward to experiencing the joy and the meltdowns. Aviva loved helping to decorate—his mother's tree had gobs of tinsel unevenly placed thanks to her—and the Christmas cookies had been a hit. Tomorrow night, he'd celebrate Hanukkah with her and Carrie, followed immediately by Christmas. If possible, he was more excited than Aviva was. Like most toddlers, she'd loved the wrapping paper and boxes as much as the toys he'd gotten her, but watching her face in the glowing candlelight had filled him with awe. He couldn't wait to share in her traditions as well.

At the shoreline, he stared at the calm water, the stars reflecting off the surface, and marveled at how lucky he was. He sent a quick message of thanks to Isaac. "You were right," he said softly. Feeling more at peace, he turned toward his home, but stopped when movement on the lake caught his eye. Two people, taking an evening stroll. He smiled. If things worked out like he hoped, one day that would be him and Carrie. And then he squinted. The woman looked like his mother. Same build, same hairstyle. When he heard her laughter, he was positive. But who was she walking with? He squinted again. At night, everything took on a monochromatic hue. But just as he was about to give up, the couple walked beneath one of the lights along the lake. The man wore a gray Stetson.

Hmm. Lots of men around these parts wore Stetsons, so it was anyone's guess who her gentleman companion could be.

Arlo paused. The idea of his mother in love was new to him. On the one hand, as her son, he really didn't want to consider romantic love and his mother with the same brain, much less in the same thought. But on the other hand, no one deserved a second chance at love more than she did. If she and her suitor were happy, he certainly wasn't going to interfere.

Nor was he going to stay out here watching them. They deserved privacy.

Turning quickly, he walked back to his house.

CARRIE AND AVIVA once again walked into total chaos when they arrived at Wendy's home for the Fortune family's Christmas Eve celebration. Holiday music played through a piped-in sound system, fir boughs, red balls and bells festooned every doorway, banister and mantle, and twinkle lights glowed everywhere.

Arlo met her at the door.

"Welcome, pretty lady," he said. He leaned forward and gave her a kiss. His lips were warm and firm, and she barely had time to notice anything else before he pulled away and pointed upward.

"Mistletoe."

She smiled. "Is that the only reason you kissed me?"

His eyes glowed, and one corner of his mouth turned up. "No, that's the reason I kissed you now."

Aviva leaned toward him and pursed her lips. "Me kiss, me kiss."

Laughing, he kissed her forehead before taking her in his arms and helping them off with their coats.

"Come on inside," he said.

With his hand on the small of Carrie's back, he led her into the living room, where the enormous Christmas tree stood in the corner. Large windows faced what she knew to be the lake, although at night they reflected the family party.

She'd been here last week with Arlo, had even been part of the decorating, but somehow, tonight, everything looked a little overwhelming.

Luckily, Arlo and his family put her at ease. Ridge and Hope gave her a hug as they entered the room. "Happy Hanukkah a little early," Ridge said to Carrie.

"Ridge tells me it starts tomorrow night?" Hope continued.

Carrie nodded, touched they'd remembered. "It does. Merry Christmas to you both."

"Thank you. Are you doing anything special to celebrate?" the auburn-haired woman asked.

"I was telling Arlo we usually have a big family meal on the last night. I'd love you two to join us if you're free."

The four of them pulled out their phones and consulted their calendars.

"Hey, you guys," another of the men said. "No playing on your phones."

"We're not playing, Nash," Arlo said. "Hi, Imani." He gave his brother a pat on the back and hugged Nash's fiancée.

"Well, definitely no business talk," she said. "It's Christmas."

Carrie smiled. "I'm sorry… It's my fault. I invited them to my *merenda*—my Hanukkah dinner—and they were checking their calendars. I'd love for you all to come as well." She looked at Arlo. "Actually, your entire family is invited if they're free."

She smiled at Arlo's siblings and their partners.

"Twee," Aviva said, pointing to the corner of the room.

The three of them walked over to the Christmas tree. With a gold star on top, ornaments both handmade and store-bought, twinkling white lights and silver garlands, Carrie thought it was beautiful.

She also thought it was way too fragile for a two-year-old to play with. Or touch. Or even breathe near.

But then she saw the brightly wrapped gifts beneath the tree—the ones she and Aviva brought included—and all thoughts of staying in the same room fled. She did not want to be known as the "tree destroyer."

Arlo must have realized her concerns, because he gently told Aviva not to touch while showing her everything she wanted to see.

Wendy walked up to them with a big smile. She kissed both Arlo and Carrie. "I'm so glad you three are here."

Taking Aviva from Arlo's arms, she played with the toddler's blond curls. "Hello, my special cookie helper! Would you like to see the cookies you made? I put them out especially for you."

Aviva nodded and happily went with Wendy to the dining area, where a large table with a red-and-green tablecloth was arranged with lots of Christmas treats.

"Relax," Arlo whispered. "She'll be fine."

"I'm not worried about Vivie," Carrie said. "I'm worried about all your Christmas decorations being destroyed by a two-year-old Grinch."

Arlo laughed, his deep baritone flooding Carrie with warmth. "With everyone who is here to keep an eye on things, the decorations are perfectly safe."

"If you say so." She wasn't convinced.

Dahlia and her husband, Rawlston, walked over and greeted

them, interrupting their conversation. "Now that you're here, we can do our gift exchange."

Carrie's heart beat a little faster. She'd asked Arlo what to get for everyone, and he'd told her books. But that was all he'd said, and what if he was wrong?

He squeezed her hand, and everyone sat on the blue tufted sofas. They were as comfortable as they looked, and Carrie reminded herself to talk to Wendy the next time she decided to redecorate her house.

Jade rose and addressed the room, her fiancé, Heath, looking at her lovingly. "Since we have a bunch of newcomers this year—" she returned Heath's loving look "—we want everyone to understand the Fortune Christmas Eve tradition. Crazy Christmas gifts aren't necessary. Most of us have everything we need, and who needs that pressure?"

Everyone laughed.

"So, on Christmas Eve, we do a book exchange." She held up her hand as people started to speak. "However, we wouldn't be this family if we didn't do things a little differently. So, everyone go take the presents you brought and come find your seat."

Carrie was totally confused but did as she was told. With a pile of wrapped gifts on her lap, she waited for Jade to continue.

"Everyone ready?"

They all nodded.

"Okay, Mom, you go first."

Wendy took the top present on her pile and handed it to Arlo. He unwrapped it, smiled and held it up. It was a hardcover of Charles Dickens's *A Christmas Carol*. Everyone oohed and ahhed, and then Dahlia spoke up.

"Sorry, brother dear, I want that." She walked over and plucked it from his hands.

Carrie and the other guests who were unfamiliar with the Fortune tradition looked at each other in confusion.

"Yup, when you unwrap the gift, anyone can steal it from you. If your book is stolen, you get to pick again. But you can only steal a book if you don't currently have one, so choose wisely."

Arlo picked a book off Dahlia's pile, unwrapped it and held it up again. This time, it was an Agatha Christie mystery.

"This is going to be great," he said. He pulled the top present from his stack and handed it to Rawlston, who laughed when he opened it.

*"Love Letters of Great Men,"* he said and showed it to the room. "A few months ago, I might have hated this book." He looked at Dahlia. "But now, I love it."

When no one moved to steal it, Rawlston took the top package off his stack and handed it to Imani.

"I'm not sure whether to be scared or excited." She chuckled as she opened the package. She held up *What To Expect, The Toddler Years.*

As she started to laugh, Carrie said, "Oh, wait, I want that!"

The two women pretended to argue, until Carrie said, "I'll let you borrow it as soon as I'm done."

Imani agreed and picked a book from Carrie's stack. *"Sephardic Heritage Cookbook?* Okay, Carrie officially wins the best books prize," Imani cried. "I can't wait to try these." She pulled the top book from her stack and handed it to Zane.

He unwrapped the gift and held it against his chest. "Nope, not trading."

"Hey, that's not part of the rules, Zane," Jade scolded. "Come on, let us see."

He glared at everyone in the room before displaying *1000 Places To See Before You Die.*

"I think Zane gets a pass on this one," Wendy said. "Because it is absolutely perfect. Imani, great job."

Imani bowed her head and then rose at the sound of a baby crying. "If you'll excuse me for a minute…"

Imani and Nash took their son into the other room.

"Let's pause the book exchange until they get back," Jade suggested, and everyone agreed.

Carrie leaned forward. "How long have you done this book exchange?"

"Since the kids were little," Wendy said, a faraway look in her eye. "The kids were always so excited about Christmas, and it was a fun way to help them deal with the excitement before Santa arrived."

Squeezing Aviva, who'd returned to her side and crawled onto her lap, Carrie nodded. "I love the tradition. My friends and I used to do something similar at Hanukkah parties in college, but with gag gifts."

Heath's gaze brightened, and he looked down at his pile of books. "That could be a lot of fun, even if we did it with books."

Shaking her head, Wendy demurred. "Absolutely not! That sounds like a perfect activity for you all to do without me in another place at another time." She grinned. "I'm really better off not participating in your sense of humor."

Everyone laughed, and Imani and Nash returned to the room.

"That was fast," Wendy added. "Everything okay?"

"It wasn't a full-blown meltdown so we're okay," Imani said. "But let's continue before one of those happens."

"Good idea," Arlo said. "Who's next?"

Zane pulled a book off the pile on his lap and handed it to Jade. "You are."

The family continued the book exchange until everyone had received, stolen, taken back and laughed at all the books. By the end, each person had a mixed pile of books to read.

"Now remember," Wendy said. "Read the ones you like and donate the ones you don't. Remi's Reads is collecting donations to send to troops overseas, so anything you don't want, someone else will."

Carrie looked around at the group of people. By all accounts, they had everything. Wealth, success and happiness. And still they found ways to help others. Even with a Christmas Eve tradition.

"What are you thinking?" Arlo asked, leaning toward her. They headed over to the dining table that was piled with all the holiday cookies they'd made.

"Just about how nice this tradition is," she said, as she took her plate and picked out a variety of confections. She saw the dreidel cookies she'd made and loved how Wendy had included them.

"Hot chocolate, egg nog and peppermint tea, with alcohol to add on if you'd like, is on the counter," Wendy said.

Carrie turned to everyone who had gathered around for their Christmas Eve snacks. "While you're all here, I want to make sure to invite all of you to my Hanukkah *merenda* on the eighth night of the holiday. I'd love to have you join me and Aviva for our celebration."

Arlo hugged her to him. "That's a lot of people," he said as they walked to one of the large sofas. "You sure you want to do that?"

"Absolutely." She smiled at him. "You've shared your holiday, and I want to share mine."

## CHAPTER NINE

ABOUT A WEEK LATER, Carrie put the finishing touches on her dining table, getting it ready for the *merenda* that evening. She'd invited Rita from the bookstore, as well as the entire Fortune family and their partners. Everyone was bringing a dish to share for the potluck celebration. She appreciated how open they were about learning about her traditions, and they'd been excited to pull recipes from some of the cookbooks she'd given them on Christmas Eve. When the sun set, they'd light the menorah.

Taking a step back, she surveyed the room, taking in the white tablecloth, blue and white napkins, and blue and silver china she'd found in Randi's closet. The menorah held pride of place on the table in front of the window, where it had stood for each of the previous seven nights. Aviva loved watching the candles flicker.

She'd hung some multicolored foil Hanukkah decorations from the ceiling—mostly dreidels—and she'd sprinkled chocolate gelt wrapped in foil on the surfaces in the room.

Delicious smells wafted from the kitchen, and she went

back in to check that nothing was burning, bubbling over, or bursting into flame.

Aviva sat on the floor in a red dress playing with Arlo's dreidel.

Carrie wiped her hands on a towel so as not to mess up her jeans and pink sweater. She couldn't wait for him to get here. Since they'd uncovered his dad's secret and Arlo had finally found peace, their life had settled into a comforting routine. They each worked during the day and then spent their meals together in the evenings. Sometimes at Arlo's, most times at Carrie's since it was easier with Aviva. He'd occasionally spend the night at her house as well. But for the last few days, she'd barely seen him. He'd said he was working on something for her, a Hanukkah surprise, so Carrie didn't push.

But she missed him. Missed being wrapped in his strong arms. Missed their quiet discussions before they fell asleep. Missed his company.

Her doorbell rang, startling her out of her musings. Aviva jumped up and ran to the door, and Carrie followed. Guests weren't due to arrive for another half hour, but when she peeked through the peephole, she smiled.

"Arlo." She wrapped her arms around him and kissed him. "I missed you," she said.

"I missed you, too," he murmured, nuzzling her neck.

"Arwo!"

"Neigh, neigh," he said, getting down on all fours and tossing his head. His shoulder muscles bulged through his white button-down.

Aviva giggled and climbed on his back. "Wide, hawsey, wide!"

He galloped her around the foyer, before depositing her on the bottom stair and rising to his full height.

"The place looks great," he said. "What can I help you with?"

Carrie shook her head. "I'm all set."

"Good, that gives me a chance to talk to you before everyone arrives." He pulled an envelope out of his shirt pocket and handed it to her.

"Oh, no. Not another mystery," she moaned. The envelope was made of heavy stock, like an invitation or a piece of stationery.

He laughed. "Well, kind of, but that's not why I'm giving it to you. Open it, please."

His intense look made her shiver. She lifted the flap of the envelope and peered inside. She pulled out an embossed invitation which invited Arlo and a guest, as well as any children or pets, to dinner.

She turned the envelope over. There was no return address.

"Who is this from?"

He shrugged. "I have no idea. It's not the first I've received. Back in July, my siblings and I all received plain invitations to a wedding to be held next month at the ballroom in the town hall."

Carrie frowned. "Oh, wait, that's where the gingerbread houses were, right?"

He nodded. "Yeah. No idea if they're part of it, since we don't even know who the bride or groom is or, really, anything about the wedding."

"You're kidding!"

"Nope. Not only that, in August, we all received texts asking our opinions on bride and groom outfits. Then we were asked to pick a quote that captures how we feel about love and family."

Carrie squeezed his hand. "What quote did you pick?"

Arlo shifted in his chair, clearly uncomfortable. He sighed, and after a bit more prodding from her, finally shared a passage from his favorite book that summed up the true meaning of family, friendship and forever love.

"I love that quote," Carrie said softly.

He smiled. "Anyway, I was hoping you'd be my plus-one?"

"Of course," she said, kissing him again. "I'd love to. You seem to get yourself caught up in a lot of surprises."

"Do you mind them?" He pulled her into his arms.

*Mind them?* If they let her be with Arlo, she'd welcome them forever. "No."

"In that case..." He kissed her again before dropping to one knee.

She gasped.

"Carrie, our relationship has progressed from one surprise to the next. Not all the surprises have been good ones, but all of them have been better with you by my side. The more we're together, the less I ever want you to leave. You and Aviva are such a wonderful part of my life. Would you spend the rest of yours with me? Will you marry me?"

"Oh, Arlo, yes." Her eyes filled with tears, but this time, they were happy ones. "You've shown me what love truly means. That as long as we're together, we can handle anything. That the only place I belong is by your side. You're my home, and there's nowhere I'd rather be than with you."

He slid a sparkling diamond ring on her finger right before Aviva ran over and hugged him.

Carrie knelt next to both of them and hugged them tight. She'd come to Chatelaine, Texas, to help out her sister, right before being plunged into the deepest despair she'd ever suffered. And through it all, Arlo had been by her side, even through all of his own troubles. Together, they were a family, despite the wrenches thrown in front of them, despite their differences. They were stronger together than apart, and Carrie couldn't think of anyone she'd rather spend her life with.

"I love you, Arlo. So, so much."

"I love you, Carrie."

"I wuv you, too!" Aviva piped up, to peals of laughter.

At that moment, Carrie's doorbell rang. She shot a questioning look at Arlo, who nodded. She rose and answered the door. Hope, Ridge and Wendy stood on her porch, holding platters covered in foil.

"Come in." She smiled at all of them as she made way for them to enter her foyer. As everyone greeted her and Arlo and Aviva, Rita and Doris arrived as well. The din in her foyer was happy and loud, something she'd missed after all this time.

They all traipsed into the kitchen with their contributions for the *merenda*. As Carrie directed everyone where to put their dishes, she tried to figure out how to tell everyone she and Arlo were engaged. Maybe he wouldn't want to tell his family now while others were present?

Just then, Hope gasped, and Carrie rushed over to where Ridge was pulling a kitchen chair out for the distraught woman. He placed a hand on her shoulder.

"What's wrong?" Concern marred his boyish features.

Hope took a deep breath. Her face reddened as she looked around the room at all of the worried guests.

"I'm sorry," she said. "I didn't mean to cause another scene."

Carrie spoke up. "You didn't. We just want to make sure you're okay."

Ridge flashed her a grateful look, and sympathy filled her.

Hope nodded. "I had another flashback. I don't know, maybe it was seeing everyone carrying things in here that prompted it, but I was carrying Evie and my baby bag. I was running for the bus—" she frowned "—I think it was near the LC Club and I thought I saw the middle-aged couple again. I missed the bus and then it was dark. I knew I needed to find shelter and it felt like I was walking forever until I found a barn." She looked up at Ridge. "And that's all I remember until I woke up with you looking over me."

"I guess we finally know what happened," Arlo murmured.

"But why was I running away from home?" Hope asked. "I still have so many questions."

Ridge knelt in front of her. "I know, honey. But as your memory comes back, we're putting pieces together, and at least we're getting closer to finding out what happened. I'll protect you from whatever happened. I promise."

"We all will." Carrie's guests murmured their assent, reminding her once again how wonderful all these people were.

"Do you want to go rest?" she asked. "You're welcome to lay down upstairs."

Hope shook her head, seeming to get ahold of herself. "No, I want to enjoy myself and spend time with all of you. You've all been so kind to me."

Carrie smiled at her. "I'm glad to have you here, and I'd like to think we can be friends."

Hope nodded. "I'd like that."

"Good." She looked out the window. "I hate to rush everyone, but the sun is setting. If everyone can join me in the living room, it's time to light the menorah."

She led them into the room, lifted up Aviva and had her pick out the candles and the order in which to place them. Of course, the child wanted lots of red ones. Before lighting, she turned to her guests.

"It's so nice to celebrate Hanukkah with all of you," she said. "Aviva and I have lit the menorah each of the other seven nights right here, using the center candle as the 'helper' and adding one candle each night. But tonight, we light all eight of them. But first, we recite a prayer…"

She sang the Hebrew blessings and then guided Aviva's hand while they lit the candles together. When they finished, Arlo turned out the lights in the room so they could all see the beautiful menorah fully lit. The candlelight glowed on Aviva's cheeks. The hush of their family and friends marked the occasion as special. Everyone remained silent for a moment. Then Arlo turned on the lights again, and the talking resumed.

"Such a beautiful tradition," Wendy said.

"Thank you so much for sharing it with us," Hope added. Ridge nodded in agreement.

"Thank *you* for joining me," Carrie told them. "It makes Hanukkah special when we can celebrate together."

"And tonight is even more special," Arlo added. He rose, sending a questioning glance her way. Her cheeks heated, and she couldn't resist the smile that spread across her face.

"Yes, it is."

He joined her at the head of the table. "We're getting married!" he announced. He kissed her, speaking as their lips touched. "I love you."

"I love you, too."

The whoops and congratulatory calls filled the air, and everyone swarmed the two of them.

The women cried happy tears, and Ridge slapped his brother on the back. Then he hugged Carrie. "Welcome to the family."

And finally, she found her home.

\* \* \* \* \*

Don't miss the stories in this mini series!

# THE FORTUNES OF TEXAS: FORTUNE'S SECRET CHILDREN

**Follow the lives and loves of a complex family with a rich history and deep ties in the Lone Star State.**

### Fortune's Holiday Surprise
JENNIFER WILCK
*November 2024*

### Fortune's Mystery Woman
ALLISON LEIGH
*December 2024*

# MILLS & BOON

# Cowboy Santa
Melinda Curtis

MILLS & BOON

Dear Reader,

Have you ever discovered a restaurant that was right around the corner but you never knew existed? And after this discovery, did you fall in love with it? That's what happens to ranch foreman Chandler Cochran. Except it isn't a restaurant. It's a woman he's known forever—Izzy Adams.

Izzy has just found her footing after her divorce. She's happy with her life. She's started a side hustle, decorating homes for the holidays, all in the hopes of giving her daughter a special Christmas gift. Who has time to love again? But when her daughter and Chandler's son get into trouble at school, she has to make time for Chandler. And given time, Izzy may just discover something special that was right there all along.

I hope you come to love the cowboys and cowgirls of The Cowboy Academy series as much as I do.

Happy reading!

*Melinda*

Award-winning *USA TODAY* bestselling author **Melinda Curtis**, when not writing romance, can be found working on a fixer-upper she and her husband purchased in Oregon's Willamette Valley. Although this is the third home they've lived in and renovated (in three different states), it's not a job for the faint of heart. But it's been a good metaphor for book writing, as sometimes you have to tear things down to the bare bones to find the core beauty and potential. In between—and during—renovations, Melinda has written over forty books for Harlequin, including her book *Dandelion Wishes*, which is now a TV movie, *Love in Harmony Valley*, starring Amber Marshall.

Brenda Novak says *Season of Change* "found a place on my keeper shelf."

### Books by Melinda Curtis

#### The Cowboy Academy

*A Cowboy Worth Waiting For*
*A Cowboy's Fourth of July*
*A Cowboy Christmas Carol*
*A Cowboy for the Twins*
*The Rodeo Star's Reunion*

#### The Blackwell Belles

*A Cowboy Never Forgets*

Visit the Author Profile page
at millsandboon.com.au for more titles.

To my family, who always nod their heads when I talk about my book characters as if they are real.

## CHAPTER ONE

THERE WAS NOTHING Chandler Cochran liked less than to be called into the principal's office.

Didn't matter that he was thirty-six. Didn't matter that Chandler had done nothing wrong or that his seven-year-old son had never been in trouble before, either. Chandler sat slumped in a chair in the lobby of the Clementine Elementary School office, knee bouncing, uncertain.

*Just like the old days.*

Chandler never knew what awaited him in the principal's office. A cop? A social worker? One of his parents? Whoever it was, it meant the same thing. Change. Uprooting. Uncertainty.

*But that's not what's happening here.*

Right.

Chandler stared at his hands while chattering kids came through the door and went back out again, while parents poked their heads in to wish the school secretaries merry Christmas, while holiday music played from a small speaker on the counter and gobs of tinsel shimmered on a small tree. No one entered from the sheriff's office or county services.

*History isn't repeating itself.*

Sam was a good kid. Chandler was a good father and an

upstanding citizen. He hadn't been called to the principal's office in decades.

But still, his knee bounced.

"What are you in here for, mister?" A stout lad of about seven or eight sat on Chandler's right. He pushed back the brim of his small, brown cowboy hat as he looked Chandler up and down. "I'm here because I wouldn't stop dancing during choir practice."

That gave Chandler pause. "I thought kids in choir did a little dancing nowadays."

The boy nodded, getting to his feet. "We were practicing our moves like this." He rocked his arms back and forth with a good bit of rhythm. "And then I did this…" He lifted his hands toward the ceiling and shimmied his entire body as if he was trying not to topple in the midst of an earthquake. "And then I was sent to the office." His arms fell to his sides, his shoulders slumped and he plunked back into his seat. "Our music teacher, Miz Cornwall, told me, *'Pete, you're too much. Go see Principal Crowder.'* So, here I am." Pete shrugged.

"Maybe you should try to tone it down," Chandler said carefully, not wanting to offend.

"Is it my fault that when I hear music I feel like dancin'?" Pete sighed, a dramatic, full-body action.

Chandler refrained from pointing out there was music playing from a small speaker on the counter and Pete wasn't dancing to the "Carol of the Bells."

"I gotta do what I gotta do," Pete continued. "That's what my grandpa says. And it works for me."

And there it was. The reason for Pete's behavior. In Chandler's experience, there was always a cause kids acted out or behaved the way they did—divorce, a death in the family, a bad influence in school or at home. As a foster kid, Chandler had seen it all, not to mention been an example of that axiom himself, reacting negatively when the status quo was challenged.

Before Chandler could respond to Pete, the boy on his left poked Chandler's arm repeatedly. *Poke-poke-poke.*

"Are you here because you parked in the principal's parking spot?" Without waiting for an answer, the boy shook his head slowly. "You shouldn't do that. My ma did it once. Spent thirty minutes with the principal."

"That's not it, Matty. Look at how his knee is jumping up-and-down." Pete leaned around Chandler to look Matty in the eye. "I bet he's the one who jumped his place in the pickup line. You drove on the sidewalk, didn't you, mister?"

"No," Chandler blurted, shocked. The line moved slower than an old nag in the hot summer sun but he'd never do something like that.

Before Chandler could ask for more details, the main office door swung open, and a reindeer pranced in—jingling all the way.

Oh, it wasn't a reindeer of the animal kingdom. It was a woman wearing brown cowboy boots, brown jeans, a brown sweater with Rudolph on the front—complete with blinking nose—and a headband with a large pair of brown antlers sprinkled with tiny, tinkling bells.

Antlers wobbling, Isobel Adams hustled into the school office like she was late delivering Chandler's feed order. Izzy was a wisp of a woman, short with white-blond hair and big blue eyes. She worked at Clementine Feed and was quiet, unassuming and efficient. So much so that Chandler never gave her more than a passing thought.

But today...

He'd never seen Izzy so bubbly. So...so *alive*.

Chandler couldn't take his eyes off her. She had a pair of tan leather gloves hanging from the back pocket of her jeans and red Christmas bulb earrings swinging from her ears. Her cheeks were flushed, and her blue eyes sparkled.

*She reminds me of Mom, full of holiday spirit and not afraid to show it.*

His foster mother, that is. Who knew how his biological mother felt about Christmas nowadays.

Reindeer Izzy trotted toward the row of chairs where Chandler waited, an out-of-character big smile gracing her fine features.

*"Ho-ho-ho!"* Izzy greeted the boys sitting with Chandler before seemingly registering there was an adult in their midst. Her eyes widened. And then she removed her antlers and turned toward the office desk with much less joviality. "Hey, Ronnie. Am I late?"

"Nope." Ronnie, one of the school secretaries, grinned at her friend from the other side of the desk. She hadn't grinned at Chandler like that when he'd arrived and she was married to Wade, one of his foster brothers. "What's seven minutes when the principal is running behind?"

Chandler refrained from rolling his eyes. He'd already been waiting more than seven minutes to see Principal Crowder. As ranch foreman at the Done Roamin' Ranch, Chandler could pay several ranch bills online in seven minutes, plus return a phone call and adjust the work schedule.

"I bet she's the one who jumped the pickup line," Pete whispered, nodding toward Izzy.

Chandler shook his head. Rudolph channeling aside, Izzy was rule-abiding and reliable.

"I was stringing lights at April Forester's place," Izzy told Ronnie, rubbing the back of the hand that held the jingling antler headband. "Got stuck in her rosebush. Took some time to free myself and the lights."

Chandler took note of a long scratch on Izzy's hand and the thinness of the leather gloves in her back pocket. He managed forty cowboys at the Done Roamin' Ranch, give or take, and hundreds of heads of stock. If Izzy worked for him, he'd make sure she had a decent pair of leather gloves. For whatever reason, it was easier thinking about Izzy and work than Izzy as the walking, talking embodiment of Santa's lead reindeer, perhaps because his foster mother was recovering from two intense rounds of chemotherapy this holiday season and, consequently, the Christmas spirit had been lacking at the Done Roamin' Ranch.

*Yeah, that's it. The cause of Izzy's suddenly magnetic effect on me.*

"How is the Christmas decorating business?" Ronnie was still making small talk with Izzy, unaware of Chandler's growing tension. "That's a cool side hustle, by the way."

"It's busy." Izzy reached over to the little Christmas tree in the corner and plucked off a paper star with a child's name and a toy request printed on it, sending a piece of tinsel drifting to the ground. She tucked the star gingerly in her front jeans pocket. Then she took two candy canes from a bowl on the counter and handed them to Pete and Matty without looking at Chandler. "I've found I have a knack for tangling strings of lights without meaning to. I'll either survive this gig victoriously with the best Christmas present for Della-Mae or Christmas will become my least favorite holiday." Izzy took a candy cane for herself, shifting from side to side while she unwrapped her sugary treat.

Reindeer Izzy was as fidgety as a bull in a rodeo chute waiting for the gate to open.

"How is Principal Crowder today?" Izzy asked.

"Ugh. Don't ask." Ronnie scrunched her nose. "He's been swamped. Too many students have a case of holiday fever. Which reminds me... He needs to move things along." She walked away from the counter, knocked on the principal's closed door and then opened it a crack, saying something Chandler didn't catch.

Probably because Chandler wasn't happy to hear the principal was in a bad mood, his knee bounced more violently. He placed a hand on it.

Humming along to "Jingle Bells," Izzy turned toward the trio of chairs where Chandler was sitting, shaking those antler bells like a tambourine. "Pete, did you get into trouble for dancing in choir again?"

"Yup." The stout boy nodded glumly.

"Matty, did you get into trouble for sneaking candy during reading time again?" she asked the boy on the other side of Chandler.

"Yup," he echoed.

"And..." Izzy's gaze landed on Chandler with unexpected impact.

His heart pounded and his boot heel planted on the gray linoleum, as if his entire being needed to freeze and pay attention. To Izzy.

*To Izzy?*

Chandler couldn't believe it.

Izzy blinked, as if she, too, had felt something unusual in that moment.

"He's here cuz he parked in Principal Crowder's spot," Matty explained to Izzy.

Pete shook his head. "Nope. He cut in the pickup line."

"Chandler? Izzy?" Ronnie gestured them to come forward as a somber Vonda Jackson exited the principal's office and shepherded her little boy toward the exit. "Principal Crowder will see you now."

"Together?" Izzy looked as shocked as Chandler felt.

"It's been a long day, so I'll get right to the point," Principal Crowder told Izzy and Chandler once they were seated across from him in his office. "It's got to stop."

Clueless as to what needed stopping, Izzy nodded anyway. She never wanted to be a bother. She slid a sidelong glance toward Chandler, who didn't look as if he knew what was going on, either. His eyes darted around the room and his knee bounced.

Izzy cleared her throat, wishing she hadn't taken the candy

cane she now held awkwardly in one hand. "Can you...uh... be more specific?"

"Your kids, Della-Mae Adams and Sam Cochran, need to tone it down," Principal Crowder said crisply.

*Mae, what have you done?*

Izzy rarely used her daughter's full name, being more likely to call her Mae. Mae was a second grader and on the shy side, like her mother. Usually... Until recently anyway. Izzy was on a journey to be less of a wallflower.

The principal selected two file folders from the corner of his desk. "Samuel Cochran and Della-Mae Adams." He flipped open both files and laid them side by side, frowning while he studied the papers on top. He was approaching middle age and the eyes Izzy had previously considered kind seemed sharp and accusing today.

*Ronnie did mention an outbreak of holiday fever.*

And here Izzy had been under the assumption that Principal Crowder had called her in because he wanted to hire Izzy to decorate his house for Christmas. She'd left a flyer on his front door earlier in the week.

Izzy turned toward Chandler, meeting his gaze this time. His confused gaze. He'd looked at her like that in the lobby a few minutes earlier after she'd greeted the kids of some of her feed store regulars. He'd stared at her as if he'd never seen her before and didn't know what to make of her.

Well, she'd seen him before. And Izzy knew what she saw when she looked at Chandler Cochran. She saw an attractive cowboy a few years older than she was. A man with light brown hair, light brown eyes and a smile that rarely ventured past polite. He was tall and wiry, a man of few words, as if he'd learned long ago that speaking too many syllables would get him into trouble—a distinct possibility since he was a former foster cowboy raised on the Done Roamin' Ranch.

"Your kids have had quite a week." The principal's voice pierced Izzy's thoughts.

Years of working the checkout counter at Clementine Feed had Izzy facing uncertainty head-on with a neutral smile. "I'm afraid you'll have to be more specific."

"Yep," Chandler said in that deep voice of his as the first line of "White Christmas" drifted into the office from the radio on Ronnie's desk.

*I bet Chandler has a lovely singing voice.*

Izzy blinked, shifting in her seat, making her antlers jingle softly. *Where had that thought come from?*

She didn't have time to ponder.

Because Principal Crowder sighed the way Izzy did when needing to explain what she assumed was common knowledge. "Every day since the Thanksgiving break, one or both of your children have been sent to the office. *My* office."

Chandler rubbed his hands down the tops of his jean-clad thighs, halting that knee bounce. "This is the fifth day back from the long weekend. I haven't heard anything about this."

"Me, either." Izzy tossed her candy cane in the small trash can to the side of the principal's sturdy oak desk. This wasn't the time for sweet moments of holiday cheer.

Chandler leaned closer to the principal's desk. "It's my ex-wife's week with Sam. She's picked him up every day after school."

"Same as my ex-husband." And Izzy would bet anything her ex and her daughter had agreed that this would be *their little secret.* Mike always treated Mae more like a friend than a child he needed to discipline and set boundaries for.

Not that Mae had ever needed much discipline before.

"We sent notices through the school's electronic messaging system," Principal Crowder repeated in a tone that implied they should be up to speed. "All parents should have received them, regardless."

"I've never been able to log in to the new app," Izzy admitted sheepishly.

"Me, either," Chandler echoed. "I tried so many times that I was locked out. Same for my ex."

Izzy doubted Mike had even tried.

"That's what everyone has been saying." With what sounded like a growl of frustration, the principal scribbled a note on a notepad: *Norma, resend parents instructions for messaging system.*

"Principal Crowder..." Izzy used her most appeasing tone of voice. "What did our kids do?"

Setting his pen aside, the principal took a moment to glance at the handwritten forms in each child's folder. "On Monday, Della-Mae and Sam convinced everyone in the lunchroom to contribute their food for a Thanksgiving feast, buffet style."

"That sounds lovely." Izzy infused her words with positivity.

The principal winced. "Yes, well, it might have been if several kids with food allergies hadn't sampled items they shouldn't have. Parents were called and the nurse was busy all afternoon."

"Oh." Deflated, Izzy slunk down in her chair.

"That was Monday." Chandler nodded slowly, turning that cool brown gaze Izzy's way just as Bing Crosby sang the closing notes of "White Christmas."

*He should frown less and sing more.*

Izzy wanted to roll her eyes or shake her head.

*This is not the time for overactive imaginations.*

"What about the rest of the week?" Chandler asked, shifting his gaze back to Principal Crowder.

"On Tuesday..." The principal flipped a page over in each file. "Their teacher—Mrs. Stodimeyer—had an...*incident.*"

"Her water broke in the classroom." Izzy had heard about this through customers in the feed store. "She had a healthy baby boy at the hospital." Izzy made a mental note to add a baby item to Mrs. Stodimeyer's teacher gift this Christmas.

"She panicked when her water broke, hyperventilated and fainted," Principal Crowder clarified in that high-and-mighty voice of his. "And when she came to, Sam had put on the plastic gloves she kept in the first aid kit, sat next to her on the floor and was telling everyone that he knew what to do."

Izzy gasped, turning to stare at Chandler. "Sam knows how to deliver a baby?"

"He watched a cow deliver a calf last spring," Chandler said flatly. "You can't fault Sam for trying to help."

"Nor can I completely fault Della-Mae," Principal Crowder allowed. "She ran to the office to report the emergency. Although her exact words were, *'Sam's delivering Teacher's baby.'*"

"Makes a good story for the teachers lounge," Izzy said, trying to make light of the episode. "Anything else?"

That earned her a critical glance from Chandler, whose large hands still rested on his knees. "He's only on Tuesday."

"Right." Of course there was more. Five days, the principal had said.

Principal Crowder flipped more pages and bent over the next set of forms. "On Wednesday, during the Kazoo and Kitchen Pan Band practice, the substitute teacher had to escort two other students to the office for having a scuffle. While she was gone, Della-Mae and Sam organized the class into a marching band. They proceeded through school hallways, banging on pans, playing kazoos and disrupting classes."

"I got nothin'." Chandler glanced toward Izzy expectantly.

*Oops.* "I can give that context, I think. Last weekend, we watched the Thanksgiving Day Parade in town and then the one on TV in New York." On repeat. Izzy bit her lip. "Are you sure it was our kids who sent them marching?" Izzy was familiar with Sam since he'd been in Mae's class the past two years. But neither one seemed like the type to stir up trouble. In fact, they were opposites and Izzy couldn't imagine them working together at all.

"He's sure," Chandler said, not a bit defensively. In fact,

Chandler sounded…like he wanted to move things along. "What about yesterday?"

The principal turned two more pages. "While making cutout reindeer and sleighs to decorate the classroom windows, Sam encouraged everyone to draw anatomically correct reindeer. He was adamant about it, going so far as to sketch things on the classroom's whiteboard."

The antlers tinkled softly in Izzy's lap. She'd let Chandler handle this one.

"You can't fault Sam with that." Chandler cleared his throat, perhaps having second thoughts about voicing that statement. "He's a ranch kid. And we're a ranching community."

"And then today," Principal Crowder continued in a tone that indicated he did find fault with what Sam had done, "Della-Mae brought a rotten egg in for show-and-tell."

"No." Izzy shook her head. "I'm sure that's not true. We have chickens but I'd notice if she was saving a rotten egg."

But would Mike?

"It's a fact." Principal Crowder's gaze was unyielding. "Your daughter cracked the egg, intending to show the class that there was a chick inside. There wasn't, by the way. The contents were spoiled. We had to evacuate the classroom for an hour because the smell was unbearable."

*Eew.* Izzy nodded slowly, and in silence. This put a damper on her excitement over earning extra money for the holiday season. "What do you need us to do?"

"Have a talk with your children." Principal Crowder closed the files and placed them on a stack in his outbox. "Impress upon them the proper behavior at school. Praise them for their creativity, their understanding of the world and their leadership abilities. But caution them to think before they act. They've become as thick as thieves since the Thanksgiving break and…" He paused, as if reconsidering what he'd been about to say. "I was going to end this conversation with an option to move one of them to a different class—"

Chandler nodded.

"—but Mrs. Stodimeyer is one of our best disciplinarians," the principal finished.

"She's on maternity leave," Chandler said in a cool voice.

"Until mid-to-late January." The principal nodded. "During which time there are two weeks' vacation. I think it's better that the children remain where they are for the moment, if only because their actions were well-meaning. We wouldn't want to send the wrong message." He leaned forward, pointing at Izzy and Chandler in turn. "But in the meantime, you both need to learn how to log in to our online messaging system."

They both promised to do their best on that score.

# CHAPTER TWO

CHANDLER HELD THE school office door open for Izzy.

Not because he wanted to work as a team to get their kids in line. No.

His brain was humming along the cause-and-effect highway. Why was Sam acting so out-of-character? Chandler kept coming back to the fact that Sam and Izzy's little girl hadn't been best buddies until they'd watched the Thanksgiving parade together last weekend.

Admittedly, Chandler didn't know Izzy's daughter that well, but she had to be the cause of all Sam's mischief.

"Well…" Izzy stepped past Chandler, stuck her antlers back on her head and looked at him without any of her previous holiday cheer, although Rudolph's nose was blinking on her sweater and had been the entire time they were on the hot seat with the principal. "We have some homework, don't we?"

Chandler made an unhappy noise and strode toward the school parking lot where he *had not* parked in the principal's space. The school grounds were nearly empty. The sun was low in the sky and the brisk wind was quickening, reminding Chandler that in his haste to get to school, he'd forgotten a jacket. His blue flannel shirt wasn't a thick enough layer.

"Hey." Izzy pranced next to him, trying to keep up on those short legs of hers. "What are we going to do about this?"

"Isn't it obvious? Keep our kids apart. It's what I do when livestock or cowhands cause trouble."

"You're... You're likening our children to livestock?" Izzy sounded flabbergasted.

Chandler nodded. "The same rules apply. Isolate. Retrain. Keep an eye on Della."

"It's Della-Mae or just Mae," Izzy muttered. "Her father insisted on naming her Della after his mother, despite the fact that it's what one of my best friends named her daughter. So, we compromised and added my mother's name, which is what I usually call her." Izzy caught hold of Chandler's arm. "Hang on. I've just realized what you're saying."

At her touch, Chandler came to a stop, facing Izzy, those big blue eyes, and that blinking reindeer nose.

"You think my daughter is to blame for all this?" Izzy sounded hurt and looked like an adorable, confused reindeer. "She didn't goad kids to draw the private parts on Rudolph or kneel down like a catcher in the big leagues and call, *'Batter up!'* when her teacher went into labor."

"You're missing the point." Chandler lowered his chin and the brim of his cowboy hat. "At the root of these events is a cause. There's a reason for an outcome. A reason a horse wants to kick up its heels. A reason a kid wants to do the same."

The confusion in Izzy's expression pinched and prickled until she was scowling at Chandler. "My daughter isn't a scapegrace. And neither is your son."

"A...a *what*?"

"A troublemaker." Izzy looked put out at having to explain. "I read historicals and sometimes a word from the past pops out when I'm upset. Like now. I'm upset at you for thinking the worst of Mae and Sam."

He'd expected Izzy to blame Sam. Her defense of both kids

silenced Chandler. But only for a moment. Because kids just didn't go causing trouble without some scapegrace involved.

*Scapegrace? Now she's got me doing it!*

Chandler resumed his retreat to the parking lot. "Regardless of what the principal said, I think we should put in a request for separate classrooms on Monday. I hear Miss Cornwall is strict. She's also the music teacher. I think she can handle Della-Mae."

Izzy scoffed, trotted next to him, antlers tinkling. "I think we should consult with Mrs. Stodimeyer first, even if she is on maternity leave." *Jingle-jingle-jingle.*

Even though her idea had merit, Chandler resisted responding. He wanted what was best for Sam. And stability was the foundation of a solid upbringing. Stability. Predictability. And no scapegraces allowed.

"Hey…um…" Izzy cleared her throat. "Did you pick up a star from the tree in the office? I hear there are a lot of kids in need at school this year."

"You're changing the subject?" *Unbelievable.* Chandler walked faster. "We're in the middle of a crisis here."

"I'm offering you an olive branch. 'Tis the season, after all. And our kids are only seven, not seventeen. Now, I took a star and…" Izzy dug in her jeans pocket and then drew a sharp intake of breath. "Ouch. Darn rosebush." She held her scraped hand over Rudolph's blinking nose.

Chandler stopped and barely kept himself from reaching for her scraped hand.

He pressed his lips together, out of sorts over the situation, over Izzy trying to brush this problem off, but mostly over his reaction to Izzy, like she was part of his family circle and to be protected. "Were you even wearing your gloves earlier?"

"In the principal's office?" Izzy stared up at him with those innocent blue eyes, antlers floating over her white-blond hair, and reindeer nose blinking at him like a beacon trying to guide him home in a snowstorm.

"Not in the office." Chandler shook his head, trying to shake off the unwanted fascination with Izzy. "Were you wearing your gloves when you were installing lights at April's around her rosebush?"

"Of course I was wearing my gloves." But Izzy didn't look Chandler in the eye when she spoke. "I know how to take care of myself."

Chandler frowned at the reindeer before him, not ready to take her at her word.

Something was happening here. Something more than Izzy's display of holiday cheer reminding him of holidays past with his Christmas-loving foster mother.

But Izzy's cell phone rang before he could puzzle the cause and effect.

And since Chandler was feeling out-of-sorts and off-kilter, he walked away.

"THIS IS FRANK HARRISON from the Done Roamin' Ranch." Chandler's foster father's voice came through Izzy's cell phone.

"Hey, Frank," Izzy said weakly, watching Chandler's tall, retreating back without having decided if he was an annoyance or a potential ally in this situation they'd found themselves in. There was something vulnerable in the way he looked at her that wouldn't allow her to classify him negatively. But still... She shivered. "If this is about an order, Frank, I can't help you. I'm not at the feed store right now." The store's biggest customers, like Frank and Chandler, had her cell phone number.

"Chandler handles most of our feed orders nowadays," Frank told her kindly. "I hear you're the one to talk to if you need help with Christmas decorating."

"That's right." Taking shelter from the strong Oklahoma wind at the corner of the last building next to the parking lot, Izzy stopped thinking about obstinate cowboys and children who tested limits and focused on Frank—a potential customer.

"You've probably heard that my wife's still recovering her strength after battling cancer most of the year," Frank continued in a voice thick with emotion. "Mary always goes all-out for the holiday—spreading cheer inside and out of every building. However, she's not up to decorating by herself this Christmas. And when I suggested the ranch hands do it, I had my butt chewed out. She wants a woman's touch. I'd dearly love it if you could see a way to fit us into your schedule."

Between working at the feed store, handling her existing holiday clients and being a mom, Izzy didn't have much time to spare for such a large job and said so.

Frank made a sympathetic noise. "You feel free to bring that little girl of yours along. I'm sure she's an angel. If you could see your way clear to doing some of the holiday baking, too, I'll make it worth your while."

*Worth my while.*

The image of the princess bed Izzy wanted to buy Della-Mae for Christmas came to mind. She'd been counting every penny from this extra work for the past two weeks and projecting her penny count for the next three. She was going to be short.

"The only way I can fit you in is to work on weekends. And maybe some nights." Izzy wanted to add, *"And not have Chandler and Sam around,"* but didn't. Instead, she said, "I don't want to intrude into your family time."

"When you're a rancher, you work 24/7. I have lots of time with family. Most of them work for me. You wouldn't be intruding," Frank reassured her.

Izzy thought Chandler would think differently.

"In fact, you'd be helping me keep Mary's spirits up," Frank said in that thick voice that gave away how important this was to him.

Having lost her mother to cancer, Izzy's heart broke for him. She relented and accepted the job.

The Done Roamin' Ranch was one of the largest spreads in the county. So what if Chandler worked there?

With any luck, Izzy and Chandler wouldn't cross paths.

## CHAPTER THREE

A FEW MINUTES after leaving school, Chandler knocked on the door to his ex-wife's small house in Clementine, full of questions.

The sun was setting. Up-and-down the Craftsman-lined street, Christmas lights were flickering on.

*Had Izzy put up any of those displays? Had she dressed in a holiday outfit while working? Had she worn her leather gloves?*

"Not my bucking bulls," Chandler muttered to himself. "Not my rodeo."

Small feet pounded across the hardwood floor inside. The porch light flicked on. And then the front door swung open.

"Dad!" Sam leaped into Chandler's arms, all gangly arms and legs, and smelling of candy canes. "I made snowflakes today. Paper ones. Can we put them in my bedroom window at the ranch?"

"Yep." Chandler shifted Sam to one hip and entered the bungalow, closing the door behind him.

Stephanie's small house always made him feel too big. On a normal day, Chandler could barely walk around the coffee table to sit in the short couch or on the single chair.

Now that there was a Christmas tree in the mix, it made him feel claustrophobic.

Stephanie was in the similarly cramped dining room on her cell phone, nodding and saying repeatedly, *"Yes."* She still wore her postal uniform and blue socks. Her long brown hair was held in two messy buns on top of her head.

No cowboy hat could fit over those hair buns.

*I should have known before I married her that Steph wouldn't take to ranching.*

His ex-wife was a town gal, through and through. But they'd been naive and believed that love could conquer their differences. He taught Steph the basics of riding. She introduced Chandler to fancy, overpriced restaurants. In the two-plus years since their divorce, she hadn't ridden a horse and he hadn't set foot in a white tablecloth restaurant.

Catching Chandler's eye, Steph held up a hand, indicating she was busy with her call.

"Hey, squirt." Whispering, Chandler lifted Sam's chin until he could see his son's expressive brown eyes beneath a thatch of unruly brown hair. "Did you spend time with Principal Crowder this week?"

"Yep." Sam nodded without a trace of guilt or remorse on his face. "Me and Della-Mae."

"What a coincidence." Still whispering, Chandler tried to make light of the situation. "Della-Mae's mom and me spent time with the principal today."

Sam grinned. "Did you have a good time?"

"With Principal Crowder?" Chandler chuckled, despite his frustration. "No. Did you?"

"Not exactly," Sam allowed, the beginnings of guardedness flattening his grin. "But sometimes you gotta do what you gotta do."

His son's words struck a familiar chord. "Have you been talking to Pete? The boy in the choir?" He'd said much the same phrase to Chandler earlier.

"I know Pete. Did you see Mom's Christmas decorations?" Sam changed subjects as adeptly as Izzy did.

"Yep. Seen 'em." Chandler nodded, considering how to turn the conversation back to Sam's school missteps.

"You haven't even looked at the decorations, Dad." Sam turned Chandler's head. "We gotta do our ranch house like this." Chandler lived alone in the foreman's house on the Done Roamin' Ranch except on weeks he had Sam. "Santa likes houses with decorations."

Chandler obediently looked around. He appreciated the Christmas spirit. Didn't mean he had to change things in his house to make room for it a few weeks every year.

Stephanie's Christmas tree stood in front of the plate glass window, glowing with colorful lights that reminded Chandler of Izzy again.

*Nope, not going there.*

Santa's sleigh and reindeer sat on a blanket of white cotton on the coffee table. Rudolph and his blinking red nose were conspicuously absent.

Chandler pressed his lips together.

Two red stockings with white trim were hung from the small fireplace mantel, which had garlands and more twinkle lights on top. A fir wreath sat on the dining room table next to a box of pink and gold Christmas ornaments, a hot glue gun and a spool of shiny red ribbon.

Last year, when he'd seen his ex-wife's Christmas decorations, Chandler had felt empty inside. This year, he felt... nothing. At least, nothing to do with Stephanie. Izzy and her antlers were still on his mind.

Chandler shook his head, not wanting impressions of Izzy to linger. They were at cross-purposes at school. He wanted action and she wanted to wait and see.

Stephanie came to stand in the arch between the living and dining rooms, slowly lowering her cell phone and looking dazed. "I got it." She wandered over to the couch, sat without any grace and repeated in a shocked voice, "I got it."

"What?" Chandler experienced a nervous swirl in his stomach, one that reminded him he'd skipped lunch. He had a hunch that whatever Stephanie had to say might make him skip dinner, too.

He set his son down. "Hey, squirt. How about you pack up what you need for the weekend while I talk to your mom?" When Sam disappeared down the hallway, Chandler came to sit in a chair near his ex. "You got what?"

"An offer. Flight attendant training school." Stephanie stared at Chandler as if seeing him for the first time. "I thought they wouldn't take me because I'd needed three tries to correctly complete my application, but they did."

"Flight attendant training… Is this an online school of some kind?" Chandler couldn't imagine flight attendant training being available in Clementine any other way. And that meant… His stomach was swirling, and his knee had begun to bounce. "When does it start?"

"It's in-person training, Chandler. It means that the airline offered me a job." Stephanie began to smile, going so far as to laugh a little. But it was a stiff, uncomfortable laugh, as if she knew he wouldn't share her happiness. "It's my dream come true. They want me to attend paid training in Fort Worth in January. Sooner if I can swing it."

For the second time that day, Chandler was blindsided by the unexpected. "But Steph, you have a job. A great one." As a mail carrier, she had job security and good benefits, including health care for Sam. Chandler took hold of his knees to keep them still. "And…and Sam. You can't fly all over the world and pick him up from school during your week. Not when we'll be here. In Clementine."

Because that's where Chandler's life and family were. Dreams were important but so was the bottom line. And the bottom line was that their divorce and custody agreements

had been based on them agreeing to make life-changing decisions together with Sam's well-being in mind. Yes, they'd
amended the agreement, most recently to expand Chandler's
weekend custody to full weeks twice a month. Was this why?

Silence stretched between them, broken only by the sound
of Sam packing in his bedroom.

"Chandler, haven't you ever had to choose between responsibility and what your heart wants?" Stephanie closed her eyes,
holding her cell phone over her heart. "It's not that easy to let
go of a dream. They gave me a few days to think about their
offer. Surely, we can work something out."

As far as Chandler was concerned, there was nothing to be
negotiated. "What's to discuss? Taking Sam to Fort Worth?"
He lowered his voice. "Not a chance, Steph. You don't have
a support system in Texas to raise him right. Sam has to stay
here. And he needs his mom." Chandler knew that was a cruel
thing to say. But he also knew firsthand the gaping hole not
having a mother put in a kid's heart.

Stephanie opened her eyes and stared at Chandler with the
saddest expression he'd seen on her face since the day she'd
told him she wanted a divorce. "I know the trade-offs I'd have
to make. But it's *my* dream."

"And *our* son." Sam would be crushed if she left…if she
chose her dream over raising him.

"Dad? Can we go swimming this weekend?" Sam shouted
from his bedroom.

"We don't swim in December," Chandler called back, not
taking his gaze from Stephanie, whose brows were drawing
down determinedly.

"Darn it," Sam said. And then it sounded like a drawer
was slid shut.

Chandler drew a deep breath, smelling fresh pine and seeing an abundance of Christmas, things that should have been
calming. But the day continued to unravel, completely out of
his control.

"You shouldn't do this, Steph." Unable to sit still, Chandler stood, moving toward the door, toward an exit and the last word.

He got so far as to gripping the doorknob. And then Chandler realized he couldn't leave. He had to wait for Sam. "Hurry up, squirt."

"Coming!" But it sounded like his son was rummaging through toys, a historically lengthy process.

"I don't work for you, Chandler." By the sound of the floorboards creaking, Stephanie got to her feet behind him. "You can't tell me what to do. And I... You know I've always wanted to see the world." Those last words were delivered as a plea for him to see her side of the situation.

Chandler could never understand choosing a life away from his child.

He turned to face her, this woman that he'd fallen in-and-out of love with. "Steph, you have to ask yourself if you want to see the world at the expense of not seeing your son. *Sam and I* aren't leaving Clementine. *Sam and I* aren't moving to Texas. At some point, you have to face the reality of the situation."

Stephanie shook her head, straightened her shoulders, looking determined. "Chandler... Can't you be happy for me? The airlines just called and... You know how much this means to me."

*She's already made up her mind. She's already put herself and her dreams ahead of our son's well-being and happiness.*

"Reconsider, Steph," Chandler pleaded, despite knowing his words were useless.

And that's why he didn't bring up the meeting with the principal. If Stephanie chose her career over raising their son, any discussion with her about Sam's behavior and subsequent parenting was a waste of breath.

"MAMA!" MAE RAN across the new car showroom floor toward Izzy, past a humongous Christmas tree, cowboy boots pounding on tile, frilly blue skirt swirling about the tights over her knees. Mae reached Izzy and wrapped her arms around Izzy's legs, staring up at her with happiness and adoration.

*As if she hadn't gotten into trouble at school all week and had nothing to be repentant about.*

Regardless, Izzy lifted Mae and held her close, breathing in her child's scent.

And if Izzy detected a lingering whiff of spoiled eggs in Mae's white-blond hair, she'd chalk it up to the power of suggestion.

"I missed you, bug," Izzy whispered.

"I missed you, too, Mama."

Izzy set her daughter down, kneeled in front of her and smoothed the wrinkles from her dress. "Where's your dad?"

"He's been making money all day." Della rolled her eyes. "I've been playing in the parts department. Did you know they have Christmas lights for license plates? I'm going to ask Daddy to buy lights for yours, Mama."

"We've talked about this before. I don't want you to ask your father to buy me anything."

"Why not?" Mae's blue eyes widened. "He buys me everything."

"And he shouldn't, remember?" They'd had these discussions before. Mike's approach to parenting was to buy Mae things to make up for the time they spent apart. He could easily buy their daughter that princess bed, but Izzy was determined that she be the one to provide something Mae would enjoy for years. And Izzy had made a point to tell Mike that very thing. "Did Daddy pick you up from school today?"

Mae turned away with a murmured, "No."

This was a sticking point with Izzy and her ex. She didn't approve of his car dealership employees covering for him so often.

"Don't tell me he sent the service driver to get you again?"

That might explain why Izzy had been called to the principal's office.

"I like Turner." Mae rose up on her toes to peer into a sedan's window, breath fogging the glass. "He tells me stories about his search for a wife." She drew a heart in the fogged section of glass and dropped back on her boot heels. "Did you know that Miss Ronnie is trying to find him his one true love for Christmas?" In addition to working as a school secretary, Ronnie was a part-time matchmaker. "Turner wants a woman who won't divorce him this time."

*Everyone wants someone who won't divorce them.*

"We'll talk about Turner and his love life later. I want to talk to your father before we leave." Izzy needed to find out if Mike had successfully logged in to the school's online messaging system and was up-to-date on their daughter's school high jinks.

"Mike is closing a sale with a customer," a cool brunette told Izzy, having somehow snuck up on them in her stilettos.

The woman—Reese per her name tag—wore a red cocktail dress, had applied makeup on the heavier side, and her hair... Not a strand was out of place. Izzy had never seen Reese before, but she knew the type—Mike's type.

With a polished smile and a flick of her wrist, Reese gestured toward the waiting area by the service desk. "We still have cookies at the coffee bar."

"No, thank you." Izzy opened the door to the car Mae had been peeking into. "Since it's getting close to dinnertime, we'll wait in here, away from the cookies."

Reese appeared shocked that Izzy wouldn't do as she'd suggested.

Izzy didn't care. Reese was new. She'd learn. Izzy did what was best for Mae, even if it went against Mike's showroom rules.

"Get in, Della-Mae Adams." Izzy waited for her daughter to hop behind the wheel before walking around to the passenger side and opening the door. "We know the rules, Reese. We'll try not to smudge anything." And then Izzy sat in the passenger seat of the sedan and closed the door behind her.

Mae stared at Izzy warily. "Am I in trouble? You don't call me by my full name unless you're mad."

"Should I be mad?" Izzy realized the nose on Rudolph was blinking and reached inside her sweater to turn it off. She should have done so when she removed her antlers on the drive over. Or before being called into the principal's office…

Her self-image as a competent person took a hit. No wonder Chandler had treated her as if all the school shenanigans were Mae's fault and hers.

Still, Izzy was determined not to shirk her parental duties. She fixed her daughter with a firm stare. "What do you think? Would I be mad if I had a talk with Principal Crowder about you? Would I be upset if you and your father hadn't prepared me for it?"

"Oh." Her daughter faced forward and slumped low in the seat.

*Guilty, as charged.*

Mae traced the circle of the steering wheel with her fingers. "You don't sound like you and Principal Crowder got along."

"Should we have?" Izzy sighed wearily. "Does Daddy know you've been in trouble?"

"No." Mae tried to pull her long white-blond locks over her face.

"Of course not. He never checks his messages." Not from Izzy. And apparently, not from the school, either. "No wonder Sam's dad and I were taken by surprise."

"Oh." Mae perked up. "You met Sam's daddy?"

"Oh, I did." And Izzy let her tone imply what a disaster that had been.

"You didn't like him, either." Mae tried harder to disappear behind her curtain of hair.

"Was I supposed to?"

She shrugged.

"We're going to talk about your behavior at school, bug. We have the entire ride home to do so." Izzy brushed Mae's hair from her eyes. "Hiding won't get you out of an explanation."

Her ex-husband rapped on the driver's window nearest Mae, not smiling. Mike wore a classy-looking teal sweater that complemented his black hair and square jaw. He opened the door and gestured for them to get out. "What's the rule about *not* sitting in the merchandise, Della?" Despite his firm words, Mike switched tack when he turned back to an older woman flashing a smile worthy of all the sales awards he received every year. "I'll get this riffraff out of your car and have Turner take it around back to gas up."

*"Riffraff."* Izzy stood on the showroom floor muttering beneath a forced smile. "It's got comfortable seats, ma'am. I'm sure you'll enjoy it."

Mae stood next to Mike, beaming up at his customer like the well-trained sales accessory she and Izzy used to be. "Your car is pretty like my mama. Isn't Mama pretty, Daddy?"

"She can be." But Mike didn't look at Izzy. And he didn't sound sincere. He wasn't sincere about much more than the dealership's bottom line. He'd be no help disciplining their daughter.

Izzy decided then and there that she'd deal with this school issue by herself.

## CHAPTER FOUR

"WHEN WAS THE last time we had a family meeting at breakfast?" Zane asked Chandler on Saturday morning, pouring a second cup of coffee from the pot before returning to his position at the pancake griddle. "Or on my day off."

"Why are you complaining? If you stop drinking coffee now, you could go back to bed when this meeting is over." Chandler used a fork to turn sizzling bacon in a large frying pan. "Unless Dad asks us to decorate the ranch for Mom for Christmas. Then you'll be busy all day."

"When can we decorate our house for Christmas?" Sam piped up from a chair at the kitchen table, feet swinging. He seemed so happy and carefree, unlike the boy who'd clammed up when Chandler had asked him point-blank about school mishaps last night.

"We can decorate after you give me answers regarding the trouble you've been causing," Chandler told his son.

Sam's feet stopped swinging. His bottom lip thrust out.

More cowboys filed into the kitchen in their stocking feet, having removed their boots and hung their hats in the mudroom. It wasn't the entire crew. A few were on vacation. Some had taken a trailer full of bucking bulls to the rodeo championship in Las Vegas. A handful of crew members had quali-

fied to compete there. But all the men had spent the majority
of their years in foster care at the Done Roamin' Ranch, a
rodeo stock company and working ranch run by Frank and
Mary Harrison, known fondly to the men as Mom and Dad.
They may have been fosters but they were family. The men
even called each other brother.

Wade entered the kitchen with his wife, Ronnie, the school
secretary, and their daughter, Ginny, who was thirteen but determined to act like she was thirty and had already achieved
the title of Rodeo Queen and Lawyer. She'd earned many
nicknames from her Done Roamin' Ranch uncles, including
"nosy gal" and "know-it-all."

But despite being precocious, Chandler couldn't remember
Ginny ever acting up at school.

"Hey, Sammy." Ginny ruffled Sam's hair. "How was school
this week? Things go the way you wanted?"

"No." Sam kept his head down, but Chandler caught a guilty
expression. Was Ginny involved in this sudden wave of mischief making?

"You're burning the bacon." Zane hip-checked Chandler
away from the frying pan and began removing the blackening
bacon to a folded paper towel resting on a plate.

Ginny moved to the other side of the room as the kitchen
filled up, chattering to cowboys about their horses as if she
didn't have a guilty bone in her body.

Cowboys continued to enter. Soon every chair was taken.
Soon every available cabinet and countertop leaned against.
Male voices blurred and blended together while Chandler tried
not to burn more bacon and Zane produced stacks of pancakes.

Dad entered the kitchen promptly at seven forty-five, the
time he'd asked them all to assemble for a family meeting.
After months helping Mom fight cancer, Dad was looking
nearly as wan and worn out as his wife. His hair seemed whiter
than ever. His face lined with concern. "Boys, I'll get right
to the point so we can eat. As you know, your mother is in

no shape to dig through boxes, climb up ladders to storage spaces or spend hours hanging ornaments, wreaths and lights around the ranch. But she refuses to let go of the Christmas decorating."

"Are we going rogue and doing it anyway?" Zane set two steaming plates of pancakes on the kitchen table.

"The thought crossed my mind." Dad leaned on the back of Sam's chair. "But then I remembered talking to someone at the Thanksgiving Day Parade in town. They'd hired a woman to help them decorate for the holidays."

*Uh-oh.*

Chandler crossed his arms over his chest, preparing an argument against hiring Izzy.

And then someone knocked on the front door.

"I'LL GIVE YOU THIS," Frank told Izzy while he waited for her and Mae to remove their cowboy boots in the foyer. He had white hair and was thinning in stature. The last year had taken its toll on him. "You sure do dress for the role."

"It's part of my service." Izzy stood, straightening her green sweater, which had green garland and red felt light bulbs sewn on it. Black jeans and a headband with a star floating above it completed her Christmas tree costume. "I bring holiday cheer from the moment I step on property."

"Me, too." Mae had gotten into the spirit as well with her red leggings beneath her red dress, and a Santa hat.

She was such a sweetheart. It was hard to reconcile Izzy's biddable little girl with her behavior at school last week.

"I'm grateful for your holiday enthusiasm." Frank patted Izzy's shoulder before indicating she should follow him. "The boys are in the kitchen."

"The boys..." *Chandler?* "You know, I work alone."

"Nonsense," Frank said, two steps ahead of her. "What's the point of having able bodies around if you don't put them to work?"

*"Della-Mae!"* Sam popped off his chair at the kitchen table the moment he saw Izzy's daughter. He ran over and hugged her before turning to the room full of cowboys standing in their stocking feet and announcing, "Everybody, this is my best friend, Della-Mae." He dragged her back to the kitchen table, where they each half sat in his chair. "Ginny, look. It's Della-Mae."

"I see her." Ginny waved hello.

"And you all know Izzy," Frank completed the introductions, although none were needed.

Izzy knew all the cowboys by name through working at the feed store. Not that she wore costumes there, which she supposed was why she was receiving so many curious stares. She fought the urge to shrink behind Frank. When she'd decided on this path of being a holiday decorator, she'd committed herself to stepping out of her comfort zone 100 percent.

And so, Izzy held out her arms and said, "I guess you all have never seen a living Christmas tree before."

That earned her some chuckles and respite from the stares.

On the other side of the kitchen table, Chandler didn't laugh.

*So much for the Done Roamin' Ranch being large enough that we wouldn't see each other.*

"This is our Christmas decorator," Frank told the cowboys. "Give her a warm welcome."

There were mumbles of hey, good morning, and howdy.

For cowboys on a Saturday before breakfast, a day most of them had off, that was practically an enthusiastic reception. Izzy should know. Most days, she worked the early shift at the feed store where cowboys picked up supplies with little more than grunts as greeting.

"Mom is going to direct Izzy regarding what she wants done," Frank went on. "And if Izzy needs any help finding decorations or putting things up per your mother's standards, I want you all to hop to it."

"I'm sure I'll be fine without an assist," Izzy assured them, although she said it mostly for Chandler's benefit. "I've got Mae to help me."

"And me!" Sam piped up, generating chuckles from the group.

Chandler turned his back on Izzy and busied himself flipping bacon.

"Grab yourself some food and coffee, Izzy," Frank instructed. "I'll go see if Mary's ready to come out to the living room and brief you." He left the kitchen.

And when he left, it was as if the tension in the room drained away. The men descended upon the bacon, pancakes and eggs. Their deep voices filled the room with welcome and warmth.

Ronnie came over to give Izzy a hug. She was a blast of strong color in her red velvet jeans, purple sweater, dark long hair and red lipstick. "You didn't tell me yesterday that Frank had hired you."

"He made me an offer after I stopped by the school."

A huffing noise came from the direction of Chandler's broad shoulders.

Ronnie linked her arm through Izzy's. "We're heading out soon to grab some things for Wade's trip to Vegas." Where he was competing in the bronc riding national championship the following weekend. "Otherwise, I'd stay and help."

"From the looks of things, I have all the help I need," Izzy assured her friend. "But any hints you can give me about pleasing Mary will be much appreciated before you leave."

Ronnie drew Izzy closer, lowering her voice. "That's easy. Mary covers every inch of the ranch in Christmas, including the bunkhouse and barn but especially this house. Just be glad you're charging by the hour."

Her husband, Wade, gestured toward the mudroom before touching his daughter Ginny's shoulder and nodding in the same direction.

"That's my cue to leave." Ronnie hugged Izzy again. "I

know you're going to have a good time today. I'll call you later." And then she was gone.

Leaving Izzy to dive into the melee for food and coffee. Mae was eating a pancake. Izzy worked her way around the table, closer to the coffeepot and Chandler. She was too self-conscious to apologize for showing up on his turf unannounced when she knew she wasn't welcome. Thankfully, Chandler paid Izzy no mind as she poured herself a cup of black coffee and took a sip.

But she was unable to squelch her curiosity. "What did Sam tell you about school?"

Chandler's turned-up nose was answer enough. *Nothing.*

Izzy sipped her coffee again before admitting, "Mae wouldn't say anything, either."

Chandler grunted.

If Izzy didn't have so much experience helping cowboys at the feed store with everything from grain orders to selecting a pair of blue jeans, she might have been put off by his crusty demeanor.

"You're burning the bacon again." Zane crowded Chandler out of his way, taking over bacon duties and as a result...

Only Izzy's coffee mug came between her and Chandler's chest. Back to the wall, with the kitchen table and cabinets on either side of her, Izzy had no room to escape.

She stared up, up, up at Chandler, expecting a frown. Not seeing one.

Her pulse kicked up, sending her body on full alert: *Warning! Handsome cowboy within kissing distance!*

Izzy didn't date cowboys. She saw cowboys all day, every day at the feed store. She'd been working there since high school. On day one, Earl Lyon, the owner, had given Izzy a bit of advice to not date the customers in case things went sideways. And honestly, it had been easy to follow that suggestion. She wasn't much of a talker, and neither were they when they came in. By now, Izzy assumed she was immune to cowboys.

But here she was—pulse pounding, gaze softening—staring up at a hunk who didn't want her around. Or did he?

Izzy's ears buzzed with the rumble of masculine voices. It might have been her imagination, but Izzy thought she heard a female tone. An escape from temptation and embarrassment. Izzy latched on to it. "Excuse me, Chandler. I hear Mary and Frank in the other room. Time to go to work."

Thankfully, she hadn't misheard. Frank and Mary were in the living room.

Mary sat lengthwise on the couch beneath a red-and-white Christmas blanket with Frank standing nearby. Mary wore a gray sweatshirt with a smiling elf on the front and a red knit cap with a cheery white pom-pom. Her cheeks were thin and her complexion sallow. But her eyes... Her eyes still had the same zest for life they always had whether she was hosting a community Fourth of July picnic or helping to organize the annual Santapalooza Christmas Day horseback parade.

"Izzy." Mary held out a frail hand toward Izzy. Her grip was surprisingly strong as she drew her to sit at the end of the couch by her legs. "Thank you for coming. Now she's here, Frank, you can shoo. I love you but I don't need you hovering."

Frank leaned over to kiss his wife's cheek before leaving them.

"I know I look like a dead fish on ice at the supermarket," Mary said in that frank way of hers, ignoring Izzy's protests. "But I'm over the worst. My hair's starting to grow back, and I've still got all my teeth. It's my stamina that's gone missing. Set me back emotionally, too. And seeing Frank worry..." Mary blinked teary eyes. "But you're here now. Everything is looking up. Including Christmas. I know my boys are all well-meaning, but their idea of decorating is putting up a tree, tossing some plain baubles on it and then forgetting to turn on the lights."

Izzy smiled because Mary had been a vital part of Clementine's community for as long as she could remember. And the contradiction between the strength and humor in her voice and the visual frailty of her body was simultaneously alarming and heartwarming. Unlike Izzy's mother, this was a woman who had defied the odds against cancer.

Izzy knew then and there that she wasn't going to charge the Harrisons for every hour she spent making Mary's Christmas perfect. That would be her gift.

Having a better idea now of what was needed, Izzy smiled more easily. "Mary, where do you want me to start?"

## CHAPTER FIVE

"DAD, CAN WE have a dog?"

"Nope." Chandler was up to his elbows in soapy water when his son's question came out of left field nearly an hour after Izzy's arrival. He handed Della-Mae a breakfast plate to dry, studying her little face, looking for any trace of mystery. "Do you have a dog, Della-Mae?"

"No, sir." The little girl was soft-spoken, well-mannered and dainty. She was dressed like one of Santa's elves, cute as a button, the opposite of a troublemaker stereotype. Certainly not a scapegrace.

But Chandler hadn't been born yesterday. Appearances could be deceiving.

"Why can't we have a dog?" Sam stood on a stepping stool on the other side of his little friend, the upper cupboard open above him. When Della-Mae handed Sam a plate, he rose up on his toes to put it on the stack in the cupboard. "You said you like dogs, Dad."

"I do, squirt." Chandler handed another plate to Izzy's little girl. "We used to have ranch dogs, but they got old and crossed the rainbow bridge."

"Which is why we need a puppy!" Sam cried, full of his usual exuberance.

Della-Mae giggled.

"What's so funny?" Chandler swiped another plate clean in the sudsy water.

"You aren't like Sam." She beamed at Chandler, looking angelic with those big blue eyes and white-blond hair. "He's loud and a talker. And you're not."

"Plus, he's taller than me and doesn't like dogs." Sam sounded very disappointed.

"I like dogs," Chandler said.

"Not enough to have one," Sam countered, full of sass and vinegar.

Chandler's father laughed. He was sitting at the kitchen table drinking his coffee, having left Mom and Izzy alone to discuss decorating strategy. After breakfast, he'd sent Zane and Dylan to select three Christmas trees of various sizes from a local lot.

Della-Mae smiled at Chandler as if she had a stake in this conversation. "My uncle Earl says that every cowboy needs a horse and a dog." She handed Sam a dry plate.

"That's a law in Oklahoma. Isn't it, Dad?" Sam stood on his toes to put the plate away.

"Nope." Chandler handed Della-Mae another wet plate. "Your pony isn't much larger than a dog, Sam. Maybe that checks both boxes."

"It's not the same," Sam lamented. "A pony isn't a horse or a dog. Besides, I'm too big for Baby Bear."

Chandler knew his boy was getting to the age where he could handle a horse of his own but something inside him continued to whisper, *"Not yet."*

"Did you have a horse and a dog when you were a kid, Dad?" Sam asked.

"Nope." Unbidden, the sound of his biological father's drunken voice filled Chandler's head along with the image of the empty hook in the hallway where his biological mother's coat had always hung. He stiffened, unsettled by the memories of unpredictability and loss. Chandler drew a calming breath, tucking the past back where it belonged. "My reals, my real parents I mean, weren't the type of people to have pets." They couldn't afford them and didn't have room in their hearts for more than themselves.

"So…" Sam frowned. "Are we like them?"

"No!" Chandler blurted. "I'm not…" A man with a hair-trigger temper or a woman who disappeared without Chandler when her husband wouldn't sober up. "I'm not like them. And you aren't like them, either."

Della-Mae regarded Chandler with wide blue eyes, so like Izzy's. And then she did the darndest thing. She reached up and patted his arm consolingly. "It's okay, Mr. Cochran."

Chandler imagined he heard the jingling of bells, imagined that he felt the warmth and promise of happy Christmases. And all because of the touch of a little girl.

*Of Izzy's little girl.*

"I'm glad we're not like your first parents." Sam grinned, yanking a plate from Della-Mae's other hand. "That means there's a horse *and* a puppy in my future."

Behind Chandler, Dad laughed again. "He's got you there, son."

"I told my dad I wanted a puppy for Christmas," Della-Mae said in a soft, wistful voice. "He told me no. My mom doesn't want a dog, either. She says we aren't home enough so it wouldn't be fair to the dog."

"Wise woman," Chandler mumbled, wishing he'd used that excuse earlier.

"But we spend a lot of time at the feed store," Della-Mae continued. "And Uncle Earl said I could bring a dog there if I had one."

Earl wasn't the girl's uncle by blood but Chandler supposed that Izzy had been working there long enough to be considered family by the old man, who had none of his own.

"Wouldn't it be great if we got puppies from the same litter?" Sam danced on the step stool. "They'd be brother and sister. Can we, Dad?"

"Nope." But it was as if Sam and Della-Mae didn't hear him.

"What kind of dog do you want, Sam?" Izzy's daughter smiled dreamily. "I want a dog that goes with me everywhere. Sits in my lap while I watch TV. Sleeps in my bed with me at night. Goes outside to play with me."

"That sounds like a Labrador, doesn't it, Dad?" Sam gripped the counter and jumped up-and-down on the step stool some more.

Chandler took in those hard-smiling young faces with suspicion. "This sounds like a setup. Did you two work this out ahead of time?"

Instead of answering, Della-Mae reached into the soapy water and took out a plate to dry.

Sam wasn't as good at hiding his emotions. His cheeks were flushing red. *"Dad,"* he said in a tone of voice that translated to, *"Don't ruin this for me, Dad. I want a puppy."*

"I wonder if Mary would benefit from having a puppy around," Dad mused from the table behind them.

"Grandma Mary would love it." Sam pounced, grinning again. "I'd share a puppy with her."

"She might need something a little less energetic than a Labrador," Dad continued in a distant voice.

Chandler turned to face his foster father. "Might be she could have one of those barn kittens instead. They're small and cuddly."

"Oh...kitties," Della-Mae cooed as if this was something she hadn't considered.

"No kittens, Della-Mae," Sam said firmly. "They scratch."

Scratches. That made Chandler think of Izzy and the way she'd trotted into the school office yesterday with that gouge on her hand.

"I'd veto kittens, too." Dad frowned. "The last time we had one in the house, it kept climbing into the Christmas tree and

trying to leap out on unsuspecting passersby…mainly, me."
He rubbed his arm as if remembering past hurts.

"We were talking about dogs, everybody," Sam gently
chided. "Dogs."

"My uncle Earl has a puppy board. He says I should wish
for one for Christmas." Della-Mae looked wistful.

"There will be no animals given as presents for Christmas
this year," Chandler said firmly. He had enough to contend
with already what with running the ranch, watching out for
his foster parents and worrying about his ex-wife's misplaced
priorities. The last thing he needed was puppies. Or a woman.
"No animals," Chandler repeated. "Especially not for kids who
won't talk about misbehaving in school."

Sam's lip jutted out. "We could talk about it if you agree
to a puppy."

"Ah, so you do admit to making mischief in school?" *Finally.*

Della-Mae ducked her head.

But Sam. He looked Chandler right in the eye and told him
exactly how he felt with one put-upon word. *"Dad."*

"THE BOXES IN the attic were exactly where you said they'd be,
Mary." Izzy set a large plastic tub on the carpet next to the coffee table, the last of that lot stored in the attic. She'd spent the
past few minutes ferrying dusty storage boxes marked *Christmas* and *Holidays* from the unfinished attic to the living room.

"Christmas!" Sam ran in from the kitchen and opened the
nearest cardboard box. "Come on, Della-Mae. We have to help
Grandma Mary decorate." He began tossing out the contents—
glittery gold garland, colorful beaded garland, fake fir tree
garland—quickly making a garland mound around his feet.

"Hold your horses, Sam." Izzy waylaid Mae before she
could open another box and do the same. "We have a plan."

Sam stared at Izzy, the spitting image of his father with
those brown eyes, soft brown hair and stubborn chin. "But

we want to help." And then he pouted, something his father would never do.

Mary and Izzy chuckled.

"And help you will," Izzy said as Chandler and Frank entered the room.

Chandler looked at the pile of garland at his son's feet and sighed, much the same reaction as Izzy had when a notoriously difficult customer entered Clementine Feed. He spared Izzy a guarded glance.

*What is going on behind those brown eyes of yours?*

Izzy didn't have time to wonder. Kids were waiting. She lifted the lid from a large plastic tub labeled *Christmas Village*. "Sam and Mae, I want you to arrange Mary's Christmas village on the coffee table."

The two kids lunged at the tub while Frank picked his way around it to sit in a recliner near Mary.

"Hang on. The Christmas village doesn't go on the coffee table." Chandler eased the children out of reach of the tub's treasures. "The Christmas village is always set up on the bookshelf behind the couch."

Izzy laid a hand on Chandler's arm, surprised at the hard length of muscle beneath her fingers, stunned that Chandler didn't immediately frown and pull away. "Mary thought the village would be easier for her to enjoy if it was on the coffee table this year." Izzy glanced at her client, waiting for confirmation. It was possible that Mary would back off from the idea.

"It was my idea, Chandler." Mary nodded. "Not to mention that I can watch the children play with it here." She gestured toward the wooden coffee table.

"Really?" Chandler sounded more hurt than sarcastic. "You never let us boys play with it. Or anything in this room."

"That's because you can't allow a houseful of rambunctious teenage boys access to fragile things." Mary smiled, softening her words. "There was always a game of catch with whatever wasn't nailed down, a fight with my best couch pillows or target practice with crumpled wrapping paper. Not to mention, noogies and pokes and jokes that had your energy levels supercharging your growing bodies until you tripped over your own feet. It's amazing to me that I have any nice things left. And now that you're all grown, I'd like to appreciate them and allow a precious few..." Mary gestured to Sam and Della-Mae. "...to enjoy them, too."

"Whatever you want, Mary," Frank said with a nod.

"Whatever you want, Mom," Chandler echoed, although he stared down at Izzy when he spoke.

And oddly, Izzy could imagine that obstinate cowboy saying those words to her in answer to whatever request she made of him.

*What do you want for dinner, Chandler?*

*Whatever you want.*

*What do you want to do on New Year's Eve, Chandler?*

*Whatever you want.*

*Can you kiss me a little bit longer, Chandler?*

*Whatever you want.*

Chandler's glance shifted to his arm...

*To my hand on his arm!*

Izzy withdrew her hand as if she'd been burned, managing to inch away from Chandler and her unexpected and mesmerizing attraction.

The room was silent. More than one pair of eyes was turned her way.

Izzy needed to say something about...something. But what? Her mind raced about nonsensically.

And then her gaze lit upon the Christmas village. *Ah, yes.* "You kids can arrange the village any way you want, as long as you don't break anything."

"We won't!" her helpers cried, leaping into action.

Chandler stared at Izzy in silence, looking like there was a lot going on in that handsome head of his. But he merely drew a deep breath and said, "I guess it's finally time to drag the outdoor lights from storage in the garage and check that they're working. You want to help me, Dad?"

"Yep." Frank got to his feet.

Together, the two cowboys headed toward the kitchen and the mudroom, presumably where they'd left their boots, jackets and cowboy hats.

Izzy opened another box of Mary's decorations and began poking through the contents.

Meanwhile, the kids had already struck gold.

"Look! Here's a horse." Mae held up a small figurine— a horse pulling a sleigh with a couple sitting close together, bundled up in coats and hats.

"And a dog!" Sam's excitement made his grandmother laugh. He held the figure toward her with a big smile and a charmer's look in his eyes. "You want a puppy for Christmas, don't you, Grandma?"

*Oh, he's going to be a heartbreaker.*

Izzy returned her attention to the box before her. She unwrapped a small, chipped Christmas mug, a pair of cracked snowmen salt and pepper shakers and two pieces of a small crystal bowl, barely big enough to hold enough mints to satisfy all Mary's cowboys on Christmas Eve.

Izzy dug deeper.

"A puppy, Sam? I hadn't thought about asking for an animal for Christmas." Mary tsked, but she was smiling at her grandson. "Puppies are a lot of hard work and I'm afraid that I've been creating more work for family lately. I won't be asking Santa for a puppy this year. But perhaps you can get me another dog for my Christmas village. That would be fun."

"How about a horse?" Sam switched tactics, smile just as bright. "Wouldn't it be great to have a new horse for Christmas?"

"I have a horse." Mary's gaze looked wistful. "I haven't ridden Taffy in months."

"But you will. You always ride in the Santapalooza,

Grandma." Sam spoke confidently, apparently unaware of Mary's frailty.

Izzy set aside a small ceramic Christmas tree since some of the bulbs were broken. The box was fast becoming a bust, mostly a testament to things broken but perhaps too precious to be discarded.

"We might need to get you on a wagon for this year's Santapalooza, Mary," Frank called from the mudroom. "Wouldn't want you to fall off Taffy."

"I've never fallen off a horse!" Mary called back with some of that spunk that had been in her eyes earlier. She gestured toward Sam and Mae, and the houses they were arranging on the coffee table. "You two are my witnesses. Mark my words. I've been through a lot, but I'm not going to start falling off horses now."

The kids dutifully nodded.

Sensing a fight brewing, Izzy jumped in. "Maybe you could ride in a wagon, Mary. I've seen some fancy ones in the Santapalooza parade over the years." And wished she could have ridden in some.

"Pish," Mary muttered.

"Posh," Frank replied in a louder voice. "That's a great idea, Izzy. My Mary will ride in a wagon on Christmas Day." He walked across the kitchen wearing his boots, pausing in the doorway in between the two rooms to waggle a finger at his wife. "Doc said to take it easy until your strength fully returned, remember?"

"How can I forget when you continuously remind me?" Mary huffed. "And how does Doc measure my strength? He asks me, that's how."

"You're still sleeping most of the day, darlin'," Frank said in a placating voice, plopping his wide white cowboy hat on his head. "A wagon will be safer."

"A wagon?" Mary's eyes narrowed. "Don't embarrass me.

I can ride. It's not like I plan to gallop through the streets of Clementine wearing my Mrs. Claus costume."

Izzy interrupted, hoping to restore the festive atmosphere. "Look at these great candle lights." She held up a pair of vintage candlesticks with light bulb flames that had been at the bottom of the box she'd been rummaging through. "Do you want me to put these in the living room windows?"

Chandler appeared behind his foster father. "Mom always puts those in the bedroom windows that face the ranch yard."

"*Always*... I'm not as predictable as all that." Mary drew herself up on the couch, in full-on contrary mode, mood at odds with that cheery elf on the front of her sweatshirt. "*I* think they'd look great in the living room windows, Izzy. And I'll be asking Doc Nabidian if I can ride in the Santapalooza this year, Frank. No wagons for me."

"And I'll be right there with you when you ask Doc," Frank told her, as if this wasn't the first time they'd quarreled about the doctor approval. "Just so we're on the same page. In the meantime, since you're turning up your nose at a wagon, I'll call around to see if anyone has a carriage we can borrow, something magical and romantic."

"We don't have a horse trained to pull a buggy," Mary protested, eyes filling with tears. "I know you're watching out for me. But you'll just create more work for everyone. I've already spent most of the year being a bother."

"This is an adorable snow globe. And it has a music box." Izzy was still trying to play peacemaker via distraction. She wound up the snow globe she'd found in another box. It began to play "Silent Night." "I wanted one of these on my nightstand when I was a kid. I thought it would help me fall asleep." The Christmas after her mother died.

"We always put that on the mantel." Chandler hadn't budged from his position behind Frank. His sense of repetition hadn't budged, either.

*Always-always-always.*

"I think I want that snow globe next to my bed this year," Mary said in her ornery tone of voice.

"But you never put it there." Chandler frowned. "In fact, every year, you tell us we can't open our stockings until the music box winds down to the last note. It's part of our holiday tradition."

"Are you going to argue with me?" Mary stared from Frank to Chandler. If her eyebrows had grown back, she might have raised them, daring those men to contradict her wishes.

"Nope. Doc said not to upset you." Frank turned on his heel and started walking. "Let's go check those lights, Chandler."

"Yep." Chandler stuck a straw cowboy hat on his head and followed his dad from the room.

The kids were quietly unpacking the Christmas village. Mary sniffed. And Izzy silently debated the importance of ranch traditions versus Mary's need for independence.

When the men had left and the back door had closed behind them, Izzy perched on the chair next to the couch and said to Mary, "I think I should put your decorations where they usually go. Just to keep the peace all around."

"Sam, can you and Della-Mae go get me a glass of water, please?" Mary waited until the kids had scampered into the kitchen. "Izzy, I believe change is good. And most of my family don't mind it. Now Chandler... He doesn't appreciate change or unpredictability. You have to give him a good reason to accept change. And if this is my last Christmas..." Mary choked up.

Izzy took Mary's hands and gave them a little shake. "It won't be."

"But if it is... If the cancer comes back..." Tears filled Mary's eyes once more. "I don't want my boys to make this house a shrine to me. Always putting things where I did."

"You should do whatever makes you happy, Mary," Izzy said softly. "*I'll* do whatever makes you happy."

"Work with me, Izzy." Mary's voice was gruff. "My boys...

even my Frank…look big and strong on the outside but underneath, they have soft centers. Mostly because they come from homes that were broken somehow."

Having grown up in Clementine, this wasn't news to Izzy. Anyone from the Done Roamin' Ranch was known to come from a less-than-perfect beginning. But she hadn't thought of Chandler in that light before.

"How was Chandler's…" Izzy shook her head. "I shouldn't ask about what circumstances he comes from."

"You should. You should ask him," Mary contradicted her. "As I understand it, yours and Chandler's children are in cahoots at school. Can't work as a team if you don't understand one another."

Speaking of… Sam and Mae were talking quietly in the kitchen. Were they plotting more mischief? Chandler might suspect them of it. But Izzy couldn't quite sell herself on the idea.

"I can tell you this. Chandler never knew what to expect from his parents," Mary continued in a low voice, drawing Izzy's attention back to her. "As a result, he sticks to schedules, watches out for others and avoids surprises as much as he can."

That explained why he'd been cranky at school yesterday, having been as blindsided by the reason for the meeting with the principal as she was. But… "No surprises? Not even at Christmas?"

Mary smiled gently. "Maybe at Christmas."

Izzy's phone dinged with a message from another client, a reminder that she had work to do. And there was an important issue at hand. "Still… I should put things where you've put them in the past." Izzy frowned at the collection of small houses the kids had left on the coffee table. "Including this village."

"I'll say it again. I want you to put things where it makes me happy." Mary took hold of Izzy's hand and gave it a determined squeeze. "Even if it's in a new place."

"But… What about Chandler?"

"Change may be difficult but it's the best way to move forward when you're stuck, like my Chandler."

Mary's smile fell away. "His house here on the ranch hasn't been decorated for Christmas since his divorce."

"Not even for Sam?"

"Not even for Sam." Mary tsked. "Sad, isn't it?"

Izzy nodded. "We should do something about that." She stared out the window thinking about Chandler alone without any decorations. And then, she felt Mary's eyes on her and added, "For Sam, of course."

Mary beamed at Izzy. "I knew you were the right person for the job."

## CHAPTER SIX

"YOUNG SAM HAS a good idea." Dad handed Chandler a bulb to replace one that wasn't working. "He needs a puppy."

Kneeling on the concrete floor, Chandler's attention in the large, chilly garage was divided between the lit string of lights in front of him, the changing state of Christmas and an unwanted fascination with Izzy's holiday exuberance. She'd touched him in the living room—just her hand on his bicep—and he'd been rendered speechless. Why? He couldn't work it out.

But at his father's comment, Chandler came completely back to the present. "A puppy? With me running stock to rodeos most of the year, I'm home less than you are nowadays. Not to mention Sam spends half his time at Stephanie's."

Although Sam would be at the ranch full-time if Stephanie moved to Texas.

"A puppy might give Sam something to think about other than mischief at school." Dad rummaged in a box for another replacement bulb while two ranch hands lifted weights at the opposite corner of the garage. "Besides, there's always someone around here to take care of a dog, including your mother."

"Then it wouldn't be Sam's dog." Chandler fit the new bulb

in place and held out his hand for another. "It would be Mom's dog. Might as well get her one for Christmas."

"Pfft." Dad pooh-poohed that idea. "Your mother and I have been talking about you. You're the one who needs a dog or a woman to make you smile again. Maybe both."

"A dog or a woman?" Chandler stood and stepped over one strand of lights to the next, moving to kneel by another bulb that wasn't working. There seemed to be a lot more burnt-out bulbs than usual this year. "Don't tell me you and Mom hired Ronnie to find me a match."

"Not yet. But we could…" Dad teased. He followed Chandler, handing him another replacement bulb when needed. "You're in a rut since the divorce. You work. You take care of Sam. You don't go into town with the rest of the boys to grab a beer on Saturday nights. You don't date. And—"

"I'm too old to date." Too set in his ways.

"Too old?" Dad checked his phone, and then tsked. "Last I checked, you were thirty-six."

"Going on thirty-seven," Chandler pointed out, sliding a bulb into a socket. It beamed cheerfully.

Dad made another disapproving noise. His wide white cowboy hat brim hid his expression from Chandler. "Is this how you see your life playing out? Single, running the ranch, raising Sam? Seems like you're missing out on more, including companionship. *Especially* companionship."

"Finally, your reason for saying I need a dog or a woman is clarified. Let me reassure you. I'm not lonely." How could he be when he was surrounded by family and an all-encompassing job?

"But are you living a satisfying life? As I recall, you used to dream about traveling the world."

"That was Stephanie's dream. Mine was to restore old cars." The bumper of the 1967 Mustang Chandler was working on caught his eye. He hadn't had much spare time to work on it lately. In fact, he couldn't remember the last time he'd tinkered underneath the hood. Two years ago? Three? It couldn't have been before Sam was born…could it?

Chandler frowned, gaze following the rest of the twisted strand of green wires, looking for more unlit bulbs. Was Dad right?

The jingle of Izzy's antlers echoed in the corner of Chandler's mind, enticing him to come out and play.

*Nope.*

Chandler firmly rejected the idea. He didn't feel as if anything was missing from his life.

He pulled the last few feet of lights closer and then removed another burnt-out bulb, pushing thoughts of Izzy and loneliness from his mind.

Dad handed Chandler another bulb. "My point is that there are places to go. There are people to meet. There's love and curiosity and limits to be explored. Son, there's more to life than working."

"Says the man who bounces in and out of retirement." Chandler got to his feet too quickly, sending blood rushing in all the wrong directions.

"How are the lights?" Izzy walked up the driveway.

And it must have been the sudden hit of vertigo because Chandler wanted to reach out and hold on to her in the hopes that she could steady him.

*Nonsense.*

"Five strings of lights are good to go." Dad returned the box of spare bulbs to the now-empty plastic tub marked *Christmas Lights.* "Since you're here, I'm going to head inside to watch over Mary and the kids. Think about what I said, son."

*Think about dating Izzy,* Chandler thought he meant.

Chandler scoffed. Dad didn't realize that Izzy was wrong for him. She'd been surprising him from the moment he'd seen her wearing those antlers yesterday. She wasn't the Izzy he was used to. Not to mention, she was at least five years younger than he was, maybe more. That was practically a generation gap. Sort of.

And Chandler was beginning to show some wear and tear. He'd started going gray last summer, everything from his whiskers to a sprinkling of hair on his head. If Izzy had noticed—*and who's to say she hadn't?*—she probably thought Chandler was ancient. Curmudgeonly, even, given his comments about decorations being put up where they always belonged.

Izzy scuffed the sole of her boot on the concrete, looking uncomfortable. "Sorry to interrupt your conversation, Chandler. But I want to apologize. I'm sorry about making new suggestions inside the house. I understand how change can be unsettling to some people."

"Yes... Uh... Thanks." Her apology was unexpected. Had Mom said something? Or was Izzy attuned to his upset? "I guess you know I'm a same-old, same-old type of guy." Emphasis on *old* and *same*.

"Normally, that's how folks describe me," Izzy said.

Chandler laughed a little, shaking his head.

Izzy's brows lowered. "Don't laugh. I know what folks in town think of me. I'm milk toast—"

There she went with another term he wasn't familiar with.

"—easily overlooked and boring. And you—"

"Not so fast." For some reason, he couldn't let Izzy describe herself that way. He pointed at her face. "You're head gear isn't easily overlooked. And if milk toast means you're boring, that sweater is anything but. Any woman who wears those outfits without shrinking when a group of cowboys look at her twice does so because she has character and Christmas means something to her." Chandler paused, in awe of his speech. And regretting it, too.

"Notice that everything in your argument relies on what I've been wearing the past two days." Her expression conveyed disappointment. "Admit it. Before yesterday, you would have said I was milk toast, forgettable and boring."

"I never would have said milk toast," Chandler tried to tease, although his words felt as if they landed wrong. "And you had my respect before yesterday. I can't say the same about everyone I deal with."

Izzy bit her lip.

Chandler was digging a hole. And he cared that he was floundering, so much so that he kept talking. "But do you know what? When I saw you yesterday, I didn't think *this can't be Izzy.* Which means I must have seen you as something more before I ever spotted those antlers of yours." He was surprised to realize that was true.

A smile took shape on Izzy's face, chipping away at Chandler's regrets. "Do you really think…" She shifted her weight, trailing off.

"Go on," Chandler urged.

"Do you really see me that way?" Her fingers twined together at her waist, an indication of unease.

Chandler wanted to take those hands in his and reassure her somehow. But he stayed where he was, hands holding a string of lights. "Yep."

Izzy turned, staring at the main ranch house. She was silent for a good while, and Chandler was okay with that, not wanting to ramble on and make a fool of himself more than he already had.

When Izzy faced Chandler once more, her smile was warm. "When I think back on my childhood, I was more like Sam than Mae. Outgoing, carefree, exuberant. But then Mom got sick, and I didn't know how to handle my emotions or everyone telling me how sorry they were. I couldn't find the words and my dad… Well, he was no help in the emotion department." Izzy sighed. "And after my mom died, I gave up trying, other than with my friends. It was as if I found a shell, closed it up with me inside and then I called it home."

Chandler nodded, more because Izzy seemed to want some kind of acknowledgment from him than because he remembered her as she described herself before her mother died.

"And then Mike came along, and, for a while, I felt different. No shell needed." Her gaze seemed more intense when she looked at Chandler. "But then things fell apart, and the shell returned."

Ah, this... This he understood. This he felt to his very bones. "Divorce."

Izzy nodded. "And then this year, two weeks before Thanksgiving, Mae was offered a role in the Christmas pageant. Mrs. Stodimeyer called to tell me about it and that Mae turned it down. When I asked Mae why, she told me that she couldn't imagine getting up on stage, because she couldn't imagine *me* getting up on stage." Izzy plucked at the green garland on her sweater, cheeks reddening. "And that made me realize I needed to be a better role model for my daughter, even if I need to pry myself out of my shell."

Chandler's interest was piqued. "You think it'll get more comfortable as time goes on?"

"I hope so." She chuckled wryly. "Look at me. Do I look comfortable to you?"

Chandler was looking. And what he saw wasn't a woman who was easily overlooked or stuck in a shell. In her own succinct way, she'd told him something personal. Her confession touched him. In foster care, they stressed that you had to keep moving forward, that you shouldn't let the past anchor you in place. He'd forgotten that. Chandler realized he'd been anchored in the ranch foreman's house. And to this ranch. His foster parents had noticed. And Sam... His son wanted something different from him. Perhaps he hadn't noticed Chandler's anchor. But he would when he got older. If Chandler didn't change.

"Chandler?" Izzy's soft voice brought him back to the present. "Earth to Chandler."

He grunted, carefully returning to the task of coiling lights. But coiling didn't require looking. And Chandler's gaze drifted until it landed on Izzy once more. The morning sunshine reflected off her hair, making everything around her look brighter, more optimistic, more...achievable.

*Like the man at her side could do anything he set his mind to.*

Chandler bumped the brim of his cowboy hat back. He wasn't usually poetic. And that was disconcerting, too. As if his anchor couldn't find purchase. Chandler risked another look at Izzy.

Her unusual hair color accented her pretty face the way silver tinsel did on the branches of a green Christmas tree. Christmas signified family. And family meant you had someone to reach out when you raised your anchor and drifted off course.

Chandler settled his cowboy hat more firmly on his head. "I'm listening to you." With caution.

"I was wondering..." Izzy began with a tentative note in her voice. "While I'm working around here, I could help you with your decorations."

Chandler's shoulders cramped. "Why?"

"Because I could use the work." She laughed self-consciously. "And because Sam seems to love Christmas so much."

Guilt speared toward Chandler's heart, hardening his voice. "Not everyone celebrates the holidays the same way."

"I know."

"I know you know," Chandler snapped. But guilt was building inside Chandler like a charging bull picking up steam, and he was having trouble diffusing it. "I admit. I don't sing Christmas carols with Sam just because. And I don't rearrange my furniture and put up a tree that's just gonna die in a few weeks and leave needles in my carpet for months. And I'm sure that's not you. I'm sure you sing carols and string popcorn with Della-Mae. You probably have Christmas kitchen towels, Christmas guest soaps and Christmas knickknacks out all over the house, just like my mom does. But that doesn't mean I don't have the Christmas spirit."

"I can check all those boxes," Izzy said, sounding like Izzy from Clementine Feed, not Reindeer Izzy.

*Retreating to her shell.*

Chandler didn't want to be the cause of that. "I was out of line. Feel free to walk away and ignore me." But selfishly, he hoped she wouldn't.

"Gosh, you're a miserabilist." Izzy tsked. "Sorry. I meant a guy who seems happy to be doom and gloom. Can you tell me why?"

"Why?" Why wasn't she demanding an apology?

"Yes, why no holiday decorations in your house? A lot of my clients are elderly who've had setbacks," Izzy explained. "They haven't had any Christmas cheer because their health hasn't been good, or their spouse has died. But you..." Her blue gaze was no longer naive. It was piercing, searching to understand Chandler. "You say you have Christmas cheer but not at your house. Enlighten me."

*It's none of your business.*

Except...a part of Chandler wished that it was.

"Are you still in the divorce funk?" she asked, still looking at him closely. "That's real, you know. It's like whatever your spouse did in the relationship is off-limits. The first year I was single again, I didn't take care of my SUV. No oil changes. No new air filter. I didn't even check the pressure in my tires. And it wasn't until I turned on the engine and it shook so much that it practically hopped out of my driveway that I put on my big-girl jeans and took it in for service."

"Divorce funk..." Chandler had never heard of such a thing. And didn't think it applied to him.

"If Stephanie is anything like Mary, that might be why you can't put up Christmas decorations." Izzy gave him a brisk nod. "Just food for thought."

"Thank you, Dr. Adams. Do I put a nickel in a jar for your diagnosis?" Chandler found his footing. "I suppose whatever reason is behind my lack of a Christmas tree makes me the Grinch."

"It makes you something," Izzy allowed, not looking at all put off. She had thick skin beneath that Christmas star on her head. "But it's not for me to judge. I could help you decorate, though. If you're too busy."

"Thanks, but your services aren't needed at this time." The last thing he needed was this woman in his personal space.

"No worries," Izzy continued, sounding as if she found this exchange awkward, too. "I have no problem putting the lights up where they've always been outside for Mary. If you give me a brief rundown as to where they go, I'll get right on that."

Chandler handed her the coil of lights. "I'll give you a hand." And then he began to coil the next string.

"No. I'm sure you have other things to do." Her gaze might have drifted toward the neglected Mustang.

*Or maybe that was an impression created by that conversation with Dad.*

"And besides, Sam is here. You need to spend time with him," Izzy barreled on, not looking Chandler in the eye. The garland on her green sweater shimmered in the sunlight. "I'll have Mae help me outside. Mary's making a list for me to do inside while supervising the kids in their effort to make cookies."

"It's too soon to bake holiday cookies," Chandler said without thinking. "I mean... Mom bakes the week before Christmas."

Izzy nodded slowly, curious gaze tempting him to move closer and share why same-old, same-old was so important to him.

He fought the impulse, wondering how Izzy kept circling around and circumventing his defenses. "Didn't we agree our kids shouldn't spend time together?"

Izzy huffed, putting a hand on one slender hip. "Oh, give it up. They're great friends."

"Yes. They're such good friends that they'd both like a puppy for Christmas." Despite everything—Sam's acting up at school, Mom's slow recovery, Stephanie considering taking a new job, Izzy being…not the Izzy he was used to—Chandler smiled. Because it was funny. "Not only that. Sam and Della-Mae suggested getting puppies from the same litter. If that isn't trouble, I don't know what is."

"Ha! Those two." Dropping her hand from her hip, Izzy shook her head, smiling a little and sending that star balanced over her head swaying. "But that doesn't mean they can't be friends."

*Or that we can't be…*

Chandler didn't finish that sentence. He was unable to take his eyes off her. His chest felt tight with an unidentified emotion but his mind… His mind counseled him to abort this fascination before it was too late for his heart. It was just that Chandler couldn't seem to act completely on that idea. "There's no telling what mischief they'll be cooking up next," he managed to say because she was waiting for him to say something.

"Hopefully that mischief today is just overly frosted sugar cookies." Izzy tugged down her Christmas tree sweater. "Let's make a pact. No puppies and no classroom changes."

"No puppies." Chandler wasn't willing to commit to the other, despite getting to know Della-Mae better this morning. He took a trick from Izzy's playbook and changed the subject. "What got you into the Christmas decorating business?"

Her cell phone buzzed. She ignored it. "I want to buy Della-Mae a canopy bed. Her father spoils her all the time while I'm just trying to make the most out of the few dollars that are left after paying our bills every month. And this bed…"

"You used to dream of one as a kid?" he guessed. She seemed the type.

Izzy nodded. "I'll probably bring it home and Mae won't

care for it at all, in which case, I'll be sleeping in it." She grinned. "Imagine that. A thirty-year-old sleeping on a canopied four-poster twin bed."

He had a sudden image of Izzy's head resting on a frilly pink pillow, a smile gracing those lips as she looked at him, and all that lustrous hair spilled out behind her. He removed his hat and ran his hand through his graying hair. Maybe if she noticed their age difference, she wouldn't smile at him like that.

"Did you have a dream when you were a kid?" Izzy asked.

"Yep." That was easy. Chandler put his hat back on his head and glanced around.

There was the arena where he'd learned to ride a horse. And the pasture where he and his brothers played musical chairs, except using horses, not chairs. There was the bunkhouse where he'd spent many a hot summer night in his youth talking to other foster boys about girls and baseball and rodeo. And that was the thing about growing up and living on the Done Roamin' Ranch. There was family everywhere. Chandler was rarely alone unless he was inside the foreman's house that was his and his alone. And if he was always willing to pick up someone's shift or walk the outbuildings before he went to bed at night when Sam was with Stephanie, that didn't make him a workaholic. His emotional well-being relied upon him keeping the ranch running smoothly, working how it was supposed to, being how it was supposed to be—a thriving family operation for generations to come.

"This ranch was my dream. Still is." Chandler cleared his throat, transferring a coil of lights to Izzy's other arm. "Not this ranch exactly. But a place I could call home with a family who cared about my well-being and happiness."

Izzy nodded. "Home and family. You put me to shame." She gave a wry laugh. "You probably think I should quit on the idea of the princess bed and get Mae something more practical, like a pair of new cowboy boots."

It was Chandler's turn to laugh. "I'm always up for a new

pair of boots, but... She doesn't own a pony, much less a horse, does she?"

"She gets invitations to ride with the children of my friends. Like Ginny." Izzy gave him a searching look.

"What's wrong?" Chandler rubbed his chin with the back of his hand. "Do I have tinsel or glitter on me?"

"No." She shook her head slowly, eyes narrowed not in scorn but in thought as she seemed to consider him. "You didn't agree to my pact about not changing the kids' classrooms."

"No." And he wasn't going to, either.

THERE WAS SOMETHING about Chandler that struck Izzy on different levels, from attraction to annoyance.

Oh, Izzy had to hand it to him. Chandler disguised his need for continuity of decoration placement beneath a thick veneer of helpfulness. Not that he fooled Izzy.

"No-no, Izzy. I'll go up the ladder." Chandler didn't give Izzy time to argue. "I know where the hooks are for the lights under the eaves. It'll save you time."

He was helpful, the way gentlemen were supposed to be.

Izzy was used to coworkers at the feed store assuming she could heft her weight in grain, dog food, hay, two-by-fours or fencing supplies. No one treated her with this much consideration at work. And it was...charming.

"Just hand me the coil of lights," Chandler told her quickly, although...not unkindly.

True to form, she'd already tangled one strand and he hadn't teased her about it.

He was nice. She'd known that for years.

What she hadn't known was his dream. Dreams told Izzy a lot about a person. Mike had told her he wanted stability that financial success would bring, having come from a family that struggled to put food on the table. But he'd never admitted he also wanted power and status.

Chandler's dreams involved intangibles, like the love of

family and security. Izzy wanted much the same, but she also wanted to give her daughter the childhood dream she'd never had. It made her feel shallow.

No wonder Chandler kept looking at Izzy as if she was speaking a foreign language and he didn't know if he should pull out his guidebook to translate or not.

"What are the tires doing over there?" Izzy asked, steadying the ladder for Chandler as he climbed down after the last strand was hung on the main house.

Tires of various sizes were stacked on the side of the garage.

"We keep them there until Mom complains about them, and then we haul them to the tire recycle place."

"It would be fun to paint them white—fun for the kids, I mean—and then we can stack them from largest to smallest like a snowman." Izzy warmed to the idea. "A little black paint for coal faces. A few sticks for arms and..." She faltered when she got to hats because Chandler had reached the ground and was frowning. "Are you telling me that you want everything in its usual place *and* nothing new?"

"That's me. Same-old, same-old."

"Old?" Instead of moving aside to give Chandler space, Izzy stayed put. Because for some reason, while he was charming, he also annoyed her with his stubbornness. "You aren't old. And you probably weren't chanting this same-same-same mantra when you were a kid."

"No." Him and that frown. It didn't impact her the way he probably thought it did.

Izzy didn't back down. "Better watch out, Chandler, or that frown crease in your forehead will become permanent." Without thinking, she pressed her thumb to his forehead.

*Yikes! What am I doing?*

"Sorry." She yanked her hand back. "That was inappropriate."

"Let's get going on the trees." The way he *didn't* react, as if her touch hadn't fazed him, had her stepping back and feeling rejected as he turned and strode toward the biggest tree in the yard. "We always start the lights at the bottom of the tree trunk. Then around and around we go. And finally, the lights always continue in a circular pattern through the branches. Always."

*Always? The man is like a brick wall.*

"Hanging them with a swoop from one branch to another is quicker," Izzy said patiently, waving to Mae, who stood inside the kitchen window, smiling face streaked with flour. "And the garland swag is just as pretty as a circular pattern."

"But it's not the same." Chandler rested one hand on the trunk and stared up into its branches.

*It's not the same.*

Standing a few feet away from him, Izzy stared up at the heavens, gritting her teeth. She bent to retrieve the pole she used to lift light strands and planted one end in the ground, standing on the grass like Poseidon and his trident. Except all her mythical power was being drained by Chandler and his need to avoid change.

She sighed, gaze dropping to her feet where she'd somehow managed to work her own brand of magic. "Oops, I tangled another strand of lights."

"On purpose?" Chandler looked from the tangled heap of lights at her feet to Izzy.

"No." *Maybe.*

Thankfully, Zane drove into the ranch yard before Chandler could challenge Izzy on that score.

Zane honked the horn, waving to them. He parked and hopped out, waving some more. "Hey, Izzy. I've got three Christmas trees for you!" Lickety-split, he and Dylan lifted them out of his truck bed, leaning them against the tailgate. "Where do you want them, Izzy?"

She opened her mouth to answer and—

Chandler butted in. "The tallest one always goes on the front porch. And the small one in the bunkhouse house. And—"

"Mary said she wanted Papa Bear's tree inside this year," Izzy cut Chandler off, using the Goldilocks reference so he wouldn't take offense. At Chandler's wrinkled brow, she added, "Mary said she wanted the biggest tree you could find so when she napped on the couch, she could wake up and that's all she'd see."

"That's not what we usually do." Chandler sounded uncertain.

"But that's what Mary wants this year," Izzy said firmly, despite feeling guilty over upsetting Chandler's apple cart. "Just a little change isn't so bad…is it?"

Chandler didn't answer, but his gaze was fixed on Izzy. Or maybe the star on her headband was off-kilter.

She fiddled with the placement of her headband.

"Change is fine by me." Zane pounded the trunk of the medium-sized tree on the ground without it shedding too many needles. "Where does Mama Bear's tree go?"

"On the porch outside Mary's bedroom window." Izzy ignored Chandler's weary sigh. "That leaves Baby Bear's tree in the bunkhouse. But before you put these trees up, can you tell me…" Izzy smiled at the cowboys the way she smiled at customers down at the feed store—*nonthreateningly*—right before she asked them if they wanted their order delivered for an additional fee. "Can you tell me what you look forward to at Christmas here on the ranch?"

"Why?" Chandler took a step back, as if she'd crossed a sensitive boundary. "Why would you ask that?"

"Because…" Izzy hung on to her smile. "…if there's something that is super-duper important to you at the holidays, I want to try and honor that for you." Even if Mary was intent upon shaking things up.

The three cowboys exchanged glances that didn't include Izzy—*fair enough*—and seemed to communicate with a language of their own, accented by the barest of shrugs, the slightest of nose scrunches, the nearly imperceptible shifting of weight.

"Mom makes sure there's Christmas everywhere. The beautiful part of Christmas, you know." Zane's nose wrinkled as he hurried to explain. "Before I came here, Christmas was something I admired from afar." He rubbed his nose, as if uncomfortable admitting that much. "At my house, we didn't have any Christmas. None. No tree. No stockings. No Santa."

Izzy's heart broke a little.

"Yeah." Dylan took up where Zane left off, shrugging. "There was Christmas at school but none at home. And what Mom does for us during the holidays…" He paused, blinking watery eyes, clearly moved. "She makes Christmas special *and* for us."

"Right down to the packages she puts so much care into wrapping," Chandler added in a low voice Izzy almost didn't catch. He was rocking slowly, side to side, as if he held a child in need of soothing.

"And the variety of cookies she bakes from scratch…" Zane had a faraway look in his eyes. "Makes Christmas last practically 'til New Year's."

"Sugar-glazed ham, homemade biscuits and sweet potatoes dripping with marshmallows." Dylan rubbed his flat stomach. "I'd never been so full before."

"She makes us sing carols before we eat Christmas dinner," Chandler murmured, almost smiling. "Taught me all the words."

Izzy was touched. Mary was right. These big strong men had soft centers.

They deserved the finest of Christmases, too. Even the annoying ones.

## CHAPTER SEVEN

"Dad!" Sam cried, standing on a chair at the kitchen counter when Chandler and Izzy had finished the outside lights on the house and yard. Sam had white frosting on his cheek and flour on his nose. "We made cookies!"

"I can see that." Chandler looked at the formerly clean counter, which was blanketed with cooling racks and sugar cookies of various shapes covered with layers of brightly colored frosting and several different kinds of sprinkles.

*Mom would freak if she saw this.*

It was all Chandler could do not to start cleaning right away.

"We're good at making cookies, too." Della-Mae stood on a chair next to Sam. She swirled her finger in a bowl of green frosting and then stuck her finger in her mouth. She had green frosting streaks in her white-blond hair and flour on her cheek. "Do you want one?"

"Try my Santa, Dad." Sam held out a cookie with a blob of red frosting. White sprinkles fell from it to the kitchen floor.

*If we had a dog, it would lick those sprinkles right up.*

Chandler accepted his son's work, took a bite, heard Izzy's footsteps and turned, inexplicably wanting to watch her enter the room. She'd been surprising him all afternoon with her honesty, while he... He'd avoided opening himself to her.

*Because I'm past the age of head-spinning romance.*

And yet…as he looked at Izzy… He regretted holding back. Izzy made him want to be a young buck, open to love and adventure, able to let others take on responsibilities he'd been bearing without complaint.

"Are you kids in here alone?" Izzy padded in, having shed her boots and star headband. Her cheeks were pink from the cold air outside and her white-blond hair was mussed.

Chandler could imagine his hand doing the mussing.

*Stop it.*

"We've only been alone a minute, Mama." Della-Mae offered her mother what might have been a Christmas tree cookie. It was triangular shaped and frosted with green.

"Where's Grandpa Frank?" Chandler glanced around, taking another bite of his cookie.

"He's putting Grandma in bed for a nap." Sam nibbled on another red-frosted cookie. Blue sprinkles tumbled to his feet on the chair. He watched them fall, laughing. "There's Christmas everywhere, Dad."

"Yep." Chandler didn't dare say more to ruin the children's holiday spirit. They meant well, but… Mom kept the kitchen spotless, tidying up as she worked.

There were several bowls filled with frosting of different colors on the counter. A big bowl sat in the sink with the remains of what looked like dough. Flour was everywhere. On the kitchen table. On the floor. The counters looked like the kids had been finger painting with frosting. And sprinkles…

They probably made a rainbow coating on the bottom of his white socks.

"I know what you're thinking, Chandler." Smiling, Izzy breezed past Chandler as if she faced chaos in the kitchen every day. "You're thinking the kitchen never looks like this when your mom bakes."

"Yep." He sighed, feeling staid and predictable. "And I'm thinking that we don't bake this early in December."

"Why not?" Sam wiped his red frosting-coated fingers on his T-shirt. "These cookies are so good."

"Grandma Mary boxes up her cookies to give as gifts the week before Christmas." Chandler popped the rest of his cookie in his mouth, which might not have been the best idea given the ratio of frosting to cookie. For a few seconds, it felt as if he'd taken a huge bite of peanut butter. But he managed not to choke when he swallowed. "Time to wash up, starting with you two."

*"Aw,"* Della-Mae and Sam chorused. But both dutifully held out their hands for Chandler to wipe the frosting off.

"And then we've got to clean the kitchen," Chandler told them.

*"Aw,"* Della-Mae and Sam chorused again, showing him their best pouts.

"Yep." Chandler moved on to wiping their faces and hair.

Izzy tsked. "Kids, we've got to hurry on the cleanup if you want to help decorate three Christmas trees."

"What?" Della-Mae's mouth dropped open. She stared up at Chandler while he tried to remove a blob of green frosting from her hair. "Three trees?"

"Yes, ma'am." She was a cute little thing. Possibly an incredible mastermind but cute nonetheless.

"And each tree is going to receive a different decoration treatment." Izzy turned on the faucet and began to fill the largest of the bowls before darting around the room and collecting all the dirty dishes. "Mary wants the tree on the front porch decorated with Sam's toys. She mentioned he has a big collection of superhero action figures."

"And villains." Sam growled, making imaginary claws with his fingers.

"How did the Christmas village turn out?" Chandler gave up on cleaning the children and went to get a broom.

"So cool." Sam hopped from the chair to the floor, landing with a thud. "Tomorrow, I'm going to move the people in a circle around the church to sing carols." He took a running start and then slid in his stocking feet, crashing into the pantry cupboard across the room.

*"Sam,"* Chandler warned.

"Ah. It was just one time, Dad." Sam proceeded to sock-skate around the kitchen, no doubt energized by all that sugar.

"The village is so pretty." Della-Mae gingerly climbed down from her chair. She was delicate in everything she did.

Chandler could see Izzy's daughter being overjoyed at the prospect of a princess bed. Now Sam... Sam would love bunk beds, especially the kind with a play cabin as the top bunk and perhaps a beanbag to leap into.

Della-Mae dragged her chair back to the table. "I wish we had a village like that, Mama."

Izzy frowned at the dirty bowls in the sink, perhaps chastising herself for not being able to grant all her daughter's wishes.

"I'm sure you'll get something just as beautiful this Christmas," Chandler told her, catching Izzy's eye and giving her a reassuring head nod.

The front door banged open. The kitchen occupants all stopped what they were doing to listen.

"Easy now." That was Zane's voice, coming from the living room.

"I'm not the one who smashed the Christmas tree into the door like a bull intent upon tossing a crash barrel," Dylan snapped with very little good cheer.

There were sounds of boots shuffling across hardwood, as if the tree they carried was heavy.

Izzy turned off the water and applied a sponge to the bowls while Chandler swept around her.

"Della-Mae, the tree is here." Sam ran into the living room, footfalls heavy for such a small tyke. "Come on!"

Della-Mae skipped after him, feet barely making a sound.

The two kids were such opposites. Why were they friends? Chandler shook his head, unable to answer his own question.

Sounds of tree branches scraping across walls reached Chandler. He resisted the urge to go out there and take charge.

*Because I'm finally alone with Izzy.*

Chandler rubbed his forehead.

*That's not it at all.*

"This tree is too tall," Dylan said from the living room.

"I told you we needed to trim the bottom before bringing it in," Zane replied, not without some agitation. "Now we've got to take it back outside."

"We'll help," Sam piped up. "Me and Della-Mae."

"You know the rule, Sam," Zane said firmly. "You can't leave the porch if you don't have your boots on."

"Then we won't leave the porch," Sam countered.

"Never-ever," Mae seconded.

Boots scuffled back across the hardwoods. And then the front door closed.

"Those two. What a pair, right?" Chandler moved chairs out of the way so he could sweep beneath the table. "And I mean Zane and Dylan, not our kids."

"Sure you did," Izzy teased. "Don't you want to help with the tree? How will you know if they put it where it belongs?"

"I deserve that, I suppose." Chandler swept sprinkles into a dustpan. Once disposed of, he searched a top cupboard for cookie tins to store all those cookies.

"By the way, Chandler, Christmas doesn't come with a rule book." Izzy had her head bent while she did the dishes. "And sometimes there's an advantage to the surprise and delight in something new, like my Christmas costumes or Mary changing things up. I know my outfits don't bring you joy, but my clients seem appreciative."

"Who said I don't appreciate you and your holiday cheer?" Chandler teased.

"What?" She glanced at him. "I don't believe that. If that was true, why haven't I seen you wear a holiday sweater?

I can't even recall you ever dressing up in costume, even for Halloween."

"My work doesn't leave me time for…"

"Personal expression? A bit of whimsy?" she guessed when he faltered.

"Are cowboys known for their whimsy? I think not." Chandler opened several tins and when Izzy didn't answer him, he added, "I told you I'm old and set in my ways."

"Does it matter what I think?" Izzy plunged her hands in the water and scrubbed vigorously, seemingly unaware that Chandler was hanging on to her every word. "And you're not old. Earl is old." Her employer at Clementine Feed.

"I have gray hair. I'm old. And stuck, like you said." And if that didn't destroy the attraction between them, Chandler didn't know what would.

"I have gray hair. And I'm not old. And look how I'm stepping outside my comfort zone." She turned to face him, resting a soapy hand on her hip. "You aren't old, either."

"You don't have gray hair," he said, countering her challenge. Chandler started loading cookies into the tins, starting at the other end of the counter and working his way toward the sink. His pulse picked up the closer he got to her. And his lips… His lips were smiling as if…as if… Chandler stopped trying to think and just let himself feel. And what he felt was a welling sense of excitement. He came to a stop next to Izzy. "Show me your roots."

"No." She laughed. "Trust me. I have grays." Izzy didn't back down. Her hand still rested on her hip. She didn't back away. Her stocking feet stayed in front of the sink. But her smile faded, and her gaze became wary. "I'm lucky. They're translucent so they blend with my hair color."

He was tall enough to see the top of her head, even if she tilted her face up to look him in the eye. He saw no grays.

"I think I got my first gray hair when my mom died," she admitted softly, working hard to hold on to her smile. Failing.

Her hand dropped to her side. "And I got another when my dad left town with her nurse," she said, just as softly.

More than anything, Chandler wanted to take that hand.

Chandler remembered those events vaguely. They'd happened at a distance from his side of Clementine. At the time, he'd considered each of those separate events sad. And Chandler must have made a mental note about her father skipping town because in this moment, standing before her, he could remember thinking back then, *"She knows how I feel."*

"My mom left when I was twelve." Chandler ran his hand through his hair. "But I didn't start going gray till this past year."

"Must mean you're tougher than me." Izzy's smile was more solid now, not so wobbly. "I found more grays when I was trying to decide whether or not to divorce Mike. Little did I know that while I was weighing the pros and cons, he was drawing up divorce papers."

"Jerk," Chandler blurted, earning a smile from Izzy.

"Well, he draws up paperwork for a living at that fancy car dealership in Friar's Creek." Izzy bobbed her head from side to side, as if trying to make light of what Chandler knew first-hand had to have been a gut-wrenching time for her. "It was all very businesslike."

"Can't say the same," Chandler admitted gruffly. "I fought hard for my marriage but…" He shrugged. "Turns out what I really wanted to fight for was Sam and his well-being." Still did.

"That's wise."

"Since I only reached that conclusion this past year, that's probably why I got these gray hairs." He tried to make light of it.

They stared at each other. Not smiling like they were falling in love. Not drowning in the depths of each other's warm gaze. Not even staring with yearning to explore the feel of each other's lips. Because despite being at odds over their children's behavior and his need for decorative status quo, they had a lot in common. And the acknowledgment of it was a bit mind-bending.

This wasn't Izzy, the quiet, polite woman from the feed store with little personality he never thought twice about.

This was Izzy, a soft-spoken, resilient woman with layers of character and more courage than he had.

Chandler didn't think he'd look at another ugly Christmas sweater without thinking of her.

Made him wonder what Izzy thought of him beyond not old but set in his ways.

"I'm just going to say this out loud." Izzy tucked a lock of white-blond hair behind her ear. "It's weird to be talking to you about gray hair and divorce. Especially when we didn't talk about much before yesterday besides feed orders and the weather."

He nodded. She was right. "Mom always says the best conversations happen in the kitchen." He moved to Izzy's side, picking up a dish towel. "You wash. I'll dry."

And they did just that for a few minutes in companionable silence.

Children's laughter drifted in from outside.

"We can't separate those two," Izzy said softly.

"Cold day today." Chandler changed the subject because he believed they could divide the pair and be better for it. Izzy may confound him but of this, he was certain. "And it'll be nippy Monday morning when I pick up my feed order."

Scoffing, Izzy shook her head.

The front door banged open again, bringing the sound of voices and branches dragging across hard surfaces.

Izzy extended her arm to put a bowl on the drying rack just as Chandler reached to take it above the sink. Wires crossed, their forearms brushed together, and they both jolted apart, staring at each other warily as if unsure what could or should happen next.

In that moment, Chandler realized that his father was right. He was living a closed-off life.

How else could he explain that one random touch from Izzy and he was consumed with the desire to kiss her? And from what he saw in her eyes, Izzy must have felt the same. Why not kiss her? In fact, Chandler was already acting on that impulse. He was slowly leaning forward, bending down, reaching for her...

"Chandler, can you give us a hand?" Zane called.

Chandler lurched upright.

"Dad?" Sam shouted.

Izzy blinked up at him and took a step back.

"I should...um...go see what they need." Chandler backed away from what would most certainly be a mistake—getting closer to Izzy and her tempting lips.

He dealt with her at the feed store. He dealt with her in the principal's office. For the good of the Done Roamin' Ranch's business, for Sam's well-being and his own peace of mind, Chandler had to keep Izzy in the place he'd discovered her years ago—the barely friend zone.

*"CAREFUL,"* IZZY MUMBLED to herself after Chandler left the kitchen, speed washing the remaining bowls and utensils. *"This isn't wise."*

She wasn't supposed to find they had things in common, things that made Chandler more appealing to her, things that made her want to share things about herself she didn't usually or ask things about a man that were personal.

She wasn't supposed to find Chandler magnetically attractive, stocking feet, gray hair, same-old, same-old and all.

She wasn't supposed to be this curious as to how Chandler's lips would feel pressed on hers.

Izzy liked her life the way it was...present dilemma with Mae's behavior excepted. She made decisions about her life with hers and her daughter's best interests at heart. And Chandler did the same. She knew that the way she knew that only hot water could melt that thick red frosting from the surface of that plastic mixing bowl. She and Chandler were too much alike—wounded by what should have been love, lost when their mothers disappeared from their lives, juggling single parenthood, gray hairs and how to keep their kids in line.

And yet, despite those similarities, they were too different from each other to work as more than friendly acquaintances. Chandler was grounded and predictable, as resistant to change as gray hair was to hair color. She'd seen the way he looked at her holiday cheer outfits. She'd never seen him wear anything holiday-related. Not Christmas. Not Halloween. And not so much as a T-shirt to support a sports team or indicate where he'd gone on his last vacation.

*Does he even take vacations?*

Izzy doubted it.

No. They weren't suited at all.

So why was she listening to Chandler's deep voice and wondering what he'd sound like during the singing portion of church service? Or singing Christmas carols around the house?

*Him? Sing around the house?* She chuckled.

Without realizing it, Izzy had washed every bowl, every spoon and spatula, every cookie sheet.

She took a wet rag to the counters and table.

She wasn't interested in male companionship and kisses. She'd had romance, a dream wedding, and then spent too many years putting herself last. In her experience, that's what relationships and being a mother were all about. Take away a husband, and she had more time for Mae and for herself, for reading and girlfriends and a quiet moment with a cup of coffee or a glass of wine.

*I don't miss the warm parts.*

Holding hands, walking arm-in-arm, whispered endearments and exchanging tender kisses.

No. They came at a cost. The risk that the warmth wouldn't

last. The risk that being part of a couple would undercut her self-worth and confidence.

Izzy turned, taking a good look at the kitchen. It was a large, open space with cupboards around three walls and a humongous table in the middle, one that could easily seat twelve, more in a pinch. There was a large bulletin board on the wall in one corner. It was covered with photographs of teenage cowboys, many Izzy recognized, having grown up in Clementine. More recent photographs were from weddings. There had been quite a few Done Roamin' Ranch cowboys married recently. But that wasn't the impression that would last in Izzy's head about the ranch kitchen. This was a room built for family. For lasting family that withstood the test of time. And family was what Chandler valued most.

"I understand," she murmured, thinking of Mary and what she'd said about Chandler and her boys.

Chandler valued the permanence the Harrisons had created on the Done Roamin' Ranch. The traditions. The bonds he'd formed…bonds that wouldn't be broken through divorce or parents abandoning him.

"Are you okay in here?" The cowboy she'd been thinking about poked his handsome head in the kitchen.

"Yes. Is the tree ready for me to decorate?" Izzy hung the wet rag she'd used over the faucet and would have hurried out of the kitchen if not for Chandler's hand held up in the universal sign for stop.

He smiled like a kid bursting to reveal a surprise. "We already decorated the tree. You'd be amazed at what three cowboys and two kids can do when they work together. But I thought you'd want to give it a once-over before Mom comes out." Still smiling, he returned to the living room.

Leaving Izzy in a brain fog that slipped past her defenses as easily as mist drifted over pasture fences.

*Chandler is nice.*

*Chandler is attractive.*

*Chandler is probably a good kisser.*

An ache filled Izzy's chest, bringing with it an acknowledgment.

*I miss the warm parts.*

Holding hands, walking arm-in-arm, whispered endearments and exchanging tender kisses.

*Oh, this is bad.*

But it wasn't bad enough.

Izzy also wanted the warmth that rare smile of Chandler's promised. She felt like she knew every single cowboy in the county and suddenly, out of the blue... *No other cowboy will do.*

She needed a few minutes to rid herself of that notion. She went to the mudroom and retrieved her headband with the gold star on top, reminding herself that she liked her life. She was finally at a place where she liked herself, too.

Why muck it up by falling in love?

## CHAPTER EIGHT

"I LIKE HER." Zane pushed back his chair after dinner that night.

"Your new mare?" Chandler asked, swiping his biscuit through the remains of his white gravy.

"My mare?" Zane grinned. "Gee, Chandler. I know you can't think of anything except running this ranch, but seriously? I'm talking about Izzy."

Chandler lost his hold on his biscuit. It dropped on his plate, an action that might have ignited a firestorm of teasing had more ranch hands been at dinner. Luckily, it was just a handful of cowboys, plus Sam, Mom and Dad.

"You know, Izzy? Our Christmas lady." Dylan nodded his agreement with Zane, gathering his dinnerware. "All these years of seeing her at the feed store... Who knew she had such a cool personality?"

"Right?" Zane got to his feet, setting his utensils on his empty plate. "She's all business at the feed store. So quiet."

"Never letting on she had something interesting to say. Kind of like you, Chandler." Dylan nodded again. "Might just ask her to dance tonight at the Buckboard if she's there."

Chandler felt an unwelcome stirring of jealousy and two pairs of eyes upon him—Mom's and Dad's.

Mom had her chin resting on her hand. "Imagine that. A woman with hidden depths."

"Might be a relationship worth exploring," Dad said, gaze drifting around the room.

"Or a fun dance partner." Mom bid Zane and Dylan farewell. "I like Izzy and little Della-Mae, don't you, Sam?"

Chandler's son nodded enthusiastically. "Della-Mae is my best friend. She has such good ideas."

Jealousy was elbowed aside by curiosity. Chandler leaned closer to his son. "What are some of her ideas?"

"She said cookies shaped like stockings don't always have to be red and white." Sam fidgeted in his chair, chewing a bite of steak. "I frosted one blue. She made one yellow."

That wasn't the idea Chandler had been hoping to hear. He'd wanted Sam to tell him little Della-Mae had been the mastermind behind the Thanksgiving buffet and the impromptu musical parade.

"Della-Mae gets her creativity from her mother." Dad rubbed a hand back-and-forth across Mom's shoulders. "You need to eat more, Mary."

Mom pushed her plate away with a hand so thin her tendons were visible. "I'm not hungry."

"That's cuz you ate a cookie before dinner." Sam was fully turned around now, spine to the table. "Can I have your biscuit?"

Mom laid the biscuit Dad had carefully buttered earlier on Sam's plate.

"Thanks." Sam ran his hands across the chair back. "I like biscuits almost as much as I like cookies."

"Me, too," Mom said, despite not touching hers.

"Table manners, Sam." Chandler used his hand to guide Sam to a normal sitting position. "What other ideas has Della-Mae had?" He really wanted ammunition against his unwanted feelings toward Izzy.

Sam reached for his biscuit and tore off a piece. "She said

a dog would run next to a horse and sleigh, not be running through our Christmas village all alone. Because if you have a horse, you need a dog." Wonder of wonders, Sam wiped his mouth with a paper napkin. "And um... Oh, yeah. She said my superhero action figures fighting villains in the porch tree would make Grandma Mary smile."

"That they did," Mom said wearily. She'd been up and about longer than usual today.

Through the window, Chandler saw Zane and Dylan go inside the bunkhouse. In no time, they'd be leaving for town. *For the Buckboard. For Izzy.*

"And what about at school?" Chandler continued his gentle interrogation. "Does Della-Mae have good ideas at school?"

"She always raises her hand in math." Sam stuffed too much biscuit in his mouth, pausing to chew, swallow, then drink milk before continuing. "And she shushes me when we have reading time."

"Sounds like your best friend does have some fine ideas." Dad nodded at Sam, and then turned his attention to Chandler. "Are you headed into town tonight?"

"Nope. Got Sam." And boy, was Chandler grateful for that. The last thing he needed to do was go into town and get caught mooning over Izzy while she danced with Zane and Dylan, especially since she was coming back to the ranch after work next week.

"We can watch Sam," Mom offered. "It's been a long time since we've seen some of his action heroes on TV. And since they're in my Christmas tree, I should get a refresher course."

"Sounds like a plan," Dad said.

"Yay!" Sam cried, running over to hug Mom.

"Yay," Chandler echoed, not nearly enthused.


"How DID IT go today at the ranch?" Ronnie asked Izzy that night at the Buckboard. "The outside lights looked pretty when I left for town tonight." She and her husband, Wade, lived in the original farmhouse next to Frank and Mary's house at the Done Roamin' Ranch. "Not to mention the porch Christmas tree was cheery."

Allison, Jo and Ronnie all looked toward Izzy expectantly. Allison was humming to the music. Never as demonstrative, Jo was bobbing her head slightly in time to the beat. And Ronnie... Well, Ronnie was leaning forward on her elbows, ready to hear every word that dropped from Izzy's lips.

*Ronnie has a nose for attraction.*

And Izzy had to be careful that her friend didn't sniff out the conflicting feelings Chandler had created in Izzy today.

The four friends had just finished nearly an hour of line dancing at the Buckboard and were receiving a round of drinks from their waitress.

"You can thank Chandler for those outside lights tonight, Ronnie." Izzy quickly explained how Sam's dad was a bit of a control freak when it came to holiday decorating, ignoring the way painting Chandler in an unflattering light felt like a lie. "To be fair, Chandler, some cowboys and our kids decorated three Christmas trees." And under Mary's direction, Izzy had redecorated two.

"Sounds like Chandler ruffled your feathers." Ronnie looked disappointed. "Is this because of your kids and their mischief?"

When Izzy didn't immediately respond, Allison stopped humming to the music being played by the DJ. "Is Mae in trouble?"

Izzy quickly explained about the mishaps at school, some of which made her friends laugh.

"They're good kids," Ronnie added when Izzy was through, which was a nice affirmation given she was one of the school secretaries.

"Thanks." Izzy smiled with pride. "They both helped put up decorations today. And they baked cookies. Mae was still talking about everything we did when I dropped her off for a slumber party earlier."

"I love the lights at the Done Roamin' Ranch," Allison said, staring off in the distance as if seeing them in her mind's eye. "Dix brought me there for Christmas dinner last year. Seeing them made me feel so happy."

"Me, too," Jo chimed in, tipping her wide white cowboy hat back. "I saw them on New Year's Eve when Ryan brought me and the boys over. I wish the Done Roamin' Ranch was closer to town or the main road. Mary always goes to so much trouble. It seems a shame more people can't enjoy her display."

"What if Frank and Mary opened the ranch to visitors?" Ronnie sat up. "We've all been concerned that she isolated herself for the most part during treatment. And now, she's taking a long time to get her strength back." She waved her hand. "Mary goes to church on Sunday, but it exhausts her. And I've had her friends mention to me that they hesitate to call or visit because they don't know how she's feeling. But this…" Ronnie frowned. "It would be a traffic nightmare, like the ranch's Fourth of July celebration. The ranch yard turns into a big parking lot. And it takes forever to get out when it's over." Ronnie shook her head. "Oh, it's a bad idea. Forget I said anything."

"Are you talking about scheduling visits to see the lights?" Izzy sipped her beer. "Or creating some kind of circular drive-through like the church's nativity scene?"

"A turnabout is brilliant, Izzy." Ronnie's eyes sparkled. "Mary could be bundled up near where cars drive past. Brief well-wishes might do her good."

"Well, you get right on that, Ronnie," Izzy said flatly. "You know, if I suggest it, Chandler will shoot it down as something they *never* do."

"I'll plant the seeds with Mary and Frank." Ronnie spoke with authority, as if the roundabout Christmas Tree Lane idea was a done deal. "And then you'll work with Chandler to re-arrange the ranch yard."

"As if." Izzy rolled her eyes and reached for her beer.

Zane appeared at their table, looking handsome in his dark blue shirt and fancy gray cowboy hat. "Ladies, I'm looking for a dance partner." And he was looking at Izzy, the only single woman in the booth.

*"Me?"* Izzy squeaked, nearly choking on her beer. "I mean, me?" she said in a deeper voice, cheeks heating as she set her beer on the table without spilling.

"Yes, you." Zane extended his hand.

Ronnie, Allison and Jo stared at Izzy with raised brows.

Izzy wanted to refuse. She shouldn't be dancing with Zane for the same reasons she shouldn't be kissing Chandler...not that any kisses had yet to occur. But still...

Beyond Zane, movement at the bar caught Izzy's eye. Chandler? When had he arrived? Regardless, he'd swung around on his barstool and was staring at her with an inscrutable look.

*It's not like he's asking.*

Izzy took Zane's hand, swinging her legs out with lady-like grace since she wore a silver sweater dress and her best dancing boots.

On the dance floor, Zane swept Izzy into his arms and led her in a skilled two-step. He was a strong and masterful dancer. He was handsome, with prominent cheekbones and thick, dark hair that was probably silky to the touch. But there was no tingle of attraction, no longing to inch closer or stare deeply into his eyes and try to make a soulful connection.

After a few songs, Zane escorted Izzy back to the booth and thanked her. "See you at the ranch."

And then he was gone, leaving Izzy under the scrutiny of her friends.

"Well?" Ronnie asked while Izzy sipped her beer.

Izzy shrugged. "He's a good dancer."

Ronnie leaned forward, slapping her palms on the table.

"He's an excellent dancer, a real looker and a hard worker. I can't tell you how many of my matchmaking clients want to date him. He's a catch. Are you honestly telling me you felt nothing?"

"Yep." Izzy channeled Chandler's monosyllabic response.

Ronnie collapsed back in her seat with a very Ronnie-like flounce. "Girl, we need to have a conversation."

"Leave her be, Ronnie." Jo raised her beer glass to clink against Izzy's. "Even I can see there was no spark."

"Izzy." Dylan appeared at their booth. He wore a burgundy shirt with leather yoke accents and a brown felt cowboy hat. He smiled at Izzy as if she was part of his inner circle. "You up for another bit of dancing?"

"Of course she is," Ronnie said before Izzy could politely say she'd rather visit with her friends. It was, after all, girls' night out. "Tell him, Izzy."

Chandler turned her way at the bar again and Izzy felt a flare of annoyance.

*Why is my dancing any of his business?*

"Of course I'm up for more dancing." Izzy put her hand in Dylan's, casting a dark look at Ronnie over her shoulder as Dylan led her away. She'd much rather send Chandler a dark look but he'd already turned to say something to Chet, the handlebar-mustached bartender.

Dylan wasn't as good of a dancer as Zane. He covered too much ground, leading them quickly around and around the dance floor. But he sang along with the chorus of every song and made small talk during the verses, which was endearing. All in all, dancing with Dylan hadn't been horrible. But again, Izzy felt nothing more than the fun of the dance.

When Dylan returned Izzy to her booth, she was breathless.

"Well?" Ronnie peered at her. "Your cheeks are flushed."

"Do not matchmake," Izzy warned.

"She's sweaty, not glowing," Allison noted.

"Yep." Izzy sipped her now-warm beer. *Ugh.* She pushed it

away, tugging the high neck of her silver sweater dress, trying to cool off. "I need to get going. I have a long day tomorrow and a long week ahead of me." Izzy gathered her phone in its wallet and her keys. She'd given up on purses years ago.

"Are you running away before someone else asks you to dance?" Jo asked slyly.

"She is," Allison confirmed.

"No." Izzy made a face.

Ronnie simply frowned at Izzy.

"Okay, I *am* running away." Izzy got to her feet and slid her arms into her coat. "But I also need to rest and recharge. Working two jobs is exhausting." With a wave, Izzy headed toward the door.

Only to draw up short when Chandler stepped in her path, coming off that barstool with a panther-like grace when to her he was generally more like a giraffe, given the significant differences in their height.

"Hey," he said, smiling, his jacket slung over his shoulder.

"Hey." Izzy jingled her keys in her coat pocket. "I was just heading out. I'm spent."

"Right. Me, too." Chandler stretched those long legs and beat Izzy to the front door, sliding into his jacket with panache, as if he dressed on the run all the time. "I'll walk you out."

The cold winter air flowed over Izzy and she had the strongest urge to run past Chandler and disappear into the night. But her knees were weak and with her luck, she'd trip over the pointed tips of her best boots.

They walked into the chill.

Izzy shivered, despite her thick wool coat, and nearly stumbled.

"Careful." Chandler's hand came to rest on her hip.

There was no way she could feel the warmth of his hand through a sweater dress and a wool coat. But she did. And, unlike with Zane or Dylan, a spark lit within her, urging her to move closer, to stare up at him, to part her lips.

Instead, Izzy walked faster. Not that she could run away from Chandler's touch. He kept pace with her. As if he could take whatever she threw at him.

But could she take whatever he threw at her?

Izzy ground to a halt. Uncertain...about too many things. The giddiness of attraction wasn't supposed to strike single moms who were happy being single.

"What? What's wrong?" Chandler stopped, hand still on her hip. "This isn't your SUV."

"Chandler..." Izzy faced him, turning the long way around so that Chandler had to either drop his hand or draw her into the circle of his arms.

And wouldn't you know it? She ended up with his arms around her.

"Chandler..." she repeated, breathless and heated and hesitant.

"Izzy?"

"I..." Izzy didn't trust herself to be this close to him. She didn't trust herself to look into those brown eyes or place her palms on his chest. But somehow... She had inched closer. She was looking into his eyes. She had placed her palms on his firm chest. "I..."

And suddenly, Chandler was kissing her. He was drawing her closer, practically lifting her off the ground and into his embrace. And Izzy... She was hot and cold and lost in a moment she hadn't seen coming and didn't want to end. Because his kiss promised joined hands and whispered endearments and private jokes and weekend afternoons spent entwined on the couch watching rodeo.

And then...

As quickly as the kiss began, it was over.

Izzy's feet landed on the ground with a spine-jolting thud, as if Chandler had suddenly come to his senses just when she was giving up on hanging on to hers.

"There... That's done..." Chandler didn't move. He just

let the words hang between them as if reporting a chore had been completed.

Izzy stared at Chandler with the distinct impression that he was withdrawing and building up his defenses so that fabulous kiss might never happen again.

That fabulous kiss…

That too-addictive kiss…

Already, she was open to him giving her another. But then his words came back to her.

*There… That's done…*

Those were the words of a man who had a unique slant on *always*. As in: *I always think one kiss is enough to test an attraction and put an end to it.*

Whereas Izzy…

Izzy *always* considered a doozy of a kiss as an avenue to a different kind of always.

*I always kiss you without holding back.*

*We always kiss goodbye, even if you're only going to the grocery store.*

Those weren't sentiments it seemed Chandler had in mind after that kiss. Which meant…

He had regrets.

"Oh no." Izzy covered her mouth with one hand, buying time as she formulated a fib. Because she could see the future at the feed store with Chandler and his regrets making things awkward year-after-year, just the way Earl had predicted. "I'm sorry. *I* shouldn't have kissed you like that."

*"You?"* Chandler frowned.

"How awkward when we're stuck in this situation at school," Izzy rushed on, dropping her hand. "And then there's me working at the ranch and you coming into the feed store. I must have had too much to drink. In fact, I'm just going to walk home. *Alone.*" Which would have been great if her boots had started moving away. But they stayed rooted where she was just in case she'd read the situation wrong.

*No-no-no. I didn't read him wrong.*

Even if he wasn't moving. Even if he wasn't voicing an opinion. And that was because...

"It *was* awkward, wasn't it?" she asked in a quiet tone she associated with the last six months of her marriage. And if that wasn't bad enough, Chandler still didn't answer.

*Please say yes. Please say yes.*

She did a mental eye roll.

*Come on, Izzy. This was a colossal mistake.*

Chandler said nothing. She said nothing. And neither one of them moved.

*Run, feet. Run!*

But Izzy was a glutton for punishment, and she wanted to gauge Chandler's reaction to her excuses, that kiss, *them.*

But none came. He was as stoic as a professional poker player.

"I guess I'll be seeing you around the ranch. Hopefully not at school. Ha ha." *Izzy, how lame!*

"I make you nervous," Chandler blurted just as Izzy was prying her right foot from the asphalt.

She stomped her boot back in place. "No?" *No?* She'd spoken the word as if it was a question. Izzy made a sound of frustration low in her throat.

"I make you nervous," Chandler said again with more conviction, a jagged smile beginning to curl into his features.

"No!" Izzy said in a stronger voice. "Let's just forget this ever happened and go on with our lives. You can be old and predictable. I can continue prying myself out of my shell. But we'll do it separately. Isn't that what you wanted?"

Chandler's mouth worked as if he was considering and rejecting several different words.

They stared at each other in silence until laughter from inside the Buckboard drifted to them.

And then Izzy ran away, leaving her vehicle and Chandler behind her.

## CHAPTER NINE

"DAD!" SAM LANDED on top of Chandler. It was Sunday morning. "Wake up."

*"Oof."* It took Chandler a moment to fill his lungs with air, to wrap his arms around his growing boy, to find the clock on his nightstand.

*Eight o'clock.* He should have been up two hours ago.

Sam rolled off Chandler, brown hair sticking up in every direction. "You never sleep in, Dad. Can we have French toast for breakfast?"

"Yep." Chandler sat up, ruing that kiss with Izzy but unable to stop thinking about it.

Was it foolish to regret something so soul-shakingly intense? *Nope. Nada.* Not even if that kiss had ignited a feeling deep inside him that said, *"You're my person, my future, my everything."* Chandler had felt that before with Stephanie. He refused to believe it a second time.

*Sam is my everything. My family is my everything.*

Regardless of how he'd felt, Izzy had taken the blame. And then she'd been the smart one and run away.

After which, Chandler had driven home and spent too many sleepless hours wondering what had possessed him to walk her out of the bar in the first place or put a hand on her waist in the second place or gather her close and kiss her in the third place.

It made no sense. She'd looked like she'd enjoyed dancing with Zane and Dylan. And he'd...

*I was jealous.*

Chandler hadn't felt jealous in years. It made no sense. He'd known Izzy for years. Overlooked her for years. And then in a span of less than forty-eight hours, she'd spoken to something inside him that had lain dormant since Stephanie broke his heart.

He should avoid Izzy. At school... In town... At the ranch...

Chandler rubbed his forehead. Ignoring her would be impossible. Smart, but impossible.

And yet, Chandler wanted to see her again. Not to hold her close and kiss her, but to look into her eyes and see what had caused this inexplicable wanting inside him.

"Dad, did you hear me?" Sam bounced at the foot of the bed.

"Nope. Say again." Chandler rolled out of bed, brain kicking into gear. He had to check on stock and get ready for church.

"If we had a puppy, we'd both be up early." Sam leaped toward Chandler, who caught him midair and swung him to the floor. "Dogs are like roosters. *Bark-a-doodle-doo!*"

"I don't need a puppy to wake me up. I have you." Chandler opened his closet. But instead of seeing his options to choose for church, he saw Izzy's face after he'd kissed her. There was that brief moment when she'd looked entirely... blissful. *"Crud."*

"What's wrong, Dad?"

Besides Izzy disrupting his every waking moment? "We're going to be late for church. Go shower and get dressed."

Instead of moving, Sam's jaw dropped. "But what about French toast?"

Chandler did a quick calculation. "Breakfast. No shower. Let's move it, cowboy."

And surprisingly, his son did.

"CAN I PUT a pair of bunnies on Christmas layaway?"

"Nope." Izzy was cranky Sunday morning. And Evie Grace wasn't one of her favorite people on the best of days.

"It says you have layaway." Evie pointed to a sign behind Izzy. Her nails were painted red and white like candy canes. Her blond hair was up in a full ponytail tied with a sparkly ribbon that looked like tinsel. She wore skinny jeans and a navy sweater that had a line of dancing elves along the hem and cuffs.

In Izzy's opinion, Evie was the epitome of holiday cuteness and although she hadn't been at the Buckboard, Evie should have been the object of Chandler's kiss last night.

Ugh. Just the thought of Chandler kissing another woman annoyed Izzy on too many levels to track. Add that to Evie's unnecessary request about layaway… And wow. Izzy's annoyance increased exponentially. "Evie, the small print says your purchase needs to be fifty dollars or more. Two baby bunnies aren't going to cost you more than twenty."

Evie huffed. "I suppose I'm going to need a cage. How much is that?"

"A small cage will get you up to forty," Izzy said evenly, and not without some satisfaction. Last year, Evie had tried to win the baking contest at the county fair by buying up all the peaches in the area so no one else could make peach anything, including Allison. A girl had to stick by their friends.

"And with bunny food it will be…?" Evie pouted and waited as if that got her what she wanted, usually.

Izzy did a quick calculation. "A large bag should get you to around sixty." Ten dollars over the minimum for layaway.

Evie rolled her eyes. "I don't want to spend sixty dollars on my nephew for Christmas."

"The bunnies are for Pete?" Izzy liked the boy. His exuberant dancing in the school choir was contagious, always bringing a smile to her face. Pete and his granddad came in most

Sundays after church to buy dog treats for his aging Saint Bernard, during which time Pete talked nonstop.

"Don't you have discount rabbits?" Evie was nothing if not a cheapskate when it came to spending on someone else. Another reason not to like her.

"Only the stuffed rabbits are discounted. Buy two, get one free." Izzy could have left it at that. But it was the Christmas season and Evie was shopping for Pete, after all. "Do you know what he'd really like, Evie? Pete would love one of those big dog toys we have in the pet aisle for your dad's dog, Thurman."

"Double bonus. Dad and Pete." Evie dashed toward the pet aisle to the closing chords of "Grandma Got Run Over by a Reindeer."

"Merry Christmas," Izzy mumbled. She glanced around the store to see where she was needed.

Since Clementine was so small, the feed store stocked a wide variety of goods. On weekdays the store was filled with ranchers needing feed and building supplies. Afternoons and evenings brought parents swinging by for an item or two as they ran other errands. Saturdays and Sundays were for families and shoppers who had a need for something they couldn't find elsewhere. But in December, folks came in on all days and at all hours to find useful gifts.

A few customers were browsing the clothing racks, looking happy to do so unassisted. Earl was helping a sturdy-looking cowboy find a pair of boots that fit his feet and budget. Stephanie Cochran, Chandler's ex, had looped her way around the aisle with the basics in underthings and feminine care. She looked frustrated.

Izzy came out from around the sales counter. "Hey, Stephanie. Can I help you find something?"

"Oh... I..." The tall brunette folded a paper, cheeks pinkening. "Honestly, Izzy. I think I'm going to have to head over to Friar's Creek."

Izzy had always liked Stephanie. She delivered the mail to

downtown businesses during the week and often stopped by for a quick chat or to refill her water bottle.

Sensing a sensitive topic, Izzy came closer to the woman. "Tell me what you're looking for."

Stephanie sighed. "Compression pantyhose."

"Compression pantyhose? Not socks?" Izzy considered other options for Stephanie. "Doc Nabidian would have compression socks for sale at his office. And the drugstore has support pantyhose."

Stephanie shook her head, biting her lower lip. "I've been offered a job that requires compression pantyhose. I was curious as to how much they cost."

Izzy's curiosity was piqued. Compression wear was for athletes, old or sick people and those who flew often. Izzy ran through the possibilities when it came to Stephanie. "Do you have your pilot's license? I heard the crop duster company in town is looking for a pilot." Flying was the only job Izzy could think of that required compression wear.

Stephanie smiled, a joyous, secretive smile. "The job is as a flight attendant," she whispered.

"Oh, wow. Congratulations." But her confession only gave rise to more questions. "Is this at a commuter airport locally?" Although Izzy couldn't think of any nearby.

"Well, I haven't actually accepted yet, so I shouldn't say," Stephanie admitted. "And the list of things I need to buy beforehand is daunting. Not to mention, compression pantyhose sound…"

"Uncomfortable." Izzy nodded, adding quickly, "But safe."

"Right? But… What am I thinking?" Stephanie laughed self-consciously, gesturing toward herself. "Do I look like I'm cut out to be a flight attendant?" She wore a white hoodie, a pair of blue jeans and sneakers. Her brown hair was in a messy ponytail on top of her head. She looked like a mom out running errands.

"Put you in a uniform with those compression hose and you

would absolutely pass as a flight attendant." Izzy didn't mention the hair. She figured Stephanie knew that would have to be spruced up, too.

"You always brighten my day." Stephanie wrapped her arms around Izzy and gave her a warm hug. "Thank you."

It was a quick hug and Izzy ended it by saying, "I think you need to take that list and shop online for this new job of yours."

"I hope I didn't hear the *O* word," Earl called from the boot department, voice carrying over a country version of "Silent Night." "I taught you better than that, Izzy Adams. We can order whatever you need, Stephanie."

"Thanks, Earl but... No, thanks." Stephanie headed toward the door, walking backward. And she walked right into Chandler.

How long had he been standing there?

"Oh. Hey," Stephanie said to him, blushing furiously. "Didn't see you there."

"Hi, Mom. Bye, Mom." Sam raced around Stephanie and toward Izzy. He had on his church clothes. "Is Della-Mae here?"

"Not yet. She was at a sleepover." Izzy adjusted Sam's cowboy hat, which was about to fall off.

When she glanced up, both Chandler and Stephanie were looking their way.

And Chandler's hand was on Stephanie's arm.

IZZY HAD BEEN hugging Steph.

And Izzy had told Stephanie to shop online for *"that new job of yours."*

Chandler had stopped by the feed store at Sam's insistence, telling himself it was best to rip off the bandage and get this first post-kiss meeting over with, never expecting to find Stephanie or overhearing that his ex-wife was leaving town. Talk about adding fuel to an already tense fire.

"Steph." Chandler's hand somehow found his ex-wife's arm without him taking his eyes off the woman he'd kissed last night. "Is there something you need to tell me?" He almost didn't recognize his own voice. It had a cold, defensive quality in it that he hadn't used in years.

*Because of change and uncertainty.*

There was safety in the status quo. But the very wood beneath his cowboy boots felt unsteady.

*Because of potential moves and unforeseen mischief and knee-knocking kisses.*

Admittedly, the latter had been his doing, but the rest... What had gotten into everyone around him? Mom... Sam... Steph... Izzy...

*I have to keep everything under control. I am the rock here.*

The peacekeeper. The problem-solver. The cowboy who was steady in a crisis.

"Nothing's been decided, Chandler." Steph shifted away from him, and Chandler's hand dropped away. "You'll be among the first to know when I make a decision." But she didn't leave.

Chandler spared Stephanie a glance. She was staring toward Sam with her heart in her eyes. With *regret* in her eyes.

She was planning to leave, all right. Chandler's shoulders tensed. Perhaps fittingly, Elvis's "Blue Christmas" began to play over the store's speaker system.

"But Della-Mae told me she'd be here this morning," Sam was saying to Izzy, whining a little. "She told me we'd look at the bulletin board with puppies."

*No.*

"Puppies?" Stephanie breathed the word with animosity. Her attention shifted to Chandler and her mood to anger. "You thought a puppy would make me stay?"

"Nope." Chandler tipped his hat to Steph and then joined Sam in front of Izzy, vaguely registering his ex-wife leaving. "What's this I hear about a puppy board, Sam? Is this one of Della-Mae's *ideas*?"

*"Dad."* Sam tapped his chest. "Puppies are my idea."

Chandler grunted, not believing him. His gaze drifted toward Izzy. He'd been hoping that seeing her in her usual feed store setting and garb—cowboy hat, gray Clementine Feed hoodie, blue jeans and boots—would vanquish his fascination with her.

He took a good long look. Gone were the perky Christmas sweaters and the cheerful, bouncing headbands. No antlers. No jingle-jingle. No garland or tinsel. And yet, he could still feel her kitschy Christmas cheer. He could still feel the near-tangible attraction. He could still feel the magnetic pull of *her.*

*Crud.*

Was it because he knew how she kissed? Or that he wanted to kiss her again? He suspected both were true.

*Double crud.*

Chandler wasn't supposed to be mesmerized by a female at his age. That was a teenage boy's purview. He hadn't searched for this. He hadn't asked for this. Like everything else in his life lately, Izzy made Chandler feel unsure of the outcome. Doubts about the future were why he'd never been a good rodeo competitor. There were too many variables outside his control—a bull with a bee in his bonnet, a steer that zagged when a rope was thrown, a balking horse spooked by a rowdy crowd.

The tension had taken hold of Chandler's neck now, too. He'd worked himself into a snippy mood. Yep, good and proper. And now, he needed something to reverse that mood.

*Kisses?*

He averted his gaze from Izzy, rejecting that notion.

*Puppies?*

He averted his gaze from Sam, rejecting that notion, as well.

"What a good friend you are, Sam." Izzy gave him a candy cane from a Santa mug on the sales counter. "I'm proud of you for admitting puppies were *your* idea."

"Dad always says I'm a good boy." Sam performed a goofy dance, kicking up his heels and waving his candy cane.

"Almost always," Chandler murmured.

"Even good boys get into mischief sometimes." Izzy tipped back her cowboy hat, a grin forming on those delicate features of hers. A grin directed at Chandler, inviting him to let go.

Chandler was focused on Izzy's cowboy hat instead. He couldn't remember her riding a horse, even during Santapalooza. And yet, she always wore a cowboy hat and boots.

Izzy's grin widened. "Sam, aren't you lucky that you're in the same class as your best friend? You'd never want to switch classrooms, would you?"

Chandler's mouth dropped open. Izzy wasn't respecting his wishes. This woman... She... She didn't understand how important it was to keep the peace. She didn't supervise scores of cowboys with erratic pasts and varying levels of ego. She didn't manage hundreds of stock. She didn't realize it was best to head things off at the pass early, to keep everything and everyone on the same even keel.

The number of cowboy terms floating in Chandler's head didn't escape his notice. Cowboying was ingrained in Chandler. *Herd first* when making ranch decisions. *Family first* when making life decisions.

*The cowboy way...*

Perhaps that was why Izzy didn't understand those two kids of theirs needed separation. She lived in town. She worked at a feed store. She may wear cowboy boots and a cowboy hat as if she was familiar with the cowboy way. But she didn't know.

"I am lucky to have my best friend with me all day." Still dancing, Sam beamed up at Izzy as if her opinion mattered most. Her opinion, not Chandler's.

That was the last straw. Chandler couldn't rein in his frustration any longer. "Izzy, have you ever owned a horse?"

"Me?" Izzy's smile fell. Around these parts, questioning someone's Western legitimacy was like tossing down a gauntlet. "I had a horse when I lived with my dad. But he

sold A.J. before he left town. Are you... Are you questioning my cowgirlness?"

"Are you two fighting?" Sam stopped dancing.

"No, honey," Izzy was quick to reassure Chandler's son.
"We're talking about the cowboy code."

"Oh." Sam shifted his cowboy hat to a jaunty angle on his
head. And then, he recited, "Every cowboy needs a hat, a
horse and a dog."

"And an understanding of how to manage a herd," Chandler
said, still frustratingly unsettled because this slip of a woman
had somehow managed to trot into his life, bells ringing, and
upended his quiet, orderly, predictable existence. Even now,
just meeting her unflinching gaze made him want to...want
to...

*Kiss her again. Longer this time.*

Chandler scoffed and shifted his feet on the wide wooden
planks beneath him. *"Cowgirlness."* He frowned. "Is that a
word? Is it from one of those old books you read?"

"Answer my question," Izzy demanded softly, chin rising.
"Are you saying you're more of a cowboy than I am? That just
because I don't currently own a horse that I have no right to
wear cowboy boots and a cowboy hat?"

"You are fighting." Sam righted his cowboy hat. "That's
not good."

"He started it," Izzy murmured.

*"Dad,"* Sam chastised in a big-boy tone of voice. "If you
hurt someone's feelings, you have to say sorry."

"That's very wise," Izzy told Sam. "You must have lots of
friends at school."

Sam bobbed his head. "Sometimes stuff happens that's an
accident. And I always say sorry." His clear brown eyes found
Chandler's. "That's why I have lots and lots of friends. Just
like my dad."

Chandler had been backed into a corner by his own testiness. "I'm sorry," he mumbled, not feeling remorseful but needing to do the right thing when his son was watching.

"You're not sorry," Izzy said, peering at him with those big blue eyes.

Sam gasped. *"Miz Izzy!"* He called her out the same way he did Chandler.

Izzy rushed on to explain. "I mean, your dad is probably sorry if he hurt my feelings, but he looks like someone put too much wood in his fire and he needs to blow some smoke."

Sam looked confused.

Chandler felt humbled. "Well, now I am truly sorry."

Someone came through the front door and said in a small voice, "Hey, everybody."

"Della-Mae!" Sam ran toward the front of the store to greet his bestie, who wore the same red outfit she'd had on yesterday and carried a backpack, sleeping bag and pillow. "I'm here, Della-Mae! And look. My dad's here, too. With your mom."

"All present and accounted for," Izzy said softly enough that only Chandler would hear. "Including the cranky kissing bandit."

Chandler choked on a laugh, dark mood taken down another notch. He was discovering that Izzy had the power to drag him—or prod him—out of his funks.

While the kids were wrestling with Della-Mae's stuff, he leaned over to say to Izzy, "Will you forgive me if I admit that I woke up on the wrong side of the bed this morning? I was confused about what happened last night, and then I walked in to hear my ex-wife talking to you about a job that will take her away from Sam. And I... I let myself get overwhelmed."

"And you got cranky." Izzy tsked, looking like she was fighting a hint of a smile. "When I get overwhelmed, I panic."

"Good to know." Chandler straightened. "Should we start the day over? You can still call me a miserabilist if it makes you feel better."

"My day starts with coffee and chocolate." Izzy waggled her finger. "That's the only way to earn a do-over."

"I'm taking notes," Chandler promised. "Coffee and chocolate." He plucked a bar of chocolate from a nearby display and handed it to her. "My treat."

"You're impossible," Izzy muttered, but she accepted the bar.

Sam towed Izzy's daughter forward, dragging her sleeping bag, which had unrolled, across the floor.

"Are you here to buy something?" Della-Mae asked, looking at Chandler with a tired yet hopeful expression.

"We're here to see you!" Sam crowed in answer, dropping the unrolled sleeping bag and bouncing around like a bunny on a sunny spring day.

"Tone it down, squirt." Chandler scooped up the sleeping bag and began rolling it up neatly.

"What are you here to buy, Mr. Cochran?" Della-Mae asked, less hopefully, looking at her mother this time.

Chandler's mischief radar kicked on. There was something going on here. He studied the faces of the two kids, searching for clues the way he did when something hinky was going on with his ranch hands.

"What's this all about, bug?" Izzy asked, kneeling in front of Della-Mae, perhaps having suspicions of her own.

Della-Mae stared at Chandler over Izzy's shoulder, lower lip starting a pout.

"Just say it, Dad." Sam tugged on Chandler's hand. "Tell Della-Mae why we came."

"To see you," he said in a gruff voice, barely stopping himself from saying it like it was a guess. But it was.

Della-Mae threw herself into Izzy's arms. And then she hugged Chandler's leg and said, "Merry Christmas, Mr. Cochran!"

Chandler's gaze sought out Izzy's, looking for answers.

She shrugged, apparently having none. And before he could interrogate the kids, they were interrupted.

"Hey, Izzy. Can you ring up Kevin's boots?" Earl dropped a boot box on the sales counter. The old man wore a black denim vest with the Clementine Feed logo over his blue flannel shirt. He tipped his black porkpie hat at the young boot buyer. "Thanks for coming in." He clapped his hands and caught the children's attention. "While Izzy rings him up, I'll show the kids the puppy board."

"Puppies," Chandler murmured. And then he plucked Sam's small cowboy hat off his head. "Do we really need one, Sam?"

*"Dad..."* Sam didn't qualify the issue. He simply took back his hat.

Evie Grace stepped into line behind Kevin, holding a large blue dog toy.

"Earl..." Izzy picked up her daughter's sleepover stuff, then returned to her position behind the register. She smiled brightly at the cowboy purchasing boots, but her words were for her boss. "Earl, I'm not getting a dog."

"Me, either," Chandler echoed.

"Every cowboy needs a horse and a dog," Earl said in a preachy tone. "Along with boots and a hat. Everybody knows that's a law in Oklahoma."

"If that were true..." Izzy scoffed, catching Chandler's gaze. "It must be why Chandler doubted my cowgirlness."

"I deserved that," Chandler admitted, trailing after the kids.

"You certainly did," Izzy said tartly but with a hint of a tease.

Chandler followed Earl and the kids into the room behind the sales counter, which was the break room. There was an office on one side with a desk cluttered with papers. A glass-paned door revealed the large warehouse crammed with goods—bags of feed, bales of hay, red-and-white metal posts, stacks of boxes and rolls of wire.

"Folks from around these parts email us their puppy litter

pictures." Earl's hair was going white and his shoulders were bent with age, but his voice was as steely as ever. "We print them out and tack them up here. They bring the staff joy."

"And puppies presumably," Chandler said under his breath, earning a dark look from Earl.

The break room smelled of green hay and popcorn. There was an old oak table in the middle with four ladder-back chairs. The floor was clean, and the light was bright. A bulletin board was hung on the wall next to a nearly full coffeepot.

Smelling fresh brew, Chandler poured himself a cup while the kids perused the board.

"Mr. Earl, we're looking for a puppy family." Sam pushed a chair over to the board and then climbed upon it.

"A brother and sister, Uncle Earl," Della-Mae clarified, lifting her arms to Chandler...kid speak for *pick me up.*

Chandler set his coffee mug down and lifted her to his hip. "We're just window-shopping, Earl."

"It's Christmas," Earl grumbled. "Are you or aren't you a cowboy in need of a dog?"

"He's a cowboy." Della-Mae poked Chandler's chest. Then she leaned over and patted Sam's hat crown, trusting Chandler not to drop her. "And he's a cowboy. And someday, I'll be a cowboy, too." She slung her little arm around his shoulders.

"Cowgirl," Chandler corrected. His heart warmed. No matter how he wished otherwise, Della-Mae didn't seem like the instigator of school mischief, not that he'd admit it to Izzy so quickly.

"What about me?" Earl asked Della-Mae in the gentlest tone Chandler had ever heard him use.

"And you're a cowboy, too." Della-Mae reached over to pat his gray-stubbled cheeks with both hands. "Even though your horse is retired, Gator crossed the rainbow bridge and you wear a funny hat."

"Do you have kids, Earl?" Sam studied the old man from head to toe.

"I've got Izzy and Della-Mae," Earl said by way of answering. "They're going to run the feed store one day."

"Mama and me run it already," Della-Mae showed a little sass that her mother would probably be tickled to see. "I feed all the baby chicks and bunnies. And Mama does everything else."

"I suppose you're right," Earl told her with a wink. And then he fixed Chandler with a threatening look. "But I'll deny it if you tell anyone else in town. I've got my pride, you know."

"Dad won't tell no one," Sam promised.

"Cuz he likes Mama." Della-Mae hugged Chandler.

And darned if Chandler's heart didn't melt again. So much so that he felt a reluctance to refuse Della-Mae anything. And she wasn't even his kid!

Earl harumphed in a way that could only be taken as disapproval over Chandler's liking of Izzy.

And even though Chandler didn't want to like Izzy, he resented Earl's reaction.

With one last disapproving look at Chandler, the old man cleared his throat. "Back to the business at hand, folks. And that's—"

"Puppies!" the kids cried.

"Yes, sirree. There's a litter of terrier puppies over in Friar's Creek." Earl pointed to a picture of scruffy little brown pups tumbling across green grass.

"That's what ranchers call a coyote snack," Chandler stated as the kids cooed over the pups and their cuteness.

Earl scowled at Chandler, but allowed, "Point taken. We need something bigger."

Sam gasped, slapping his hand on a picture of roly-poly puppies. "Are these Labradors?"

"The doodly kind." Earl nodded, rubbing a hand over gray stubble. "Pricey, if you ask me. Are you allergic to pet dander?"

"What's that?" Sam asked.

"He's not." Chandler adopted his most serious expression. "But we're just looking."

"My Della-Mae isn't allergic, either," Earl said, taking the girl from Chandler. "I'm partial to a hunting dog, though."

"We don't hunt," Chandler grumbled.

"Hunting dogs are smart. Short-haired don't shed a blanket of hair every week," Earl continued. "Got this picture of some German shorthair pups from a breeder just over the county line. What do you think, sweet thing?" he asked Della-Mae.

She examined the picture with a serious expression while twirling a lock of white-blond hair. "Do they have girl pups?"

"Might," Earl said.

"What about boys?" Sam leaned in for a close look, practically pressing his nose on the picture.

"Might," Earl repeated.

"Are they free?" Chandler wondered aloud, thinking of Izzy saving for her daughter's fancy bed.

Sam gasped, turning on the chair and losing his balance. He would have fallen if not for Chandler grabbing hold of his arm. "Dad, can we have a puppy if it's free?"

"Now isn't the right time of year to bring a pup home." Chandler tried to evade, shifting his feet on the old floorboards. "They say puppies are more likely to be hurt at Christmas, choking on chewed bows and glass ornaments because they don't know any better."

"Even the Grinch had a dog." Frowning, Earl pointed out another photograph. "Here are some cocker spaniels."

"They look like Lady," Della-Mae whispered. "I love that movie. Lady falls in love with the Tramp."

Sam didn't look impressed, possibly because his taste in movies ran more toward cartoon superheroes.

"Earl." Izzy stuck her head in the break room. "No dogs."

"Amen," Chandler echoed.

"Oh, man." Sam looked at Della-Mae. "We're in trouble. What moms say goes." And Izzy wasn't even his mother.

"Have a heart, Izzy," Earl called toward the now-closed door. "We could use a dog at the feed store."

"A pretty dog?" Della-Mae asked sweetly.

"Any kind of dog you want, Della-Mae." Earl chuckled. "We'll find the right dog for you. Just don't tell your mother I said that."

Sam set his finger on the picture of Labradoodle puppies, then pouted at Chandler. "If Della-Mae gets a puppy, I want one, too."

A SMALL, FAMILIAR body took hold of Izzy's leg as she was helping Dix Youngblood select outdoor extension cords.

"Mama. Mr. Cochran said no to Lady and Tramp. But Uncle Earl said—"

"Bug, I told you we aren't getting a dog. We have chickens." She gave Dix an apologetic smile. "Do you need anything else, Dix? Replacement light bulbs? Maybe a star made of lights for your front window?"

"Just the extension cords." Dix knelt to her daughter's level. "Don't give up on a puppy, Della-Mae. Santa Claus is coming to town."

"But I didn't ask Santa for a puppy," Della-Mae moaned.

"What did you ask for?" Izzy was curious but her daughter pressed her lips together and ran toward the back of the store.

Dix stood, grinning. "Now, Izzy. You know that requests for Santa are secret."

"Thanks, Dix," Izzy said dryly. "But that works both ways. Better watch out if you bring your littles into the store. I may show them the adorable baby bunnies." She rang him up and sent him on his way, nose still bent out of shape. *"Puppies."*

Della-Mae and Sam were playing checkers at the small table behind the sales counter, debating the merits of different pups, as if they were indeed getting a pair.

"Izzy, can I talk to you?" Chandler had been leaning against the wall near the break room while she was busy with Dix.

He pushed away, staring at her in that manner of his that she couldn't read.

Apprehension skittered through Izzy's veins as if she was the one who didn't like surprises, not Chandler. She needed to draw some boundaries. There would be no more kisses. She was banning them along with puppies.

"Why are you still here? I'm working," Izzy told Chandler, moving into the boot department and away from their kids. "If you placed a call asking about puppy availability, I'm going to go all Scrooge on you."

"This isn't about puppies." His gaze grazed her mouth.

And suddenly, the powerful kiss they'd shared the night before was top-of-mind. Izzy lost some of her bluster. *Evade. Evade.* And tried to emotionally regroup. Her chin came up. "Do you finally agree with me that the kids shouldn't be separated at school?"

Chandler shook his head. "Earlier... When we came in... Stephanie was saying something to you about a new job?" He wasn't looking Izzy in the eye. He straightened out a display of boots.

Chandler wanted to know about his ex-wife? Not their kiss? That was a relief, although Izzy wasn't going to blab.

"Chandler..." Izzy began. "If you have questions and you're feeling overwhelmed, you should ask Stephanie. She was excited and seemed like she really wanted to talk to someone about her job."

He gave a barely perceptible nod.

"Izzy, do we have any inflatable Santas left in the back room?" Earl called from the front of the store.

"We're sold out," she called back. "We still have abominable snowmen, though." And then she placed a hand on Chandler's arm, just a brief touch before his gaze moved to it. She removed her hand and took a step back. "I know you're not a chatterbox. But I imagine you're a good listener. Listen to her."

Actually, that was Izzy's new hope—that Chandler preferred listening to speaking. A talker would ask about that kiss. Over and over until he got answers. And the last thing Izzy wanted to do was talk that through. She couldn't even think it through on her own. How was she supposed to put it into words?

"I did listen to her." Chandler straightened more boots on display. "She told me she was thinking about taking a job in Texas. And…" His gaze drifted in the direction of his son. "If she took the job in Texas, does that mean she wants to take Sam, too? In which case, I need to assert my parental rights. Or is she taking the job and leaving Sam behind, in which case… He'll be crushed."

*The way I was when Dad left me. And I was an adult.*

"I'm sorry. I hadn't realized the implications to Sam," Izzy said sympathetically. For a man who didn't like change, Stephanie's decisions had a huge impact on Chandler. "No wonder you're worried. If you ever want to talk, I'm good at listening."

Chandler glanced at her hand on his arm again.

Izzy quickly removed it. "How did that get there?"

"That's what I wondered, too…" Chandler murmured, gaze moving from his hands to Izzy's lips. "…when *I* kissed you."

"Oh, no. You're not allowed to take the blame." Izzy back-pedaled, practically leaping away from him and toward the corner of the store.

Chandler matched her step-for-step, a smile growing on that attractive face. "Maybe we're both to blame."

Izzy scoffed, coming to a stop with her back to a display of hat and boot bands. She grabbed a leather hatband with a peacock feather decoration, holding it in front of her like a shield. Although that might have been hypocritical because she was taking inventory of Chandler's lips.

He had a wide mouth, well-suited for smiling. And he was clean-shaven, well-suited for prolonged kisses. And unlike other times he'd been in the feed store, he wasn't looking distant and distracted.

*It's been a long time since a man has looked at me like that.*

"Dad, I'm hungry," Sam called.

"Me, too," Mae seconded.

"Me, three," Chandler said softly, although it was clear to Izzy that he wasn't hungry for food but for kisses.

Izzy couldn't catch her breath.

"Dad?"

"Mama?"

Chandler took the hatband from Izzy and returned it to the display. "There's something going on between us but…" He looked deep into her eyes. "…I'm not looking for something."

"Me, either," Izzy wheezed.

Chandler turned and walked away.

But she was afraid whatever this was between them wasn't over yet.

# *CHAPTER TEN*

"UNCLE CHANDLER, we have to stop at Clementine Coffee Roasters for hot chocolate," Ginny said from the back seat of Chandler's truck on Monday after school. "I have coupons. Buy one hot chocolate and get one free. That covers me and Sam. Right, buddy?"

"Right," Sam piped up.

Chandler was hoping to head back to the ranch to work on the new year's rodeo schedule. Requests were already coming in from rodeos to provide them with stock for their events. It was a balancing act since Chandler had to make sure he didn't overpromise and be short on bucking bulls or roping steers or underbook and have stock sitting idle.

Chandler inched forward in the slow-moving pickup line without seeing Izzy's blue-gray SUV, either in front of him or behind him.

*Not that I'm looking.*

After seeing Izzy at the feed store yesterday and confessing that he felt something pulling him into her orbit, and also stating that he was going to resist that pull, Chandler planned to give the woman a wide berth.

If only he didn't keep having conversations with her in his head.

*I'm going to a rodeo in Denver this spring. The wildflowers will be in bloom. Have you ever seen them? Would you like to?*

Romantic nonsense. Chandler had better things to do with his brain cells than to think about Izzy.

"Can we stop, Dad?" Sam sat behind Chandler, repeatedly tossing his cowboy hat to the ceiling. "I heard a lot of kids are going to use their coupons."

"Which means it's going to be crowded and take a long time." The Grinch was back, sitting on Chandler's shoulder.

*What would Izzy think of me ixnaying hot cocoa?*

*"You're something, all right," she'd told him Saturday.*

For his own peace of mind, Chandler had to get Izzy out of his head.

Chandler sighed. "I suppose since you didn't get called into the principal's office today that we can stop for hot chocolate."

"Yay!" Sam cried, high-fiving Ginny. And then he tossed his cowboy hat too enthusiastically. It bumped against Chandler's hat and then ricocheted into the front seat. "Oops. Sorry, Dad."

"Not cool or safe." Chandler made the turn toward the center of town, not looking for a blue-gray SUV or white-blond hair with antlers floating above. "Now, just so we're clear. We're not staying to drink our hot chocolate. It's to-go." The stress of scheduling pressed on him but he'd give the kids this special treat.

Chandler found a parking spot on the street a block away. "Sam, cowboy hats aren't for tossing," he told his son before plopping the stray hat back on Sam's head.

Sam pulled down the brim on either side of his ears. "My hat is for everything."

"Your hat will be in the trash bin if you don't take care of it." Ginny gently pried Sam's hands clear. "My dad says cowboy hats don't grow on trees."

Chandler chuckled. "He told you that after yours was chewed on by those goats, Ginny."

"There was nothing left!" Ginny settled her straw cowboy hat more firmly over her brown braids. And then she stuffed her hands back into her pink puffy vest, which was the same color as her pink boots. "A cowgirl has to have a hat."

Sam made a go of jumping over all the cracks in the sidewalk. "I'm so glad Ginny had a cocoa coupon."

"I got them from Mom." Ginny slowed to check out the merchandise in the local boutique's window.

There were lots of holiday doodads on display, including a snow globe with a music box base, which made Chandler want to think of Izzy. But he refused to think of Izzy.

Even when Sam asked, "Can we get a Christmas tree today?"

Nope. Chandler did not think of Izzy.

*Because I'm a man in control of my own destiny.*

"This week is kind of busy, squirt," Chandler told Sam, thinking that at some point, he'd have to pull himself out of the divorce funk, haul up his anchor and put up Christmas at the house. "We'll do it soon."

"That's what my dad says when he doesn't want to do something ever," Ginny quipped. "I could decorate for you, Uncle Chandler. Me and Mama Ronnie already put up our decorations."

"That's kind of you to offer, but no thanks."

"You could pay me." Ginny was just as industrious as Ronnie. Or Izzy for that matter. "Mama Ronnie said I'm old enough to babysit and get paid for doing other stuff, too."

"I bet you are, but I've got to clean and move furniture around first," Chandler said.

"I could clean," Sam said, stepping over Ginny trying to say the same thing.

"It's just something I've got to do myself," Chandler said, more firmly this time.

The two kids looked at each other and exchanged shrugs. They were too young to understand that it was the past holding Chandler back, not cleaning or furniture moving. Still, his reluctance to leap into Christmas with an eager embrace made him feel sullen. Something had to be done. And he was the only one able to do it.

When they reached the coffee shop, Chandler opened the door to let the kids in first, and spotted Izzy, Christmas personified, in line with her daughter.

*I've been set up. By two kids, no less.*

But Chandler didn't feel as grumpy and stressed for time as he had a minute ago.

He'd like to attribute that to the wreath with bells on the front door or the decorated Christmas tree by the front window. But he was afraid that he knew the truth behind this cheerier mood.

And his truth had hair the color of tinsel.

"Della-Mae!" Sam sprinted to the little girl's side, as much as a gangly boy in cowboy boots could sprint. "We're here, too!"

The pair hugged. Ginny joined them in line, laughing and whispering, as if she was in on the joke.

Chandler mostly ignored them. He drank in Christmas Izzy. She'd changed out of the feed store garb he'd seen her in this morning. Now, she wore gray jeans beneath a red-and-white-striped sweater, topped with red-and-white-striped earmuffs, currently hanging around her neck. "Miss Candy Cane, fancy meeting you here."

Izzy wore a quizzical expression where he'd come to expect a smile.

"Did you have a coupon for a free hot chocolate, too?" Chandler asked, giving Ginny—who was clearly up to something—a stern look.

Course, it couldn't be too stern of a look.

Chandler didn't go telling the world, but he was fond of candy canes, especially life-size ones. That may have explained why his stern expression had been broken apart by what felt like a broad smile. For Izzy.

"We have a coupon, too," Izzy confirmed. She glanced at Sam and Della-Mae. "Did you two plan this?"

"No," the younger kids chorused innocently.

But Ginny... Ginny didn't wear guilty well. She blushed furiously.

"Yep, there's nothing for it, I guess, but to..." Chandler glanced toward the exit, hoping to make the kids suffer a little by making them think they were leaving empty-handed. And then he tilted the brim of his cowboy hat back and grinned. "There's nothing for it but to get our hot cocoas."

The kids cheered.

And truth be told, Chandler was cheering a little inside, too. So much so, that he allowed himself to be talked into drinking their hot chocolate with Izzy and Della-Mae instead of taking it to go.


"WHY ARE WE sitting at this little table *alone*?" Izzy asked Chandler, torn between enjoying herself and being a grump because there was matchmaking in the air but no Ronnie around to blame it on. "And why are the kids sitting way up at the front without us?"

"We're suckers." Chandler shrugged, but he was smiling a smidge, like a man who'd surrendered to his fate and found it wasn't horrible. "Didn't you take a good look at those drink coupons? On the bottom, mine said, '*Complements of Ronnie Keller, Matchmaker.*'"

"You think this was Ronnie's doing?" Izzy tossed and turned that idea around in her head for a minute, staring into Chandler's warm brown eyes as if she had a right to. "Did *you* hire Ronnie?"

"Me?" Chandler chuckled. "I did not. And I can't imagine you did, either. You'd have told me this morning when I picked up my feed order if you'd hired her. I hear her clients go out of their way to make small talk."

"So your theory about the drink coupons is…"

"Oh, Ginny took them. No question." Chandler glanced at the kids as the opening verse of "The Twelve Days of Christmas" filled the coffee shop.

"Have you ever sung this song?" Izzy wondered aloud.

He quirked a brow. "What kid hasn't belted out the five golden rings part?"

"There are eleven more gifts to sing about."

"No one remembers gifts seven through ten." Chandler slowly spun his hot chocolate cup. "I bet you another kiss that our kids will sing the line about the gold rings in a minute. And *only* the line about those gold rings."

What a tempting bet. Izzy chewed her lip. "Are you…?" She leaned forward, filled with suspicion. "Are you sure Ronnie didn't put you up to this?"

"Ronnie has nothing to do with this conversation and…" Chandler held a finger in the air and sang along with every kid in the room, *"Five gold-en rings!"*

He had a strong singing voice. Deep and rich. And that smile…

"You owe me a kiss," Chandler whispered, smiling in a way that made kissing him seem as natural as breathing.

"I never agreed…" Izzy trailed off when Chandler laughed. She slapped a hand on her forehead.

He laughed some more.

"That's not fair." She was the one trying to come out of her shell and here Chandler was *outshelling* her. A week ago, she'd never have imagined him laughing so freely with her, singing in a place that wasn't church or kissing a woman he barely knew with complete and utter abandon.

Izzy tugged at the neck of her candy-cane-striped sweater and tried to make small talk. "I decorated Harper Dye's place before picking up Mae from school today. Harper is going through a Christmas gnome phase. But she hasn't quite let go of her white turtledove phase. I think we hit the right balance in her living room."

"Of gnomes and turtledoves?" None of the amusement had drained from his face.

She nodded, still fighting the urge to accept his kisses in her future. Kisses—plural—promised things. Dates—casual, formal, legal. A Saturday night dinner, a big wedding, a wedding certificate. Izzy shook her head at her thoughts. "How was your day?"

"We're tabling bets?"

"Yes," she said nervously, still thrown by thoughts of dates and marriage.

"Okay. I'll play along," Chandler capitulated. "I've got a crick in my neck from bending over the computer." Chandler rubbed a hand around the back of his neck. "I was trying to figure out the schedule for the new year, but Dad kept interrupting me."

"Earl does the same when I'm trying to manage our inventory." Izzy sipped her hot chocolate.

*"Five golden rings!"* the kids chorused.

"You missed that one," Izzy couldn't resist teasing Chandler.

"I was thinking about..." Chandler stared into her eyes without speaking, as if he'd lost his train of thought. "Truth be told, I was thinking about checking in with Ronnie when I got back to the ranch. And that made me think of Wade, who's flying out tomorrow to compete at the national championships in Las Vegas. And that reminded me to check in with our ranch hands who're transporting a couple of our bulls to that competition. And that had me wondering how I was going to have time to work rodeos in person next year if Stephanie takes that job and I have custody of Sam every week." He sat back with a defeated sigh.

And here Izzy had imagined he'd been lost in romantic

thoughts about her. Not that having a romance with him was her goal, far from it. But this was a reality check.

Izzy reached for her sense of humor. "That sounds like what goes on in my head. But it's more like… Shoot, Mae has a stain on her leggings. Am I out of laundry detergent? I should probably stock up. And speaking of stocking up, did I remember to place an order for summer bulbs at the feed store? Those always sell out quickly, just like Christmas merchandise. Which reminds me that I haven't ordered a fruit and nut basket to send to my father and stepmother this Christmas. And I should put in a request for a babysitter the Saturday before Christmas for girls' night out. But shoot… Mae has a stain on her leggings."

*"Five golden rings!"* the kids and Chandler chorused.

Izzy and Chandler shared a laugh, a laugh with everyone in the coffee shop actually.

"And here I thought I was the only one carrying too many responsibilities to think straight." Chandler's gaze was warm, but also tender.

*The way he looks at me…*

*It probably doesn't mean what I think it means.*

"We're having a normal conversation." Izzy picked up her hot chocolate cup. "Did you notice?"

"Yep. No disagreements about where ornaments, trees or lights usually go." Chandler smiled.

"No discussion about separating our kids in school." Izzy nodded. "You know what this means."

"I do *not*." Chandler set his cup aside, expression turning serious.

"It means that we're becoming friends." As soon as Izzy spoke the words, she knew this was true. She leaned forward and whispered, "We don't need to be something more."

Chandler opened his mouth but said nothing.

*"Five golden rings,"* the kids and Chandler chorused along to the music, creating another cascade of laughter afterward.

"We'll be fine like this," Izzy went on, reassuring herself.

Chandler tapped his finger on top of his cup, keeping time to the music. "Are you coming out to the ranch later?"

"Yes." Izzy noticed Chandler changed the subject. That was a tactic they both used when they wanted to avoid the sticky conversations.

He continued tapping his cocoa cup. "Maybe you could... help me put up lights or decorations at my house."

"Outside or inside?" Izzy held her breath, thinking about how Mary had told her Chandler hadn't put up any Christmas anything since his divorce.

Chandler's gaze roamed toward the kids. "Inside? Sam's been wanting a tree."

"Do you need me to buy a tree for you?" She had for some of her older clients.

Chandler frowned, attention coming back to her. "No. That's something Sam and I should do together."

*He's a good man.*

But Izzy wasn't in the market for one. Christmas would be here before she knew it and she had to use every spare minute to earn money for Mae's Christmas gift. She couldn't afford to be distracted by Chandler.

"I suppose if I want you to help me today, I've got to buy a tree now." How Chandler-like. The Chandler that she used to know. Stoic. Businesslike. Pragmatic.

Izzy laughed. "Well, Mr. Grinch, if it's Christmas that's gotta be done, you wouldn't want to make it fun, would you?"

"So, you'll help me?"

"Just today." Izzy nodded. She had time. And she wouldn't accept payment. Sam would be overjoyed.

"There's just one thing we need to agree on, though," Chandler said slowly, pausing to join the kids to sing, *"Five golden rings."*

"Oh, here we go." Izzy sat back in her chair and crossed

her arms over her chest. "Is this about the bet you offered me earlier? The one I didn't agree to?"

"Not that... It's two things, really," Chandler allowed. "First, we decorate my way."

Izzy might have been slower than usual to nod her agreement. She was Team Mary first, after all, when it came to shaking things up at the ranch. Any decor at all was a win. "And second?"

"And second, I'm not sure this *something* between us is going to hit Pause in the friend zone." At Izzy's gasp, he added, "We'll either be *something* to each other or we won't be *anything* to each other."

Izzy didn't answer.

She didn't want to admit that he might be right.

"CHANDLER, ARE YOU ready for me?" Izzy called across the dark ranch yard near dinnertime. The sun had set. She carried a large cardboard box.

The bright Christmas lights and colorful yard decorations lit her way from the main house to Chandler's. Although with her candy cane sweater and white-blond hair, she looked like she could be a part of the cheerful display.

And Chandler might have been cheered to see her if he hadn't been suspicious of the box she carried. "Did my mother send you over here with decorations?"

"She did." Izzy came into the glow of the lights Zane and Ryan had hung around Chandler's front porch earlier that afternoon.

"I thought we agreed that we'd do things my way." Chandler took the box from Izzy. "These aren't my decorations."

"Mary didn't think you had enough." Izzy had her sights on that box Chandler was holding. She should have been concerned about the cold. She wasn't wearing a jacket, just that candy-cane-striped sweater. And the temperature was quickly dropping below fifty. "We don't have to open the box if you have sufficient decorations at your place."

"Sufficient?" Chandler rolled his eyes toward the white twinkling lights outlining his front porch. "Why do I get the impression that your idea of sufficient and my idea of sufficient when it comes to holiday baubles aren't the same?"

"Because you're one smart cowboy."

Chandler grunted. "Now you're just trying to butter me up."

"Is it working?" She grinned. And even though she wasn't wearing any bells, Chandler thought he heard the soft jingle-jangle of sleigh bells.

"Is it working?" Chandler echoed, thinking about all the undone tasks on his to-do list.

Instead of working on the rodeo stock schedule for the new year, Chandler had bought the first tree Sam chose, put the Christmas tree in a stand in the living room and done a quick clean of the house. Not that his house wasn't always orderly and relatively dirt-and dust-free. It just hadn't been giving a guest-cleaning recently. And while he'd cleaned, Chandler had fretted about the work he wasn't doing, wondered how Izzy would see his house and chastised himself for throwing down the relationship gauntlet at the coffee shop.

*We'll either be something to each other or we won't be anything to each other.*

*Izzy probably thinks I'm a pompous jerk.*

And that bet about the kids singing *five golden rings...*

She hadn't taken him up on it. And he'd brought up his reward.

*Again, jerk.*

"Is something else bothering you?" Izzy seemed to have switched tactics. She'd apparently given up on reclaiming the box of decorations and was inching toward his front door.

"Something else is always bothering me." The workload. His ex-wife's plans and intentions. Keeping Sam happy and well-behaved. And Izzy... She'd recently taken up too much of his mental space and he wasn't the better for giving in earlier today to spend time with her when she very clearly wanted to park him in the friend zone. "But if you must know, I promised Dad I'd go with him tomorrow to check out some livestock."

"Which meant you were trying to do double your work managing the ranch today." Izzy nodded, hand reaching for his doorknob. "And now, you can't catch up tonight because of Christmas frivolity. Is that what you're thinking?"

Without answering, Chandler eased over to block Izzy's easy entry. Truth be told, he'd had second—and third— thoughts about her coming inside. "At least there's one place where we're on the same page."

Izzy's brow quirked. "You don't want me inside your house."

"Correct. It seems like an important step." Chandler hesitated before pushing on. "And since we don't know what to do with each other, I'm not sure I want to open myself up to your judgment."

"Is that what you think I'd do?" She crossed her arms over her candy-cane-striped chest. "Explain yourself, cowboy."

Chandler drew a deep breath. "When I see a cowboy and his horse, it gives me a good idea of who he is."

"Really." Izzy gestured for him to continue.

"Is his tack well taken care of? Is his horse well-behaved? Does he respect his livestock?"

Her brow was wrinkled. "Did I judge Harper Dye for her gnome and turtledove obsessions? I think not."

She had him there. He opted for honesty. "I don't really know what message my house gives off. No one's been inside except Sam and my parents since Stephanie moved out."

Izzy nodded slowly. "And you prioritize taking care of this ranch and others more than you do sprucing up the place where you lay your head at night."

"Exactly."

"Ah." Understanding dawned in her pretty blue eyes. "You're like Earl. Utilitarian."

"Earl?" The stooped-shouldered, white-haired, slow and crotchety old man who owned the feed store. "You're likening me to Earl?" Chandler's ego was bruised.

"It sounds as if you're just like Earl." Izzy was nodding, moving closer to him and the door as she warmed to her topic. "Let me assure you that Earl has nothing on his walls. No throw pillows on the sofa. No guest soaps in the bathroom. And do you know what? I don't feel any different about Earl. He's a smart businessman with a big heart. When my dad left town after I graduated high school, Earl offered me a chance to turn a part-time job into full-time work. Plus, he let me rent out the studio apartment over the office." She glossed over what was surely a rough time in her life.

And that made him like her all the more.

"He's good people," Izzy said matter-of-factly. "And guess what? You're good people, too. Why does it matter if you've only got the basics inside your living space?"

He'd run out of excuses.

"Don't say I didn't warn you." Chandler nodded toward the door. "Let's go in." And if she was turned off by what she found, this *will they, won't they* feeling might hit a hard stop.

A small, foolish part of him pulled for *will they.*

They entered his house.

"You need a wreath outside on the front door," Izzy said, almost like an afterthought.

Chandler reluctantly agreed, setting the box of decorations down on the entry bench. They removed their boots before going any farther. Standing next to Izzy in his socks in his home felt somehow…intimate. But then his gaze went to the visible parts of the house—the couch almost completely blocking the entry, the bare walls, the sparse collection of mismatched furniture. It was definitely a bachelor pad, furnished with castoffs.

Izzy didn't pull a face or make a quick exit. She moved slowly inside, inching around the too-large couch. "The tree has got to be in front of the big window facing the ranch yard. You should have something Christmassy that Sam can play with in the living room, like Mary's village."

"A train set? But isn't that a little much? It's just me most of the time."

"Sam is seven." Back to Chandler, she ran her fingers along the Christmas tree branches. "Christmas is still magical to him. A train would create a wonderful memory for him." She turned to the fireplace. "And you should have candles on the mantel with some garland woven in, plus a Christmas blanket on the couch."

"I'm surprised you didn't say I needed Christmas throw pillows." Chandler kept his distance from Izzy, standing behind the couch, still in the foyer.

"Christmas should be comfortable for you, too." Izzy turned and removed her candy-cane-striped earmuffs, hanging them around her neck the way she had at the coffee shop. "I like pillows but if you don't…" She shrugged. "And then stockings on the mantel, of course."

Chandler was still dwelling on Izzy liking Christmas throw pillows. It took a moment for her last words about stockings to sink in. "Stephanie does the stockings with Sam on Christmas morning. And Mom fills one for me at the main house."

Izzy studied him. "That doesn't mean you shouldn't hang some stockings in here for both of you. Remember what you told me about Mary making Christmas special for you. You can make Christmas special for you and Sam. What I saw in your eyes when you talked about Christmas that day told me it was important to you."

"Like what might be ahead for us," Chandler murmured.

That something between us.

With a guarded expression, Izzy moved into the dining room where three small cardboard boxes of Christmas decorations sat on the table. "A tablecloth and some kind of holiday centerpiece would liven this up."

Chandler followed her, drawn as if connected by a string. "Why? We don't use the dining room at all."

Izzy gave him a questioning look. "Don't tell me you eat in the living room all the time?"

"Most of the time we eat at the main house." She was making him reevaluate his parenting style and his bachelor habit of eating in the kitchen standing up.

"Forgive me. I'm not here to judge." Izzy moved on to the kitchen. "You might hang a pine garland between these rooms. Mary has some plastic ones you could use. A Christmas cactus on the counter over there would bring some festiveness into your kitchen. And maybe a holiday dish towel if you can stand it." Before Chandler could stop Izzy, she was marching down the hallway.

"The rest of the house doesn't need holiday cheer." Chandler hurried after her, heart pounding. She wasn't going to go into his bedroom... Was she?

"Really? Mae and I each have little Christmas trees in our bedrooms. As for the bathrooms—"

"That's Mae and you. Sam and I—"

"He's going to love a little tree in his man cave. You can get some twinkle lights and let him put whatever he wants in the branches." She smiled at Chandler the way he liked, easy and unguarded. "When spring comes, you can plant it in a bigger pot outside so that you can use it again next Christmas."

This was all new territory to Chandler. "Is that what you do?" He wasn't even sure if that's what Stephanie did.

Izzy nodded. "We've replanted our little trees twice since we got them. They were almost too heavy to bring in this year." She glanced around Sam's room. "Do you know what else you're missing? An advent calendar. Kids love those, especially the ones with chocolate. We still have a few at the feed store. I can set one aside for you."

"Sam isn't here every day." Chandler rubbed his neck. "I mean, he might be if things change and..."

"He'll happily eat the chocolate on the days he misses." Izzy seemed to sense she'd waded into uncertain waters. She moved passed Chandler, headed toward the living room. "What are you getting Sam for Christmas?"

"There's a mini-quad in the ranch garage. It doesn't go very fast."

"He'll love that." Izzy chuckled. "And frankly, I love that you aren't getting him a puppy." She leaned against his couch, gaze roaming the room once more. "Mae would never let me hear the end of it."

"Are you sure Earl isn't giving Mae a puppy?"

"You called her Mae." Izzy smiled, blinking watery eyes. "Twice since we've been in here."

"Seemed natural, I guess." Chandler leaned against a bare wall, hands behind his back so he wouldn't reach for Izzy. "Is it okay that I do?"

"I… I'd like that." Izzy smiled. But it was a careful smile. "And here we are again. Dancing around *something*."

Chandler nodded. He felt it, too.

"Or maybe we're dancing around the furniture in this room." Izzy looked from one end to the other. "It's laid out weird. There's no flow. You can't walk inside and directly into the hall or the dining room. There's no space for that Christmas tree. Where it is now, if you light a fire in the fireplace, you might start a fire. Did you lay it out this way on purpose? Or leave it the way the previous foreman did?"

"I arranged it like this." Chandler wobbled gently against the wall, which was probably because he wasn't sitting. If he was sitting, his knee would have been bouncing.

"So…you…like it this way?" Izzy's gaze fell on him, causing what felt like a significant *ka-thump* inside his chest.

"Yes." Chandler rubbed a hand over his chest. *This.* This was where he should stop. Instead, he said, "Like this."

Izzy opened her mouth, closed it, and then said, "You wouldn't like it better if we rearranged it?"

"No."

"Why not?" Izzy took a few steps until she stood in front of Chandler. She touched his arm, something she'd done frequently over the past few days, a connection she barely seemed aware of making. "You don't have to tell me, but I'll ask again. You're so utilitarian. Why would you keep your furniture arranged in a way that slows you down?"

*I don't have to tell her. I can change the subject.*

Relief unstuck the shoulders Chandler hadn't realized were approaching his ears. But what she was offering...not having to tell her... It was an easy out. And yet...

"I do have to tell you." He had to tell someone. And he'd never told Stephanie. "My dad was a drinker. He used to tell my mom that he could handle it." Chandler rolled his shoulders back. "And maybe he could. He showed up to work every day on time. Didn't drink a drop while on duty as a construction worker." Or so he'd claimed. "But come five o'clock, it was time to hit the bar. And he didn't come home until whatever game was on TV at the bar was over. Dad was like a cat. He could walk into our apartment in the dark—no matter where we lived—" and they'd moved around a lot "—and navigate his way to the bedroom without bumping into furniture." It was something of an art form. "But he always woke Mom up when he got to the bedroom. And then the yelling would start." Waking Chandler up. Making him tense into a ball on his bed, listening, waiting. For the crash of something fragile, human or otherwise.

Izzy gave his arm a gentle, understanding squeeze.

Chandler covered her hand with his own. "They were competitive. Mom didn't like Dad drinking. Dad didn't want to give in. I never knew what the night would bring. What would be broken. What situation I'd be greeted with in the morning." He'd felt so small back then. So helpless. "I tried to be invisible."

"Oh, Chandler."

"Mom started moving the furniture around before Dad came home, but she'd always deny doing it. She'd tell him he was so drunk that he couldn't remember. Things…escalated. And I… I didn't help matters. Sleep deprived, on edge, I had a short fuse at school. Hence my aversion to the principal's office the other day."

The angry words of his parents, shouting at him, shouting at each other, reverberated in Chandler's head, tunneling his vision, tensing his shoulders.

But through the brain fog, one voice reached him. A calm voice. A caring voice. Izzy's voice.

"It's okay, Chandler."

And surprisingly, with a deep breath, it was better. Chandler focused on Izzy's face. Those empathetic blue eyes. Her delicate features framed by that silver-blond hair. The nod of her head. "One time, my mom shoved all the furniture in front of the door. Dad couldn't get in. Not without things hitting the fan anyway."

"Those days are long gone." Izzy slipped her arms around Chandler's waist and gave him a hug, laying her head over his heart.

It seemed natural to bring Izzy closer, to feel the steadiness of her breath, to picture her as the oar he needed when he was adrift because he'd lifted his anchor, sailing into uncharted waters. With her.

"Is that why you arrange your furniture to block the entry?" Izzy spoke into Chandler's chest. "In case your dad shows up?"

Chandler nodded, realized she probably couldn't see or feel him nodding since her head barely reached his sternum, and said, "Yep. I know it's not likely but it makes me feel better."

"That's sad."

"Yep." It wasn't something to be proud of, either. Chandler tried to make a joke of it. "You should see my bedroom."

Izzy stiffened.

"That was a joke," Chandler said gruffly.

"I knew that." But Izzy eased out of Chandler's embrace and turned her back on him. "How about we change things now in the living room? Are you up to moving furniture?"

"Yep."

But he suspected they both knew he was lying.

## CHAPTER ELEVEN

"HOW ARE YOU FEELING?" Izzy asked when they'd rearranged Chandler's living room into something that had more feng shui.

The couch was opposite the fireplace, not blocking the entry. His chairs faced the tree, which they'd moved in the middle of the big front window. Now, anyone could come in and reach the hallway or the kitchen without having to shimmy around the couch.

Chandler hadn't spoken much while they moved things around, perhaps because he was uncomfortable with how much he'd shared about his past.

Or the length of their hug.

Or the comment about his bedroom.

Why was the room silent?

Izzy realized Chandler hadn't answered her question. He stood near the Christmas tree, staring at the carpet and the clear path to the door.

"Hey." Izzy waved at him. "Are you woolgathering?"

He blinked slowly. "Wool *what*? Is that another of your historical terms?"

"Yes, sir." Was it nice that he remembered her love of reading historicals? Izzy decided it was. "Woolgathering. It means you're lost in thought."

"I was." Chandler's warm brown gaze was encompassing. *Like his hug.*

It had seemed so natural to embrace him.

And when he'd looked at her... It was as if he could stare into her eyes all day.

*I know I'd be able to do the same.*

"Now who's woolgathering?" Chandler's smile was infectious. "Aren't you going to ask me what I was thinking about?"

"Nope." Izzy was afraid to. "I asked you how you were feeling about removing your defense against the past. I'm still waiting for an answer. We can move it back if we need to."

"One thing at a time," Chandler murmured, a small smile on his lips. He came over to her side of the couch. "I was just noticing the deep imprint of the legs in the rug and thinking how I wasn't able to do this when I was married. Not the talking. Not the moving."

*If he couldn't do this when Stephanie was here, that must mean...*

Izzy's cheeks began to feel hot. She pressed her hands to her face. "We should get your Christmas decorations out. Or at least the lights for the tree." She took a step toward the dining room.

Chandler caught her hand. "You're changing the subject."

"We're both good at doing that," Izzy said softly, not daring to look at him.

Voices and the sound of feet on the porch stairs announced the arrival of others.

Slipping her hand free, Izzy hurried to open the door. "Sam! Mae! Come see the tree."

The kids barreled in, not even removing their boots before running into the living room.

Moving at a slower pace, Frank helped Mary ascend the stairs.

"Thought we'd see what was taking you so long." Frank didn't look up. He had one arm around Mary's waist and a hand supporting her arm.

"Took us ten minutes to get out the door." Mary wore black snow pants and a very thick white parka. From what Izzy could see of Mary's face beneath a knit cap and infinity scarf bundled over her chin, the older woman had a healthy burst of color. "Frank wanted me swaddled tighter than a newborn. Can't hardly move my arms and legs."

"A chill does no one any good." This was Frank at his best. Patient and unflappable. Must have been why he was such a success at taking in dozens of teenage foster boys over the years. "You'll thank me tomorrow, Mary."

"Oh, I'm grateful," Mary grumbled, reaching the front door. "Overheated and exhausted. But grateful. You will always be the best of my blessings, Frank."

"And you, the love of my life." Frank kissed his wife's cheek.

Izzy was humbled by their comfortable love for each other. It was out in the open for everyone to see.

Izzy's love for Mike had been a private thing. They whispered endearments but only when they were alone. And those words came less and less often the longer they were married, until Izzy had felt that she didn't know what love was. That she'd been attracted to Mike and to his ambition because she wanted something more—more financial stability, more emotional stability and a future that included being a mother. But she hadn't loved Mike as deeply as Frank and Mary loved each other.

And maybe that was why the feelings she had for Chandler were so frightening. Would their feelings grow like the Harrisons? Or wither as her feelings toward Mike had? She didn't know.

Frank helped Mary over the threshold. "Well, will you look at that. Do you see that pretty tree, Mary?"

"I do." Mary leaned on the doorjamb, staring at the rearranged living room. And then she reached for Izzy and whispered, "Thank you for this change."

"It was him," Izzy whispered back.

"If it was Chandler, it would have happened long ago." Mary tugged off her knit cap and scarf. "It was you, Izzy. Now, help me shed these layers, Frank. My son needs a little expert advice creating Christmas cheer for my grandson."

Izzy's phone beeped with an alarm. She'd set it to remind her when it was time to go, so that she could get Mae to bed at a decent hour and limit her time with Chandler, if necessary. And boy, was it necessary. She was at risk of getting too close to Chandler before she thought things through. "We've got to go. It's getting late."

She needed time to figure out what love was supposed to be. And if love was possible with him.

"I'LL WALK YOU OUT, IZZY." Chandler practically bolted to the front door for his hat, boots and jacket. Only Izzy's wary gaze had him slowing down and saying, "Come on, Mae. Wouldn't want you out late on a school night."

"*Della*-Mae," Sam said. "Her name is *Della*-Mae, Dad."

"My mama calls me Mae," Izzy's little girl said in that innocent voice of hers. "Your daddy can call me Mae, too."

"Oh, like family," Sam said as if understanding was dawning. "Should I call you Mae?"

"I think I'd like that." Mae beamed.

Chandler had no time to dwell on his son's reaction. Izzy had her boots on and was in possession of Mae's hand. He stumbled after her, heels finding purchase in his boots, arms punching into jacket sleeves, his hat left behind.

"While you take care of that fire, Chandler," Mom called after him, sounding like her precancerous self, "we'll talk about what decorations Sam wants on his tree."

"Monster trucks!" Sam cried. "And apples, in case I get hungry."

His son was anything but traditional.

"Izzy." Chandler stretched his legs to catch up to Izzy and Mae with only a vague notion in his head about what needed to be said. His heart was racing in circles, urging him to slow Izzy's departure. "I think… I think we need to talk."

"About what?" Mae asked, all adorable and sweet. The winter wind tossed her long white-blond hair this way and that.

"Can't talk right now." Izzy was working those short legs of hers double time. A candy cane escaping through the ranch's winter wonderland. "It's a school night. Gotta get home. I'll be back here tomorrow afternoon."

"Did I…say something wrong? Or…say too much?" Chandler's movements felt stiff, wooden, yet wobbly. "Like you said at the feed store. I'm more of a listener. Probably put my foot in my mouth." Scared Izzy off, more like. A man who didn't feel comfortable moving his furniture? Izzy was probably wondering what else was wrong with him.

They reached her SUV.

Izzy opened the back door. "Mae, get in and buckle up, please." When her daughter was safely inside and the door shut behind her, Izzy faced Chandler, arms crossed, shoulders hunched against the cold prairie wind. "You didn't say too much. I'm… I'm *honored* that you told me about your dad. But this…this *something*…" She gestured back and forth between them. "I have no foundation to judge it with. I don't have the depth of experience—*successful experience*—to trust these feelings. I have responsibilities… Mae… Earl and the feed store…my holiday decorating… Christmas. I'm already stretched too thin. And then you…"

"Put you over the edge." Chandler nodded. "I get it." It made his chest ache, but he understood. "Not rushing in… It's a sensible decision." The wrong one, he was sure.

She sighed in apparent relief. "Thank you for understanding."

Chandler nodded again.

Izzy turned, taking hold of the car door handle.

And that's when an urgent feeling took hold of Chandler, a

feeling that propelled him forward and had him taking gentle hold of Izzy's arm covered in red-and-white knit.

Izzy paused, glancing up at him over her shoulder.

"We won't always be this stressed out and time crunched." Chandler released Izzy's arm and put her candy-striped earmuffs over her ears, holding them out so she couldn't claim not to hear his next words. "We should keep the channels of communication open." And then, he settled those round muffs over her ears. "Good night, Candy Cane Izzy."

She stared at him in silence for another moment before nodding briefly and opening her SUV's door. "Good night."

"Good night, Mr. Cochran!" Mae called from the back seat.

Chandler waved, and then waited for them to drive off before he walked back to his house. Along the way, he admired the exterior lights hung where they'd always been. There was permanence in those lights. And safety.

Not surprisingly, when Chandler looked at Izzy, he didn't feel any of that permanence or safety. Instead, nerves trotted along a repeating, circular path in his stomach. When Chandler looked at Izzy, he didn't know where she fit in his life.

But when he'd held her in his arms... The nerves came to a halt, dropping anchor. And certainty... Certainty settled in his chest.

*Izzy could mean something to me.*

He was afraid she already did.

"Everything all right, son?" Dad asked Chandler when he'd shed his boots and jacket and joined them in the living room.

"It could be." Chandler took another look around the open layout of his space.

On the couch, Sam and Mom were exploring the treasures in the box Mom had sent over with Izzy earlier, the one Chandler had taken from Izzy for fear she'd use every last item in that box to decorate his home. Now, he wished she'd stayed to do just that. If they spent more time together, she might figure out how she really felt about him.

"There's a fresh feeling in here since you rearranged the furniture." Mom blew dust, real or imagined, off a red bird ornament before handing it to Sam to hang on the tree. "Like a fresh start."

Chandler grunted.

"Gives the room balance with the tree in here," Dad said, still studying Chandler. "Speaking of the tree, I tossed a string of lights on it because young Sam was determined to put ornaments on tonight."

"Christmas trees can't be naked, Grandpa." Sam was putting all the ornaments in a one-foot-square area on the tree. The rest was bare. "That's what Grandma says."

"I do, indeed." Mom spared Chandler a smile. "Everything about Christmas should make you feel joy."

Chandler nodded. From now on, he wouldn't think about the holiday without also thinking of Izzy—her over-the-top Christmas spirit and tinsel-colored hair. And speaking of... "We need tinsel."

"I might have some in a box somewhere." Mom's gaze found Dad's. "Frank, would you—"

"Nope." Dad got to his feet. "Izzy had the right idea. It's time to head home. Chandler and I can pick up tinsel in town tomorrow when we go look at that stock."

"I suppose you're right." Mom allowed Dad to bundle her up again while Sam continued to put ornaments in a one-foot radius on the tree. "Big day for you today, Chandler. Can't tell you how proud I am."

"Of what?" Sam piped up. "Of our tree? Does it look pretty, Grandma?"

"Sure does." Mom patted Chandler's cheek. "Nothing is easy. Not even love."

"It was easy the first time." And Chandler bet Izzy would say the same.

"But look how that turned out," Dad pointed out, not unkindly. "No offense but easy isn't always forever."

"That's a shame." Chandler nodded, opening the door for them. "Easy is something you look for when you get older."

Mom tsked. "Easy should only be something you look for in a chair."

# CHAPTER TWELVE

"Izzy, you've got the face of a woman burning the candle at both ends."

Izzy grumbled something in the affirmative to Earl early Tuesday morning.

Earl handed Izzy a cup of coffee. And then gave bright-eyed Mae a mug of hot cocoa, ushering her to the table in the break room. "Usually, it's Mae who drags her feet in before school."

"I'm wide awake," Mae said. She wore a bright blue dress with yellow tights, colors as wide awake as she was. "I woke Mama up this morning. She didn't hear her alarm."

"You worried about something?" Earl stared at Izzy, raising his bushy white eyebrows.

"I'm counting down the days to Christmas is all," Izzy said. And counting every penny toward buying that princess bed. If only the furniture store in Friar's Creek offered layaway. It would be one less thing to worry about because Chandler... He expected them to figure this *something* out after the holiday. He was willing to wait. That had to mean their *something* could lead to something real. "This month is flying by," Izzy said. December was nearly half-gone.

"The best days often do," Earl remarked.

Izzy chugged half her cup of coffee, hoping it would chase

away the cobwebs in her head where thoughts of Chandler had stuck last night. And this morning. And threatened to stay all day long.

In the warehouse, Stan was driving the loader, filling the store's delivery truck with pallets of hay. The steady hum of the Bobcat matched the steady thread of thoughts regarding Chandler in Izzy's head.

*He's a good man. He's a good father. He's a good kisser.*

Izzy performed an imaginary eye roll as she drained the rest of her coffee.

*A good kisser didn't guarantee a future together.*

Mae stared into the contents in her mug. "Can I add marshmallows, Mama?"

"Of course," Earl answered for Izzy, reaching for his stash of mini-marshmallows, undoing the rubber band sealing the bag. He was like a grandfather to her. Always spoiling Mae.

Chandler's suspicions might be right. Earl could get Mae a puppy for Christmas.

"That's a lot of sugar before school, Mae," Izzy felt compelled to point out. Point out. Not reject. She wasn't feeling up to snuff in regards to winning any argument, no matter how small.

"Sam says sugar makes you run faster." Mae held out her mug for Earl.

"Tell me when." Earl poured the white puffs into her mug until the hot chocolate couldn't be seen. "Or we can stop here." He closed the bag when Mae would have taken more. "Wouldn't want to get into trouble with your mama."

Mae began eating the marshmallows one at a time off the mountain in her mug. "I'm going to be the fastest kid at school today."

Earl refilled Izzy's mug with coffee. "I hear someone in the front. You look like you need a distraction."

Izzy shed her jacket, picked up her coffee, settled her cowboy hat more firmly on her head and went out to face the day.

She stopped just on the other side of the door, shocked to see her ex-husband standing at the sales counter. Not being a cowboy or a rancher, and not living in Clementine anymore, Mike never came in the feed store.

But here he stood in front of her in his unwrinkled khakis, crisp blue polo shirt and black leather jacket.

"Mike." Izzy hurried forward, keeping her voice low. "What are you doing here?"

"Is Della-Mae around?" he asked, voice nearly a whisper.

Izzy nodded, set her coffee down, grabbed hold of the edge of the sales counter and braced herself for bad news. A death. A disaster of some kind. Conversations with Mike were rarely about the weather. And then, she realized what else he might have come for. "Did you check the school's online messaging system?"

"No. Should I have?"

Izzy shrugged, trying to ignore the guilt of not telling him Mae had been in trouble. "I can never sign in and you said you were going to."

"I've been too busy." Her ex-husband shifted his weight, checking a message on his phone before pocketing it.

Izzy reached for her coffee, needing to hold something. "Mike, why are you here?"

"First, I want to thank you for not being difficult about the divorce or the custody agreement." Although Mike's voice was low, Izzy recognized that tone. It was his deal-closing tone—smooth, nonthreatening, trying to establish trust while he laid out the terms that benefited him. "We've had a good few years of co-parenting."

The hair on the back of Izzy's neck rose. Mike hadn't come to deliver bad news. Mike was here to renegotiate. But what? All Izzy could decipher was that Mike considered this a potentially difficult negotiation. "And..."

"Second," Mike continued in that easygoing liar's voice. "You had to know that at some point, our relationship status would change for one or both of us. And that change will affect Della-Mae."

"It shouldn't." Annoyance—*or perhaps mainlining caffeine*—heated Izzy from the inside out. She let go of the sales counter and crossed her arms over her chest. "And…"

"I'm getting serious about someone." Mike was still in negotiation mode. "And she doesn't want to have kids."

"Does she have a dislike of kittens and puppies, too?" Izzy blurted, laughing nervously.

Mike shoved his hands in his black leather jacket pockets, frowning. "Izzy."

"I'm sorry. That was uncalled for." Izzy's arms stayed locked tight over her chest because she had the oddest suspicion that Mike wasn't done. But what was she missing?

And then a thought surfaced. And her stomach dropped.

She'd been in this situation before. With her own father.

"This woman you're serious about doesn't just not want children, she doesn't want stepchildren, either." Izzy's voice trembled. "And since you're here, you've *chosen…*" She choked on the word, swallowing before she could start again. "You've chosen *her* over your own daughter."

Oh, those words hurt to say, if only because they'd break Mae's heart. *He'd* break her little girl's heart. *Just like Dad did mine.*

"What kind of man are you?" Izzy whispered, voice strained, releasing a hand to tip her cowboy hat back.

"I want to change our custody agreement." Mike tried for his salesman's smile, but it didn't fool Izzy. She'd gotten under his skin and made him feel uncomfortable.

*Good.*

"Are you relinquishing all rights?" Izzy's temperature changed from hot to cold. Her toes stung with it in her cowboy boots. "Or are you only going to see her once in the summer and once at the holidays? Is that what kind of father you're turning out to be?" Izzy lowered her voice. "How could you do this to Mae? This is low even for you."

"Let's keep this civil." Mike's voice had taken on a gravelly quality, a warning of sorts if one knew him well.

Which Izzy did. "Oh. I can be civil. That doesn't mean I won't judge you." She sucked in a breath, blinking back tears. "I'll gladly take Mae most of the year. I won't fight you on that. But I won't make excuses for you."

Mike scowled. "I'm not asking you to make excuses for me."

"But you expect me to talk about you in a good light." Izzy grabbed her coffee cup, wishing she was the type of woman to give vent to her anger by dousing him in coffee. But she wasn't. She was just Izzy, a woman who avoided confrontation.

*Candy Cane Izzy.*

That's what Chandler had called her last night.

Chandler. His tall, steady, *honorable* presence came to mind. The strength of his arms when they wrapped around her. The sturdiness of his torso when she leaned into him. He wouldn't abandon his child for a woman. How she wished he was here beside her to tell Mike to get lost.

*To tell Mike that he'd adopt Mae.*

Izzy's breath caught. She shouldn't be thinking such things.

"Have your lawyer contact my lawyer," Izzy told Mike coldly. "And get out of here before Mae sees you and I make you tell her how coldhearted you are to her face."

"*Della*-Mae," Mike said, clearly being ornery just because. "Her name is *Della*-Mae Adams."

Zane entered the store carrying what looked like a frayed pair of braided reins.

"Move along, Mike." Izzy gave her ex-husband a shooing motion. "When Mae's older, she'll decide what she wants to be called. And what she thinks of you."

"TURN HERE," Dad instructed Chandler late Tuesday morning. "This is the place. Sooner Wagon Wheels."

The turn put them on a weedy, dirt road lined by barbed wire fences. Pastures on either side held large draft horses with swaybacks and long white whiskers. Those old horses had literally been put out to pasture.

"Sooner Wagon Wheels." Chandler scoffed after hitting a deep pothole. "They should have called it the Retirement Home for Draft Horses. I hope the wagons are in better shape." He and Dad were shopping for a horse and cart for Mom to ride in on Christmas Day. Ever since Izzy had mentioned it, Dad had bitten into the idea and wouldn't let go.

"I called around." Dad was smiling. He'd been smiling all morning.

And if buying a horse and buggy gave the older man's smile back to him after Mom's cancer battle, Chandler was willing to consider it. He'd been considering a lot of things he wouldn't normally lately. Moving things around in his well-ordered life. Opening his heart to Izzy. Keeping it open while she sorted through things.

"Sooner Wagon Wheels has a good reputation," Dad continued. "And you know how your mother loves a horse with character. I bet every one of these big fellas has character to spare." He leaned to look out the passenger window. "Look at them. They're trotting along with us."

Sure enough, the horses were keeping pace with Chandler's truck. He had to admit, it was magical.

"What if I slow down?" Chandler took his foot off the gas and coasted.

The horses paced him, slowing.

He sped up again. And so did they.

*Sam would love to see this.*

And Izzy. She'd love it, too. She and Mae.

"Your mother would love to see this," Dad said in a thick voice, echoing Chandler's thoughts. He sat back in his seat. "We aren't leaving until we get what we came for."

The ranch was a mile down the road. The horses followed them the entire way.

When they reached the ranch yard, Chandler was impressed by the grandeur. Two double-decker barns, a covered arena, an outdoor racetrack—all in good repair. A large sign on the side of the barn proclaimed it as Sooner Wagon Wheels, Established in 1950, C.D. Sutton, Proprietor.

A man of unusual height and girth strode out of one barn with an aura of authority. His boots and jeans were worn and faded, nearly as colorless as his shaggy white hair. *Was that a new plaid shirt?* His narrow-brimmed straw cowboy hat looked as if a horse had nibbled its crown.

"I'm Clarence Dwayne Sutton." The big cowboy was taller than Chandler and had a firm handshake with hard calluses. "But you can call me C.D."

"Impressive operation you have here." Chandler knew how difficult it was to stay on top of maintenance on a large spread.

C.D. chuckled. "Quite a difference from our driveway, ain't it? Most folks forget the potholes when the herd escorts them here."

Chandler nodded.

"I'm not interested in one of them," Dad told C.D., hitching up his blue jeans. "You've got more to offer than our escorts, I'm hoping." And instead of waiting for C.D. to respond, he hurriedly added, "I want a well-trained, well-behaved cart horse with personality and I'm willing to pay extra for it."

"No sense spilling your hand." Chandler shook his head at his father's naïveté. "What happened to my father? Frank Harrison, master stock negotiator?"

Dad crossed his arms over his chest. "This is an important purchase for your mother. When you think about the woman you love, the woman you almost lost to the Big C, you'll spare any expense to make her happy."

"Merry Christmas to me is what I'm hearing." C.D. chuckled, hooking his thumbs in his belt loops. "Never fear, Chandler. My family hasn't been in business for three generations because we take advantage of our buyers."

"That's a relief." Dad clapped a hand on Chandler's back. "Isn't it, son?"

"Yep." Chandler gestured to C.D. "Let's see what you've got."

"I've got two different horses and rigs ready for you to check out in the arena." He led the way toward the open gate to the covered arena. "Dinah is a Clydesdale. She's in her prime at ten. She enjoys pulling a bigger wagon. If you've got children or grandchildren, or you're interested in taking a group of folks for a ride on the regular, she's the way to go."

They entered the arena. A large chestnut Clydesdale with huge hooves was hitched to a wooden wagon that looked like it could sit eight burly cowboys.

"Much as I like to include the family in everything we do," Dad said, planting his boots in the loamy arena soil, "my Mary would treat that like a cubic zirconia."

C.D. scratched the gray hair at his temple.

"Translation…" Chandler began. "My dad wants Mom to be as thrilled with this gift as she would be if she received a real diamond."

C.D. pivoted toward the other end of the arena toward a large gray horse hitched to a black buggy with two forward-facing bench seats, yellow wheels and a black fringed canopy on top. "If you want a fancier rig, you'll like the surrey and Shirley."

The gray whinnied, making C.D. chuckle, which given how often he'd chuckled since they arrived didn't seem such a hard thing to do.

"She knows her name?" The enthusiasm in Dad's tone matched that of his smile. Despite his shorter legs, he hurried past Chandler.

"Sure does," C.D. said with a nod. "She's a Percheron.

Knows she's a beaut and likes to prance. Gets impatient if you go too slow."

"Can't prance when you walk," Dad agreed.

"Is she headstrong?" Chandler was going to reject her if she was. "Mom isn't—"

"My Mary would sure like something with flash and character." Dad walked up to the mare and reached up to run a hand over her withers, and then down her front leg. She politely shifted her weight so that he could pick up her large hoof. "That's my girl. I like her."

*That's my dad. Forgetting how to negotiate.*

*"Dad."* Chandler sounded as put-upon as when Sam used the moniker. "You don't buy a car without a test drive. Same goes for livestock."

"He'll get his test drive, Chandler." C.D. had his thumbs hooked through his belt loops again. He rocked back on his boot heels. "You both will. And since you told me in your call that you didn't have driving experience, we'll do a bit of training first."

"Sounds good," Dad said, happily running his hands up Shirley's neck. The mare lowered her head, nudging Dad's chest like a cat seeking attention. "We've got all day."

*All day?*

Chandler's eye twitched. He checked the time on his cell phone, mentally rearranging his afternoon schedule. Zane could swing by and pick up Sam from school, if necessary. And if things dragged on here, what did it matter? It was probably for the best that Chandler didn't see Izzy as she went about decorating the ranch tonight.

*"Snowy white horse, yellow wheels, fringe."* Dad was practically singing. "I feel like Curly."

"I have no idea what that means." Chandler walked around the mare assessing her confirmation, which seemed excellent.

"It's an *Oklahoma!* reference." Dad laughed. "Our parents

were fans of a good musical and *Oklahoma!* is one of the best, especially if you live in Oklahoma."

Chandler was vaguely aware of the musical.

"There's a song where Curly sings to Laurey about a rig and pair of horses fit for a bride to ride in." Dad stroked beneath the gray's forelock. "And Shirley—"

The mare whinnied, nudging Dad and pushing him back a step.

Chandler rushed to his side, grabbing his arm to prevent him from falling over.

"—Jones played Laurey in the movie version. This is Curly's buggy and Shirley..." Dad paused, grinning.

The mare blew a raspberry and pawed the ground.

"Why isn't she named Laurey or Curly?" Dad wondered aloud.

"Laurey was this girl's mama." C.D. climbed into the front seat with surprising grace for being such a large man. "Hop in, gents. I'll take you for a ride and then teach you about driving."

Chandler made sure his foster father was in the front seat safely before he scooted into the back, ducking a little when the crown of his cowboy hat brushed the canopy above him. His knees bumped the backside of the front seat. "Not much legroom back here."

"These surreys are made for women." C.D. picked up the reins and signaled for the cowboy holding Shirley's headstall to release her. "And off we go."

Shirley leaped into action, jerking the buggy forward before settling into a bouncy trot, a pace Chandler assumed was the prancing the owner was talking about.

"You fellas should note how I'm holding the reins. I've got them coming below my ring fingers, up and over my index fingers, and I hold them in place with my thumbs." The owner showed his hands to Dad. "Shirley—"

She whinnied.

"—has a light mouth. So, if you want to go left, don't saw on the reins. Ease her into it." C.D. guided her to the left, crossing the arena. "Same when you bring her to a stop. Whoa, now. Whoa." He eased the reins back.

Shirley came to a bouncy halt, tossing her head a little as if she was annoyed at being denied her prancing.

"You feel like trying?" The owner handed Dad the reins.

"I'm game." Dad threaded the reins through his fingers. "Giddyap, Shirley."

The large mare lunged forward with a shrill whistle, practically giving Chandler whiplash.

"Not so much rein when you start," C.D. advised.

"Let's see what she can do." Dad drove the buggy the way he drove a motor vehicle—too fast and like he had a death wish.

C.D. white-knuckled the bar at the front of the rig.

"Slow down," Chandler cautioned when Shirley broke into a gallop.

"This is like a ride at one of those amusement parks!" Dad shouted. "*Hoo-whee!* Mary's going to love this."

"Dad!" Chandler clapped a hand on his foster father's shoulder. "Reel it in."

Someone was going to have to act like the adult. And Chandler was afraid that role was on him.

"WE NEED MORE WREATHS." Mary held a pine sprig to her nose on Tuesday afternoon. She sat at the kitchen table across from Izzy, wearing a gray sweatshirt appliquéd with a teddy bear and a sprig of mistletoe. "This smells like Christmas. And we need more of it."

Izzy agreed. "I can pick up some more wreaths tomorrow before I drive out. You can never have too much Christmas cheer." Although Chandler might argue that.

Or he would have last week. He was...different now.

But maybe, so was Izzy. Every time she heard a truck pull up in the ranch yard, she held her breath, waiting for Chandler to enter. She wanted to tell Chandler about Mike. She hadn't even shared the news with Earl. What Mike was doing... It sent her blood pressure soaring.

"Never have too much Christmas cheer. That's what I always say this time of year." Mary gazed around the kitchen, smiling contentedly. She seemed to have more energy than she had on Saturday. "The house is shaping up, thanks to you."

"My pleasure." Izzy smiled. "We've done a lot in just a few days."

The tree was up and decorated in the living room, along with the Christmas village and lighted boughs on the mantel. The vintage candle lights were in the front windows and twenty stockings had been hung from the mantel—one for every foster cowboy spending Christmas at the ranch this year.

And the kitchen...

There were ceramic reindeer at one corner of the counter and jolly knit gnomes tucked in between the sugar and flour canisters, while white twinkle lights sparkled beneath the upper cupboards and around the large kitchen window. A red-flowering Christmas cactus sat in a pot in the middle of the kitchen table, sporting bright red blooms. A bright red tea towel hung from the oven handle, alongside a green hot pad with a Santa on it.

And that was just the inside.

Mary reached over to squeeze Izzy's hand. "I've been enjoying your Christmas outfits. Just seeing them lifts my spirits."

Izzy's sweater today was also pink, decorated with a team of pink flamingos sporting antlers and pulling Santa's sleigh. She wore her antlers, and they jingled as she helped the two kids prepare felt cowboy hats to be hung on the bunkhouse Christmas tree. Izzy was gluing turtledove ornaments onto two wreaths Mary had selected, chuckling to herself about how Harper would appreciate this. Mary was supposed to be signing and addressing Christmas cards, but she was easily distracted and had only done a few.

"I changed after school so me and Mama match." Mae's white knit dress had pink flamingos and presents in an alternating pattern around the skirt. She was gluing gold cords on the felt cowboy hat ornaments Izzy had found in a box in the garage.

"I don't have any sweaters for Christmas." Sam's job was to glue green ribbon hatbands over the crown of the felt cowboy hats.

"Maybe you should ask for a sweater for Christmas," Izzy suggested, then lifted her head because she thought she heard another truck pull in.

"I wrote my letter to Santa already." Sam coated his fingertips with glue from the glue stick, then stuck them together and pried them apart. Repeatedly. "We both did. Miz Stodimeyer was going to mail them to Santa."

"That was the day Miz Stodimeyer had her baby." Mae gasped. "Do you think she mailed our letters?"

Sam's eyes widened. "What if our letters don't get to Santa on time?"

"I'll get in touch with Mrs. Stodimeyer," Izzy promised. She'd been meaning to anyway. "I'll try tonight after dinner."

"I'm sure she mailed those letters," Mary said reassuringly, but she gave Izzy a worried glance. "She knows how important they are to all you kids."

"If you don't write a letter to Santa, do you get a lump of coal?" Sam whispered, big brown eyes wide.

"No." Izzy laughed, taking the opportunity to wipe the boy's glue-covered fingers. "Coal is for kids on the very naughty list." Like Mike, who deserved a stocking full of coal.

"Are we on the very naughty list?" Mae looked scared.

"You've been in trouble, but I don't think it's enough to put you on the naughty list." Mary was still trying to reassure the kids.

"And besides, I hear they give you cauliflower nowadays instead of coal if you've been misbehaving." Izzy did something with the cookie dough. "If you get a stalk of cauliflower, Sam, Mary will cook it."

"But… I don't like cauliflower." Sam turned up his nose.

"Do you know the best way to make sure you aren't on the naughty list?" Izzy asked them. When they shook their heads, she said, "Stay out of trouble at school and be a blessing at home."

The kids went back to mixing. Still worried, if their pouts were any indication.

"I'll send Mrs. Stodimeyer a text now in case the baby is sleeping later." Izzy opened her phone screen and scrolled through her contacts with only a twinge of guilt for not trying to use the school's online messaging system, which she had yet to try and figure out. "If your teacher hasn't mailed your letters, I'll swing by on the way home and get them."

"And my mom will get them in the mail," Sam said happily, referring to Stephanie. "I can't wait to show her my Christmas tree. I had Dad take a picture with his phone and send it to her."

"That's half the joy of the holiday." Mary nodded. "Seeing what other folks decorate with."

Her words reminded Izzy of another conversation about folks enjoying the festive displays at the Done Roamin' Ranch. "Mary, have you ever considered opening up your holiday display to friends and family?"

"Ronnie mentioned that the other night." The older woman tsked. "She seems to think it would do me good. Everyone has an opinion about what would do me good."

"Think about it." Izzy gave up on Chandler arriving and focused on Mary. "I bet you'd have fun seeing people enjoying your decorations. If we rearranged the trucks in the ranch yard, we could make a loop so that your friends could drive past, say hello and then drive back out."

Mary thought about that for a moment before saying, "I don't know. Frank will complain if they come at all hours. He likes to go to bed early." She chuckled. "Or fall asleep in his recliner early in front of the TV."

"We could post a sign saying the lights switch off at ten." Izzy hadn't thought this through but for every argument Mary presented, she seemed to have an answer. "Maybe nine if you prefer."

"Can my friends come, too?" Sam asked.

"Oh, and me." Mae perked up.

"All right. I'm making an executive decision." Mary chuckled. "If I don't go for it, Chandler will never agree. Let's get it going before the boys get back."

"Why don't we call them?" The last thing Izzy wanted was to upset Chandler and his status quo.

"I'll call and have *you* ask Chandler." Mary's eyes twinkled with mischief.

Izzy's cheeks heated. "What makes you think I have any sway over Chandler?"

Mary laughed louder, but she wouldn't answer the question.

And it was a moot point. Neither Chandler nor Frank answered their phones.

# CHAPTER THIRTEEN

"WHAT'S GOING ON HERE?" Chandler drove into the ranch yard after sunset on Tuesday.

After taking the horse and buggy for an extended test drive, receiving a time-consuming tour of C.D.'s operation and haggling with the Sooner Wagon Wheels owner, Chandler and Dad had purchased a horse and buggy for Mom. Shirley and the rig were to be delivered next week. All he wanted was a hot meal and a little rest and relaxation with Sam before bed. But there was mischief afoot at the ranch.

"Looks like someone's rearranging the yard." Dad picked his white cowboy hat from the dash and put it on his head. "And look at all those tires. Are they supposed to be round pyramids?"

"Snowmen," Chandler mumbled, recalling Izzy's idea from days before.

Zane waved his arms, directing Chandler to park nearer the side pasture.

"What's going on?" Chandler demanded as soon as he'd parked and his boots had hit the ground.

"We're making a turnabout." Izzy came into the glow of the ranch yard lights, wearing several tones of pink and looking like she was ready to celebrate Christmas somewhere tropical.

And if Chandler hadn't been upset over things changing without his or Dad's approval, he might have spent more time dwelling on thoughts of pretty, tropical Izzy.

But he was upset and so images of bikinis and umbrella drinks were banished. "Izzy, why didn't you think to check with me? The ranch foreman?" Chandler pointed at the many stacks of old, bald tires that formed the circle he assumed vehicles were supposed to drive around. "I told you that we save those tires until we have a truckload and then we haul them to the recycle center."

"You can still do that." Her antlers jingled, defying his sour mood, encouraging him to join in the joyous spirit of Christmas and change. "We're going to spray-paint them white, use black markers to make blocks of coal for a face, and *voila!* We'll have recyclable snowmen defining the turnabout. Mary suggested we put the nativity scene in the middle."

"Haven't seen the nativity here in years." Dad was noticeably not entering this fight.

"All this effort for more holiday cheer?" Chandler washed a hand over his face.

"Chandler..." Izzy's voice softened. "If you want to help Mary recuperate this season, you need to be supportive. We thought it would be fun to open up the ranch a few hours after sundown a few times a week for the community to do a drive-through. Zane and Dylan moved a couch from the bunkhouse onto the front porch so Mary can wave or talk to friends who swing through. It'll lift her spirits."

"In the cold." Chandler huffed, looking to Dad for support. Getting none.

"She's agreed to bundle up," Izzy assured him, also appealing to Chandler's foster father. "Plus, Zane found her a portable heater."

"We *have* gone along with Mary being a hermit during and after her treatments," Dad allowed. "These outdoor visits might be good for her spirits. It was her idea, you say?"

Izzy looked uncertain for the first time since their arrival. "It was Ronnie's and my idea first. But when we floated it by Mary, she wanted to run with it and…" Izzy blew out a breath. "Frank, when you hired me, you did say you wanted me to go the extra mile. And when Mary tried reaching you two this afternoon, she rolled to voice mail."

"We had no signal where we were," Dad admitted.

"She didn't leave a message," Chandler stated. He'd texted Zane, asking if there was an emergency. Zane had indicated everything was fine.

And that would be the last time Chandler trusted Zane. He should have clued Chandler in.

"Dad! Come see what we did!" Sam appeared out of the darkness and crashed into Chandler's legs. Sam stared up at him with one hand holding his cowboy hat on. "Mae and me have been working on bunkhouse decorations so we won't be on the naughty list."

And Sam was so happy…

Chandler very nearly gave this Christmas Tree Lane idea of Izzy's his blessing.

"And Miz Izzy brought me a chocolate calendar." Sam pranced around. "Yummy, yummy, yummy. Happy, happy, happy tummy."

"I guess that's what's important," Chandler told Izzy, leaving her and Dad and submitting to Sam's tugging. "Happy, happy, Sammy."

"I'm sorry!" Izzy called after him.

"Give it a chance, son," Dad hollered after him.

"Give it a chance, Dad." Sam bounced happily next to him.

Chandler's son led him to the bunkhouse, where white lights outlined the wreath-adorned door. Inside, there was a small tree decorated with red-and-green paper chain garlands, white lights and cowboy hat ornaments that Chandler had never seen before. Stockings with each ranch hand's name were pinned to each bunk bed. A small pillow with a reindeer had been tossed onto each bed. A red plaid runner crossed the length of the dining table. White lights, red glass balls and fir boughs made a cheerful centerpiece. A glass jar on the small kitchen counter held candy canes. Another held sugar cookies. Next to that was a stack of paper napkins with Santa printed on them.

"I bet Grandma Mary was happy with this." Even if it wasn't what she normally did. Chandler bet the other ranch hands were happy with it, too.

"She was." Sam looped an arm around Chandler's leg. "I glued so-o-o-o many cowboy hatbands on these ornaments."

"All by yourself?"

"Mae helped." He used Chandler's leg like a pole and swung around.

"We'll have all the ranch hands thank her." And Izzy. The space looked warm and welcoming, just the way he, Zane and Dylan had described to Izzy. She'd come through for them. And what had Chandler done? Nitpicked. Harping on about the same old place for lights and decorations. Snapping at her about the drive-through. "Where is Mae?"

"We were playing with the Christmas village inside with Ginny and Grandma." He laughed. "I like Della-Mae. Do you?"

"Why wouldn't I?" He lifted Sam to his hip. "Mae's your best friend."

"Yep. She's practically family." Sam placed his hat on top of Chandler's.

"That's good to hear," Izzy said from behind them, having entered the bunkhouse without Chandler noticing. "I've got to get Mae home. We haven't eaten yet."

"Why not stay for dinner?" Chandler surprised himself by asking. So much for giving her space.

"Yay!" Sam leaped to his feet and dragged Chandler toward Izzy. "We're having pork chops and potatoes." Sam stopped an arm's length from Izzy and tried to join her hand with Chandler's, something he used to do when Chandler and Stephanie were together. "Come on, everybody."

Chandler's fingers brushed against Izzy's before they each pulled back. Her cheeks turned an appealing shade of pink. Appealing, because it was Chandler's touch that had created that blush. Pride filled his chest.

*I'm not so old, after all.*

"Wait until I tell Mae she's eating with us." Sam ran out of the bunkhouse calling, "Mae! Mae!" Chandler's son ran on a long-lasting battery. His energy and enthusiasm never seemed to wane.

Izzy snuck a glance at Chandler...at his lips, reminding him of how combustible their kiss had been, making him want to kiss her again. Maybe on a tropical beach given her hot pink holiday attire.

"I guess we're staying for dinner," Izzy said softly, still blushing, still not quite looking Chandler in the eye.

"Pork chops and potatoes." Good thing the rule at the Done Roamin' Ranch was to always make extra. "I guess I should give the roundabout my blessing." Because Dad didn't seem to mind, and the last thing Chandler wanted was to start a fight with Izzy.

"Are you sure you don't want to talk about it some more?" Izzy's soft blue gaze finally met his, tentatively. At his shaking head, she added, "I'm so glad. Mary is excited about it."

"She knew I'd cave in." Chandler shook his head, feeling the tension inside him ease. "Have you decorated all the outbuildings? Mom won't want to throw open the gates to visitors until you do."

"No. Honestly, I haven't even been inside anything but the main house, your house and here." Now that he'd given the roundabout his blessing, the more she talked, the more comfortable she seemed with him. "Do the barns and outbuildings really need decoration?"

"Mom would insist." They should be moving toward the

kitchen and dinner. But Chandler wanted more time alone with Izzy. "Let me give you a brief tour of the barn to give you a chance to come up with some new ideas."

"New ideas? I thought you didn't want anything that hasn't been done before?" Her gaze turned wary. "Or does the tour include you trying to talk about *something*…?" Izzy gestured between them.

"Your suspicion wounds me." Chandler held the door for Izzy without answering her question. The cold air and chill wind wrapped him in its chilly embrace. "I heard you before when you said now wasn't the time to pursue anything."

"Good." She walked out past him.

"But it's nice, isn't it?" Chandler moved to her side as they headed for the large barn, head bent to catch anything she might say, be it muttered or murmured. "This *something*?"

"You're fishing." Her antlers jingled. "We're not pursuing whatever this is, remember?"

"Talking isn't really pursuing." If they never talked about this hum between them, they'd never kiss again. And Chandler had an inkling that never kissing Izzy again would be a crying shame.

"Are you flirting with me?" Izzy gave Chandler a quick glance before hurrying onward. "You don't flirt."

"Like I shouldn't flirt with you…ever?" Oh, this was completely not like him, but he couldn't seem to stop. "Or you don't want me to flirt *with you*?"

Izzy huffed, accented by her antlers jingling. "How can you be flirting with me? Weren't you annoyed with me fifteen minutes ago?"

"Yes, but then the way you looked at me reminded me of Saturday night, obviously because it was one of the worst experiences of your life." And if that wasn't a blatant play for a compliment, Chandler didn't know what was. "Regardless of who kissed who, it sounds like you were disappointed."

"It wasn't bad." Izzy walked faster. Her white-blond hair

shimmered in the overhead ranch yard lights. "And that's as much as I'll say."

*It wasn't bad.* From Izzy, that was practically high praise. Chandler's chest swelled with unexpected pride. *Go, me!*

"And that's why we aren't going to talk about it," Izzy continued, hanging on to her antlers when the wind nearly blew them off.

He recognized that tone of voice. It was the efficient tone Izzy used when handling his business calls at the feed store. That wouldn't do. "Well, we have to talk about something." Even if it wasn't the spark between them.

"Tell me what your mother usually does in terms of decoration in the barn." Izzy practically broke into a jog.

"I can't talk to you when you run away." Unfortunately, Izzy wasn't stopping. "I know I make you nervous and we've been in awkward situations the past few days but…"

"But?" She slowed, glancing up at the barn looming before them.

Izzy not running away was a win Chandler would analyze later. Instinctively, he knew that he'd miss sleep while taking his feelings and her words apart tonight. For now, it was time to put her at ease. "Outside the barn, there are wreaths and lights. Mom loves her wreaths and lights. And mistletoe."

"Why is there mistletoe at the barn?" Izzy asked, still studying the barn.

Chandler took a moment to think about that, having never really considered it before. "I think it's Mom's way of encouraging opportunities for romantic moments. Ronnie isn't the only starry-eyed woman on the ranch."

"We didn't need mistletoe to…" Izzy turned to him, cheeks blooming with color, revealed by the exterior barn lights. "Never mind. It's been a long day, starting with my ex."

A gust of wind kicked up. Izzy shivered, not surprising given she only wore that pink sweater. That seemed like her work uniform and if she wasn't careful, she was going to burn too many calories shivering outside at night. That could lead to dangerously low blood sugar levels.

"Let's get out of the wind and get you warm." Chandler opened the barn door for her. The smell of hay and horse greeted them. Up and down the breezeway, horses poked their heads over stall doors. "You saw your ex-husband this morning?"

"Yeah. He wants to change our custody agreement." Izzy's voice had a fragile note in it. "He's getting serious about a woman who doesn't want to be a mom. Not to Mae. Not to anyone."

"The good news is that you'll have Mae more often." Chandler frowned, making a mental note to check in with Stephanie.

"And the bad news is that she'll realize at some point that Mike was willing to give her up." Izzy had stopped. Her shoulders drew inward. "For a woman. Just like my father did with me."

Chandler dared rub the small of her back. "Hey. Don't crawl into your shell over this. We can get through it. Together."

Izzy drew a shaky breath. "You're right. I can get through this. With the help of my friends. Like you. I can only control so much, right? The rest... The rest I have to weather with grace, the way you all do here at the ranch."

Chandler couldn't speak. No one but his foster parents had ever spoken so powerfully about what he'd overcome, the way he moved forward. He and his foster brothers.

"You honor me...us..." But Chandler didn't want to talk about strength and perseverance. He didn't want to talk about ex-spouses. They were alone. And they were so rarely alone that he wanted to make the most of it. He pointed upward. "Here's where the first sprig of mistletoe goes."

Izzy glanced up, and then at him. "You're teasing me."

"A little. But I'm also telling the truth." He led her to the first stall, which held Baby Bear, the pony Ginny had ridden until a few years ago, and was now Sam's. "Mom hangs a sprig of plastic mistletoe outside each stall door, too."

"Plastic?" Izzy's brow wrinkled.

"Real mistletoe can give a horse colic, which can be deadly."

"Wouldn't want that." She nodded, ruffling Baby Bear's dark forelock. "My mother loved Christmas. And since money was tight, she had a ton of plastic decorations we reused every year. It was my job to clean the dust off the wreath for the front door." She glanced up at Chandler. "Did your mother love Christmas? Your biological mother, I mean."

Chandler's throat clogged unexpectedly with the sharp pain of abandonment. It made no sense. That had been over twenty years ago.

One glance at his face and Izzy withdrew, inching away from him as if sensing he needed space. "I didn't mean to pry or upset you."

Chandler nodded, moving because he needed to, walking away even if his heart didn't want him to put distance between them. He was used to evading questions about his past, including with Stephanie. But if he'd learned anything from his failed marriage, it was that you couldn't open your heart to a woman without opening the door to your past, as well.

Chandler stopped at the stall of Cisco, a palomino, making a low noise to call the horse over. And while he gave the gelding pats on the neck, Izzy joined him at the stall. Cisco tried to nibble on her antlers.

Izzy removed her headpiece with a sleigh-like series of jingles and held it out of reach. "Hey, not edible, young man."

Cisco blew a raspberry.

"About my mother..."

Izzy's blue gaze met his. She waited for him to say more.

"My biological mother was a coffee shop waitress. She always worked on holidays, like Christmas. She said the tips were better. And I..." Chandler drew a bracing amount of air in his lungs. "I already told you about my dad. Neither one was interested in celebrating Christmas the way a lot of families do, like my ranch family does."

Izzy touched his arm briefly, making him wish her hand remained. "You were only a child. That must have been terrible."

"Some kids who were lucky enough to end up here experienced worse." Chandler speared his fingers through Cisco's thick mane, grabbing hold, trying to find emotional balance. "The thing about kids is... They're really good at adapting." To loneliness, to hunger, to lack.

Izzy stared at Chandler with those big blue eyes that he'd forever associate with Christmas. "*You* were good at adapting. None of this third-person stuff. You. And you shouldn't let them haunt you."

Cisco stretched his head over the stall, making another play at nibbling on Izzy's antlers.

Chandler gently pushed the gelding back. "My mother doesn't haunt me. In a way, I have a lot to thank her for. She went to work one day and never came back." Leaving Chandler with only the memory of her words—*take care of yourself, kiddo.* "I kept going to school. At least they gave me two meals a day. And then Dad had a streak where he couldn't stay out of jail. Social services found out and... Here I am."

"Oh, Chandler." Izzy laid her hand on Chandler's arm once more. "Don't ever make light of it."

"I guess we shouldn't judge Mike's new girlfriend." Chandler tried to smile. Failed. Placed a hand over hers. Kept talking. "It might be for the best."

"My dad wasn't a drinker, but he wasn't interested in raising a kid, either," Izzy said in a faraway voice. "Especially not a grieving one when he'd already moved on."

"Kids deserve better than they get sometimes." That seemed like a gross understatement.

"Agreed." Izzy had moved closer as she spoke, brows slanted with curiosity, gaze trained on his mouth.

Chandler was curious, too. And Izzy was too close not to kiss.

He leaned forward, pausing with his lips a hair's breadth away from hers, waiting for Izzy to meet him halfway.

And on a sigh, she did.

It was a gentle kiss this time, a kiss that didn't burst with barely contained heat. This kiss said there was more between them than a surprising attraction. There was a sense of shared experience, of shared values, of respect.

But underneath that tender kiss, there was a growing unease inside Chandler. Because this attraction...this connection... It required change. And change made him twitchy.

So, it made no sense that Chandler kept kissing Izzy. Or that he held on to her as if he never wanted to let her go.

The barn door opened.

Their kiss didn't end. Chandler imagined Izzy didn't hear.

"Oh, hey, Chandler. *Dinner?*" Zane's voice. Surprised.

And then the barn door closed.

## CHAPTER FOURTEEN

"WHAT WAS THAT?" Izzy hurried to the main house, trying—*and failing*—to outwalk Chandler after she'd belatedly realized they'd been discovered kissing and had bolted out of the barn. "No. Don't tell me. I don't want to know. It was bad enough you said that Zane saw us. Go back to looking at me like I'm an alien in Christmas clothing."

Because that kiss had been gentle but powerful. Emotionally powerful. She was just regaining her internal footing after the divorce. She didn't want or need to be plunged into the turbulent waters that love brought.

Izzy suspected Chandler would argue or laugh off her reaction. But they passed beneath the twinkle lights illuminating the trees without speaking. They walked between an inflatable Santa and Frosty without speaking. The main house loomed with gutters and gables lit up with colorful lights. Sam's Christmas tree on the front porch had racing lights. And still, they didn't speak.

She risked a glance at Chandler as they walked across the path toward the stairs and the mudroom. He looked as shell-shocked as she was.

Their gazes met. And it was just as Izzy had requested.

Chandler regarded her as if she was an alien dressed in Christmas clothing—shocking, surprising, someone to be wary of.

*Be careful what you wish for, Izzy.*

"Kissing isn't supposed to be like this," Izzy muttered, charging up the stairs. "Like the Buffalo Diner gave me a double-slice of Coronet's famous pecan pie when I've sworn off desserts."

"If you liked it that much, it means we should be kissing, and kissing frequently," Chandler muttered back, matching her step for step. Still, he managed to reach the mudroom door first and open it for her.

"That's not what it means." Or at least, it wasn't what Izzy wanted it to mean.

There was chatter in the kitchen that quieted to whispers as they removed their boots.

*Great. Zane blabbed about what he saw.*

She couldn't bolt. Mae was in there. But her cheeks were heating and her courage failing.

A touch on her hand made her jump. But Chandler didn't recoil. His fingers curled about hers.

Izzy lifted her gaze to his. She saw understanding there. He knew she wanted to run.

But she'd heard the reputation of the Done Roamin' Ranch boys. And she knew many of them. They didn't run from hard times.

*And I won't, either.*

Izzy straightened her boots, hooking her jingling antler headband in one, and then entered the kitchen, head held high. "Sorry to keep everyone waiting." She slid into a chair next to Mae.

"We didn't wait." Sam had a pork chop and a mountain of potatoes on his plate with a lake of gravy on top surrounded by a forest of green beans.

"Mr. Zane said you were talking to Mr. Cochran in the

barn." Mae had only a dollop of mashed potatoes and five string beans on her plate. She ate like a bird.

Izzy ladled green beans on her plate, and then took two pork chops from a serving tray, placing one on Mae's plate. She quickly cut the meat into Mae-sized bites.

"Mae, why are you calling Zane by his first name and my dad by my last name?" Sam broke the dam on his potato lake, sending gravy streaming onto his plate. It flooded his pork chop and green beans.

"I don't know Mr. Zane's last name." Mae ate a dainty bite of pork chop.

"You don't have to call me mister," Zane said from down the table. "Zane will do."

"And you can call me Chandler." He with the power of drugging kisses took a seat across from Izzy.

"You want me to call you Chandler because you and Mama were talking in the barn?" Mae asked in a hopeful voice.

Zane suffered a coughing fit, resulting in cowboys on either side of him slapping his back.

Zane, who'd most likely witnessed that kiss.

Izzy's cheeks heated once more.

"Everyone at the Done Roamin' Ranch is family," Mary told Mae. "And that means there's no mister or ma'am."

*"Oh..."* Mae drew out the word, small brow furrowed. And then she brightened. "Family? Does that mean they're married now?"

"Yippee!" Sam cried, raising his fork in the air.

Those who'd started dinner before Izzy stilled. Only their heads moved, shifting focus toward Chandler and Izzy's end of the table.

Izzy didn't dare look at Chandler for fear she'd die of embarrassment. "Mae, allowing you to use Chandler's first name doesn't mean we're married. We were just...talking in the barn. About holiday decorations." No one but the kids would believe that whopper of a fib.

"Were you talking about me and Mae?" Sam asked.

"Or about getting married?" Mae asked.

"Or about holiday decorations?" Mary jumped into the fray with a barely contained smile.

"Or about the Christmas turnabout?" Frank asked, better at hiding his amusement than his wife.

"I bet they were talking about specks of dirt in someone's eye," Zane managed to choke out.

Izzy wished there was a way she and Mae could disappear. This not-running stuff was hard.

"What does it matter what we were talking about?" Chandler grumbled, filling his plate with the last of the mashed potatoes. "Pass the gravy, please."

"Oh," Mary said, looking pleased.

"Oh?" Frank said, looking speculative.

"Oh, yeah," Zane said, looking smug.

Izzy wouldn't have thought it was possible, but her cheeks grew hotter. This was worse than the time she tried to ask Tate Oakley out only to find he was in the midst of a date at the time. "Anyway, it's nice to be included in the Done Roamin' Ranch family without having to marry into it."

"Although that's still on the table," Zane said in a stage whisper.

"Sweet." Sam nudged Mae with his elbow. "Now, is anyone going to get me and Mae puppies for Christmas?"

A CONTINGENT OF Done Roamin' Ranch cowboys escorted Izzy and Mae to their SUV after dinner.

The stars were out and the night was crisp and cold. The prairie wind buffeted the inflatable Santa Claus.

And if he was being honest with himself, Chandler wasn't upset about not having time alone with Izzy. He hadn't counted on their kids assuming their time together meant there was marriage on the horizon. That was too much, too soon.

"Well..." Dad turned after Izzy's taillights disappeared over the first rise separating the ranch from the main road, holding on to the top of his cowboy hat when the wind tried to carry it away. "Never a dull moment around here."

"I'll say." Zane covered Sam's ears with his hands, tucking them under his hat brim. "Are you staking a claim on our Christmas flamingo?"

"Hey!" Sam squirmed free.

Chandler frowned at Zane. "We're navigating *something.*" He didn't know how to describe what was going on between them. "There's no claim." *Yet,* a voice whispered in his head.

"Then you won't mind if I ask her to dance next time we're both at the Buckboard." Zane had always been comfortable dancing at the edge of fire.

"I won't stand in anyone's way if that's what you mean," Chandler growled.

"What?" Sam scaled three stacked tires that were soon to be snowmen. "Who are we talking about?"

Chandler lifted Sam into his arms. "Not who. What. We were talking about Christmas decorations."

Zane snorted.

"Dancing ones?" Sam snuggled close, nearly knocking off his hat.

"Yep." Chandler took hold of it.

"Our decorations sure look pretty," Dad said, playing along. "That was a good call on my part. Hiring Izzy, I mean. Why if I hadn't, we might have been stuck."

Chandler grunted.

Laughing, Zane bid them good-night, heading for the cheery lights in the bunkhouse.

"Do you want to talk?" Dad asked Chandler.

"Nope." Chandler headed for the main house. "We're just walking you home." His job was to make sure his parents were safely tucked in at night, same as their stock.

"We could go inside for a few of those Christmas cookies." Sam tucked his head on Chandler's shoulder, beneath the brim of Chandler's cowboy hat, a sure sign that his batteries were running low. "Nothing puts me to sleep better than milk and sweets."

"You made cookies again today?" If so, Chandler hadn't seen the evidence.

"Ronnie and Ginny made fudge." Sam was drooping, limbs turning slack. He yawned.

"You should follow your instincts," Dad said. "If you find something you like that makes you feel good inside, you should stick with it."

"Are we talking about fudge?" Chandler teased.

Dad chuckled. "If you want to be."

"I think this is going to be the best Christmas ever." Sam yawned again. "Decorations, puppies, family. Can we have fudge, Dad?"

"Nope. Time for bed. Plenty of time for fudge at Christmas." Chandler smirked. Sometimes he couldn't believe the parental dreck that came out of his mouth. Chandler stopped at the first porch step.

Sam snored softly.

Dad rubbed Sam's back. "You and Izzy seem to be getting along."

"You've got to preheat an oven, Dad." Chandler didn't want expectations about the two of them to race ahead of their actual progress.

Dad nodded his head. "Well, that's the thing about getting in the kitchen. Sometimes you whip things right up. And sometimes you take hours to create a masterpiece. Don't always know what you'll get as a result."

"You're always so optimistic." And unless Chandler was kissing Izzy, he didn't share that sentiment where they were concerned.

"I know my glass is half-full, son." Dad smiled, slowly scaling the porch steps. He turned when he reached the top. "But the fact remains that if you never go back in the kitchen, you'll never know what happiness awaits you at the dinner table."

## CHAPTER FIFTEEN

"Izzy, do you have a Santapalooza costume?" Earl led Lois Pierce through the jeans section of the feed store on Friday morning toward the sales counter. "You and Mae?"

Earl was walking with noodle legs, and he kept glancing over his shoulder at Lois with an unusually large smile. He'd had a crush on Lois since Izzy couldn't remember when. Lois had taken up dying her grays last Christmas when she began dating again. She usually went around town in worn ranch clothes, carrying a tote with whatever craft project she was working on. In the summer, it was knitting. And with Christmas approaching, she'd be working on costumes for the annual Santapalooza ride on Christmas Day, where all participants had to dress like Santa or his missus.

"A Santapalooza costume?" Izzy set aside the Christmas-scented candles she'd been pricing and thoughts of Chandler. Who would have thought that beneath that stoic exterior lived a man who was so passionate and impulsive? Probably the same folks who would have predicted Izzy would go around town in holiday-themed outfits getting paid to decorate for Christmas.

"Izzy," Earl said, bearing down on the sales counter. "Do you have a Santapalooza costume?"

"Nope," Izzy said. "Why do you ask?"

"Last year, we broke the record for the most Santas in a parade ride." Lois set her large purple tote on the counter. It was stuffed with red velvet and white faux fur trim. "Now some yahoo town in New Mexico is trying to break our record. We're recruiting riders, preferably those who already have costumes. Clementine must defend Santapalooza."

"We don't have horses or costumes." Izzy smiled apologetically. "My last ride was when I was a teenager. When my dad sold my horse, I gave my costume away." And every year since, she'd watched with just a twinge of envy.

"I asked Frank over at the Done Roamin' Ranch if we could borrow some horses." Lois stared at Izzy from beneath a worn brown hat. "And I'm going around town this morning to recruit Santas. If I can make you costumes in time, can we count on you and Mae?"

"Course you can," Earl answered for Izzy. "You can count on me, too. Whatever you need. You just call me. Day or night. You have my number, don't ya?"

"I'm glad you said that, Earl." Lois smiled at him without a trace of reciprocal opposite-sex admiration. "I've never been able to get you to ride in Santapalooza. Can we count on you this year?"

"I... I... I... I..." Earl stammered. He hadn't ridden for years due to a bum hip he kept putting off replacing. Riding for him was a bit painful, not that anyone but Izzy knew it. But after being blindsided by Lois's offer, he recovered, standing taller. "Course, I will. If you need me."

Izzy hid her amusement behind a small cough. "If someone has a wagon, Earl, Mae and I will gladly climb on board in our Santa costumes. We'd be proud to represent Clementine."

Earl beamed at Izzy. "That's a right good idea. Count us in for a wagon ride."

A few minutes later, having taken note of their clothing sizes and promising to deliver costumes next week, Lois made her leave. No one else was in the store. Stan was out making deliveries.

It was the perfect time to tease Earl about his crush.

"You should ask Lois out." Izzy returned the priced candles to their display box. "You'd make a cute couple."

Earl removed his cowboy hat and ran his hand through his white hair, scoffing. "She's been dating Chet for a year."

"Then you should attend some of those socials at the retirement home to find yourself a dance partner." Izzy carried the box toward the Christmas aisle. "Studies show that men live longer with a romantic partner. Love keeps you young."

"I've got you and Mae to keep me young," Earl stated matter-of-factly. "Speaking of, when are we going to set up Mae's princess bed?"

Mae's Christmas gift. Izzy bit her lip. "Mike is supposed to have Mae on Christmas Eve." Izzy made room for the candles on the shelf, wondering if her ex-husband would still want Mae given the self-serving choice he'd made. "And I need a few more payments to come in from my holiday services before I can buy that bed."

"Our girl's going to have big dreams beneath that canopy," Earl mused.

"I hope so." Satisfied with the way the shelf looked, Izzy returned to the sales counter, still thinking about Mike. "Earl, why didn't you ever get married and have kids of your own?"

His back to her, the old man was restocking the candy display. He didn't answer for some time.

Izzy opened a file on the store's computer to check online orders.

"I wanted to have a family," Earl said, turning slowly to face Izzy. His eyes were filled with sadness. "I never met the right woman at the right time. It's like this attraction I have to Lois. She wasn't ready to date for years. And then when she was ready, I didn't notice." He snapped his fingers. "And just like that, she got snapped up."

"I'm sorry." Was that how it would be with her and Chandler?

"Don't be." He carried empty candy boxes to the counter, breaking them down until they were flat. "I have you and Mae."

"That you do. We're lucky to have you." Izzy's father lived in Oklahoma City and had little interest in staying in touch other than with birthday and Christmas cards. But who would take Mike's place as a reliable father figure for Mae? Chandler? He was a good father.

Izzy bit her lip. Love shouldn't be judged by the other attributes a man brought to the relationship.

"Izzy..." Earl pressed his palms on top of the stack of flattened boxes. "If you feel something for little Sam's father the way I think you do, don't wait."

"Whose team are you on?" Izzy tried to make light of Earl's advice, even as a tiny voice in her head agreed with him. "Haven't you ever heard the phrase about fools rushing in?"

"Try telling that to all those friends of yours who've gotten engaged in the past year or so." Earl's chin thrust out. "They're rushing in, the same way customers barrel in here on Black Friday for our annual cowboy boot sale. And why? Because they know a good man is as hard to find as the right pair of boots."

Izzy laughed. She couldn't help it.

Her laughter riled Earl all the more. "Mark my words, Izzy. If you hesitate, you'll end up like me. Alone. Sending signals to the person you pine for but whose radar is oblivious to your frequency."

"Don't you worry about me." Izzy came around the counter to hug Earl. "Or my love life."

"That's just it, girl." When Izzy would have pulled away, Earl clung tight. "You're all I've got to worry about."

"THERE'S MY LITTLE MAN." Stephanie opened the door and smiled at Sam, who stomped past her and headed for his room. "What's wrong with him?"

It was Friday night and dark outside even though it wasn't yet dinnertime. The prairie wind had died down but there was promise of cold in the air.

Chandler handed Stephanie Sam's duffel. "Sam is super excited about things going on at the ranch." The Christmas roundabout, the decorations inside his room at the ranch and the fact that Mae was there practically every day. "He really wanted to stay the weekend."

"That's not like Sam." Stephanie frowned, tugging at the collar of her mail uniform. Her thick-soled work boots were in a heap next to the door. "He's always so good-natured."

"There's a lot going on everywhere right now, including you and that job offer." Chandler tipped his cowboy hat back. "Sam told me he wanted to buy you a suitcase for Christmas. Seems like he might know something that I don't."

"He might have heard me and Mom talk about it on Thanksgiving." Stephanie crossed her arms over her chest. "You'll be happy to know that she doesn't approve of the job, either."

It felt petty to acknowledge how happy that statement made him. "Have you made your choice?"

"That's what I wanted to talk to you about." Stephanie hugged herself tighter, a stubborn look in her eyes. "I took next week off to go to Fort Worth for orientation. Monday through Friday."

"Steph." Frustration at his ex, worry for his son's heartbreak and annoyance that Steph could be this selfish... Those emotions tangled up inside Chandler, tighter and tighter until he thought his control might shatter. That he might rant and rail at Stephanie for throwing away their son's love and trust.

"You're freaking out. I knew this would happen." Steph drew a deep breath. "It's just five days. And I might not like the work, or they might not like me. But if I do move to Texas, I want to take Sam with me."

"No!" Sam cried, running for the front door. "I won't go."

And before either of them could stop Sam, he'd bolted out the door into the darkness.

"Sam!" Stephanie shouted, eyes filling with tears. She reached for her shoes.

But Chandler had already crossed the threshold. He turned back. "Wait here. I'll talk to him."

Steph stood, wiping a tear from her cheek. She looked away, and then slowly closed the door, shutting him out.

Chandler hurried to the sidewalk, then walked down the street, calling for Sam. He didn't have to go far. Christmas lights were shining up and down the avenue, all except at one house. But there was activity on that lawn. Chandler could just make out the silhouette of a ladder and beside it a small figure, possibly a child.

"She wants to take me, Mae. Can you believe it?" Sam's voice carried to Chandler, who was still a few houses away. "I won't go. I won't."

A crack, like a branch snapping under unexpected weight, cut through the air.

"Take a breath, Sam. You're not going anywhere right now until I can get out of this tree." Izzy's voice. "Mae, can you shine that flashlight up here. *Ugh, n*ot in my eyes, bug. There. That's better."

"Your dad won't let you go, Sam." Mae sounded worried. "Will he, Mama?"

Another crack was followed by Izzy's cry of, *"Ouch!"*

Chandler broke into a jog, heading for Paula Lincoln's house. She was a retired schoolteacher and a member of the Santapalooza planning committee, always cheerful with a kind word for Sam. And it seemed she'd hired Izzy to help her put up lights. Why Izzy was working in the dark and in a tree, no less, was beyond Chandler.

"Ouch!" Izzy cried again, followed by the slightest of jingling bells.

"Are you gonna fall, Miz Izzy?" Sam's voice. "Do we need to get out of the way?"

"Yes," Chandler answered for Izzy, charging across the lawn and into the meager light spilling out of Paula's front windows.

"Do you want me to climb up there, Mama? I can get those lights untangled for you." Mae now sat on the bottom rung of the ladder. She shined the flashlight at Chandler, luckily not into his eyes. "Hi, Chandler."

A branch cracked. Izzy made a sound that was half gasp, half curse.

"Hey." Chandler took one of Mae's cold hands and drew her to her feet. And then he took possession of her flashlight. "Sam, if that's you hiding behind the tree trunk, kindly step out where I can see you and Izzy won't fall on you. I want both you kids to move over by the front door."

"Dad, I'm not going back. I'm going to live with you at the ranch." Sam leaned his head around the tree trunk.

"We'll talk about this in a minute, squirt. Right now, I need you and Mae on the front walk." When they did as he'd directed, Chandler glanced up into the tree. "Trouble, Izzy?"

"Nothing I can't handle." Izzy was balanced precariously on a branch above Chandler that bent to support her weight a few feet from the trunk. She was dressed as Rudolph, whose nose blinked like a beacon. And she was struggling to free a section of lights tangled with a branch. "I've got this. I just need to get a little farther out."

Chandler aimed the flashlight into the tree, assessing the bouncy bend to the branch every time Izzy moved and the determined look on her face. "I thought you didn't do circular lights in trees."

"I had a client request." Izzy's frustration was showing. Her chin was out. Her sweater had a big snag with a small branch stuck in it. And her antlers had sunk to the back of her head and were at risk of sliding off. "Now, don't say another word."

"Where's that fancy pole we used the other day at the ranch?"

Izzy made an indecipherable noise. "That's twelve words, Chandler. And I have three words for you. *At the ranch.*" Izzy was losing her cool, lunging more precariously for the stuck strand of lights every time.

"I think she can do it," Mae said. "Mama does everything she says she will."

Sam made a sound of disgust. "My mom, too. And she wants to take me to *Texas.*"

Chandler ignored them. "Come down, Izzy. You can tell Paula that you'll finish tomorrow. I'll bring the pole into town first thing in the morning." He'd even untangle the strand from the branches for her.

"You'll come in at dawn?" Izzy scoffed. "Paula wants her lights up before her grandkids arrive for lunch. I promised her we'd be done tonight and..." Izzy swiped her hand out toward the stuck strand, but the foot she was standing on slipped. She contorted, seemingly balancing midair. And then she plunged, torso landing on the branch where her foot used to be. And her feet...

One boot kicked Chandler's hat off.

Her hands flailed toward him. But she was out of reach, sliding off the branch backward.

Young cries filled the air, accented by Chandler's flashlight beam highlighting the fear in Izzy's eyes.

"I've got you." Chandler held out his arms, grabbing Izzy's legs as she fell, but lost his balance and toppled backward onto the ground.

*Oof.*

"I'm okay," Izzy wheezed but it sounded as if she was taking her last breath.

"Mama!" Della-Mae dogpiled them. "You're safe."

*Oof.*

"Dad!" Sam fell on top of them all. "You saved her."

"I can't breathe," Izzy wheezed, fainter this time.

Chandler slowly rolled over, sending the kids gently tumbling to the grass and Izzy listing next to him.

"Can't..." Izzy repeated, not gasping, just wheezing, like a hooked fish taken from water.

"You've got the wind knocked out of you." Chandler had seen it often enough when someone got thrown from a bull or bronc.

"Mama?" Mae sounded woeful.

"I've got you." Chandler moved to his knees, bringing Izzy with him, pushing her into a crouched position. And then he wacked her on the back with the flat of his hand. "It's all right. It's all right." But he was scared to death that he wouldn't be able to get her lungs working properly again.

"What are you doing?" Mae hollered, moving closer. "Don't hit Mama!"

"Dad, what are you doing?" Sam scrambled to his feet, sounding aghast.

Chandler kept giving Izzy bracing backslaps. "Come on, honey. Fill those lungs with air."

"What's going on out there?" Paula Lincoln opened her front door, sending light spilling out to the lawn. "I can't hear *Jeopardy.*"

Izzy drew a deep, raspy breath.

And without thinking, Chandler wrapped his arms around her. "It's okay. It's going to be okay."

He'd save the lectures for later—after he was certain Izzy was fine, after he calmed the kids and reassured Paula that her lights would be up on time in the morning, and after he and Sam drove Izzy and Mae home.

"I'M FINE." Izzy couldn't count how many times she'd told Chandler those same words in the past hour.

He'd insisted on driving them home, insisted on coming inside, insisted on staying. "I've seen plenty of cowboys get the wind knocked out of them when they get thrown. There's a possibility that your diaphragm will cramp up again, seizing up your lungs. Just so you're aware. You shouldn't be alone."

"Dr. Cochran," she'd scoffed. But while he'd ordered pizza and found a movie suitable for the kids to watch, Izzy had searched for information on follow-up care on her cell phone and was humbled to find Chandler was correct. "Thank you," she told him when he sat next to her on the couch. "I appreciate you watching out for me. But it's been nearly an hour."

"I don't mind staying." Chandler settled her red-and-green Christmas blanket over his legs, too, and slid his arm behind her neck. "Better safe than sorry. How are your ribs?"

"It hurts to breathe," she admitted. And because he'd been her hero, she added, "If you hadn't been there..." Her voice cracked and her heart clenched because she couldn't imagine how she would have survived if Chandler hadn't been there. "I could have..."

"But you didn't. I was there. Mae and Sam were troupers, just like when Mrs. Stodimeyer's water broke. If I hadn't been there, Mae would have pounded on Paula's door. As a teacher, Paula would have received medical training. She'd have come to your rescue."

What-if scenarios continued to swirl through Izzy's head, but eventually she had to admit that Chandler was right. And about that time, the pizza arrived.

Chandler didn't let Izzy get up. He found plates. He brought them drinks. And when they were all seated around Izzy's small dining room table, it seemed so natural, like they were a family, and Izzy started to cry.

"Mama?" Mae abandoned her chair for a seat in Izzy's lap.

"It's okay. I promise not to cry for long." But when she wrapped her arms around Mae, more tears fell than dried up. The pressure of the week had caught up to her—the expensive bed for Mae, Mike's startling announcement, all her running around without proper rest, Chandler's confusing kisses and that horribly scary fall.

Her meltdown didn't stop the males at the table from de-
vouring their pizza.

"Dad?" Sam asked when Izzy blew her nose in a napkin. "I
don't want to go with Mom. Not anywhere. Not ever again."

Suddenly, Izzy remembered how Sam had shown up, bursting out of the shadows full of upset. She glanced at Chandler.

He took Sam's outburst calmly, laying a hand on Sam's
shoulder. "Do you remember what Grandpa always says about
bull riding?"

Eyes wide, Sam nodded. "You gotta hang on and roll with
whatever happens."

"That's right." Chandler's smile looked brittle, and Izzy's
heart went out to him. "Your mother was offered a job in
Texas and—"

"I'm not going." Sam's lips thrust out.

"I don't want you to go, either," Chandler said quietly. "But
this is just like a bucking bull suddenly putting on a spin move.
We've got to hang on to each other and figure this out."

"I'll tell somebody I want to stay with you." Sam wasn't
ready to be mollified. "Just like you told somebody you wanted
to stay with Grandma and Grandpa."

"A judge," Chandler murmured, gaze drifting Izzy's way.

"That's right." Sam gained steam. "You told a judge cuz
your mom came out of nowhere and wanted you back."

Izzy gasped. Taken to court and forced to choose between
that family he'd dreamed of and a mother who'd left him behind. What a horrible position to be put in.

Chandler ran a hand through his hair. "I was older than you,
squirt. And it wasn't easy to look my mother in the eyes and
tell her I was better off where I was."

"I could." Sam picked a pepperoni from his pizza, and then
stared up at Chandler. "But maybe you could do it for me?"

"This is something your mom and I have to work out."
Chandler moved his hand from Sam's shoulder to his hair,

giving it a playful ruffle. "And who knows? She may spend next week in Texas and realize she hates it."

"I can't leave." Sam laid his arm on the table and then put his hand on Chandler's. "My life is ruined. I had it all planned out."

Mae slipped off Izzy's lap and worked her way around the table to Sam's side. She patted his head. "We'll figure this out, Sam. The same way we work on math in school."

That seemed to cheer Sam up.

Later, after the pizza had been devoured and another movie found for the kids to watch, Izzy and Chandler still had the couch to themselves. He'd texted Stephanie. They'd agreed that Sam would spend the night with Chandler at the ranch. Hopefully, by morning the worst of Sam's rebellion would have passed.

Izzy snuggled closer to Chandler, trying not to breathe too deeply and make her ribs hurt, or too shallowly and give herself a panic attack for thinking her lungs weren't working the way they should. She replayed Earl's conversation about missed opportunities in her head. Decided that was demoralizing and somehow replayed Chandler talking about their something either being fabulous or ending up a bust all around. Since that was depressing, her thoughts went to someone else's problems—Lois and the need for more Santas on horseback, the unexpected run on tinsel at the feed store and Stephanie deciding to follow her dreams.

"I need to think about something other than my ribs," she whispered to Chandler. *Or problems in general.*

"You want to talk?" he whispered back. "About what?"

"About something that doesn't matter." Oh, that wasn't it at all. She wanted to talk about important things, topics that would help her decide if there was hope for a future with Chandler or if they were doomed to fail. She needed to be careful that Mae didn't get too attached to Chandler. Her daughter was already attached to Sam. But was this the right time for romance?

The kids were sprawled out on pillows on the floor, engrossed in their animated movie. She was tucked in next to Chandler as if they were a real couple. It was very domestic, almost...safe.

"Actually, the truth is... I was angry with my mom for dying," Izzy admitted in that same whisper. "Probably the same way you were angry at your mother for leaving without saying goodbye."

Chandler said nothing. But he didn't push her away or bolt for the door.

So, Izzy continued. "Other people go through cancer successfully, with their kids or spouses by their side. But my dad... He couldn't handle adversity of any kind. He worked for the power company when I was a kid until he got a bad performance review." She'd overheard Mom telling someone that he'd quit because of pride. "And then he managed a grocery store in Friar's Creek but when someone else was promoted over him, he quit. Each time, he tried to explain things to me. And even though I didn't really understand..." She'd been a kid, after all. "I wanted to believe in him. You know, to root for him. But then, Mom got sick, and I realized that he couldn't stand loss of any kind." She'd tried talking to him but that hadn't worked.

Chandler said nothing. The kids still looked engrossed in their movie.

"I was relieved when Dad left town but also sad, the way I imagine you felt after choosing your foster family over your mother. But my dad didn't give me a choice. Stay here, he said." And that had made Izzy feel relief, as well. Her father had lost her respect and she'd wondered how long it would take for her to lose his, for him to turn his back on her the way he had on Mom. "But there was a happy ending. Because of Earl..." Izzy drew too big a breath and winced, taking a moment to allow the pain to fade before continuing. "I had a place to call home and someone to watch over me. And then... I fell in love with Mike."

Chandler grunted.

"Mike had a life plan. Find a woman with the same work ethic as he had. Start a family young so that he could enjoy his later years as an empty nester." It had all sounded good to Izzy, like they were on the same team.

Chandler released a deep breath.

"Are you listening?" Izzy glanced up at him. "Should I stop?"

"Don't stop." Chandler shook his head, compassion in those soft brown eyes. "I heard every word. Mom. Anger. Dad. Anger. Mike. Getting to the anger."

She supposed he was right. "The point is... We've both had our share of folks breaking our hearts. I never wanted that for Mae."

He made a deep sound in his throat. "Or me for Sam."

Their gazes met and held. And she knew... Izzy knew that neither one of them wanted their hearts broken again. Not by family. And not by the person who promised to cherish you till death tore them apart.

There was a long pause, during which time the hero in the movie disappointed everyone important to him. And the difference between that character and someone like Izzy's father was that the animated hero was self-aware enough to realize he'd made a mistake and apologize.

Izzy eased away from Chandler. The movie would be ending soon, and she didn't want to give the kids ideas about weddings again.

But Chandler drew her back to him, turning his head to whisper in her ear. "I resented my mom for disappearing. Well... I told the police my dad might have done something to her. But that turned out to be untrue."

"The spouse is the first suspect on every police show I

watch," Izzy whispered back. "And from what you've told me, they were a volatile couple."

Chandler nodded. "I bounced around in foster care. Hurt. Angry. Resentful that no one wanted me."

Izzy found his hand and gave it a squeeze. "Unlike me, you probably let it all go."

"Yep."

"I can't imagine leaving Mae."

"Or me, Sam."

His statement warmed Izzy's heart immensely.

"Mike canceled having Mae this weekend because there's a big car sale at his dealership." She was afraid that was the end of him taking Mae for anything. The revised custody agreement was sitting on her bedroom dresser awaiting her signature.

"Can I call Mike a jerk?"

Izzy smiled, but it was a sad sort of smile. "Why not? I do. Can I call Stephanie scared for wanting to take Sam with her to Texas?"

"She's selfish," Chandler said quietly. "Not scared."

Izzy shook her head. "She's afraid and I'll tell you why. You understand how scary change is. I know you do because you hate change so much that you hadn't moved a couch that disrupts the flow of traffic in your house."

He made a face. "So what?"

"Stephanie wants to take Sam because she's scared, too. Scared of reaching for a dream and falling flat on her face. And there's nothing that makes a parent feel better than a hug from their child."

And even if Chandler said nothing, Izzy could tell by the way his brow was furrowed that she'd given him something to think about.

## CHAPTER SIXTEEN

"DAD." SAM PADDED into Chandler's bedroom and crawled into bed with him while it was still dark outside. "Are you awake?"

"Yep." Chandler had merely been waiting for his alarm to go off in…another twenty minutes. Funny how just thinking about Izzy made him lose sleep. Funnier how he didn't feel sleep-deprived. He felt energized, ready to see her, curious to know how she was feeling today.

"Can we go into town for breakfast at the Buffalo Diner?"

"Yep." Chandler didn't move, though. If they went into town, he'd need to let Stephanie know and broker peace between her and Sam. Considering he wasn't a neutral party in the negotiations—he wanted Sam to stay in Clementine—that was a conversation he wasn't looking forward to.

Sam kicked out his feet and moved his arms as if he was swimming in bed. "Dad?"

"Hmm?"

"You're not moving."

"Right." Chandler rolled out of bed. It being Saturday, he didn't need to feed stock or manage work on the ranch.

He didn't shower. He didn't shave. He just threw on some clothes, same as his kid. He stepped out on his front porch, taking stock of the ranch buildings, the Christmas decorations, the roundabout with its snowmen surrounding the nativity scene.

It was dark. The Christmas lights were still on.

That wasn't unusual. Mom liked her light show on all night. Said it reminded her that there was good in the world and that there would be good in the world when she got up the next day. Sometimes those lights got too much for Chandler's brothers in the bunkhouse and they unplugged a strand or two in the name of a good night's sleep. But this morning, the lights were all still on, still bright and cheerful.

Enduring cheerfulness. Enduring...love.

When Chandler thought of his foster mother, that's what he thought of. When he thought of his biological mother, he thought of selfishness, of weakness, of bitterness. Thinking of her left a bad taste in his mouth.

But last night, when he and Izzy were sharing confidences, she'd said something about Stephanie that had given Chandler pause.

*Stephanie wants to take Sam because she's scared.*

*Was my mother scared? Scared she'd be stuck in that unpredictable, unhappy life?*

Chandler had washed his hands of his biological mother out of self-preservation. If she left him once, who could promise she wouldn't leave him again? No one, that's who.

"Dad?" Sam took Chandler's hand. "Are you gonna look at the lights all day?"

"Nope." But he'd like to. Chandler didn't think he'd look at Christmas lights again without thinking of his foster mother and Izzy. "But we need to find that pole Izzy used to string lights in the high places. I think Zane and Ryan used it to put up our porch lights."

Sam whooped. "I know where it is!" He ran down the porch stairs, pulling Chandler along behind him. Across the ranch yard. Into the roundabout. "Zane said it looked like a shepherd's staff."

Sure enough. Izzy's wooden pole was in the lean-to shielding the baby Jesus from the elements.

Sam used it like a staff as they walked to Chandler's truck. Staff in the truck bed, Cochran fellas buckled in, they drove into town. The sky to the east was cloudy, a mixture of purple and red.

"I'm not going to Texas," Sam said from the back seat. "Not ever."

"Not ever?" Chandler glanced in the rearview mirror, making out the shadowy features of Sam. "What if I'm working a rodeo in Dallas?"

"You never take me to rodeos." Sullen.

"You're old enough now to compete in junior rodeos."

"I am? Wow." Sam was less sullen now. "Can I ride bulls?"

"Most kids start with sheep."

Silence. It stretched for a mile or so.

"Mom doesn't like rodeos."

There was a test for Chandler in that statement. Sam might just as well have asked, *"Whose side are you on, Dad?"* Chandler chose his words carefully. "Your mom doesn't want you to get hurt."

Silence. The pastures of the Oklahoma prairie gave way to smaller ranchettes. The horizon showed a sliver of yellow.

"I'm not going to Texas," Sam said, less sullen, more feisty.

"Not even to visit your mom?"

"Do you want me to leave you?" Small, booted feet kicked Chandler's seat back. Small fists bumped the truck's ceiling. "Are you trying to get rid of me?"

Chandler slowed down, pulled over. Put his truck in Park so he could turn and face his little mini-me. "Sam, I love you. I don't want you to go anywhere." His arms were long enough that he could rest a hand on Sam's jean-clad leg. "But your mom… She wants to do something more exciting than deliver the mail. And she can't do it here."

"I'm not—"

"Going to Texas," Chandler finished for him. "Yeah. I know. I'm going to talk to your mom. But you have to understand that if I can convince her to let you stay with me that it's going to break her heart to leave you."

"Then she shouldn't go." Sam crossed his arms over his chest. "She's supposed to take care of me."

Chandler nodded slowly, trying to channel Izzy. She always seemed to know what to say and when to say it. Even if it wasn't what Chandler wanted to hear. "Sometimes you have to make hard choices, squirt. Like your uncle Wade. He had to leave Ronnie and Ginny home to compete in bronc riding."

"They could have gone."

"Nope. They had responsibilities and commitments. To work and school."

"Then Wade could have stayed."

"But then he wouldn't be able to do the thing he loves."

Sam slumped in his seat. "I don't want to grow up."

"But you will, squirt." Chandler turned around and put the truck in gear. "And when you do, you're going to make me proud."

Sam was quiet the rest of the ride into town.

Of course, as soon as Sam's boots hit pavement, he ran for the Buffalo Diner's front door. "Come on, Dad!"

Chandler hadn't taken two steps into the coffee shop when a young, feminine squeal rose in the air, bringing Coronet and her coffeepot to a halt midpour.

"Look! It's Sam!" Mae cried, rising to her knees in a window booth.

"Look! It's Mae!" Sam cried, running toward his bestie, who sat with her mother.

*With Izzy.*

The sky outside seemed to lighten.

Chandler felt the beginnings of a smile. And of a thought…

*What are the chances that this was a coincidence?*

But when Chandler's gaze connected with Izzy's, he didn't

care if fate was lending him a hand in winning her heart or if two seven year-olds were in cahoots and trying to set them up. Izzy was his ray of sunshine. She made change worth the risk.

Sam scooted into the booth, taking a seat next to Mae. "Come on, Dad." He glanced back at Chandler and pointed to the seat next to Izzy.

*Oh, yeah. There was mischief afoot.*

Chandler eagerly walked across the diner to join them.

Chandler's boots came to a stop at Izzy's booth, their tips nearly touching the base right where there were scuff marks on the linoleum. Someone had bolted into or out of this booth lickety-split. *Bolting into...* That had practically been Chandler. "Sam, were you invited to take a seat? Maybe Izzy and Mae want to eat alone."

Mae and Sam bumped shoulders and giggled...*nervously?*

What did it matter what mischief was afoot when Izzy was smiling so warmly at him?

"Invited? *Dad,*" Sam said after their laughter died away. "It's Mae. We have to sit with her."

"Because we're best friends," Mae echoed, smiling so sweetly...so innocently.

*Maybe I have an overactive imagination.*

"Best not to paddle upstream." Izzy patted the seat next to her. She was dressed to decorate houses today—green sweater with a squirrel on the front and a Santa hat. The squirrel had antlers and...

"I see you're finally owning up to the fact that tangling Christmas lights is your holiday superpower." Chandler chuckled, taking a seat next to her. The squirrel on her sweater was tangled in blinking lights.

"Hardy-har." Izzy sipped her coffee. "Did you bring my pole?"

"Yep." Chandler sat back to give Coronet room to slide a steaming mug of coffee in front of him. She also dropped off crayons and place mats to color for the kids. "Not that you're going to use that light-stringing pole. I'll put up lights for you today." He cataloged Izzy's posture. "How are you? Sore?"

She nodded. "Now I know how bull riders feel the day after they've been thrown."

"Then you need to learn the secret to a speedy recovery, sworn to by every Done Roamin' Ranch cowboy." Chandler smiled at Sam, not that his son noticed. He was playing tic-tac-toe with Mae. "It's pancakes and bacon." *And love.*

He didn't dare say that last part out loud.

LATER, AFTER A filling breakfast and an hour spent preparing Paula Lincoln's front yard with enough holiday cheer to please any Scrooge, Chandler stood on Stephanie's front porch with Sam. Izzy and Mae had moved on to decorate Destiny Rogers's room inside the retirement home.

Chandler glanced at Sam. "Remember what I said."

Sam nodded, staring at the front door. "Mom is scared and needs us."

The front door swung open. Stephanie looked a right mess—dark circles under her eyes, uncombed hair ends sticking out from under a knit cap, baggy gray sweats. She dropped down to her knees and opened her arms. "Sam…"

Their son propelled himself forward, throwing his arms around Stephanie. They both started to cry.

After a moment's hesitation, Chandler knelt on the ground next to them, drew them close and said the most natural thing. "We're going to figure this out. Together."

"WE PULLED IT OFF." Ronnie gave Izzy a side hug on Saturday night. "Cars are beginning to pull through the First Annual Done Roamin' Ranch Christmas Roundabout." She squeezed Izzy harder.

"Ouch." Izzy grimaced through a wave of rib pain, easing a step away from her friend where they stood on Ronnie's front porch.

"Sorry." Ronnie's mittened hands hovered over Izzy's mid-section. "I forgot you're among the walking wounded."

Izzy drew a careful breath. "No hugs until the new year. Doc Nabidian said it'll takes weeks to heal." He'd wrapped Izzy's ribs in gauze, prescribed rest and pain pills. "He wants me to slow down."

"To which you vaguely nodded, all the while thinking you'll slow down after Christmas." Ronnie fussed with Izzy's heavy coat, gently pulling the ends closer together before zipping it closed. "I know how you think."

"That's because you and I think alike." As many single mothers were wont to do. Izzy watched the first truck make the U-turn around the circle of tire snowmen ringing the nativity scene.

The ranch was ablaze with light and color. Every building outlined in lights. Every tree ringed with the same. Wreaths on every door. Inflatable Santa and Frosty waving toward visitors. Christmas music was playing on a speaker set on the main house's front porch, currently playing "Deck the Halls." All they needed was snow to make folks think they weren't in Clementine, Oklahoma, anymore.

Ginny, Mae, Sam and some kids from the junior rodeo team were working a hot chocolate and cookie station at the beginning of the circle, overseen by Bess and Griff, the high school team's coaches. That had been Mary's idea, very much last minute. But she'd contacted various local teams and clubs offering to let them take over for a night to raise money. Or, in the case of Lois and her quest for more horseback riding Santas, a chance to recruit volunteers.

Chandler, Frank and a few other cowboys flanked Mary, who sat bundled in a chair between two tire snowmen. She was covered in several layers of blankets, wore Christmas-themed knit—cap, scarf, mittens—and was ready to greet visitors as they pulled through. She'd rejected the idea of sitting on the front porch as being too far from her visitors.

Chandler glanced Izzy's way and waved.

And then the visiting truck rolled to a stop between them, blocking Izzy's view of Chandler and Mary.

"You've got an admirer," Ronnie teased, fussing with the pink scarf around her neck before slipping her hands into her purple swing jacket pockets. "How's that going?"

Two more vehicles appeared on the rise, their headlights sweeping down on the ranch as they approached. Laughter emanating from those around Mary filled the air.

"Things with Chandler are...confusing." Izzy drew another careful breath. "For me more so than him, I think. I've been trying to remember back to when I thought I was in love with Mike because I don't want to be in a relationship just because a man is nice to me and kisses my socks off. If I'm going to do this again, I want it to be real and lasting, like what Frank and Mary have. Or what you found with Wade."

"Love doesn't come with checkboxes." Ronnie smiled gently.

"If this isn't the kind of love songs are written about, it isn't fair to Mae. She's fond of Chandler."

More vehicles were arriving.

"Not to mention she and Sam are suddenly best friends." Ronnie nodded. "I understand where you're coming from. But nothing worth having comes without a risk. And if what you're feeling for Chandler and he's feeling for you has the foundation of deep, everlasting love, it's worth taking a chance."

Izzy nodded. "A few weeks ago, I wouldn't have been open to risking our safe little life." And then Mae had turned down a role in the Christmas pageant. "I wouldn't have ordered a week's worth of ugly Christmas sweaters or matching head-gear."

"Or fallen out of a tree?" Ronnie asked. "Perhaps never kissed a tall, handsome cowboy?"

"There are disadvantages to you knowing me so well." Izzy tried to laugh, but that still hurt. "One of which is that it's hard to keep a secret from you. But... What would you do if you were in my boots?"

The roundabout was filled with trucks and the Done Roamin' Ranch cowboys had spread out to greet them. The hot chocolate and cookie table looked to be doing a good business.

"What would I do..." Ronnie began, then laughed. "I'd think about it and then go for it. It's what I did with Wade—all in." Ronnie rubbed a hand across Izzy's back. "But that's me. We may think alike but you've treaded carefully since your divorce. If you have doubts, slow things down."

More vehicles were coming over the rise now. Mary was due to have lots of visitors tonight.

"I have doubts, but..." Izzy leaned her head on Ronnie's shoulder, thinking of Earl. And letting the warm, excited emotion toward Chandler roll through her. Was this love? "I'm worried that this is something I could lose out on if I don't take hold of it now."

# CHAPTER SEVENTEEN

"MERRY CHRISTMAS, IZZY."

The female voice first thing in the morning had Izzy looking up from reconciling feed store inventory to find Della-Mae's teacher holding the handle of a car seat cradling a thickly bundled newborn. The woman's normally smooth brown hair stuck out in spots and she had the air of exhaustion about her.

Truth be told, Izzy was having a hard time concentrating on checks and balances. She hadn't seen Chandler in two days, but he was never far from her thoughts. Partly because he texted her several times a day, asking how she was feeling. Her ribs didn't ache as badly as they had but the holiday decorating business wasn't helping. Nor were her worries about earning enough to buy Mae that princess bed or the wait for a new set of papers from Mike. If it wasn't Chandler keeping her awake at night, it was her achy ribs, the size of her checking account or the revised custody agreement she and her lawyer were waiting for.

So, the appearance of Theresa Stodimeyer was a joyful and welcome distraction.

"Merry Christmas, Theresa." Izzy hurried to usher the new mom to a chair behind the sales counter. "What can I get for you? Water? Help shopping for Christmas gifts? Wrapping paper? Dog food?" Izzy ran through a litany of things Theresa might need.

"I'm not here to trouble you with requests, Izzy. I brought you Della-Mae's letter to Santa. I meant to deliver them two weeks ago...but..." Theresa stared lovingly into the face of her baby boy. "I was interrupted. And since some parents in our class didn't want me to mail them to the North Pole, I knew it was important to deliver them to parents as soon as I was cleared to drive." She reached into her diaper bag and withdrew an envelope with *Santa* written on the front in big, wobbly letters.

"For the record, I voted to mail them to Santa," Izzy told her. She opened the envelope carefully, trying not to rip it. "It's risky getting these letters back. Heaven forbid Mae finds it in my possession." She took a moment to read her daughter's Christmas wish before looking at Theresa in shock. "This is unexpected."

"I bet." Theresa nodded, swaying side to side in her chair. "I helped her and Sam with the wording."

"They wrote these after Thanksgiving? Together?"

"Yes. They wrote the same Christmas wish." Theresa smiled warmly at Izzy. "It's not a bad wish."

"Says you." Izzy shook her head. "If you have Sam's, I can save you a trip to the Done Roamin' Ranch and give it to Chandler myself." She'd call and see if he could make a trip into town. This seemed important. It was certainly unsettling.

But first, Izzy spent a few minutes visiting with Theresa. Luckily, she had her Christmas gift under the sales counter. It was always fun to hear moms talk about their babies. Thankfully, it was slow at the store, allowing them some privacy.

Finally, when the baby started to fuss and Theresa got slowly to her feet, Izzy was about to wish Theresa a Merry Christmas when she remembered something.

"Did you hear about Sam and Mae getting into trouble the week you gave birth?"

"I did." Theresa smiled apologetically. "They're good kids. But even good kids get caught up in the moment once in a while."

"They were caught up in moments five days in a row," Izzy felt compelled to point out. "And Chandler seems to think one of them should be moved to a different classroom."

"Oh, I wouldn't do that." Theresa reached for the diaper bag, but Izzy got there first.

"I'll carry this out for you." It was lighter than a baby in a car seat and it didn't hurt her ribs to heft it. "And not only because I'm hoping you'll tell me why the kids shouldn't be separated."

"They're really a good influence on each other." Theresa chuckled, heading toward the door. "Sam is a dynamo and Mae is too much in her head. They balance each other out."

Mae is too much in her head? That didn't sound good. But Izzy wanted to wrap up one conversation before starting another. "You don't think they egg each other on?"

"I think their experiences after Thanksgiving were a product of a new and surprising found friendship. They haven't misbehaved since, have they?"

"No." But then again, Izzy hadn't checked the online message system. She made a mental note to ask Ronnie to help her log in.

After Izzy got Theresa to her car, she came back inside and called Chandler, feeling tense and out of sorts.

"Yeah." Chandler sounded distracted when he answered his phone.

Izzy explained about the Santa letters their kids had written and how she had them in her possession. "Can you swing by the feed store and take a look at Sam's before school gets out? I don't feel right opening his. But if his wish is the same as Mae's… Well, there might be trouble." If what she felt for Chandler wasn't love.

"What's this I hear about letters to Santa?" Earl came out

of the back room after she'd disconnected. He carried a box containing multiple sets of outdoor holiday lights.

Izzy put her hand on her hip. "Were you eavesdropping?" The man was as bad as Ronnie when it came to keeping a pulse on other folks' business.

"Nope." Earl set the box down on the counter and picked up the envelopes addressed to Santa. "I saw these. Did Mae ask for a puppy in that letter?"

"No." At this point, Izzy would have loved it if her daughter had. She was feeling a bit panicky.

"Hasn't been the same since we lost Gator a year ago." Earl's beloved Labrador. He made as if to read Mae's letter.

Izzy grabbed the envelope before he could open it. "You feel free to get a dog, Earl."

The old man gasped. "She *did* ask Santa for a puppy. You wouldn't snatch it if she hadn't."

Izzy picked up the box he'd brought and placed it in his arms. "Butt out, Earl."

"We're on the same team." Earl stomped off and disappeared down the Christmas aisle. "A dog will always be there for Mae, even if that car salesman isn't."

"A dog will always be there..." Izzy picked up the stack of paper invoices but couldn't concentrate on them. She stared at the two Santa envelopes. What had come over those two?

There were sounds of Earl restocking the shelves. A few minutes later, he returned with the empty box. "I don't suppose we can get in any more tinsel before the holiday?"

Izzy shook her head, glad for the interruption. "It would take more than a week. We'd be stuck with it until next year. I'll make a note to buy more next summer when we order." She scribbled on her calendar.

"You should also make a note of this." Earl leaned on the counter and tipped his porkpie hat back. "Mae needs something permanent to take from one house to another. And a puppy—"

"You think Mike will care for a puppy properly?" Izzy slapped her pen on the counter, so touchy about the situation that she had an unusually short fuse. "Mike can't even pick up his daughter from school when it's his week. Not to mention he's giving up custody."

"What?" Earl's mouth dropped open.

"He was here a few days ago. He's found someone new and..." Izzy sighed. But that wouldn't get rid of the uneasy feeling in the area of her heart whenever she thought about Mike abandoning Mae. "I signed his paperwork. He'll only see Mae a few days a year. If that."

Earl tossed the empty box toward the break room door. "All the more reason to get Mae a dog." Earl shook his finger, first at Izzy, then pointing up at the ceiling. "A dog can get you through the worst of times."

"Earl... I can't... I can't think about puppies right now. Or... Or...inventory." Izzy was horrified to find herself near tears. "There's so much uncertainty in my head. And I just... I don't know what to do."

"Oh, darling, come here." Earl threw his arms around her and held her close.

"YOU NEEDED SOMEWHERE?" Scotty, the Done Roamin' Ranch's regular blacksmith, asked Chandler when he tucked his cell phone back in his pocket.

"I need to go into town." Although why Izzy sounded so panicked over letters to Santa Claus was beyond him. And yet... Chandler was worried because she was worried. "I can help you finish shooing Baby Bear before I leave."

The pony always misbehaved when shod. He tried to lean his body weight on Scotty while the man balanced Baby Bear's rear hoof between his thighs.

"Hey, none of that." Chandler gave the pony a few pokes in the ribs when he tried to misbehave again.

Baby Bear adjusted his center of gravity with an impatient puff of air.

"Ponies and draft horses are always a shooing challenge." Scotty finished fitting the pony's shoe and then set his hoof down.

"Draft horses? Why?" Chandler thought about Shirley and the buggy arriving tomorrow.

"Those large breeds have very thin hoof walls." Scotty heated the pony's shoe and then pounded it with a hammer to achieve a shape closer to Baby Bear's hoof. "It's better to let them go barefoot and develop calluses on the bottom of the hooves than to have nails split the hoof wall."

"Interesting." Chandler trusted Scotty's opinion. He'd been their farrier for over a decade. "Does it take long to develop calluses?" A key question since Shirley had been shod when they'd bought her.

"It does. At least a season. In the meantime, once their shoes are off, they need rubber boots if they do any work—riding or pulling." Scotty finished hammering Baby Bear's rear shoe on. "Are you thinking about adding a draft horse around here?"

"More than thinking. It's a surprise, but..." Chandler told Scotty about Dad's purchase of Shirley.

"My next visit is scheduled before Christmas. I'd love to take a look at her hooves and come up with a plan for care. I can order boots for her, guaranteed to fit."

Chandler thanked him.

A few minutes later, Scotty was done, paid and loading his tools in his van. Chandler headed out of the barn and toward his truck.

"Chandler, are you going into town?" Dad caught him in the ranch yard. "I sure wouldn't mind a lift."

Chandler agreed and soon the pair were on their way.

"What errand are you on?" Dad asked, plopping his wide white hat on the dashboard.

Chandler explained about the letters to Santa. "Izzy wouldn't tell me what was in Mae's, but she sounded upset."

"Those kids aren't in trouble again, are they?"

"Not as far as I know." Izzy would have mentioned it to him... If she'd been able to log in to the school messaging system. He couldn't begrudge her that. Chandler was guilty of not trying. He made a mental note to ask Ronnie about it tonight.

Dad fiddled with the brim of his cowboy hat. "Nice to see you with a woman in your life."

"*Dad.* You're jumping the gun." Chandler had respected Izzy's request to go slow. "I can't even label what this is as dating."

"I'm not planning your wedding." Dad chuckled. "Although I think young Sam wouldn't mind it if you did and made his best bud his sister. Still, you can enjoy Izzy's company. She's sweet and good-natured. And your mother is growing very fond of her."

Chandler kept silent.

"Whatever it is you're feeling for Izzy deserves to be explored. And weathered." Dad turned his wedding ring on his finger. "True love weathers the good and the bad. And in life, there's always the good and the bad. Why can't you just go with the flow where Izzy's concerned?"

"Because Izzy..." Chandler slowed as they approached the center of Clementine. "Izzy's reduced the flow down to a trickle. She's being careful where her heart and Mae's are concerned, which makes me..."

"Overthink your feelings, too." Dad nodded slowly, seemingly considering the problem at hand. "If there's one thing I've learned about life, it's that you can't rely on it to be predictable. And when things between you two get unpredictable, you'll know."

"Know what?"

"If she's the one."

IZZY HAD JUST realized she'd entered alfalfa under the oats code in the computer program when Chandler entered the feed store.

*It's about time.*

His boots rang out on the hardwood floor as he approached the sales counter. He wore a blue flannel shirt beneath a sleeveless tan jacket. He looked stressed, yet when their eyes met, he smiled.

And it was in the glow of that smile that Izzy felt the world slow down, felt the moment stretch, felt again the inner pull to smile back, to meet him halfway, to offer her hand to twine with his and say they were stronger together.

The feed store phone rang, jolting Izzy back into the present, turned her attention to the laptop screen in front of her.

"Clementine Feed." Earl's voice drifted to her from the break room.

"Thanks for coming in, Chandler," Izzy said in her best businesslike voice as she closed the laptop. Then she opened a drawer beneath the cash register and took out the two envelopes with letters to Santa, handing them to him.

She waited for Chandler to read both, listening to a bouncy rendition of "Jingle Bell Rock."

"Well…" Chandler returned both letters to their envelopes. "That explains a lot."

Izzy nodded. "They both wished for a new parent—a mom for Sam and a dad for Mae. This explains why Mae asked me if I liked meeting the principal after we saw him in his office. And you. She wanted to know if I liked you."

He grunted but didn't reply.

Chandler stared at Izzy without speaking for so long, that she had to ask, "What's going on in that handsome head of yours?"

*Shoot.* She hadn't meant to add the word *handsome*.

Chandler's guarded smile appeared, making him look more handsome, more…kissable. "I'm thinking that the reason the kids have been behaving at school ever since their mischief-making spree is because you've been working out at the ranch, often with me. And this also explains how we ended up having breakfast with you on Saturday. And…a half-dozen other things that didn't seem like a coincidence." Chandler leaned over the counter, bringing those tempting lips closer. "They'd be absolute angels if they knew about *our kisses*." He whispered those last two words.

And those last two words made Izzy shiver, made her want him closer.

The sound of a phone being dropped back in a cradle reminded Izzy that they weren't alone.

"But the question is… What do we do about it?" Izzy whispered, trying not to be overheard. "Because they want us paired up and committed by Christmas. That's ridiculous."

"Is it?"

There were no customers in the store. It sounded as if Earl was making another pot of coffee in the break room. Stan was off delivering feed. The store was unusually quiet. Except for the blood rushing in Izzy's ears.

*Because no matter what I just said about commitment being off the table by Christmas, I wouldn't mind it.*

And Chandler seemed to suspect as much. He hadn't budged from midcounter. He was within reach, barely smiling, letting Izzy decide.

*Is commitment off the table?*

Impulsively, Izzy rose up on her toes and planted a kiss on Chandler's cheek. And then she dropped down on her heels, jarring her ribs.

"What was that?" Chandler didn't relinquish the ground he'd taken.

"Merry Christmas," Izzy said breathlessly. "But… We have to be careful considering those letters."

"Hmm." It was when Chandler was stingy with his words that Izzy suspected there was a lot going on behind those warm brown eyes.

Izzy had plenty of words, enough for both of them. She'd had lots of time to think about their situation. "We should write letters back, telling our kids that there are some things Santa can't deliver for Christmas."

"Hmm," Chandler repeated.

"You're not taking this seriously," Izzy complained.

"If you knew how seriously I'm taking this, you wouldn't peck me on the cheek." He smiled. Wickedly.

*Oh, my.*

Izzy's heart pounded faster. She'd never seen Chandler smile like that. He was Mr. Staid. Mr. Tall and Silent. Mr. Frown at My Antlers.

Where was that Chandler? Izzy could resist that Chandler.

"Something's happened," she murmured.

"Besides these letters?" Chandler asked.

She nodded.

And then Chandler did draw away, resettling his cowboy hat on his head. "I dropped my dad off at the pharmacy. I'm paraphrasing. He told me that when things got unpredictable that we'd know what to do and how to feel about each other." Chandler tapped the Santa letters on the counter. "This could be our sign. Our sign to move forward."

"I disagree." Izzy barely got the words out, mind spinning with the idea that Chandler had talked to his father about her. "We barely know each other."

Chandler shook his head. His gaze was gentle, as if he knew this conversation would scare her. "I know you, Izzy. I know you're honest and trustworthy. You work hard and love to dance. You're a good mom. You have a deep love of Christmas. You don't always take yourself too seriously, but you don't always take care of yourself the way you should." He gestured toward her ribs. "Men who were supposed to love you didn't do a good job. And that makes you afraid to trust me, even when your kiss says you want to." He paused, walking around the sales counter to stand in front of her. "Am I close?"

Her eyes were filling with tears and her breath was ragged and all she could manage was a whispered, "Yes."

"You set aside your dreams when your mom died but you want your daughter to be free to dream and to pursue them, too. And I..." Chandler took one of her hands. "I'm afraid that you'll swoop into my life like a colorful, chattery finch, only to flit away when you finally realize that you have dreams that need cherishing just as much as Mae does."

He was afraid she'd be like Stephanie, harboring dreams that could only take flight elsewhere.

"I don't have dreams," Izzy said in a hoarse, subdued voice because it felt like a betrayal of herself to admit that. "I don't have the luxury to have dreams."

Chandler took hold of her other hand, standing with her behind the outdated cash register like it was an altar and they were about to exchange vows. "You have dreams, Isobel Adams. You dream of family and permanence."

Izzy nodded, blinking back tears. He did know her.

"We could find that together," Chandler said in a voice as soft as his touch.

The front door opened. Two cowboys walked in, heading for the boot department.

Izzy put her hands on Chandler's firm chest and shooed him out from behind the counter. "Now isn't the time for serious talk. We need to decide what to do about the Santa letters."

Chandler shook his head again, slow like the pendulum in Earl's grandfather clock. "My dad recommended we go with the flow. Regardless of what he meant by that, I take it to mean the kissing flow, if I'm being honest, because I do like your kisses. And they seem like a requirement after the serious talk we just had." He leaned over, making a show of puckering up.

*Boy, is he tempting.*

The cowboys in the boot department laughed.

Common sense returned to Izzy like a plunge in Lolly Creek

in spring. There was no kissing in the feed store. Certainly not any exchange of cowboy kisses.

She took a step back and kept her voice down. "Whoever we kiss this holiday season… Or for that matter in the coming months, will be seen as marriage material by our kids. The last thing I want is for Mae to be hurt if you get bored kissing me."

"Like that's going to happen." Chandler huffed, crossing his arms over his chest. "If you're agreeing to go with the flow, you can't want us to sneak around."

"No." Izzy backstepped. "That's no way to start a relationship."

"Neither is kissing *before* a first date." Chandler raised his brows, flashing that wicked smile as if to say, *point to me*.

The front door swung open once more.

"Chandler, I got your mother's meds." Frank walked into the feed store. "Are you ready to go?"

"Yes," Izzy replied for Chandler. "Yes, he is. We're done here."

Chandler gave her a hard look before reaching out to touch her chin with his fingers. "We're done. For now."

## CHAPTER EIGHTEEN

*WE'RE DONE. FOR NOW.*

Chandler's voice echoed in Izzy's head all day while she worked at the feed store. He'd knocked her off her game. She'd very nearly sent a cowboy home with the wrong size boots (he caught her error). She'd had to ask another cowboy twice what he needed help finding in the tack department (he found a replacement bit himself). And Earl had to repeat himself three times before it sunk in that he was asking her something (if they had anymore white extension cords).

How could Chandler be so certain they had a chance at forever?

*Because he knows me. He knows who I am, and what's important to me. He knows what I want out of life. And we want the same thing.*

But wasn't that checking boxes? Every woman wanted that, along with a man who had a good job, a good sense of humor and no glaring bad habits.

Izzy talked herself in and out of love all day long, drank too much coffee and got very little done.

"Mama, are we going to Sam's ranch?" Mae asked as she climbed into the back seat of Izzy's SUV after school that day.

"I told Sam I'd help him make cookies for the hot chocolate table for tonight's roundabout."

"We're not going to the ranch today, bug." Izzy carefully navigated the traffic out of the pickup line. "We have some clients we need to decorate for in town." John Stottle and… Someone else…

*"Mama."* Mae's disappointed voice, so seldom heard.

Izzy chewed her lip.

Once Mae learned that Mike was making a quick exit from her life, she'd latch on to Chandler as a replacement father figure.

*And I don't even know if I love him. Or could love him. Or should love him.*

It wasn't fair to Mae to lose two important men in her life. It was imperative that they stay away from Chandler and the impression that Mae was getting a new daddy for Christmas until Izzy knew how she felt about Chandler.

*How do I feel about Chandler?*

"Mama? Are you okay?"

*Nope. Nope, I'm panicking.*

But she needed to answer. "You know… I've… I've been thinking about puppies."

Della-Mae squealed. *"Puppies? Puppies?"*

"Yes. Yay," Izzy said with absolutely no enthusiasm whatsoever. "Puppies. A dog… A dog will always be there for you, no matter what." No matter what man let Mae down.

"And Sam? He's getting one, too? He has to get one, too." Mae was on a roll now, so excited, so hyped up. "Call Chandler, Mama. Call Chandler. He's picking up Sam. We can go to the feed store and decide on the puppies on the board."

Mae continued to rattle off ideas as Izzy drove them to the feed store because she had to get back to work and finish her shift before they transitioned to decorating some houses downtown. *If* they got to decorating houses in town. Puppies would throw everything off.

But Mae kept rambling and repeating, "Call Chandler, Mama. Sam needs a puppy, too."

And finally, Izzy did.

"THIS IS A bad idea," Chandler said to Izzy twenty minutes after she'd called him. "You complicated everything."

"I'm going with the flow, Chandler." Izzy sounded flustered and vulnerable as she stood behind the feed store sales counter. "It was either puppies or you. Mama Claus made a choice."

"I know what I would have picked," Chandler muttered. And it wasn't a puppy.

But he dutifully headed for the break room, thinking how odd this turn of events was.

He'd never seen Izzy have a meltdown. When she'd called, he'd been waiting in the school pickup line while kids slowly got in cars ahead of him and were even slower to buckle up. Chandler was tied up in knots inside and he wasn't honking his horn and inching up on the bumper of the truck ahead of him to reach Sam, who was talking to one of the school aides four cars ahead.

Oh, and those knots…

Chandler inched forward. They were there because Izzy…

That woman could second-guess a course of action when she roped the business end of a charging steer.

As he inched forward again, a call came in through the truck's Bluetooth link.

"Yeah," he'd shouted at the rearview mirror, which was where he'd always assumed the telephone microphone was. And after Izzy had identified herself and told him her idea, his initial reaction was to reject it.

A puppy was chaotic. And having Izzy around…

She was leaving a trail of chaos in her wake—her holiday decorations in Mom's house, the moved furniture in his house, the constant need to kiss her. Why did Chandler need more unpredictability, more…more…responsibility? Without any of the benefits of kisses?

He hadn't quite put it that way, but Izzy got the gist.

"Stop complaining or Santa will put you on the naughty list, Chandler. Pick up Sam and meet us at the feed store." And then she hung up.

And amazingly, Chandler smiled.

"Hi, Dad." Sam opened the back door of the truck and threw his backpack in. "Can we get milkshakes?"

"Hold that thought." Chandler really should have kept quiet, but he couldn't. "What do you think about getting a puppy today?"

Sam went so excited, he rolled down his window and yelled over and over, "I'm getting a puppy! I'm getting a puppy!"

And because the pickup line was so slow, Sam was practically hoarse when they finally reached the feed store.

"You get yellow, and I get brown." Sam giggled, falling prey to the joy of happy, loving puppies.

"But I like the black one." Mae had a black puppy in her lap.

Izzy stood on the other side of the puppy enclosure, hands shoved in the pockets of her gray Clementine Feed hoodie. "I like the black one, bug."

The black puppy was a male, and the male puppies were several hundred dollars less than the females. The kids and Chandler had chosen the Labradoodles from Earl's puppy board. The most expensive puppies, it seemed. They were practically the price of that princess bed Izzy had her eye on.

*So much for dreams…*

Chandler pointed toward the yellow Labradoodle. "But I think that one is—"

"Not going home with us," Izzy cut him off. The yellow ones were all females.

"Don't get mad at me," Chandler whispered. "This was your notion."

"I'm having second thoughts." There'd be vet bills. Dog food bills. Potty training. Leash training. The things destroyed that would need replacing. "It's all a bit overwhelming."

"More overwhelming than you and me?" Chandler laid his hand over the small of her back.

Izzy wanted to snuggle closer and let him settle her nerves with a touch, a kiss. But that would defeat the purpose of this puppy business. "Right now, you and the puppy are tied."

The kids laughed as a brown puppy lost his balance trying to wrestle a stuffed rabbit to the ground.

Chandler inched closer. "I was wondering if you could pencil me into your busy schedule this week."

Izzy stared at him incredulously. "Are you asking me out on a date? We're here to get puppies. And tomorrow I'll put letters in the mail from Santa, just as we discussed." Explaining to the kids how Santa couldn't deliver something like love.

But boy, Izzy did like the way Chandler smiled at her. Not to mention the warmth of his hand on her back. But she had to think of Mae. What if Chandler wasn't permanent? Mae's heart would be broken a second time.

"We'll need to make puppy playdates," Chandler said with a hint of that wicked smile. "The pups are siblings, after all. Wouldn't want to keep siblings apart."

"Or best friends," Izzy muttered, shaking her head. "Have you always been this incorrigible and I just didn't notice?"

"I think you bring it out in me."

And despite herself, or maybe because of it, Izzy laughed.

"GRANDMA MARY! GRANDMA MARY!" Sam ran ahead of Chandler through the main ranch house, carrying a brown puppy in his arms without the leash they'd entered with. "Come see our new dog!"

"Sam! Come back here." Chandler finished removing his boots and grabbed the discarded leash.

"This is unexpected." Dad turned from the stove where he

was taking out two trays of lasagna. There was hardly any room to cook given the plethora of holiday decorations on the kitchen counter. "I thought you weren't getting a dog."

"Me, too." Chandler continued through the kitchen. "Izzy and I are going with the flow." Not exactly the flow he wanted but there was hope for that. He saw it in Izzy's eyes.

The living room was also crammed with decorations, making it seem small, even if it was empty of people.

"Isn't he adorable?" Mom said from down the hall. "Who is this?"

"This is Rusty." Sam gushed. "He likes chewing on my jacket sleeve."

"Hand over that little squiggle worm." Mom sounded happy. "Oh… Puppies like to chew on everything, don't they?"

"Even Grandma's pillows."

Chandler hurried into his parents' bedroom, not wanting little puppy teeth to sink into Mom.

"That's right, Sam." Mom had one hand on the football-sized brown puppy and the other on a small decorative pillow, which Rusty was gnawing on. "We'll have to make sure there aren't any Christmas decorations down low that Rusty can chew on."

"Sam, we agreed that Rusty needs to be on a leash," Chandler said gently. "For exactly the reason Grandma Mary mentioned. Don't want him to choke on pillow stuffing or cut his mouth if he takes a bite of a glass Christmas ornament."

"But Rusty doesn't like the leash." Sam climbed up on the bed and scooped the squirming puppy into his arms.

"He'll learn to like it if you give him treats." Mom stroked Rusty's curly fur. "Puppies are a big responsibility, just like babies."

Sam snorted. He hadn't been around any babies. "Rusty is smart. He'll be fine."

"He's still a baby." Chandler moved closer to chuck the puppy beneath its furry little chin, dodging his sharp little teeth. "We have to take care of him the way we do our other livestock. We don't let horses or cattle wander around unsupervised. And you did promise to take good care of him."

Sam gathered the energetic puppy close, giggling when Rusty licked his nose. "I'll be careful."

Chandler clipped the leash on Rusty. "And you'll keep his leash on? Even in the house?"

"Yes, Dad."

Chandler handed Sam a small bag of dog treats they'd purchased at the feed store. "Every time he does what you ask him to, give him a treat."

"Yes, Dad."

Rusty looked around the bed, and then lunged for the pillow once more.

Sam giggled.

"Go run around with him outside," Chandler instructed. "We want to tire him out."

"Okay." Sam slid off the bed and then carefully put Rusty on the floor. "Come on, pup. Come on, boy." He scampered out, followed by his new best friend.

Mom captured Chandler's hand. "What brought this on?"

Chandler explained about the letters Sam and Mae had written to Santa requesting he and Izzy find new spouses for Christmas. And how Izzy felt the puppies would be a suitable distraction because she didn't want to risk Mae getting attached.

"I love that little boy." Mom patted his hand and then leaned back on her pillows. "You could stand to learn something from him."

"Really? Like what?"

"Sam goes through life with such a big heart. He wants everyone to be happy."

"Here we go," Chandler teased. "Did you and Dad write a letter to Santa requesting I find a new wife, too?"

"No." Mom's expression turned serious, although her eyes

sparkled with mirth. "But there's still time. Where's Izzy? If Mae got a puppy, I'd expect to see them here, too." She glanced behind him.

"She's... She's not coming." Chandler's throat was suddenly thick. "I just don't know..."

"Oh, honey." Mom understood without him having to say more. "Izzy may not be ready to love you today, but that doesn't mean she won't realize she loves you tomorrow."

"Sure."

Mom hugged him, still too thin and fragile feeling. "Well, neither of you wanted a puppy. And look how quickly that turned around."

"BIFF IS THE best dog ever," Mae said to Izzy when she was being tucked in that night.

"He's a keeper," Izzy agreed.

The little black puppy was the runt of the litter and had collapsed from exhaustion before Mae's bath time. They'd put him to bed in Gator's old crate in the kitchen near a heating vent. But Izzy fully expected the pup to wake up later, disoriented and missing his litter mates.

"Now, go to sleep. We have a big day tomorrow. School and work."

"At the ranch?" Mae asked hopefully. "Biff could play with Rusty."

"No. Here in town. I played hooky from Christmas decorating today. Sleep now." Izzy kissed Mae good-night and made sure the small lamp was on by her bed before turning off the overhead light.

But she didn't leave the room, not immediately. She'd spent her savings for that princess bed buying a puppy. And she paused to mourn that fact.

Biff was adorable. Mae and Earl were ecstatic. What did it matter that Mae wouldn't have a dream princess bed?

The puppy whimpered tentatively, its cry carrying down the hall.

Sighing, Izzy hurried to the kitchen. "What's wrong, Biff?" She knelt at the crate, fingers reaching through the frame.

Biff licked her fingers, still whining.

She and the puppy hadn't bonded. Izzy had been too busy making sure Mae knew how to handle Biff safely and gathering all the puppy paraphernalia they needed. And then she'd been preoccupied mourning the loss of her dream.

It had been a frivolous dream. An impractical dream.

*But just once, I want to be frivolous and impractical.*

Chandler's wicked smile came to mind.

The puppy sat back, whining.

"All right, Biff." Izzy unlatched the kennel, resolved to do baby duty. Feeding, playing, potty, and then back to the crate. "Go easy on me, honey. It's been a while since I've taken care of a baby." Because she fully expected this to be just like nurturing a newborn.

Biff leaped out of the cage and into her lap and, without another sound, closed his eyes, apparently ready to fall back asleep.

And Izzy...

She fell instantly in love.

## CHAPTER NINETEEN

"WHAT ARE YOU doing out here?" Chandler asked Mom, surprised to find her in the barn on Tuesday afternoon, standing at her horse's stall while holding Rusty's leash. It was good to see her wearing her usual ranch garb—white blouse, jeans, her cowboy boots and hat.

But Shirley and the surrey were due to arrive any minute. Dad had wanted his gift to be a surprise.

"Am I not allowed outside unsupervised anymore?" Mom stood at Taffy's stall, stroking the palomino's nose while Rusty sat at her feet staring up at the horse warily. "If you must know, I'm checking the property for Christmas decorations. There aren't any around inside here." She gave Chandler a sly look. "You know I always put decorations inside in the barn. You need to call Izzy and get her out here."

"That'll make Sam and Rusty happy." And Chandler.

A grinding sound cut through the air, like a large truck shifting gears. A few of the horses poked their heads over their stall doors.

"How about I walk you back to the house?" Chandler stepped forward. "*Rusty* looks like he could use a nap." He reached for the puppy's leash.

"This pup and I are bonding." Mom's fingers curled tighter

around the leash. "I was considering going for a ride," she admitted wistfully. "Talking to my friends at the roundabout every night has reminded me what I'm missing."

"Uh-huh." The engine noise grew louder. "Nobody's ridden Taffy in months, Mom. I should ride her first."

"Kid gloves," Mom murmured, glancing down and catching Rusty's eye. "I'm not as fragile as they all make me."

"You'll be back to full strength soon enough," Chandler promised.

Outside, that loud engine sputtered and backfired. This wasn't going to be the surprise Dad imagined.

"Are we getting a feed delivery?" Mom moved carefully toward the barn door leading to the ranch yard, Rusty scrambling ahead, straining the leash. "I didn't think they delivered on Tuesdays. No matter. Rusty needs to get used to the sound of big rigs."

"Chandler, come quick! They're here!" Dad called from outside, clearly excited.

"What has that man done now?" But Mom chuckled. "Did he buy a new bucking bull?"

"Let's go see." Chandler held Mom's arm as they walked out of the barn and into the bright winter afternoon sunlight.

A big rig drove toward the roundabout towing an open stock trailer.

"Your father did buy another bucking bull." Mom tipped her hat brim back.

"Nope."

Mom scoffed. "It has to be a bull, Chandler. Nothing else could be that tall."

Chandler picked up the pup while the trailer came closer, letting reality speak for itself.

"What to my wondering eyes should appear..." Mom spoke in a soft voice. "Did your father buy a draft horse for the rodeo clowns?"

"Mary!" Dad appeared, hurrying to her side. "I wanted this to be a surprise."

The big truck pulled slowly into the roundabout, revealing the surrey in the truck bed, yellow wheels and all, and an inquisitive Shirley taking a gander at them all.

Dad thrust out his arms and burst into song.

Chandler supposed it was the tune from *Oklahoma!* Dad had referenced the day they'd made their purchase. It sounded off-key and corny.

But Mom started to cry. Happy tears.

"DAD! DID YOU bring Rusty?" Sam scrambled into Chandler's truck Thursday after school.

The puppy whined from inside the cat carrier Chandler had used to transport him in, scratching at the door.

Putting the truck in Park, Chandler lifted the carrier from the front seat and put it in the back with Sam. "Don't let him out until we get to the feed store." They needed more chew toys and Chandler wanted to check in on Izzy. Were her ribs healing? Were she and Mae faring better at puppy care than he and Sam were?

Yes, he'd gotten to making excuses to see her. Rusty was getting along just fine.

A few minutes later, they pulled up in front of the feed store. There was a brief scramble to get Rusty's leash on and Sam safely to the ground with the pup in his arms. And then Sam made a mad dash inside, shouting, "Della-Mae! Della-Mae!"

Chandler hurried after them.

The two kids found each other behind the sales counter. They were giggling and squealing, ecstatically.

Izzy finished ringing up a sale for Sheriff Underwood. She was decked out to decorate someone's house. Her Christmas sweater was green with a cat batting at a string of lights on a Christmas tree. She wore a plain Santa hat. A tame holiday outfit compared with her previous wardrobe choices.

And darned if just looking at Izzy didn't fill his head with sleigh bells ringing.

Izzy's weary gaze found Chandler's. "How many times did you get up on puppy duty last night?"

"Too many times." Chandler came around the counter to see the kids with their puppies.

"It's worth it to see them with Rusty and Biff, though." She leaned against the counter, the pom of her Santa hat resting on her cheek.

"Ask me on Saturday," Chandler said. "Let's see how much REM sleep I have then."

Earl came from the break room to join them. "Toughen up, you two." He put his hands on his hips and smiled at the kids and puppies. "What a Christmas gift."

"Oh, this ain't our Christmas gift," Sam told him, glancing back at Chandler and Izzy. "We wrote letters to Santa."

Mae nodded, smiling up at Chandler like an angel. "We asked Santa to bring us something special."

"Santa always delivers the goods," Earl said gruffly.

"Oh." Izzy gripped the sales counter.

"Bet you aren't feeling so great about your decision now, are you?" Chandler couldn't resist asking.

"Ha, ha." Izzy sighed.

"Nancy's here for her shift." Earl waved at a teen with black hair who wore all black, even her Clementine Feed sweatshirt. "Kids, I'll treat those pups to a new toy. Why don't you go find one on the shelf."

Excited cheers filled the air. And then the kids ran around the sales counter and into the store, puppies trailing them. Nancy barely avoided being tripped by leashes.

"Let me get a coffee," Nancy told Izzy. "And then I'll be ready for my shift." She disappeared in the back.

Earl gave Chandler a searching look. "Are you helping Izzy decorate today? I heard tell she's running behind."

"Just a day," Izzy hastened to say. "Because of the puppies. I'll catch up on Saturday."

"What if someone cancels?" Earl leaned closer to her to whisper, "You need that money for Mae's Christmas gift."

"I'll be fine." But Izzy blushed.

"What are you working on today?" Chandler gestured toward her cat sweater with its tangle of lights. "Outdoor lights?"

"Yes. And no, I'm not worried about snarling string lights." But she wouldn't look him in the eye.

"Good. We'll tag along. Gotta tire out the puppies." And make sure Izzy took care of her bruised ribs.

Izzy shook her head.

The kids appeared from the pet aisle, each carrying a squeaker toy and chattering nonstop.

"Sam, you want to help Izzy decorate for Christmas?" he asked.

"Yeah, I do." Sam hopped around.

"Yeah, he does," Chandler echoed. "We'll get you back on track, Izzy."

"Chandler and Sam to the rescue!" Mae raised her chew toy in the air. "Yay!"

"Yay," Izzy muttered.

"HERE'S THE PLAN." Izzy began unpacking the tubs that contained Braxton McDavid's holiday lights, moving slowly and breathing shallowly. "Gables and porch, bushes and tree. Braxton said he had an inflatable snowman, but he can't remember where he left it in his garage." And Izzy hadn't been able to find it when she'd rummaged around.

Chandler had set up Braxton's ladder in front of the gables.

The kids and puppies were being watched by her elderly client. Braxton had a screened-in porch in his backyard so the puppies could meander safely.

If only Izzy could find that snowman, things would be great.

*If only Chandler wasn't here, looking at her with a smile and making her nervous.*

Except he wasn't looking at her now. He climbed the ladder—which was her job—and said, "Feed me the lights."

She glanced up at him. "Shouldn't we check to see if they work first?"

"I already did." He sat on the top of the ladder, staring down at her. "You were in the garage looking for Frosty."

"You're a step ahead of me." She fed him a strand, trying to be careful not to tangle them. "Is this what it's like to work for you?"

"Nope." Chandler made quick work of attaching the strand to the hooks that were already in place. "Mom wants you to come out to the ranch and decorate the inside of the horse barn. Caught her in there the other day."

Izzy nodded. "Your mom called me. She's on the schedule. But I'm—"

"Behind, yeah. I know." Chandler smiled at her. "If you get caught up, are you going to the Buckboard on Saturday night? I didn't get a dance with you the last time we were there."

Instead, he'd gotten a kiss.

Izzy felt her cheeks heat. "Are you asking me on a date?"

"Might be. Are you amenable to one?"

"Might be." The words were out before she thought about them. "You've got this. I'm going to go looking for Frosty again."

"Running away doesn't look good on you," Chandler quipped.

Izzy did it anyway.

She poked around Baxter's garage, lifting boxes of old books, moving an old stroller covered in cobwebs, shifting containers of antifreeze that were in front of a box that held an aboveground pool.

"Found Frosty!" Izzy called, peering over the pool box. "I could use some help dragging it out."

Chandler came to stand next to her. "Thank you for asking for help."

"My ribs appreciate you."

His arm curled around her waist. "I like standing next to you."

Chandler was so honest. He deserved honesty in return.

"I'm sorry I twisted your arm to get a puppy." Izzy turned to face him, except she stared at a shirt button over his heart. "I panicked and boxed you into a corner."

"Rusty is part of the family now." With a tender touch, Chandler lifted her chin until she had to look him in the eye. "With some work, you could be part of the family, too."

"Some work." Izzy chuckled. "Those are practically fighting words."

"No," he murmured.

"No?"

Chandler shook his head, leaning down to whisper in her ear, "When I say *some work*, I mean you and I need to work on that something between us to see what could be."

*What could be...*

That sounded like a partnership more so than a decision that rested on Izzy. The tension inside her, that knot in her stomach, it eased.

And then Chandler drew back, but only a smidge, because that's all he needed to fit his lips over hers.

The interior garage door opened.

Izzy and Chandler shifted apart.

The puppies tumbled forward, each leading a child holding a leash.

"Look, kids. We found Frosty," Izzy said, although she was staring up at Chandler with what she imagined were stars in her eyes.

They may have found Frosty, but so did the puppies. While they were inflating it, one of the pups chewed a hole in the white plastic, requiring an apology to Braxton and a patch kit.

## CHAPTER TWENTY

"I LOVE SHIRLEY."

The large gray horse whinnied at the mention of her name.

Mom stood close to the Percheron with one hand on her headstall. With the other, she reached up and gave Shirley a loving pat on the neck. "But Frank, I'm really more comfortable with riding Taffy than driving a rig."

"What's going on?" Sam came to stand next to Chandler at the arena gate. He had a firm grip on Rusty's leash. "Sit, Rusty. Sit."

The little roly-poly sat, staring at Sam intently.

"Good boy." Sam dug a small dog treat from his blue jeans pocket and fed it to the pup. Rusty gulped it down without chewing. "Is Grandma taking to cart driving?"

"I'm an excellent buggy driver," Mom said from mid-arena, pride in every syllable. "Me and Shirley—"

The gray whinnied.

"—are getting along famously."

"It's me she's not getting along with." Dad moseyed over to where Chandler and Sam were standing. "All I tried to do was spoil her. And what do I get?"

"Nag, nag, nag," Mom answered. "I'm still new to driving a buggy and Christmas is just a few days away. What if I can't control her?"

"Can I try?" Sam asked, handing Dad the leash, and raced over to Mom and the rig. "Let me try, Grandma."

Deprived of his dog treat supplier, Rusty tried to reach Sam, using a racing start to jerk the leash right out of Dad's hand. The rascal charged after Sam, leash dragging behind him.

Shirley startled, tossing her head and sidestepping away from the approaching youngsters as her flight instinct kicked in.

Which would have been fine, if Mom had let go of her leather headstall.

Or if the puppy's trailing leash didn't vaguely resemble a snake, which caused Shirley to rear and those big hooves landed...

Where they shouldn't.

"Is Mary all right? I came as soon as I heard." Izzy burst into the hospital waiting room, spotted Chandler amid all the other cowboys and ran over to him. "Is anyone else hurt? You? Or...or Sam?"

Chandler sat slumped in a chair, knee bouncing, hat brim pulled down low. He looked... He looked the way he had that day in the principal's office. Demoralized, waiting to hear the worst.

Izzy came to a stop in front of him. "Is Sam okay? Are you?"

Chandler didn't look up. Didn't acknowledge Izzy in any way.

"We're fine," Frank said from a chair on the other side of the room. His face was pale and lined with worry. His wide white cowboy hat rested on his knee. "We're all wishing it had been us instead of her."

"What happened?" Izzy sank into the chair next to Chandler, worried for Mary but also worried for him. Something didn't feel right. "All Earl heard was that a horse bolted and knocked Mary down."

"It all happened so fast," Frank said in a faraway voice. "One minute we were teasing each other, the way we do. And the next..."

"Mom's in surgery." Zane was standing rigidly against a wall, as if the structure needed him to stay upright. "Doc said she needs pins to hold the wrist bones together."

"Oh, poor thing. I'm sure she was a trouper." Izzy couldn't imagine anything less from Mary.

Chandler grunted.

Wanting to comfort him, Izzy reached over and rested her hand on Chandler's bouncing knee. "Is there anything I can do?"

"You should go," Chandler said in a low, thick voice. A tone that sounded like...the day he'd first told her their kids should be in separate classrooms. "None of this would have happened if you hadn't started changing things. Dad wouldn't have gotten the idea to buy a horse and buggy. Sam would never have gotten a puppy."

Everyone in the room stilled. All those hurting cowboys. It was as if they all stopped breathing.

And Izzy... Izzy stopped breathing.

"Now, Chandler," Frank began.

"We all know it's the truth." Chandler jolted to his feet, staring down at Izzy with hurt in his eyes. "Izzy came in and changed everything."

"That's not fair," Zane said, bless him.

But Chandler was on a roll. "There's a cause for everything bad that happens. You can trace it back. And in this case, Mom would be fine right now if Izzy hadn't come to the ranch and changed everything."

Izzy's chest hurt. It hurt because her heart was breaking, and she was bent over and that always aggravated her bruised ribs. But the physical pain wasn't near as sharp as the emotional pain. And she knew why. Oh, she knew. And it hurt.

"Chandler, go take a walk." Frank was standing now, too. "Before you say something you'll regret."

"No." Izzy found her footing, coming to stand, finding her voice. "This was what I was afraid of." *I should go. I should go.* But Izzy couldn't seem to move because she felt so...broken. And betrayed. And it was all because of *him*. "I didn't ask to come into your life. I was in a safe space. I could handle what was on my plate. Alone. But then you... You all opened your hearts to me and Mae." Oh, no. Mae. Mae would be crushed. "And I knew deep down... I knew *something* didn't fit right. That you... That I...didn't belong." That those kisses and those feelings weren't to be trusted. "And maybe Chandler's right. Maybe some things shouldn't be changed or moved or tested or examined or..." *Loved.*

And that was it. She'd fallen in love with Chandler and the idea of a big extended family who loved each other through thick and thin. But from the very beginning she'd just been an outsider. Someone who was allowed to visit and experience that special place that was the Done Roamin' Ranch. But she didn't quite fit in, not all the way. She'd been so close to laying her heart at Chandler's feet except she knew. She knew with absolute certainty that this would happen.

She tried to draw a breath, but she'd clamped her lips and was fighting tears and that told everyone in that waiting room that she was going to cry.

"If Rusty isn't going to be a good ranch dog, Mae and I will take him." She sniffed again. A loud, watery sniff that had her stiffening. "But you better be quick about it so that you won't break his heart like..."

*You broke mine.*

The HOSPITAL WAITING room was quiet after Izzy left.

The only sound Chandler heard was the echo of his harsh

words in his head. The words fueled by fear because the foundation of the family he'd found in Clementine had been threatened.

*You came in and changed everything.*

*There's a cause for everything bad that happens.*

And when those words receded, Izzy's words took their place. Her frail, soft words that were like arrows shot through his heart.

*This is what I was afraid of.*

*I didn't ask to come into your life.*

*Maybe some things shouldn't be changed or moved or tested or examined...*

Her words faded away except for that last bit.

*Maybe some things shouldn't be changed...*

*Like me. Like her.*

Chandler's body felt heavy. He sank down into the chair Izzy had vacated. He stared at his hands without seeing them.

She'd held him when he'd recounted those days from his childhood.

She'd counseled him when he got defensive about Stephanie taking a new job. She said to listen. She'd said Stephanie was afraid.

He'd laughed when Izzy panicked the other day and practically demanded they get puppies because she... She was afraid, too. Afraid of change and risk and...love.

And today... Today when he'd panicked because seeing Mom go down, seeing that large hoof come down on top of her...

For a moment, Chandler had thought Shirley's hoof had landed on Mom's midsection.

And that fear... That cold, prickly fear had clung to him all the way into town, all during the exam and the wait and the arrival of Izzy.

The woman he'd fallen in love with.

"He looks like he's going to faint."

"Somebody get him some water."
"And a candy bar. I don't think he's eaten anything."
The words of his family surrounded him like a fog.
And Chandler couldn't say anything. Not a word.
Why would he?
He'd already said too much.

# CHAPTER TWENTY-ONE

"YOU SHOULD ALL just go to the Buckboard without me," Izzy told her friends that night, hugging a throw pillow because Mae and Biff were spending the night with Earl. "I'm not good company."

Plus, her girlfriends all looked ready for Saturday night at the local honky-tonk while Izzy still wore her ugly Christmas sweater.

"I'm already making margaritas," Ronnie called from Izzy's kitchen, the proof of which was the mighty roar of Izzy's old blender.

"I brought a whole batch of chocolate chip cookies." Raising her voice to be heard above the blender, Allison opened the canister and set it on Izzy's coffee table. "Baked them today."

"I brought chips and salsa." Bess came out of the kitchen carrying two bowls. "Bought them today."

"And I bought guacamole." Jo appeared from down the hallway. "I hung up the Mrs. Claus dresses in your closet, along with Earl's Santa costume. Ma said to try them on in case she needs to make any adjustments." Ma being Lois, the object of Earl's unrequited love. "She said to tell you that she'll swing by with a wagon to pick you up on Christmas morning. I thought you were getting Mae a princess bed for Christmas."

Izzy explained about the puppy purchase.

"That's a shame." Allison selected a cookie from the tin. "Every girl needs a special place to dream."

The blender quieted.

"The princess bed was more for me than Mae," Izzy admitted. "And Mae already whispers secrets to Biff. He's such a sweet little puppy." Less rambunctious than Rusty, who had just as boisterous a personality as Sam.

Izzy's heart squeezed. It wasn't just Chandler she'd lost today. She'd grown fond of Sam, too.

"You need a place to dream, Izzy," Ronnie called from the kitchen.

"Oh… I'm past the dreaming stage," Izzy was quick to point out.

"You're never past the dreaming stage," Bess said.

"Agreed," Jo said.

Izzy felt all eyes upon her. Waiting for her to say something, no doubt. Izzy squeezed the throw pillow tighter to her chest. "If you all leave now, you'll still be there in time to line dance."

"If we leave now," Ronnie called from the kitchen, "we'll only sit in our booth and worry about you all night."

*Sit in our booth.*

"By Sunday church, the whole town will want to know why we aren't there tonight." A familiar wave of embarrassment washed over Izzy with a chill that quickly morphed into a hot, prickly skin tingle. She'd experienced the same feeling before—when Mom was sick, when Dad left, when Mike told her he wanted a divorce. "Isn't it funny how you think you're just you? And then you realize that you're interwoven into other lives."

"Our friendship circle." Allison nodded, taking a bite of chocolate chip cookie.

"The high school rodeo team." Bess nodded, scooping salsa with a chip.

"The roping circuit." Jo called from the kitchen, where presumably she was giving the guacamole a stir.

"The Done Roamin' Ranch." Ronnie nodded, setting a tray of margaritas in plastic glasses on the coffee table. "We're all tied to the Done Roamin' Ranch since that's where the men we love were raised."

"God bless those Harrisons." Jo returned from the kitchen with the bowl of guacamole. "And our fellas, the ones Frank and Mary raised right."

Izzy felt all eyes on her because this was a test, of sorts. If Izzy bad-mouthed Chandler, the others would support her, at least as far as admitting that Chandler had done Izzy wrong. But she didn't want to cause a rift.

"I'm not going to lie and tell you that Chandler's words didn't hurt." Izzy released the pillow, setting it in her lap and smoothing out the creases. In time, that's what she'd do with her emotions, too. Smooth over the scars Chandler had given her. "But everybody copes differently. And he… There was truth to what he said."

Ronnie scoffed, passing out drinks. "Didn't mean he had to say it."

"You'd rather he lie?" Izzy sipped her icy drink. "You'd rather he held it inside?"

"Are we making excuses for him now?" Allison demanded. "I came over here expecting to spend at least an hour bad-mouthing Chandler."

"But this is Izzy." Bess gave Izzy a sad smile. "Unlike me, she doesn't bear grudges against anybody."

"No." Jo raised her glass as if in toast. "Izzy is great at turning the other cheek."

"That bodes well for Chandler, I suppose," Ronnie said.

Izzy shook her head. "I close the door. I turn the page. I move on. But I don't think I ever completely get over it. I haven't tried to forge a relationship with my dad. Or with Mike.

Evie Grace came in last week and I wasn't exactly charitable to her, Allison."

Allison chuckled. "Even I've given her a pass for cornering the market on peaches to try and sabotage my county fair baking."

"I hear what Izzy's saying." Ronnie set down her margarita glass. "This doesn't bode well for Chandler, does it?"

Izzy shrugged, dying a little inside. "His words showed me what's important to him, and that's not me."

"Idiot."

"Jerk."

"Fool."

"Troll."

Izzy stared at her drink. "He's scared. Scared of a future he can't predict. He's scared of losing Mary and the family dynamic that saved him. You can't fault someone for being scared. We've all got our fears and they all shape who we are. And Chandler's fear… That's probably part of what drew me to him. He's had family fold beneath him. And that's where we're the same. But he never learned to face his fears and make his way on his own."

"Like you did." Ronnie took hold of Izzy's hand. "Over and over. Our dear, sweet Izzy has picked herself up and moved on every time someone's broken her heart."

"Correction. I closed the door, *then* picked myself up and moved on." It was just that Izzy wasn't ready to close the door on those newly discovered feelings with Chandler.

But she had to. For Mae's sake, if not her own.

"Chandler… Is that you?"

Chandler jerked awake, nearly tipping the too-small hospital chair over in his haste to sit up. "Mom?" He blinked blurry eyes. "I'm here. What do you need?"

The hospital room came into focus. Beige walls. White bedsheets. Pale blue blanket.

And Mom. Tubes and wires every which way. Her injured

left wrist bandaged and propped up on pillows. Metal screws rising up from the gauze, a reminder of how fragile she was becoming.

"You should go home," Mom said weakly. "I'll be fine here."

Chandler refused. He stood and came around the bed to hold her right hand. It was thin and cold. He gently cradled it between his larger ones, trying to transfer some warmth. "I'm the oldest. I took the night shift."

"Stubborn." Mom closed her eyes but not to sleep. "The oldest are always the most stubborn. And the most likely to take the blame when someone else gets hurt on their watch."

"True. But it was my fault. I should have held Rusty's leash instead of Dad." The little pup had an unexpected strength. "And I should have told Dad not to buy Shirley and the buggy. Makes no financial sense."

"Ah. You're in charge of the finances now, too." Mom's eyes were still closed. "And Izzy? I heard you blamed her for what happened to me."

"I'm not proud of that," Chandler said gruffly.

"You've always been too much in your head. Overthinking." Mom heaved a sigh. "Do you remember the early days? You were our only child for a few months. And then in came another. And another. And another, until we had a full house."

"Those were the days, weren't they?" Chandler could remember each new face. The guardedness that eventually gave way to careful smiles that eventually gave way to carefree laughter.

"You asked me how you could help." Mom squeezed his hand. "You watched over them. You noticed what upset them and you tried to put bumpers around them so that they'd never get upset again."

"Cause and effect." Chandler nodded.

"You were like a detective back then. Told all the boys they had to be honest and confess their transgressions. But you've forgotten one thing. I forgive everybody because nobody is perfect."

Chandler froze.

"I don't want you to take this wrong, honey. But just because someone is part of the chain of events that led up to an accident doesn't mean they're to blame. I don't blame you. Or Sam or Rusty or Shirley or your dad. And I certainly don't blame Izzy."

"I know. I let my emotions get the best of me because I thought…"

"I know. I heard you tell your father you thought Shirley had stomped on something vital." She smiled. "I'm getting older. And yes, at some point, I'm gonna take my last horseback ride. But I'm a gal who has to live her life on her own terms. I may get knocked down or set back, but deep down inside where it matters, I'm like all my boys. I get back up and keep moving forward."

"That's good to hear."

"Is it? Because it pertains to you. You made a mistake when you let your temper get the best of you. Whatever happens or doesn't happen with you and Izzy will be decided in the next few hours. The next few days."

"Oh, good. You're awake." A nurse wheeled in a cart with a computer on top. "Time to take your vitals."

"You think about what I said, Chandler."

"I will." But after the things he'd said to Izzy, he wouldn't blame her if she never forgave him.

"THERE YOU ARE." Ronnie panted, sounding like she'd been running. "Found him, Ginny."

Chandler was drinking coffee in the kitchen of the main ranch house on Sunday morning, testing and discarding different apologies for Izzy. Rusty slept in his lap. "You were looking for me?"

"Yes. Ginny has something to say to you."

There were sounds of boots and jackets being removed.

Finally, Ronnie propelled Ginny into the kitchen with her hands on the girl's shoulders. "We're here to make an apology."

"Sorry, Uncle Chandler," Ginny recited woodenly.

"Sorry for what?" Rusty stirred. Chandler rubbed the brown pup behind his ears.

Ginny bit her bottom lip and glanced over her shoulder at Ronnie.

With a put-upon sigh, Ronnie took a seat across from Chandler. "Ginny asked me to take her Christmas shopping after church. She wants to buy Wade something special for Christmas—a pair of new boots he's been wanting."

"The limited-edition ones?" Chandler whistled, which startled Rusty out of his doze. The pup sat up, blinking blue eyes over the edge of the table at Ronnie. "But those cost close to five hundred dollars."

"That's what I said." Ronnie clasped her hands on the table and glanced up at Ginny. "And then I asked her who she thought was going to pay for those boots."

"And she said..." Chandler prompted, studying Ginny's guilt-ridden face.

"I have money." Ginny's gaze dropped down to her toes. "I didn't realize I didn't have enough, though."

"Have you been saving?" Chandler asked, setting a squirming Rusty on the kitchen floor.

"Her allowance?" Ronnie gave a wry laugh. "No."

Again, Ginny looked tortured. "I started a home business. Like Mama Ronnie."

Ronnie's head bobbed. "Just like Mama Ronnie. She's been giving out relationship advice to kids at school. *For their single parents*, including Sam and Mae."

Chandler wasn't surprised, still... "That explains a lot."

"I don't think you understand, Chandler. Ginny told Sam and Mae to get into trouble to try and bring you two together. She's been recruiting underage clients ever since. She's been taking their allowance and lunch money."

"Not to mention she swiped a bunch of your buy one/get one free coffee, or in our case, hot chocolate coupons," Chandler teased. "Essentially, she's performing matchmaking without a license, stealing your clientele and your promotional items. Do I have that right?"

Ronnie made a growling noise.

"I'm sorry. Okay." Ginny sounded like she was sorry she'd been caught. In fact, she crossed her arms over her chest. "But I'm good at this. Look at Chandler and Miss Izzy. Look at Merick and Miss Dora. And I have tons of other works in progress."

"I thought you wanted to be a lawyer." Chandler reached down and pulled Rusty away from his sock before his sharp little teeth ripped a hole in it or sunk into his skin.

"Yes. A lawyer and a rodeo queen. But also an entrepreneur, like Mama Ronnie, Miss Jo and Miss Allison." Ginny folded her legs and sat down on the floor, reaching for Rusty. "I'm showing initiative. I'm pursuing my dreams. Isn't that what you and Dad always tell me I should do?"

Ronnie's head came down to rest on her hands. "I've created a monster."

"I don't think love is as easy as you're making it out to be, Ginny," Chandler said slowly. "Izzy and I smashed into the guardrails. And I don't think she'll listen to anything I say or do to try and win her back."

Ronnie raised her head. "Do you want to win her back? Do you deserve to? You accused her of being the cause of Mary's accident."

"I was wrong. And I've been sitting here this morning trying to come up with the words to make things right." He peered at Ronnie. "Unless you think I've ruined everything."

"Your window of opportunity is very small," Ronnie said cryptically. "Or should I say your door of opportunity is closing?" She shook her head. "Never mind. I have an idea but we have to act fast."

## CHAPTER TWENTY-TWO

"MERRY CHRISTMAS!" Izzy bid the last feed store customer farewell and locked the door behind them.

It was Christmas Eve. She hadn't seen Chandler in two days. Not since he broke her heart.

Every time she heard the door open, Izzy glanced up with eager anticipation, only to chastise herself for hoping. Whatever she and Chandler had together was done and dusted.

"Earl, are you ready to close up?" Izzy had a turkey breast cooking in a slow cooker back home. It was a tradition that she and Mae hosted Earl for the holiday.

"Can't wait for our supper." He came out of the break room catching sight of Mae and Biff playing with a squeaker toy on the floor, who'd taken a cancellation of evening plans with her father well. "Best hurry, Mae." He grabbed hold of a small, flat box beneath the counter. "Or I'll get the biggest slice of pumpkin pie."

"We have to eat turkey and vegetables first." Mae stood, gripping both the dog toy and the leash tightly. Since she'd heard about Mary's mishap, she'd always taken a strong hold on Biff's leash. "Mama, are you sure we can't invite Chandler and Sam over for dinner?"

"I'm sure, bug." Izzy slipped on her coat and then helped Mae with hers.

"But Biff misses Rusty."

"I'm still sure, bug." Chandler was done with them. Izzy filled her lungs with air and her mind with the will to move on. "Earl, what have you got there?"

"Turkey platter. Destiny Rogers returned it today. Said it was too small for her bird but I thought it'd be just right for that turkey breast you always make."

"What a nice gift." Izzy herded her little family toward the door.

*They are enough.*

She didn't quite believe it. So, while they walked home with Earl and Mae chattering, Izzy kept telling herself reasons why she was fine.

*My heart can't be broken. I didn't really fall in love with Chandler because I never told him those three words.*

*The nights aren't so bad. I've got the entire bed to myself.*

*Mae and I will retain control of the TV remote.*

*If Mae gets married someday, I'll walk her down the aisle.*

"And tomorrow after *the real Santa* comes," Mae was telling Earl, "we'll dress up like Mrs. Claus and be part of the Santapalooza parade."

"I'll dress up as *Mr.* Claus," Earl clarified.

"Hey. What's that on our door?" Mae ran ahead, crossing the lawn just as the outdoor lights came on. The sudden flash spooked Biff, making him leap into the air, but he recovered, racing Mae to the front porch. "It's a letter, Mama."

Someone had stuck an envelope between the front door and the doorjamb.

"Looks like a Christmas card." Earl took it from Mae. "More square than rectangular. And it's thick." He passed it to Izzy.

Her name was written on the front in neat, block letters. Izzy handed Earl her keys, heart pounding. Was this from

Chandler? She followed Earl and Mae into the house, which was filled with the smells of Christmas—turkey and pine. They all set their cowboy hats and jackets on a hook behind the door.

Mae unclipped Biff's leash before plopping on the floor and pulling off her pink cowboy boots.

"Who's it from? Not *him*, I hope." Earl took up residence in a chair before removing his boots.

"I haven't opened it yet." Izzy padded over to the couch in her stocking feet.

"It's from him. I can tell from the way you're staring at it." Earl wiggled his toes and leaned back in the chair. "Throw it in the trash. That's what I say."

"Without reading it?" Was it an apology? A request to try again?

"Open it, Mama." Mae came over to stand between Izzy's knees. "Read it to me."

"Just the good parts," Izzy hedged, hoping there would be good parts.

She tore open the envelope and withdrew the card inside.

"Puppies!" Mae leaned closer for a better look at the front.

There were indeed puppies on the front of the card. Their cute little faces poked out of a doghouse that had been decorated with lights and ornaments for Christmas. And the words above the visual read…

*"I know I'm in the doghouse this Christmas…"* Izzy opened the card. *"But I wanted to wish you all the best this holiday season."*

"That's it?" Earl scoffed, clasping his hands over his chest. "Wake me when the turkey's ready."

"There's more." Izzy read it silently first. "It says, *'I was wrong. Please forgive me. You've been making everyone else's dreams come true. I hope you don't mind that I tried to make yours a reality.'* It's from Chandler."

"What does that mean?" Mae's shoulders fell. She headed

down the hall, calling for Biff to follow her. "I don't know what it means, do you, Biffy?"

"I don't know what it means, either," Izzy murmured, setting the card on the coffee table.

*"Mama! Mama, come quick!"*

At her daughter's shriek, Izzy came running.

"Look." Mae stood in the hallway, pointing inside her open bedroom door.

"What is it? A critter? Did something fall?" Izzy swung into the doorway and came to a dead stop. "Oh."

There were Christmas lights hanging from the ceiling above Mae's bed, strung from the overhead light to her plain wooden headboard. Almost like half of a canopy bed. And Mae's bed... A pink unicorn bedspread replaced the sunflower quilt Izzy's grandmother had made. The pillows also had unicorns appliquéd on them.

"Mama, my room is so pretty." Mae walked slowly inside, looking around. "I have my Christmas tree and now a unicorn bed."

"What's all the ruckus?" Earl joined them. "Why, this is as pretty as a daydream, Mae."

"And it's mine." Mae flopped on the bed on her stomach, only to slide to the floor since the material was slippery. "Is it from Santa?"

"No, bug. It's from Chandler."

"And Sam," Mae said with certainty.

"Most likely." Izzy nodded, smelling turkey and thinking that she needed to get the rest of their meal started. But first, she wanted her slippers. Izzy opened her bedroom door and turned on the light. "What the heck?"

Mae ran past her. "He did it for your room, too, Mama."

Izzy's bedroom had a new pink and fuzzy bedspread emblazoned with the word *Dream* appliquéd in the middle in large letters. Lights outlined her bedroom windows. Lights

ran along the top of the walls. And just like in Mae's room, lights streamed from the ceiling light in swooping lines that ended at her headboard.

*Oh, Chandler.*

He knew her so well. She had to forgive him.

"You should change the locks on your doors." And with that, Earl stomped back to the living room.

But Izzy and Mae?

Izzy imagined they had dreamy looks in their eyes the rest of the night.

CHRISTMAS MORNING DAWNED clear and bright with nary a blast of wind or frost on the ground.

Izzy and Mae wore long johns beneath their Mrs. Claus red dresses. They'd been given a pair of clear glass spectacles and a Santa hat to complete their wardrobe. They both wore cowboy boots and big grins, standing at the front window waiting for Earl to arrive.

Poor Biff was whining in his crate in the kitchen. He wasn't coming with them.

"There he is!" Mae jumped up and down in a circle very much the way Sam would have had he been here. "There's Santa Earl!" She ran to the front door, flung it open and began to sing "Here Comes Santa Claus."

"Ho-ho-ho. Merry Christmas, Mae!" Earl's suit had no padding. But he had a lovely white beard that hid his mouth and nose. "Merry Christmas, Izzy!"

They spent a few moments admiring each other's costumes.

The clip-clop of a horse had them turning to look down the street.

"There's another Mrs. Claus!" Mae hopped up and down again.

Sure enough, Mrs. Claus—or in this case, Lois Pierce—drove a horse and wooden wagon down their street. Next to her sat a Santa Claus, most likely her beau, Chet. His face was hidden behind a full white beard. The wagon had been outfitted with colorful Christmas lights, a small Christmas tree and red cushions for folks to sit on. Several Santas and Mrs. Clauses were in the passenger area, many with colorful Christmas blankets on their laps.

"That's Destiny Rogers sitting in there. And she's waving at me." Earl perked up. "Come along, Mae. If we're real nice to Destiny, she might invite us over for Christmas dinner."

"Hey," Izzy protested. "You always come to our house for Christmas dinner after the parade." Izzy had left a ham warming in the oven.

"Izzy, don't ruin this for me." Earl lowered his voice. "Look at the way Destiny is waving at me. That's a finger waggle. And finger waggles are a flirting tactic."

"I've never heard of finger waggles." Izzy followed Earl to the end of the wagon.

"You've never lived until someone finger waggles at you," Earl whispered, giving Destiny a jolly finger waggle in return. "Makes your heart flutter."

The sound of jingling bells at the end of the block had everyone turning.

A huge gray horse pranced toward them while pulling a fancy cart. There were bells on the horse's harness and a wreath around its neck.

"That's Sam," Mae cried. "That's Sam and... *Chandler Claus.*" Mae grabbed Izzy's hand and tugged her away from the waiting wagon.

"I'm getting in this wagon." Earl ascended the small ladder in the back. "You girls should get in here, too."

"Gotta get moving," Lois added from the front.

Chandler pulled up to the curb behind the wagon. And then he...he...

Izzy couldn't believe it.

Chandler waggled his fingers at them. "Ho-ho-ho! Merry Christmas!"

*Oh, my.* Earl was right. Being on the receiving end of a finger waggle sent flutters through Izzy's chest.

Chandler was dressed in a Santa costume from head to toe, as was Sam, who had his hands beneath his chin and Santa beard and was waving the white fluffy whiskers like a flag. Frank and Mary made a perfect Mr. and Mrs. Claus on the bench behind him. Mary's arm was in a sling held close to her chest.

The big gray impatiently pawed the sidewalk with a gigantic hoof, sending the harness bells tinkling.

"We're here to pick up a pair of Mrs. Santas," Chandler continued, warm brown eyes focused on Izzy.

"Come on, Mama." Mae tugged Izzy, trying to draw her closer to Chandler and Sam.

"Don't fall for it, Izzy," Earl called from the wagon. "Destiny says the retirement center has plenty of turkey and has invited us over to her place for Christmas dinner."

Chandler handed Sam the reins and leaped to the sidewalk.

*Oh, my.* That caused Izzy's heart to flutter, as well.

"Santa Chandler." Mae tugged his red pants leg. "Do you know what my Christmas wish was?"

"Yes, I do," Chandler said in a deep booming voice, turning his gaze to Mae. "You wanted your mama to find someone to love."

Mae nodded solemnly. "Someone good. Someone kind."

"Someone like my dad!" Sam yelled, eliciting chuckles from the elderly Clauses in both wagon and cart.

"Someone who wouldn't make her quiet and sad," Mae went on. "Someone to tell her she's pretty and smart and the best mama ever." And then she sniffed as if she was going to cry. "But that man wasn't under our Christmas tree this morning."

Chandler nodded, gaze turning back to Izzy. "That's because I was afraid, Mae."

Mae gasped. "You're too big to be afraid."

"Nope." Chandler reached for Izzy's hand. "Nobody is too big to be afraid. But I'm too big to let those fears put words in my mouth anymore. It took hurting you to make me see." His voice lowered, gentled. "I was wrong, Izzy. I said things I didn't mean. I'm sorry I hurt you. Sorry that I panicked."

"I panic, too, sometimes," Izzy admitted softly, having already forgiven him upon discovering his gift of dreams in her bedroom.

"But I learned something important that day, Izzy." He moved closer, taking her other hand in his. "I learned that I can't go back to living in a box. The world isn't a box. It rotates and changes and expands and contracts. The world... My world... It's wherever you are. I love you, Izzy."

Izzy's heart had lodged in her throat. Everyone heard those words. There were gasps and a smattering of applause from those in the wagon.

"He waggled at her, you know," Earl said knowingly.

Izzy smiled. "I love you, too, Chandler..." There was supposed to be a *but* in there. She'd closed the door on her feelings for him, after all.

"Can you find it in your heart to forgive me?" Chandler pressed a kiss on her forehead. "I was callous and a fool. And I promise to make every day we're together a joyous one."

"No one can promise that." But oh, how glad she was that Chandler wanted to try.

The big gray pawed the road once more, filling the street with the ripple of bells.

"Behave, Shirley," Chandler said.

The gray whinnied, making most of the folks around them laugh.

"I love you, Izzy," Chandler said again, loud and clear enough for everyone to hear. "And I'm just as bad of a negotiator as my father because I'm telling you that I have marriage in mind when I think of you. Marriage, love and a lifetime of happiness. With you. Only you."

"We're getting married?" Mae squealed, whirling to face Sam. "We're getting married!"

"Hurry up and kiss her, then," Lois called back to them. "I've got other pickups." She whistled and the wagon with Earl in it moved slowly forward.

"What do you say?" Chandler had his arms around Izzy now. "Are you up for a lifetime of family and dreams coming true?"

"I am." Izzy grabbed hold of his white faux fur trim. "But first, Lois is right. We've got to seal this deal and to do that—"

He kissed her.

# EPILOGUE

"WE'RE JUST WAITING on Izzy," Ronnie told Chandler, smiling from behind the school office counter on Valentine's Day. "Have a seat."

"Got it." Chandler sat in the same seat he'd occupied in the office the day Reindeer Izzy had trotted into his life. And just like that fateful day, his knee bounced nervously. "Are you going to tell me what they've done this time?"

"And steal Principal Crowder's thunder?" Ronnie tsked. "Nope."

Chandler couldn't imagine why Sam and Mae had misbehaved. They'd been such angels since Christmas break.

Izzy blew in with the same intensity she'd blown into Chandler's life. She wore blue jeans and a Clementine Feed T-shirt beneath her red jacket. Her silver-blond hair brushed her shoulders. "I came as soon as I could. Ronnie, you said not to worry. No blood, right?"

"The kids are sitting in the library room. No blood," Ronnie assured them.

Principal Crowder opened his office door and gestured for Izzy and Chandler to come inside.

Chandler took a seat. Before he even settled back in the stiff chair, his knee was bobbing.

While the principal reviewed a sheet of paper, Izzy took a significant glance at Chandler's bouncing knee and then said softly, *"I love you."*

She laid her hand on his knee, her pretty engagement ring sparkling on her finger. Once they'd moved past the fears about change and the permanence of love, he'd proposed. That had been on New Year's Day. And she'd said yes. They'd rushed to commit but they weren't rushing to the altar. They'd agreed that too much change wouldn't be good for the kids. Stephanie had left town, taking that job in Texas. And Mike was almost completely out of the picture.

"I suppose you're wondering why I called you in today." Principal Crowder didn't sound happy as he returned the paper to the file.

"I was hoping you needed volunteers for something." Izzy chuckled. "Or perhaps the support of the Done Roamin' Ranch and Clementine Feed for the spring carnival?"

"We ran out of pizza today at lunchtime," the principal said instead of reassuring them.

"Mae loves pizza day," Izzy murmured.

"Sam, too." Chandler nodded, covering Izzy's hand with his own.

Principal Crowder frowned. "They loved pizza day so much that they staged a protest in the cafeteria when we ran out."

"They're seven," Izzy reminded him. "It can't have been much of a protest."

"Oh." Chandler thought of Ginny's side hustle, a business she was supposed to have closed down.

Izzy and the principal turned to Chandler for answers. Both saying, *"Oh?"*

"It's nothing. I just remembered something I forgot to do at the ranch."

"Your children are very impressionable," the principal said coolly. "As I understand it, the protest was a coordinated effort between Sam and Della-Mae." The principal rested his folded hands on the desk. "The cafeteria monitors didn't know what hit them, and only managed to reclaim control by promising everyone chocolate milk. Your children have been waiting for you in the library."

Chandler cleared his throat. "We're sorry. It won't happen again." He got to his feet and led Izzy out the door.

"I don't think the principal was finished," Izzy said from behind him.

"What else could he say that we haven't heard already?" Months ago. "Home lectures and reading messages sent on the online messaging system."

"We haven't managed to figure out the online messaging system," Izzy teased. "He might have recommended our children should be in separate classrooms?"

"Mrs. Stodimeyer didn't want them separated," Chandler reminded her. "And neither do we."

At the library door, he turned and drew Izzy close. "I don't like the principal's office."

Her arms wound around his neck. "Then, let's make sure we don't get called there again."

Chandler kissed Izzy. And in that kiss, he found the equilibrium and humor he needed to face their hooligans.

They entered the library. Chandler breathed in the smell of books.

Sam and Mae sat at a table in a corner, books open in front of them. They both looked very small.

"Hey, kids," Chandler said.

The librarian shushed him.

*"Hey, kids,"* Izzy whispered, sliding into a child-sized seat across from Mae. She leaned forward, still whispering, "Would Santa approve of a pizza protest?"

Chandler stood behind her. "I wouldn't."

That earned him another dark look from the librarian.

"Mama," Mae whispered. "We've been talking in school about Cupid."

"And love," Sam added, also in a whisper.

"We're in love," Chandler reassured them in his outdoor voice.

The librarian shushed him again.

"You hurt the lunch ladies' feelings with that protest," Izzy whispered gently.

"We're sorry," they chorused back.

The librarian rolled her eyes and moved to another section of the library.

"Explain to me what Cupid has to do with pizza," Chandler said as softly as he could.

"Pizza? Pizza had nothing to do with Cupid," Sam said, as if this was common knowledge.

Chandler was speechless.

"Cupid is a baby, Mama," Mae whispered urgently, leaning forward as if this was an important concept that was hard to grasp.

Chandler's head hurt. He rubbed his temple.

"A baby, Mama," Mae whispered. "And that's what we want."

"A baby...ducky?" Izzy guessed, glancing up at Chandler with mischief in her blue eyes.

"A baby brother," Sam said at the same time that Mae said, "A baby sister."

The kids stared at each other. And then grinned and chorused, *"Twins!"*

The librarian shushed them from the other side of a bookrack.

And Chandler... He couldn't help himself. He laughed. He laughed so hard and so long that tears spilled over his cheeks. And those tears...

They had Izzy, Sam and Mae fawning all over him to make sure he was all right.

"I'm fine," he managed to say when his tears had dried, and he'd caught his breath. "I'm just surprised."

"Surprised?" Izzy shepherded them out of the library, waving apologetically at the librarian. "That our kids would make a ruckus at school instead of asking us if we planned on having more kids?"

"No. Not that." Chandler got on his knees and gathered Sam and Mae into his arms. And then he stared up at Izzy until she relented and crouched down to be included in a family hug. "I've been trying to start this conversation for weeks and every time I do, you change the subject, Izzy."

"That's not true." Izzy scoffed without looking him in the eye.

But the kids nodded. Smart ones, those two.

"We need to do a better job at communicating," Chandler told the kids. "There will be no more visits to the principal's office. And no more dodging important questions."

"Like when can I get a horse," Sam said.

"And me a kitten," Mae said.

"And me a baby," Chandler added.

A tear tracked down Izzy's cheek. "I changed the subject because... I thought you wanted to talk about *not* having any more kids."

Two wide-eyed young gazes swiveled around to focus on Chandler.

"See?" Chandler kept his calm. "This is what I'm saying. We need to talk freely about what we want in this family."

"Babies," the two kids chorused again.

"And a horse," Sam added.

"A kitten," Mae whispered.

"We need to talk about whatever is on our minds. That includes you." Chandler kissed Izzy's forehead. "And you two..." He kissed Sam's and Mae's foreheads. "And most importantly what we need to talk about now is—"

"Babies!" they all chorused together, including Izzy.

Someone behind Chandler cleared their throat.

He turned. And stumbled to his feet. "Hey, sorry, Principal

Crowder. We were just adjourning our family meeting. You won't have any more trouble from us. Will he, kids?"

"Oh, no," the kids agreed with faux innocence, standing.

Izzy chuckled and rose, too. "They're good kids, Principal Crowder, but the truth is we can't guarantee they'll always be angels. That's the way life is. That's the way love is and I love Mae and Sam, but there's no telling what they'll do from one day to the next."

Three months ago, the truth and unpredictability of that statement would have made Chandler nervous. Not now.

"There's no predicting what they'll do in the next hour." Chandler drew his family close. "And amen to that."

\* \* \* \* \*

# WESTERN

*Rugged men looking for love...*

## Available Next Month

**The Maverick's Resolution** Brenda Harlen
**A Match For The Sheriff** Lisa Childs

.........................................................................................

**Fortune's Mystery Woman** Allison Leigh
**The Cowboy's Rodeo Redemption** Susan Breeden

.........................................................................................

LOVE INSPIRED
**The Texan's Journey Home** Jolene Navarro
**A Faithful Guardian** Louise M. Gouge